CATFANTASTIC

Nine Lives and Fifteen Tales

EDITED BY
Andre Norton &
Martin H. Greenberg

DAW BOOKS, INC.

DONALD A. WOLLHEIM, PUBLISHER

1633 Broadway, New York, NY 10019

Introduction: Speaking of Cats—A Very Weighty Subject © 1989
  by Andre Norton.
The Gate of the Kittens © 1989 by Wilanne Schneider Belden.
The Damcat © 1989 by Clare Bell.
Borrowing Trouble © 1989 by Elizabeth H. Boyer.
Day of Discovery © 1989 by Blake Cahoon.
Wart © 1989 by Jayge Carr.
Yellow Eyes © 1989 by Marylois Dunn.
It Must Be Some Place © 1989 by Donna Farley.
The Dreaming Kind © 1989 by C. S. Friedman.
Trouble © 1989 by P. M. Griffin.
SKitty © 1989 by Mercedes Lackey.
The Game of Cat and Rabbit © 1989 by Patricia Shaw Mathews.
From the Diary of Hermione © 1989 by Ardath Mayhar.
It's A Bird, It's A Plane It's . . . SUPERCAT! © 1989 by Ann Miller
  and Karen Elizabeth Rigley.
Noble Warrior © 1989 by Andre Norton.
Bastet's Blessing © 1989 by Elizabeth Ann Scarborough.

DAW Book Collectors No. 785

First Printing, July 1989

1 2 3 4 5 6 7 8 9

PRINTED IN THE U.S.A.

HUNTERS, GUARDIANS, COMPANIONS . . .

With fur fluffed and claws unsheathed, they stalk their prey or stand against their foes . . . With tails raised and rumbling purrs, they name and welcome their friends. . . . With instincts beyond those of mere humans, they ward off unseen dangers, working a kind of magic beyond our ken. . . . They are Cats, and these are their stories:

"The Damcat"—Could one small bobcat stand against an evil magic which threatened to destroy a major dam project?

"The Dreaming Kind"—When a scientific experiment goes terribly awry only a genetically altered cat and one kitten can see the terror that is being unleashed. . . .

"It's A Bird, It's A Plane, It's . . . SUPERCAT!"—It all began with a UFO sighting, a science fiction writer, and a cat's stalk of an alien. . . .

These are just a few of the fabulous felines you'll meet in—

CATFANTASTIC

CONTENTS

INTRODUCTION

Speaking of Cats—
A Very Weighty Subject

There is an affinity between writers and cats and perhaps there always has been. Doctor Johnson's concern
(expressed in his will) about that well-developed
household despot Hodge (who greatly favored oysters
for tea) is quoted to this day in most of the biographi-
cal material dealing with that sage, critic and author of
the eighteenth century.

Having been declared divine in Egypt and in the
legends of the north (as witness that the chariot of the
Goddess Freya was drawn by cats), fortune favored
and then abruptly failed the feline species. Still they
survived both the worship in temples and the obscene
tortures they were later subjected to as the familiars of
witches.

The tales and legends dealing with cats always present them as being not only mysterious but also superior in good sense and understanding to our own species.
There was Dick Whittington's cat who made his master's fortune as surely as Puss-In-Boots wrought favor-
ably for the somewhat stupid and feckless young man
who inherited his services.

Perhaps it is because cats do not live by human
patterns, do not fit themselves into prescribed behavior, that they are so united to creative people. Always
the cat remains a little beyond the limits we try to set
for him in our blind folly. A cat does not live with
one; rather, one lives with a cat.

Each season in the publishing world brings a crop of
feline studies both in pictures and words. There are
Garfield and Heathcliff to hammer home indepen-
dence and the pitying attitude of cat for person, as

well as such heartwarming stories as those written by such authors as James Herriot.

Herein are neither Heathcliff nor Garfield but some others who have as definite personalities to make forceful impressions within their territories. The matter of magic familiars (much more practical then the wizards they company with) is competently dealt with. For cats have been linked to magic, the more intricate the better, from time immemorial.

These fifteen histories deal not only with spells but also with diplomatic relations on other planets, with forbidden research, engineering on a grand scale, and with guardians who know their duty and expertly do it.

Cats are presented in all shapes, colors, sizes, alike in self-confidence and general ingenuity. There seems never to have been a cat who was not entirely equal to the situation which confronts him or her. In other words, there are no extraordinary cats, merely ones to whom unusual opportunities present themselves.

—Andre Norton

THE GATE
OF THE KITTENS

by Wilanne Schneider Belden

Feathers was the only kitten of Silk's last litter who did not yet have a permanent home when the man came to obtain a mouser.

"Isn't she small?" he inquired.

"She's a fearsome huntress," Anja informed him. "We don't think she'll ever be large. But are you interested in size or in effectiveness?"

The man smiled. "I need a mouser—and a ratter."

"Rats don't come full-grown," Anja responded.

The man nodded.

"You couldn't want a better," Anja said. She padded a carrying cage with another blanket. "Just don't make her an outdoor cat—the foxes'll get her. A safe way indoors, her rug by the fireside in winter, a cool place in summer, water, and care if she needs it."

"Well, I'll take her if she'll come."

Time I had a home of my own, Feathers thought. But she was far too small to become a cat who lived alone. She'd refused other homes where they wanted a baby-sitter, lap cat, and dependent animal. But this man wanted a working cat, and Feathers accepted.

"Think to me every morning," Silk advised her daughter. "Or I shall worry." Feathers knew her small size concerned her mother. She agreed.

Feathers set about eliminating the small rodent population of the long-untenanted holding her humans were putting back into some sort of order. The man who had come for her saw that she was well cared for—although she understood clearly that she was not

9

his cat. All in and on the property belonged (human term) to a man called the Master. Feathers was not entirely sure he knew of her existence. She would have taught him the Proper Order of Things with her teeth and claws—had he not been one who made her ears lie back when he entered a room. Cats *know* about Power, its creatures and its uses. Even young and inexperienced cats are instinctively aware of Good and Evil. Feathers knew that what went on in the part of the establishment set aside for his exclusive use was Bad, Wrong, Evil. She felt things that made her long fur stand on end and her mouth open in a silent hiss. Her solution was to avoid all contact with him.

When her first breeding season occurred, she should have been closed indoors, to take no chances that she would conceive so young. But no one thought another cat was within miles, and few paid suffcient attention even to know of her condition.

Stranger and stranger were the behaviors of the Master. Lights of distorted colors accompanied even more disgusting odors and quite indescribably hideous sounds. The servants became silent, frightened of their own shadows, and drank more than too much. They went on long journeys carrying peculiar bundles. People of dubious aspect and, Feathers suspected, even more doubtful character came to the holding in the darkest hours and left well before dawn. The Master would be gone for days, even weeks, then return, usually furious, and cause upset and perturbation. Awaiting kittens, Feathers welcomed his presence even less than usual.

She knew him and his behaviors to be Evil, but she could not contain her raging curiosity. When she thought to Silk, her mother was horrified. Disturbed both by this reaction and her own uncharacteristic mania, Feathers agreed that she would seek to discover what the Master did only if she could locate a way to see without being seen, to find out without being found out. Conscientious searching located no way into his private workroom. Every mousehole and ratway was blocked with material that made her ill when she smelled it. Still, she watched.

While she observed the only door one night, her dark fur with its shadow stripes and spots making her utterly unnoticeable, a man who came and went (always at night, always surreptitiously, always on a horse with muffled hooves) brought three other men with him to the steading. He led them to the door of the workroom. When they entered, so did Feathers. They did not notice.

"You have no doubts that you have located the Gate," the tallest man said.

The Master nodded. "And established the requirements to bring to it that we seek. It has but to be tested."

The three men stared at one another.

"Tested? How can you test that—something—will come through it?"

"By sending something the other way."

The men moved uneasily. The tall one rested his hand on his sword hilt.

"When?" the fattest one asked.

"Tomorrow is the night of the Cat," the master replied.

"Why the cat?"

"What do we seek to have enter through the Gate?" the Master asked—as if only the abysmally stupid would have to be reminded.

"The Puma," the little man said. Softly.

The men nodded.

"And the fee to pass the Gate?"

"The Puma will bring with him one we do not need."

"You're sure it will be he who . . . pays?"

The Master's brows almost met. "You doubt me?"

The men assured him they did not doubt.

Feathers wanted to yowl, to hiss and scratch. She sat glued to the floor instead, filled with a combination of terror and disgust. She had never heard of Gates, knew nothing of what the men spoke, and had no idea what a Puma was. But paying the fee she understood. They planned to kill.

Why should it matter? She cared little for people.

Because to kill to eat or to protect was in the natural order of life. To kill to do a wrong was not.

A hand came down, grabbed her by the back of the neck, and dropped her into a lidded basket. A voice chuckled. "A good choice, I think, to test the Gate. A small cat in exchange for a Puma."

"Mother!" Feathers screamed. She was, after all, not quite nine months old, and she was terribly frightened.

They all laughed, and if Feathers had not been a cat, she would have fainted from dread.

The next night she saw nothing, heard things that, had she not been a cat, would have driven her mad, and, at the last, was grabbed by those bloodless, bony, cruel fingers and pushed *through* something. She fell into an icy rain puddle. Inside her, one of her babies died.

Librarians, in general, are pretty nice people. What faults and failings they have as individuals rarely cause them to run down old ladies in crosswalks or kick puppies. Consequently, when Judith Justin, MLS, in charge of the Bookmobile, made out the form of a cat half-crawling across the rainy road, she applied the brakes with caution—and prayer. As she had been driving twenty miles an hour for over twenty miles, crouching forward on the seat and peering anxiously through the rain-drenched windows, the opportunity to rest was sufficient inducement to overcome her dread of attempting to bring the heavy vehicle to a safe stop.

Several members of the staff accused her of minor witchcraft—if sorcery could have any effect on machinery or other examples of cold iron. They insisted that the Bookmobile liked her. It did what she asked it to: started when she turned the key, rocked out of sandtraps with alacrity, and steered between obstacles without even scratching the top coat of paint. It invariably had its flat tires, broken fuel lines, and burned out light bulbs for other Bookmobile drivers. Never for Judith. So the brakes, wet as they were, took hold smoothly and effectively, the rear half of the bus followed the front half instead of skidding into the middle of the street, and the Bookmobile sat waiting patiently for the cat to cross.

Judith turned on the interior lights and opened the front door. An oblong of light wavered into the rainy afternoon—dark, almost, as night.

"Here, kitty, kitty, kitty," Judith called. She never insulted her own cats with the phrase, but cats somehow knew that people who called, "Here, kitty, kitty, kitty," offered food and shelter.

The most woebegone wail ever to issue from feline throat responded. Judith's heart turned over. She shielded her face against the cold windshield and squinted out. Yes, the cat had turned and scrunched under the bus.

Judith stood at the top of the steps and called again. The cat answered, but it did not enter.

Maybe it can't get up the first step, she thought. Not a big step for a healthy cat, but this one looked almost as if a car had hit it.

Judith pulled on her poncho, scrunched it around her legs as she stooped, and squatted on the bottom step.

"Kitty?"

"Mrow." The cat was right below the steps.

"C'mon," Judith said encouragingly. "I'll help you. I promise I don't kick cats."

A scraggly head on a long, scrawny neck, both sopping and dripping, poked out from beneath the step.

"Farther," Judith encouraged. "I don't want to pick you up like a kitten. You're too big a cat for that to be good for you."

The cat peered up, blinking. It inched out until Judith could get her hands around its body behind the front legs. She reached down.

"This could hurt," she warned the cat, now knowing whether the drenched animal was really injured or not. "I'm only trying to help. Don't scratch."

She might have been picking up a fur stole that had

been soaking in ice water for a week. Judith hissed. "Poor thing," she murmured. As she slid a hand down to support the back half of the cat's body, she realized that, hurt or not, the cat was certainly pregnant. Very pregnant.

"This is no weather to have kittens," Judith protested. "Let's see if I can at least get you warm and dry."

She carried odd things in the librarian's closet: her sleeping bag and knapsack, for example, because on two of her routes she stayed overnight. The county paid twenty dollars toward lodging, but Judith could use that twenty dollars. She didn't remember removing her swimming suit and towels, either. Those, she carried all summer. Camps had pools, and several camps were regular Bookmobile stops. *Yup*.

Judith was worried about the cat. She didn't seem to be damaged, but the woman was no veterinarian, and she couldn't be sure. By the time the animal was as dry as Judith could rub her and curled up on the beach towel next to the heater vent, she was making a sound Judith interpreted as a rusty purr.

Better, anyway, she thought. She ducked out from under the dash and sat back. *Odd.* That marvelous, dark feathery fur somehow masked the animalness of the cat—turned it into a blob of nothing in the semi-darkness. Pretty fur, really, black and a dozen shades of gray, with no distinct pattern. She petted the cat's head. It purred again.

Caring for the cat had restored the blood supply to several places Judith had tensed it out of, relaxed her amazingly, and made her feel a little less inadequate to the task of getting the Bookmobile down the mountain in the dark. Only eight more winding, precipitous miles to the intersection with the state route, another twenty-five across the flat, then the last long drive on the freeway into town. She'd called to say she was going to try to beat the snow so the Bookmobile wouldn't get stuck on the mountaintop for who knew how long. The dispatcher was appreciative, but she'd insisted that Judith call from the filling station at the intersection, then again from the motel at the freeway. According to the weather report, the valley floor should be clear. But if all did not go well, she wasn't to try to come into town tonight.

All did not go well. The rain became sleet. The temperature outside dropped too rapidly—the snowline might be as far down the mountain as the motel. The roadway, not the best at any time, became actively dangerous. If she hadn't been more scared to try to stop—this stretch hadn't a single pullout big enough for the bus—than she was to drive, Judith would have given up. But damned fools acted as if they had nine lives and none of them could be lost to the conditions tonight. She was passed by three vehicles—one coming, two going—a four-wheel drive affair, a sports car, and a light truck. The latter two went swishing around the bus at twice the speed Judith considered safe. The driver of the RV seemed to believe himself late for his own wake, but he was also, obviously, a professional driver. Moves Judith considered suicidal proved to be only highly dangerous. She shook her head. "Well," she told the cat, "I guess if they can, I can."

The filling station was already closed, and Judith didn't blame the high school kid who pumped gas on weekends for going home a little early. She knew where the attendant hid the restroom keys, thank heavens, but the public phone was almost unprotected. Judith was wet to the waist by the time she could return to the warm Bookmobile. The cat indicated it wanted to go out, so Judith put it under her poncho and took it to the least windy side of the building. "Hurry up," she said, shivering. The cat hurried.

"Part of my funk is hunger," she told the cat. "I'll bet you're hungry, too." The cat meowed.

"Well, there should be something."

She changed into her camping clothes and dug into the emergency drawer. In addition to flashlights and adhesive bandages and similar other assistances for the minor emergencies a Bookmobile librarian might be expected to meet, she'd seen, well, she thought she'd seen . . . *Hmm. Yes. Candy bar. Old, but not too old.*

Unfortunately, cats didn't eat chocolate. What else? *Ah-ha*! Trust Cal's hollow leg. A tightly-lidded tin box of English biscuits that rattled loudly. Probably canned meat, as Cal was a diabetic and couldn't eat sweets. So it was. The good kind, without too much salt. Judith pulled the top off and let the cat lick its dinner off her fingers.

She didn't want to go on, but she'd waited as long as she dared.

"We're stopping at the motel," she told the cat. *Positive thinking*, she added to herself. The likelihood that they'd get as far as the motel seemed less and less probable every second. But experience in these mountains warned Judith that the snowline would be well below the elevation of the station. No one manned the place on Sunday night, and the amount of food in Cal's can wouldn't keep them for another couple of days. She probably wouldn't starve before somebody showed up, but she wasn't sure the cat could make it. Only later would someone point out to her the oddity of failing to call the sheriff for help and, even odder, of placing the importance of feeding the stray cat before that of quite possibly losing her own life.

Unwillingness to commit herself and the bus to the dubious mercies of the weather kept her from starting. She wondered if she should get out in the rain again and check to be sure the chains were there, just in case she needed them. But where in the world *would* they be if they weren't in their stow space? Putting on chains would be no easy task, but she'd had to master it to get the job, so she could, if she had to.

She examined what she could see of the roadway, peering into the darkness intently. Incredulous, she watched headlights become attached to a bus even larger than hers, rather like a transcontinental Greyhound. It rumbled past at a speed that made her wonder why it was not flying. Certainly it had worked up adequate speed to take off.

Well, if they can, I guess I can, she informed herself. *On we go*. She shoved her hands into her fur-lined gloves and turned the key.

The bus purred into life. They inched onto the road.
This part of the trip really is the easiest, she tried to
reassure herself. *Straight, and the wind isn't strong
enough to be a problem.* Often, high winds whipped
across the flatlands, winds so strong that the county
office canceled the Bookmobile visits. But the state
road was well maintained, most of it was three lanes
wide and some of it four, and at this end of the valley
one could make out the lights of isolated homes. To
Judith's considerable surprise, the radio condescended
to work, due, doubtless, to an unusual inversion layer
that reflected the signal into the valley. Judith grinned,
demanded Bach—and got it. She snorted. Things
seemed to be going better.

Then the snow began.

In five minutes she knew it was chains now or give
up. She got them all on in less than an hour, and by
that time almost was unable to drive out of the hollow
the presence of the bus had made in the swiftly piled
snowbank. But the chains were new and sharp, and
they dug in. She drove down a whirling white tunnel
beyond which was only darkness, solid, like ebony or
granite. She dared not go on. She dared not stop. She
shifted into a lower gear and continued. For as long as
the bus would move, she'd drive. Every quarter mile
brought them closer to the freeway, to the motel and
people and safety. Every turn of the wheels made one
step she need not take in the cold and snow when the
storm was over, and she had to move or die.

The man had a name, and most people knew what it
was, but he was never referred or spoken to as anything but General. He deserved it. He made the essential breakthrough in the scientific aspect himself, and
he convinced men who could take that information
and turn it into a completed system that they could
and must do so. Whatever they needed he earned or
developed or bought or stole—ahead of time.

When it was done, he named it the Puma. The
name seemed particularly appropriate. The puma was
the big cat of the American west, the most deadly

carnivore that hunted alone. It moved with stealth, erupted into powerful movement, and destroyed with strength and speed. Yet a sleeping puma was harmless— and could rarely be found, so camouflaging was its color, so clever were its habits of concealment. All of these traits were to be found in the Puma. It was deadly, and it was powerful, but it was nowhere near the size of previous—objects—of its kind. It and its transport and launching systems were approximately the size of a large bus which, as a sensible precaution, the exterior was designed to resemble. Just as the puma slept upwind of possible pursuers and could not be located by scent, the Puma disseminated no telltale radiation. And after it had done its work, its target area would be free of animal life, but clean. Troops could go in at once. That was the General's personal contribution.

"Tests start tomorrow," the General said.

Someone commented that the weather was not ideal.

The General indicated that if a puma was hungry, the weather didn't matter a damn. If the Puma couldn't be transported and launched in a *hurricane*, it had better be redesigned. Did anyone need to do his job over again, and if so, why hadn't he spoken up before this?

Nobody mentioned blizzard because nobody thought of blizzard.

"It pounces on Sunday," the General said. "I've arranged for the test grounds to be empty. Except for us. Any indications that we've been breached?"

There hadn't better be, so there weren't.

Nobody asked if it wouldn't be better to use a dummy warhead. Half the point of the test was to see what the real one would do.

The bus started Friday morning. On orders, the driver took it easy, crossing the desert at fifty-five, climbing the mountains at forty, slowing down in the tricky spots. They were to spend tonight at the summit in the lodge, then start down tomorrow to the flats. Two-thirds of the way to the highway the land conformation made radio or other wave-born communication erratic and chancy at best. A roughly circular area some ten miles in diameter held not a single human habitation. Unusual autumn rains had filled an arm of the sometimes-lake so they could park the bus on the shoreline and take no chances of setting a major fire and getting caught when they unleashed the Puma. Then only a few more miles to the freeway and on to the coast.

Except that the obvious is always the enemy. They got a flat tire and the driver became stubborn. No way was he going to drive that bus without a good spare. Unhitch the four-wheel RV off the back, take the tire to the station and get it patched, return and stow it. The schedule would have to be put back one day. The General was not pleased but, to everyone's relief, he was not unduly upset.

And that's what they did.

Then the rain began, and it started to look and smell like snow. They had to get the bus out of the mountains, down to the flat, and they might not be able to for a week or so if that snow . . .

They started about four. Driving conditions were very, very bad. Snow hit them halfway across the flats. In the whiteout, the driver became totally disoriented. By the time they found themselves trying to go back up into the mountains, it was too late to do anything but wait it out.

The General was not pleased.

He should have been.

Each morning, Silk became more concerned for Feather's safety. The little one became more and more determined to solve the mystery of the man she would never call Master. Silk could not shake her feeling of impending doom and began acting strangely. Someone suggested that a Wise Woman or a veterinary Healer might find out what troubled their usually self-possessed mother cat. Not until she leaped into wakefulness one night yowling like a scalded ice-demon and stalked about the house growling, her tail switching, her eyes blazing, did anyone take the suggestion seriously. Then

Anja requested the presence of a member of the race of sentient beings who coexisted in their land (although separately, for the most part), and who could speak with both animals and humans.

The word passed. A woman of those people appeared at the steading. Silk met her. What she told Anja sent the fastest rider on the best horse to another place—and the word flew.

A man who knew of Gates, and what might come through them, and the horror caused by Alizon while their Gate was open, took horse and rode day and night. Others joined him.

They were too late. The Gate was open, the Call sent, and death was the payment for passage. They established a defense perimeter outside that of the entities who had opened the Gate, and waited.

Silk stalked and growled. She continued yowling. Her fur sparked blue stars when she swished her tail.

Beyond the standing stones—or beyond the opening framed by the three stones—was a sunlit day.

Judith was no longer young, and she had never been pretty. She was far too bright and independent for a girl of her generation. Loneliness was a curse she did not suffer as a child—not with eleven others in the family, and she in the middle. As a young woman, getting out, away, earning college money, then working her way through in the company of her best friends, those in books, had taken every moment. When the time to be lonely arrived, she had learned how to handle it.

Fantasy was so much more satisfactory a place to live than reality that Judith spent much of her life there. Doing so was both reasoned and intentional. She had a clear, biting sense of what was and what was not. She simply preferred what was not. Life in books—and beyond them, in places where only her imagination created worlds—sufficed. Satisfy, it did not, but reality offered so much less that Judith had long since relegated living in it to such times as she was with others. She wished she could reject it completely.

As she tried, unsuccessfully, to reject the sunlit world beyond the stones.

The cat would not let her. She crawled from under the dashboard screaming in demand to be allowed out of the door. Shocked, Judith watched the contractions of labor begin in her sides. The cat clawed the door and screamed again.

"No, no," Judith exclaimed. She reached for the animal, to be met with teeth and claws and infuriated noises. The cat ripped and tore at the rubber edges of the doors, squirming to get her head between the flanges. She would kill herself—or her babies.

"All right, all right," Judith yelled at her. "I'll take you out. Wait a minute."

She shoved her arms first into her down jacket, then into the knapsack straps. The cat continued to scream. Judith picked up the beach towel, threw it over the cat, and stuffed cat and towel into the backpack. The cat became suddenly silent.

Judith almost stopped. "No, I said I would," she whispered. *This time I have really flipped,* she thought. *Keeping a promise to a cat, yet?*

She could not take her eyes off the brilliant rectangle of sunshine, the green, grassy hills, the hint of a stream, the likelihood of wildflowers, the . . . She grabbed the lever and opened the door. The balky back door chose this time to open, too. Before she could stop herself, she jumped down into the snow and stamped to the front of the bus. She could smell spring! She could feel warm wind on her face!

Almost, she waded forward to pass through the open . . . gate? Space?

"No," she said aloud. To do that was foolish. She had no way of knowing what really was . . . *there.* If anything. The Bookmobile had brought them this far; it could take them through. Remaining inside it was the only protection she had.

She knew the lintel stone to be more than a foot above the top of the bus, the side stones of the . . . entryway . . . just far enough apart to let it through—if she folded the rearview mirror back.

As she got ready, she could feel the cat inside the knapsack. The kittens must be coming. A pained yowl made her wonder if the first one was here. She could not stop.

When she climbed back into the driver's seat, she did not close the door, she just gripped the wheel until her knuckles went white, then pried her right hand free so she could turn the ignition key. The bus responded. It was perfectly lined up, as if things were planned—as things were in fantasy. Forward in the lowest gear.

The front bumper contacted something invisible. It gave slowly, as if it was heavy but movable. The bus dug its chains in and shoved. Judith held her breath. The cat squalled again.

They rolled almost through, suddenly, as if the bus was a cork coming out of a bottle . . . and stopped.

The back doors had never fit properly. They always stuck out farther than the front ones. The bus was wedged by the strong, steel doors.

Judith shifted into neutral. She stepped down onto grass. Everything was fuzzy, half-there. She could see and not see that the bus must have pushed aside a great block of stone. On the other side of the stone was something concealed by a putrid red-orange flare. She looked away quickly. Even half-seen, it made her ill. She blinked and looked up, beyond. Whatever was there, and she could but dimly perceive this, also, was cloaked in living blue-green light. It confused her completely.

She felt fury from the evil red entity. She was not the one they expected. She had taken that one's place, and all their time and effort had gone for naught. They were determined to clear the Gate and try again. She must move the bus immediately. Why this sensible demand seemed evil she did not know, but she had no doubt whatever.

From the benificent beings lapped in their cool loveliness, she felt . . . rejection? No, they did not reject her, they warned her. She must not remove the blockage in the gate. What the red entities sought to replace it with was Wrong. She must return or die, but she must not return!

The cat squirmed and cried. Judith swung the knapsack off and set it on the sunny earth in front of the bus. She opened it and turned back the towel. The cat lay on her side panting. Two small dark lumps lay where she had pushed them. Judith touched each gently. Dead kittens. Poor little things. She hoped this next one would live. Maybe it would if she blew into its nostrils or massaged it to get its heart beating. Her whole world became too small to hold the impossibilities outside the knapsack. There, in the cat giving birth, was reality.

The kitten slid out smoothly. The cat panted a moment, then sat up and checked the small, damp baby. She opened her mouth and made an almost inaudible sound. Judith found herself crying. This one was dead, too. There could be more. She'd better take the dead ones away now, before the new mother could worry about them.

She reached in. The cat had chewed off the cords, licked away the cawls, and the lifeless infants were still warm and soft. Judith continued to cry. She wasn't quite sure why, because she knew it was better for them to die at birth than to have to be put to sleep or to go homeless. But they were so perfect and so innocent. She held them in her cupped palms and cried.

She didn't want to set them on the bare, scraped dirt while she went back in for something with which to dig. So, without thinking, she put them on the great block of stone.

The sound, the sensation of being drowned in blood-red flame, the incredible shock of the reaction to that simple move took her senses. When she regained consciousness, she was lying on soft grass and the cat was meowing in her ear. Judith sat up. The surface of the stone had been burned black—except for three small-kitten shaped white spots. The entity concealed by the red-orange light was gone. No longer fuzzy, whatever she looked at seemed too sharp-edged, too real.

The cat meowed.

"Oh, the knapsack tipped over." Judith righted it. The cat leaped in and pawed at the towel. Judith removed it carefully, supporting it as fully as she could. She set it down and parted the folds. Two small black and gray kittens mewled and wriggled. The cat pushed between Judith's hands and settled herself by her babies. She purred.

Someone chuckled softly.

Judith, her mouth open in shock, turned her head to look up so quickly that she became dizzy again. She decided she was hearing things and lay down.

Someone said something her ears heard as gibberish but her mind understood as, "It's too soon. Give her more time. Come away for now."

Nothing was real, and she was absolutely sure she was dead. This was neither heaven nor hell, though it seemed to have attributes of both, but it was outside the world of what was and what was not. Judith knew no other ways of going outside, beyond, than those of conscious fantasy, madness, or death. She had not made up any of this, if she was mad she could do nothing about it, but if she was dead, she found she didn't mind. She sat up very slowly this time. The dizziness seemed to have passed.

Even more slowly, she got to her feet. The lovely spring world she had seen through the opening was all around her. Holding onto the Bookmobile, she began circling it to the right. The vehicle just stopped—ceased to exist—not as if cut, she could not see into the interior—at the rear edge of the blocked opening from there to here. She continued on around the stones and along the side of the bus to the open door. She entered and walked to the rear seat under the window. Snow whirled around the back of the bus; cold penetrated through the windows.

Shaking her head, Judith returned to the driver's seat and stared through the windshield. A blob of black was racing toward them across the sunny grass. It yowled, and the cat, her cat, Judith almost thought, responded. Judith was quite beyond astonishment, so when the blob became a large black cat she merely continued to watch. The two cats greeted each other with an enthusiastic abandon that culminated in the big one giving the small one a thorough bath. New mama or not, her mama wanted to show how glad she was to see her offspring. Judith cupped her chin in her palms and leaned forward on her elbows to watch. She felt wonderful: relieved and happy and wanted and safe and loved.

She felt even better ten minutes later. The big black cat bounded over the rectangular stone as if she would not have used it for a litter box. Turning, she made a second leap that landed her at Judith's side. Purring so loudly that the windows rattled, the cat butted the top of her head into Judith's middle.

That's love, Judith thought, stunned. Not rub-the-side-of-the-jaw-along what you're claiming, but the highest compliment a cat can pay. She had wondered if she should be a little afraid. The older cat wasn't quite the size of an ocelot, more long-tailed bobcat size, and gave the general impression of being a domesticated animal. But it was no tame tabby. Moving slowly, she brought her hands over and rubbed the top of the cat's head. It purred even louder.

"Silk!" Judith exclaimed. The cat's fur was so exquisite to the touch that she could think of no other comparison.

The cat pulled back, looked at her, and nodded.

Nodded

"Your *name* is Silk?" Judith ventured.

The cat nodded again.

"Judith Justin," she murmured.

Silk licked her hand once.

If she was going to have a conversation with a cat, she must find a topic of interest to both of them.

"Have you seen the babies?"

Silk was out of the Bookmobile so rapidly one might have thought her to disappear. Together, Judith and Silk admired Feather's babies.

This time when somebody chuckled, Judith looked up, smiling. The man was big and bearded and about her age, and he was dressed as nobody dressed where she came from, nor had for several hundred years, and

he smelled distinctly of horse and sweat, but he reached
out to help her to her feet, shook her hand in a
perfectly normal manner, and greeted her in English.

"The name's Tregarth," he said. "Call me Simon.
It's a well-known name here, though I'm by no means
the first to wear it."

"Judith Justin," Judy replied.

"Librarian," Simon added. "That is a Bookmobile,
isn't it?"

Judith nodded, nonplussed.

The man shook his head slowly. "What a surprise
that must have been," he said softly, "when they were
expecting the Puma."

"The Puma?" Judith asked.

"Suppose you turn off the engine and join us over
there." The man waved toward a low hill that seemed
to have sprouted several people. "We wanted to wait
until you'd sorted yourself out. But food and drink are
in order now, aren't they?" He grinned. "And explanations—at least as many as we can give."

Judith nodded, swallowed, and got out, "Very much
so. Do you have anything a cat can eat?"

He chuckled again. "Several things," he said.

After all the explanations that could be made had
been made, and Silk and the people had returned to
their domiciles, after the blizzard had blown itself out,
and Judith had removed the screws and hinges from
the rear door of the bus so that it could be moved,
Judith sat on the bus steps with Feathers and the
kittens on her lap. Either the grass or the seats in the
Bookmobile would have been more comfortable, but
she felt in transition, neither here nor there, neither
real nor not-real. She grinned. "Halfway down the
stairs is a stair where I sit," she quoted Milne to the
uninterested cat. "There isn't any other stair quite like
it."

No, there wasn't. Never would be. Shouldn't have
been. Shouldn't be. The poor bus was taking an enor-
mous strain. If she didn't move it one way or the
other—if she could bring it into this world—it would

disintegrate, possibly lethally. She had to make a decision now. Back to books and not-real as the only worth? Or forward to maybe?

Judith was no child. She knew that the maybe was ninety-five percent likely to be identical to the other world's reality. Was five percent chance worth hoping for when one might have toothache and sinus trouble and infections that, back there, were solvable?

Feathers stood up on her lap, looked at Judith as if she had suddenly become a week-old dead fish, and picked up a kitten in her mouth. As well as possible, considering the circumstances, she climbed down and stalked into the tall grass growling in a tone that clearly indicated her complete contempt.

Judith felt bereft, lost, dismayed, deserted. She cuddled the other kitten to her cheek and stood up. How could she possibly feel as if she were losing her only friend? She had several close friends back there through the snow. All she needed to do was to go back.

But she followed the cat.

"Wait a minute," she called. "I want to get a lot of things from the bus. Don't go. I'm coming. I'm going to stay."

You idiot! she condemned herself. *Talking to a cat as if it understood!*

It did, and she knew it would. It came back and waited while she got her backpack and her sleeping bag, her towels and her swimming suit, her harmonica and her guitar, her twenty-seven favorite books (for which she wrote a note indicating they could use her uncollected salary to pay) and any number of other things of possible usefulness in her new situation.

The cat sat behind the big stone and purred.

"Okay. Wait for me. I'll be right back."

For the last time, Judy turned the key in the Bookmobile's ignition. The motor had great difficulty starting. "Come on, old friend." Judith patted the dash. "Don't fail me now."

She shook her head. *Now I'm talking to machines,* she thought. But that was nothing new. She always had.

Encouraged, the motor caught and, coughing in protest, came to life. Judy shifted into reverse and backed the vehicle carefully. When the front bumper was just inside the edge of the marking stones, she turned off the ignition, but she did not set the brakes.

She climbed up onto the roof, lay flat, and slid forward feet first. Her body barely fit under the top stone. She wiggled her legs free and down, slithered over, and dropped off. Then she got up, set her back against the front of the bus, and pushed.

When it moved back, she ran as hard as she could run and threw herself flat behind the stone block. The Gate closed.

Things were most unusual for a considerable period of time. Judy lay curled around the cat and the kittens until things settled back to normal—if this was what was to be normal for them from now on.

She stood up. Feathers left the kittens for a moment and leaped onto the stone to sit beside her.

They saw three stones, not four. Two stood upright, one lay here to shelter them. What had happened to the lintel-stone would never be explained, Judy felt sure, but she wasn't interested. What did interest her was that between the two upright stones she could see grass and sunshine and wildflowers and hear birdsong and smell water. The anomaly had been removed, and the Gate . . .

" 'Gate of the Puma,' faff!" she stated, remembering Simon's explanation. "The Puma had nothing to do with it." She stroked the feathery fur on the cat's head and neck. Feathers purred so loudly that Judith wondered what people on the other side of the Gate would believe the rumble to be.

The cat looked up at her, then jumped down and sat by her kittens.

Judith's gaze shifted from the living kittens to the three white shapes on the stone. *A signature*, she thought. Deliberately, she refused to think what had caused the slick black soot that rain wouldn't wash off.

"The Gate of the Kittens," she said softly.

She put everything she didn't plan to carry on the

stone, covered it with her poncho and tucked the ends in securely. Then she put the living kittens on her towel in the top of the backpack and held it open for their mother. She sat.

"Hmm," Judith murmured. "You'd rather see where you're going than where you've been?"

Feathers nodded.

"Let's see what I can do."

Judy slung on the pack, then covered her left shoulder with the folded beach towel and leaned down. The cat jumped up and crouched beside her ear. "Good girl." Judy rubbed her head against the cat's feathery side. "On we go," she said. They started off in the direction of the blue-green light, Judith laying out a path that would allow them safely to avoid the areas where the red-orange and sick yellow-green flared. She supposed it should bother her that she'd been told few other . . . inhabitants . . . of this reality could see the lights, but it didn't. Aside from having one-sided conversations with cats—and Bookmobiles—she had to have some reason for being the one they said was "called." Somewhere on the route between here and the light, she'd been told, would be food and shelter and whatever else she was going to earn or be granted by this world. She hoped that the five percent maybe would be worth it.

She sighed, a long, anticipatory sigh. *It really doesn't matter*, she thought. She'd made existing in reality but living in fantasy enough back in her old world. She could make herself believe it to be enough here, if she had to.

Feathers spat.

Judy smiled. "Nope, it's already better," she agreed, leaning her head into the black-and-gray fur. *It has to be*, she thought. Her mind brought back the sight of the three little bodies whose deaths had paid her way, and their mother's, safe, into their world. *Not for me. For them.*

The cat purred loudly against her left ear.

THE DAMCAT

by Clare Bell

The young folks don't think much of dams these days.
I mean the big dams—Grand Coulee, Shasta, Hoover—
the ones that went up in the first half of this century.
Back in the thirties, when I was an engineer on the
Black Canyon project, we were heroes. Our dams
provided the water and power needed to feed a growing West. Now all you hear about is silt backup that
may turn the big dams into waterfalls in less than a
century. Why, there's even talk of tearing them down
and letting nature reclaim the flooded lands. Maybe
it's a good idea and maybe it isn't. We did push the
dam-building too far and we overlooked things we
should have paid attention to. But, as for tearing
down the dams, well, they better not try it with Black
Canyon. Tell 'em that from old Dale Curtis.

You think I'm just a sentimental, senile cuss who
can't forget that he worked on one of the greatest
dams in the world. Well, there's some of that feeling
there, I'll admit. But, like it or not, that dam is here to
stay. She won't be knocked down. The fellows with
the dynamite and the bulldozers will find out if they
try.

Hell, yes, it's a good dam. We built 'em strong back
then. But that's not the reason Black Canyon will
never fall. You know why? Because that dam is protected and I do mean with a capital "P." Magic.

Now I know you want to find out why, so just have
yourself a sit over there and mind the splinters. It's a
strange story about some Indians and some queer things
that happened while we were building Black Canyon.
And the bobcat. . . .

People say the dam would never have been completed without that cat. The truth is, not only would Black Canyon have remained incomplete, it would have broken when the reservoir was still filling. There's a plaque at the dam site telling about Tonochpa and the cable she pulled through a conduit too small for a man to crawl through. That's what it says on the brass inscription, but I know better. What that little wildcat hauled through the tunnel was more than a bundle of wires.

The reason I got involved in the whole thing was because the government contract said that the dam would not be considered technically complete unless it was instrumented. The Feds wanted all kinds of measurement devices such as strain gauges, contraction joint meters, thermometers and so forth installed in the dam and monitored during construction. Now all these instruments had to be wired to a power source and remote chart recorder. In the hustle and bustle to build the dam (Black Canyon went up in record time), certain details got overlooked. The concrete jockeys were pouring so fast that they didn't think about laying access tunnels or conduits for instrumentation wiring.

A few weeks after I got hired and figured out the situation, I swore at them under my breath and laid temporary cables along the downstream face of the dam to my monitoring shack. We had to have the output from those instruments to tell whether the dam was undergoing any unusual stress or strain that might foretell a collapse. My arrangement worked, but I knew that it would never satisfy the federal inspectors. Those guys had a tendency to follow the letter of the law, not the intent. The contract specified that the monitoring installation had to be permanently installed in conduit that ran inside the dam. I was tearing out what remained of my hair over this problem when I met Mike and Tonochpa.

Actually I met Tonochpa before I met Mike. About a minute before. I don't think either she or I will ever forget that introduction. And neither will a certain pair of pants, though I kept them as a memento of the occasion.

It was the summer of '34, a few months after I had been hired. At that time the crews had finished most of the blasting, but high-scalers still worked the canyon walls upriver from the dam itself. Some days it seemed as though more dust than air hung above the construction site. The deep canyon blocked any breeze from the surrounding desert country and the black basalt sucked up the sun until it was hot as a griddle and you could literally fry flapjacks on the boulders if you didn't mind grit.

To get from the trailer that housed the company field office (all plastered over with the blue NRA eagle like everything else in sight) to the chart-recorder shack, I had to cross an open area in front of the cement mixing plant.

Back in those days, we didn't have the kind of cement trucks with the rotary mixers you see now. We used flatbed diesels with eight-foot wheels, equipped with huge bins bolted to their flatbeds. Those trucks were built like huge hay wagons, with a buckboard seat and no cab over the top. The wet cement would start hardening when it hit the bins so the trucks lined up to load and go as fast as they could. This encouraged some unique driving styles.

One fellow used to stand up on the seat, facing backward so he could watch his bins fill from the overhead hopper. The stream of wet portland cement shot out so fast that he didn't have to stop his truck. The monster ground forward at low throttle while he steered by way of one muddy boot on the wheel. Others soon picked up that cowboy trick from him and the loading area soon resembled a rodeo arena.

With my hard hat banging my glasses down on the bridge of my nose and my clipboard tucked underneath my arm, I played the daily game of dodging the cement haulers. I was nearly in the clear when I saw something shooting up the slope that led to the construction site. I caught a glimpse of blurred legs and long ears. We often spook jackrabbits on the site, so I didn't think much of it until I spotted another animal pelting along behind the rabbit. It moved so fast and churned up so much dust that I couldn't tell what it was. A rope or leash whipped back and forth in the dirt behind the animal. I could tell the critter was after the jackrabbit and not paying attention to much else. Trouble was that the jackrabbit was making a run for the trucks.

I knew the rabbit would make it; I've seen them dash right between those rolling tires. But its pursuer looked like someone's pet and with the handicap of a dragging leash. . . .

I can't say I'm much of an animal lover, but I hate the job of peeling flattened carcasses out of the dirt. As the rattling diesel of the nearest truck battered my ears, I lunged and stamped hard on the trailing rope as the creature shot past me.

I nearly lost my footing as something heavy and furry rebounded against my shins. I heard a strangled caterwaul, then claws began shredding my pantsleg so fast I didn't even feel the pain. Twelve pounds of desert bobcat raked my knee and was heading up for strategic territory by the time I unfroze and tried to grab the beast.

"Tonochpa, no!"

The Indian's voice was a lilting tenor and his accent different from that of the Navajo workers. His hands got to the bobcat before mine and I'm probably lucky they did, since I might not have kept all my fingers. I doubted that he would keep all his either, but the bobcat didn't put one scratch on those dark-skinned hands. He spoke a few words of a language I didn't understand, but the bobcat did. She loosed her hold on me and climbed into his arms. I stood up and found myself facing a short stocky young man dressed in Ben Davis overalls, no shirt, and a dented hard hat.

The cement truck added insult to injury with a derisive blat from its power horn that sent the young Indian scrambling downslope toward the construction site, clutching his bobcat. Not knowing what I intended to do, I followed him. My knee stung like it

had been dragged through a patch of mesquite, my
pants had two-foot long rents in the left leg and my
disposition was out of joint.

When I caught up with the guy, I saw him cradling
the bobcat. Something seemed to be wrong with her;
she gulped and her breathing sounded wheezy. I felt a
pang of guilt for stamping on the rope even though it
probably saved her life. I could see the worry in the
young man's face as he tried to soothe the animal. I
tapped the Indian's bare shoulder and pointed to the
recorder shack on the other side of the canyon bottom.

When we reached the shack, he put his pet on a
rough-hewn workbench and felt in the fur around her
neck. She balanced on her long legs with her little tail
flicking up and down, leaning against him and watching me warily. She coughed once or twice, shook her
wiry fur, then seemed okay. I imagine that yank on
the collar gave her a whack on the windpipe and she
just needed a little time to recover.

Which gave me time to wonder what the hell she
was doing here in the first place. A stinging and tickling sensation on my left leg reminded me that she was
not the only casualty of the incident. I caught her
master's eye and inflated myself, ready to act the part
of the aggrieved white, irritated by the careless ways
of the Indian worker. But somehow he and I didn't fit
those roles. Perhaps the reason was the bobcat.

She was small for a bobcat, judging from the size of
the skins I'd seen tacked on plyboard after some friends
of mine had been out varmint-hunting. Her build was
heavier than a housecat's, her head larger in proportion to her body. That and her legginess gave her a
kittenish look.

The Indian bent over her and whispered a few words
of his language. She lifted her nose and prrruped back
at him.

"She gives you apology," he said in a soft sandy
voice that seemed to match the tone of his skin and
hair. "I, too. My name here is Mike. I call her
Tonochpa."

"Curtis," I said, trying to keep my voice gruff, but

without much success. "Dale Curtis. Pleased to meetcha both, I guess."

Tonochpa swiveled her head, pricking black-tufted ears toward me. Tiger-stripes marked her face, with black bands running out into wide muttonchop whiskers. The rest of her was tawny with black spots that smeared out into bands encircling her legs.

When I moved closer and she didn't spit or hump her back in cat-fashion, I decided she might be in a good mood. She pivoted to face me, leaning forward and hunching up her shoulders. I felt Mike's hand on my elbow, drawing me back.

"What's wrong?" I asked. "She didn't give me the Halloween cat treatment."

Mike shook his head. "Bobcats aren't like your pet cats, Mr. Curtis. Tonochpa won't arch her back to warn you. Instead she'll face you and hump her shoulders to make herself look bigger." He clucked to get the bobcat's attention, then stroked her. "I have learned her language. She is saying that she will get used to you, but she needs time."

He smiled shyly, then looked solemn. "Bobcat scratches can fester, Mr. Curtis. Sit and I will heal the wounds."

I was already reaching for my battered, metal first aid kit. I sat down on a nearby orange crate with the kit on my lap. Mike dug in the side pouch of a knapsack he carried.

"Don't you need anything from here? Alcohol? Iodine? Merthiolate?"

He shook his head. The only items he would accept were a clean rag and the little bottle of alcohol. Once he had rolled up my pants leg and dabbed the wounds clean, he took what looked like the fleshy leaf of an agave, broke it, dusted the gel oozing from the leaf with powder and smeared the resulting concoction on the gashes. I stiffened, expecting the fierce burning you get with iodine or other antiseptics, but all I felt was a soothing coolness that gradually subdued the pain.

I expected him to bind up the wound with the rag,

but he only smeared more of the agave on my leg and told me to keep still until it dried, forming a thick film.

"Indian bandage," he said. "Sticks by itself until scab forms, then falls off."

I eyed him. Somehow, in that gentle way of his, the young Indian had dissolved the barrier of class and color that should have separated him from me. I felt almost as if I should try to reestablish it. But I had no pigeonholes, no places to put him, since I knew almost nothing about him. Two things were obvious; he was trained as a healer, but for some reason, he was working construction.

"Who's your foreman?" I asked. "Isn't he going to be missing you?"

He named someone I'd never heard of.

"And what are you doing with a pet bobcat at a construction site?" I said, trying to reassert my status above him in the hierarchy.

He scooped up Tonochpa, let her climb up his shoulder. "She is my partner," he said, as if it were perfectly obvious. I watched as he clipped the end of her tether to a metal ring riveted to his overalls. He made a clucking noise with his tongue. The bobcat clawed open the flap of his pack and crawled in. The packflap lifted briefly to show two agate-colored eyes.

Mike told me he worked as a "cherry-picker" or high-scaler. Each day he lowered himself in a flimsy bosun's chair from the canyon rim, with rock drill, crowbar and sometimes a load of dynamite. Though most of the loose rock had been blasted and chipped from the walls of Black Canyon, scalers were still hewing out the foundations for the inlet gate towers that would stand behind the dam.

That explained a lot about him. High-scalers were an ornery and independent lot, valued for their skills and their disregard of danger. They could do pretty much as they pleased within certain limits and the bosses looked the other way. Even if it came to having your own mascot along, I suppose.

"Do you really take her with you up there?" I

asked, thinking I was reasonable in believing that hanging from a cable in the midst of noise, blasting and confusion would be sheer hell for any creature, let alone such a nervous and timid animal as a wild cat.

"She is my partner," he said again. "We trust each other."

She is my partner. It sounded so simple, so obvious and yet so strange to this white man's way of thinking. My face must have betrayed my skepticism.

"Tonochpa keeps me from harm. Other high-scalers, they have accidents. Falls. Blow fingers, eyes, out with explosives. Not me."

I'd done some reading on Indian anthropology. "Is Tonochpa your totem?"

Mike's smile was just a twitch at the corners of his mouth. He eyed me in that odd, indirect way. "Because you try to understand, even if it is for the white man's purpose and in the white man's way, I will share a secret with you."

He motioned me toward the bobcat, who seemed willing to accept my presence now. I approached, still aware of my ragged trouser leg and the drying agave gel pulling my leg hairs. He chucked the cat under the chin, making her raise her head. In the buff and gray fur at her throat, I saw a pair of oddly curved short stripes, each with their ends nested in the concavity of the other's arc.

Mike ruffled the fur with a square, blunt thumbnail. "She had this marking when I found her as a half-drowned kitten after a flash flood. This symbol is the *nakwatch*, the sign of brotherhood among my people."

I peered at the *nakwatch* marking, amused that the Indian would take such a thing so seriously.

"Touch it," he said. "You have earned the right."

The right to make a damned fool of myself, I thought, wondering why I didn't have the guts to send him on his way. I thanked my own version of a guardian spirit that no one else was around the recording shack. I made a tentative poke at the bobcat, fearing she would retaliate, but she only eyed me steadily with pupil slits that seemed to pulse to my heartbeat. When I withdrew my finger, she ducked her head and washed the marking as if she took pride in it.

"Are you a *hatathli*?" I asked Mike, drawing on my book-learned wisdom.

His smile became tolerant. "*Hatathli* is Navajo. A medicine man who heals with sand paintings. I am a healer of the Hopi tribe."

I felt vaguely embarrassed. The little reading I had done said no love was lost between the Hopi and Navajo tribes. To mistake one for the other was a typical outsider's blunder. I took refuge in skepticism.

"Do you really take the cat on the high-wire act with you?"

"I would not go there without her. If you doubt, come visit us at the north inlet tower site." His smile became a grin, covering his wide face. "I must go now, Mr. Curtis," he added, gathering up the knapsack and Tonochpa."

I wasn't ready for his departure. We had some unfinished business, namely the state of my pants. He read my face, then followed my gaze down to the rents the bobcat had made.

"You bring that pair of pants when you come up to the tower site." He winked. "I am good at mending the holes Tonochpa makes."

I refrained from asking how many holes the wildcat had made and who she'd made them in. I watched the two of them leave, scratching my incipient bald patch beneath the band of my hard hat. I decided to pay a visit to the high-scalers on the north tower site even if it meant skipping some day's lunch. The young Indian who called himself Mike and his guardian spirit disguised as a bobcat intrigued the hell out of me. I had to know whether he was pulling my leg or not. I stashed a pair of field glasses in the recorder shack and waited for a piece of slack time long enough for a trip up the canyon wall.

Several days later, I rode old truck-shuttle number 160 from the workers' tract city to the dam site early enough to slip in a visit to the tower site before work. Because the foundations for the inlet tower were being hacked from the canyon wall, the only way to reach it was the inclined tramway we dubbed the Monkeyslide. I got on with the last group of first shift stragglers and clung to the welded pipe railing as the Monkeyslide ratcheted its way up.

My fellow riders watched me from the corners of their eyes while they told tales of the previous night's carousing in nearby Glitter Gulch. They spat from the tramcar and rolled cigarettes from pipe-tin tobacco. Feeling as out of place as an oyster in the desert, I searched among the press of bodies, tormented by the unreasonable fear that Mike had decided to skip work that day, had been taken ill, or had been fired.

With its gears clashing and groaning, the Monkeyslide lurched to a halt, the guard chain fell aside, and everyone piled out onto a plank catwalk overlooking the black basalt ledge forming the inlet gate tower foundation. The "cherry-pickers" around me all seemed to become alpine spiders, for they disdained the plankwalk to clamber away over the rocks and lower themselves on cables to their places below. Soon I was alone on the catwalk except for the clinking of chisels and the tearing rattle of rock-drills.

I tiptoed as close to the edge of the unguarded plankwalk as I dared and peered over. I found it hard to look down without breaking into a cold sweat. I don't have much trouble with heights; I've clambered about on enough bridges and girders to know that part of myself. But knowing that a misstep meant a fall through half a mile worth of nothing gave me a new respect for gravity. The planks underfoot seemed to take delight in sagging in such a way as to tip me while the grit slithered my feet toward the treacherous edge.

I finally found a secure perch and scanned for Mike with my field glasses. There he was, a tiny figure in overalls, hard hat and knapsack, whaling away at the fissured rock from the end of a long line. He looked too distant to see my wave. I decided it would be better not to distract him, so I just watched. I saw no sign of Tonochpa.

He scaled away the rock loosened by previous blasting then drilled holes for new charges. After drilling a square grid of holes, he paused, planted both boots against the cliff face and leaned out over empty air as if he were relaxing on a sofa. As if that was a signal, I saw the packflap stir, then the bobcat emerged.

She climbed over his shoulder and onto his chest, nestling beneath his chin. He fed her bits of flattened baloney sandwich from an overall pocket. I could see that she wore a makeshift safety harness and a tether shackled to Mike's cable. Even so, I thought, a short fall would still have a nasty jolt at the end of it. But my criticism was lost in fascination as I kept my glasses trained on the two. It was an amazing picture of man and animal in precarious balance against the panorama of cliff, sky and canyon.

Bursts of noise from other scalers drilling on either side didn't appear to bother the bobcat in the least. She sat on Mike's chest, kneading the front of his overalls as if she were a household moggy sitting on someone's knee before a cozy fire. When another scaler flipped a cigarette butt at Mike, telling him to quit fooling with the cat and get back to work, Tonochpa only yawned derisively and crawled back into the knapsack.

I watched from overhead as Mike packed explosive into the holes he drilled, set the charges, then jerked the line as a signal for someone to haul him up before the stuff blew. It was close. I glimpsed his feet disappearing out of my view field only a breath before the rockface puffed out and a rumbling growl shook the cliff.

I picked my way along the plankwalk, arriving just as the other men hauled him up. His face was masked in gray from sweat and rockdust, making him look as though he were wearing pancake makeup. He spat grit, then grinned as he saw me.

"You saw us, Dale Curtis? Tonochpa and me at the end of the long line? Now you believe, hey?"

"I believe," I said.

"You got the pants she ripped?"

I handed over the bundle wrapped in brown paper.

Flinging one hand behind him, Mike flipped up the knapsack flap and let the bobcat scramble out. Perched on his shoulder, she appraised me. I expected that she might be slightly ruffled by the nearness of the blast Mike had just set, but not one hair was awry. Mike stroked her with rough affection. "I'm not afraid, she's not afraid," he announced proudly. "Best team on the high walls."

A whistle shrilled from the canyon floor, echoing between the walls. It reminded me that my own work hours would soon begin. I had to catch the Monkeyslide on its return trip.

"You come see me again," Mike said as I took my leave of him, "you get your pants back. Fixed. Deal?" He clucked his tongue at Tonochpa, who returned to the knapsack.

"Deal," I agreed. I didn't even wince when he shoved my parcel in with the bobcat.

I braved the Monkeyslide to retrieve my pants and then a few times more just to watch Mike and Tonochpa. Mike did a good job with the pants. They couldn't be made good as new, but he'd sewed up the rents with small strong stitches that would probably outlast the cloth itself. The repair on my leg proved equally successful. The wound healed rapidly and the dried agave peeled off by itself, just as Mike said it would.

My problem with the instrument cabling remained, though my temporary wiring functioned well enough to postpone the final version. Each day I monitored the health of the growing dam via the signals sent from a network of strain gauges and joint contraction meters. From these instruments, I could tell if the concrete was hardening to design strength and whether stress was concentrating at vulnerable points or distributing evenly throughout the structure.

The wiggling traces of the Beckman strip chart recorder pens formed patterns, first on the paper, then in my notebook and ultimately in my mind. For me, the dam was an interconnected web of signals, all making up an entity that seemed almost alive. I could watch the great structure "breathe" slowly over intervals of several hours. I could see it expand and contract from the effects of temperature and shift to accommodate itself to the mass of new concrete pours. To me it was a great concrete beast, expanding, waking, and gathering strength for the task of holding back the river.

The multiple channels of information coming from my instruments had their own ranges of variation between parameters I had established by experience. The recorder pens wandered on the chart grids, but always remained within the bounds I expected and returned to the averages I had calculated.

One morning, about three weeks after I first visited Mike and Tonochpa, I noticed one of my strain gauge readings had drifted up overnight. Not beyond limits, but enough to be noticeable. I checked the channel for electrical problems, then the instrument's calibration. Everything came out clean.

Over the next few days I watched the trace closely, ready to call the construction engineers if the strain gauge should indicate a problem. I'd installed this one near a recent concrete pour and counted on it to give warning if the cement was going rotten. Its reading stabilized, staying rock steady at the new set point. I was about to relax my watch when a second gauge, located in the same sector, showed an upward drift.

I called Nelson, the construction engineer and had him out to the sector to probe the hardening cement and do chemical tests. Everything indicated that the pour was hardening as it should within the forms. Nelson suggested, none too diplomatically, that I should recheck my instruments.

I scratched my thinning hair beneath my hard hat. Should I be alarmed about such slight deviations? The instrument readings had kept to their expected levels ever since I'd installed the first strain gauge in the rising foundations of the dam. Why should they change now?

I spoke first to another engineer who'd had training

in the new technology of instrumenting construction projects such as this one. He only scratched his head beneath his hard hat and said that my readings were within acceptable bounds. My boss looked at the traces and said I worried too much. The concrete engineers told me to have faith—after all, it was they who were building Black Canyon.

I'm a guy who knows when worrying is counterproductive, so I shrugged my shoulders and quit sweating. I started reading the paper again during lunch instead of spending the time trying to analyze my data. I didn't expect much out of the local scandal sheet, but I was surprised to find an interesting column by a guy who bylined himself Ernie Pyle. His writing was terse and to the point, not high-flown or fancy. It seemed he had taken a few years off to roam around the Southwest, describing his experiences in little squibs that he sent to the syndicate. They were refreshing to read after all the bad news about Europe and the threat of impending war.

Other guys on the site took to reading Pyle and I remember my boss saying that this fellow would make a good war correspondent, if it came down to that. The writer really made himself popular with our crew when he did his "Dambuilders" column, describing his impressions of the men at another construction site just north of Black Canyon. I thought that if Ernie had been impressed with the hard hat he'd seen who rode the cable hook from gorge to rim without giving the trip a second thought, what might flow from his pen on meeting not only an Indian worker with a similar disregard for the hazards of height, but a bobcat who shared his attitude and his place on the end of a high-scaler's line?

Well, Ernie went on to the other end of the state to write about rutted roads and Navajos and Mike's Tonochpa never found immortality in the lines of his column. Ernie did serve one purpose and that was to get me thinking I hadn't paid the two a visit lately.

By that time, the tower crew had nearly finished the inlet gate foundations. They rerouted the Monkeyslide to stop at the rock ledge instead of the overhead plankwalk. When I got off, I found Mike with a gang of other high-sçalers, amusing them with the bobcat. Mike put her at one end of a coolant pipe that seemed impossibly small for her and took bets on whether she'd make it through.

I'd seen housecats pull some amazing contortions in getting themselves in and out of tight spots, but this bobcat put them all to shame. Although two or three times the size of a regular cat, she could shinny in and out of the tiniest places. She seemed to be able to elongate herself into a big furry caterpillar, for no sooner had her stub tail disappeared down one end than her whiskers appeared at the other. Mike was raking in a pile when I sauntered up.

"Aren't you afraid she'll get stuck?" I asked him.

He grinned and shook his head, his eyes glinting in his dark face beneath the battered steel hard hat. "She knows. If she can't get through, she won't go. Never got stuck yet."

He shooed the other men away, picked up Tonochpa and went with me to the shade cast by a boulder. There we could sit and look out over the rising dam. Mike's mood seemed to change, becoming pensive. He asked me what work I did, what all the equipment in the recorder shack was for. Carefully I explained the study of stresses and strains within the structure and how they must be monitored to ensure the strength of the completed dam.

He looked at me piercingly from beneath the rim of his hard hat. "I did not know that you are a medicine man."

I blinked and shook my head, taken completely aback by his remark.

"You do not know it yourself? Think about what it is you do. You guard the wholeness of this thing, this big dam we build. You use your white man's magic to seek out weakness or bad influences and you tell others how to cure these things."

I didn't know whether to burst out laughing or take

him seriously. It was a strange way to characterize my profession, but in a way, he was right.

"And so," he said, picking up Tonochpa and stroking her, "is this dam whole and strong?"

He did not look directly into my eyes, but I felt as if he could read the story of the wandering traces, the subtle shifts in balance within the structure that might be early warnings of trouble.

I don't know why, but I spilled it all to him. The strange readings, the uncertainties, the attempts to convince my boss and the construction engineers that something just might be wrong.

"The thing is, I don't have any real indications. Just these strange little shifts in my equipment and my bad feelings." I concluded.

"Feelings," said Mike. "That is what's important and what you must trust. The others are not wise to ignore their own medicine man. I also have bad feelings about the dam. I will show you why."

He asked me if I'd brought my field glasses and took me to a spot where we'd be isolated from the other scalers on the tower site and yet could have a clear view down to the construction atop the dam.

I looked where he directed me, although I had no idea what I was searching for. I watched the crew on the section almost directly below me.

Though I'd never worked the cement gangs, I knew what was involved in mixing and pouring concrete for a structure such as this. I'd gained a sense for the rhythms of the work. Things happened in a certain order; the forms went up, the twelve-ton bucket was filled on the canyon rim and dropped on the cableway, the concrete was dumped and spread—all this the men did quickly, smoothly, and with few unnecessary movements. Thus I was good at detecting even small disruptions, such as the one that occurred when a worker, stopping to glance over his shoulder, slipped his hand into his overall pocket and poked something into the gray cement sludge alongside a coolant pipe.

I noticed something else. As the man shaded his eyes against the sun, I caught a glimpse of leathery

skin and a hawklike Indian profile. I felt Mike touch
my elbow.

"Put the glasses down and turn away," he said softly.
I did. We both walked away from the edge, leaned
against a rock. Mike asked me what I'd seen. I told
him.

"That guy was an Indian, wasn't he?" I asked. "One
of your people?"

"No. I'm the only Hopituh on this site. Others
Pima, Hualapai, Navajo."

"Well, he looked to be doing something crooked," I
said. "Look, I think we ought to go down there and
tell the gang boss."

"No good," Mike said. "I tell you what he find.
Something that looks like a pebble."

Now I was completely lost. "Why would someone
take all the trouble to plant one rock in a pour that
has a million of 'em?"

"Not rock," the Hopi said. "Bead carved from bone.
Used to cause people to get sick or bad things to
happen."

"He thinks he's putting some kind of hex on the
dam?"

"Not just him," Mike answered. "Others. From
here, I see. I have sharp eyes. And in town, I hear."

I considered his implication of an Indian conspiracy
against Black Canyon. If certain workers were plant-
ing hidden charges or doing other things that might
weaken the dam, that was one thing. But an attack
using magic?

"Come on," I said. "Hasn't this gone far enough? I
believed you about the bobcat, but I can't accept that
anyone can knock down tons of steel and concrete
with fetishes and incantations."

For a minute I thought he was going to go all sullen
on me, but he only cradled Tonochpa in the crook of
his arm and ruffled the place on her neck where the
nakwatch lay. Mildly he asked, "Then what does your
own magic tell you, white medicine man?"

Those readings. Those damned readings that could
mean anything. But I wasn't ready to take Mike's

explanation. I was a little angry at him for using my own uncertainties to stampede me toward a ridiculous conclusion.

"I'm sorry," I said to him, a little more curtly than I meant to. "I don't think we're talking the same language, sport. Look, I have to get back to my job."

"It is all right. You must wait and watch. Then you will see."

I only hunched my shoulders and walked away from him, his strange ideas, and his damned bobcat.

It was just past noon on the following day when a worker fell from his scaffold into wet concrete that had just been dumped by the bucket. Rescuers stirred and probed the heavy cement, but the scaffold was so high that the fall took the victim far under the surface and suffocated him before he could claw his way to the top. They could not even recover the body before the cement in the form began to harden.

Though a few roustabouts cursed, the rest shrugged their shoulders and went on with their labor. I knew that men were expendable to Black Canyon; the project consumed them as it did explosives and cement. There was no pause in the work and no investigation.

Two days later a cement pour atop the dam refused to harden. While people were scrambling around trying to figure out why, a scaffold broke and two men fell to their deaths. The only thing anyone found was a strange ring woven of yucca fibers and feathers that floated atop the still-heaving mass of concrete. And another strain gauge left its previous value and started to drift up.

For some reason, Mike stopped by my recorder shack the next day during lunch. As always, he had Tonochpa with him. Watching him feed her bits of baloney sandwich made me remember the shinny-through-the-pipe game he played with her at the tower site. Something tickled my mind. Hadn't a concrete engineer said he'd laid a pipe through which coolant had been pumped while the concrete around it was curing? Now the run of pipe lay empty and could serve as a conduit for my instrument cable, if I could feed the cable through. Trouble was that the pipe ran from one end of the dam to the other, but only had a fourteen-inch diameter. A man couldn't get through, but a compact creature like Tonochpa. . . .

I asked Mike if she could do it. I said I'd pay him for her services.

"Sure." He grinned.

"Is she strong enough? We'll run a rope first and tie it to the cable, but a few thousand feet of rope is going to be heavy."

"Only way to know is to try," said Mike. He stroked the bobcat, who arched her back against his hand.

"Okay," I said. "How about a week from today? We'll do it when everyone's eating lunch." I didn't mention that having a bunch of my colleagues observing this stunt wouldn't add much to my reputation, especially if the idea didn't work.

Mike became interested in the recorder traces and raised his eyebrows at me knowingly.

"You really think that this is being caused by . . . magic?" I blurted and added, "Don't get the idea I believe such mumbo jumbo."

He just shrugged his shoulders. "To me, this is magic," he said, indicating the banks of recorders and their wiggling pens. "To you it is the way the world works. Perhaps the same is true of what you call Indian magic. It is all part of the way the world works." He paused. "Are you worried about the dam?"

"Hell, yes! Aren't you? You've put sweat into it."

"And I have gotten out of it what I want," he said. "A living. And that will end when they no longer need us high-scalers on the tower sites."

I stared at him, unsure of what he meant. I'd seen how hard he worked and the pride he took in his job. I thought he was like the rest of us, eager to see the dam completed and the river harnessed for power and agriculture. But I could see that my assumption was completely wrong. It occurred to me that Black Canyon might not be a boon to the Indians, but instead a means by which more of their land might be wrenched from them.

"If that's how you feel, why are you worried that the dam might collapse?" I challenged.

"I have an uncle who has settled with his relatives in the Imperial Valley," he said quietly. "You know how much water will be backed up behind this dam."

I knew and I could well imagine how a dam break could send a wall of water rushing down into the agricultural areas below Black Canyon.

"Why don't you just warn him?" I asked, trying not to sound resentful.

"He has worked hard to get the farm and resettle his family. Also, he does not judge me old enough to give him advice," Mike answered.

I sighed and rubbed the back of my neck. I should have known that the only thing that would motivate an Indian would be concern for his relatives. To me, relatives were nothing but a pain in the tailfeathers. Well, at least Mike and I had the same goal in mind, even if our reasons were different. At least he would let me use Tonochpa to get my cable placed.

I continued logging my observations daily, hoping that the record I made would not have to be used in an investigation should Black Canyon Dam collapse during filling. The changes remained small in magnitude, and although more deviations appeared, none grew to alarming proportions. Perhaps the stress and strain numbers were not what they'd been calculated to be. Perhaps my previous experience on other projects was misleading me on this one.

Yet I couldn't help the feeling that the dam itself was trying to send me messages through the wiring of my equipment, trying to tell me that something was going quietly wrong inside the rising mass of steel and concrete.

Government inspectors came and went, praising the speed of construction. They said that my discoveries were nothing to worry about. At close to eight hundred feet, Black Canyon was the tallest gravity-arch dam yet built and it should not be expected to conform to rules built up by experiences with lesser structures.

If men who were supposed to know said the dam was safe, then who was I to argue? I decided to pay attention to petty things I was sure I could handle, such as laying the instrument cable through the coolant pipe.

The day came and Mike showed up with Tonochpa at my recorder shack, as promised. He seemed ill at ease and told me he felt other Indian workers were watching him. And as we made our way up, I swear we got several dirty looks from hard-hatted Navajos. One moved to follow us.

"What the hell's he worried about," I hissed to Mike. "We're only placing a damned cable, for Pete's sake."

Mike, however, didn't answer. I heard him chanting something under his breath. I was wondering whether all the Indians on the site were going slightly loco, this one included. Perhaps this wasn't the best time after all.

As if Mike read my hesitation, he took my sleeve and drew me after him. I shrugged and went. We ducked into a maze of two-by-fours and plywood making up the forms for the next cement pours. He led me over, around and through the framings in a wily trail intended to throw off the Navajo. At last we came to a frame butting up against a finished pour. The end of the coolant pipe stuck out of the concrete block at a distance two feet above the floor we stood on. I spied a panel of plywood on the ground, picked it up and propped it into place to close the way we had come.

We crouched there in the rough chamber made by the plywood sides of the concrete forms: Mike, Tonochpa, and I. Behind us was the roll of cable on its unreeling frame, one end tied to a coil of rope. Mike brought out something else from his knapsack, a leather pouch decorated with symbols. He made a motion as if to attach this to Tonochpa, then hesitated.

"Sacred blue cornmeal in this bag. It will disturb the net of witchcraft woven through this dam. If I put this talisman on her, the sorcerers will know," he muttered, "but she must have protection." He turned to me, looking worried, then his brow cleared. "Bind the rope to her harness. Quickly." A few knots and I made the end fast while he held Tonochpa.

A sudden tapping rattled the plywood sheet beside the one I had propped hastily between two posts to block anyone from interfering once we had started.

"The witches know what I am doing," Mike whispered. With deft fingers, he bound the medicine pouch of cornmeal around the bobcat's neck on the opposite side from where we tied the rope. He placed her at the opening to the coolant pipe, where it emerged from the cement face. Then, to my surprise, he made a tiny tear in the bag with his knife. To my eyes the hole appeared useless, for it would only allow an insignificant dribble and would probably clog up. Mike only smiled and shook his head.

"The hole is large enough for the guarding power of the cornmeal to pass through," he said.

The bobcat nosed the pipe's end, tested it with her whiskers. To me, the diameter looked too small. Had we miscalculated? Tonochpa seemed ready to agree with me, for she drew back her whiskers as if to retreat. Something made her halt. She eyed the dark interior of the pipe, then thrust her muzzle inside. One front paw slid in, then another. She shinnied her way into the coolant pipe, pulling the rope behind her. I could barely contain a cheer.

"No time for that," said Mike harshly as someone struck the plywood again. "The witches are moving against us."

"I only hope that isn't the gang foreman on the other side wanting to know what in hell we're doing," I said, and added, "Or my boss." I grabbed the slithering rope and helped to feed it into the tunnel. The Hopi stooped, laying out a line of powder from another leather pouch. He ran it around me, around the spooling cable, up to the concrete wall and even sprinkled some on top of the coolant pipe.

From the other side of the plywood came a strange chanting song that made me feel as if I had prickles all over my body. I noticed that it affected Mike even more than I, for he had to fight to keep moving.

He paused, wiping sweat from his brow. "I pray this will be all I have to do, Dale Curtis," he said. I felt baffled. Tonochpa was safely into the pipe now. No one could reach her or drag her out, except by the rope that Mike and I guarded. I continued to feed the rope in response to Tonochpa's steady pull. And then, suddenly, the pull ceased at the same time as the chanting from the other side became louder.

"Damn. Either she's stuck, or she got cold feet."

"No." I saw Mike's throat move as he swallowed, caught the sheen of sweat on his wide face. "She has been stopped. I feel what is happening." He snatched up his knapsack and began pulling things out. A kilt of white leather. Body paints. Spruce branches.

"White medicine man, you must help me now," he said and surprised the hell out of me by wiggling out of his overalls. He whipped off his shirt, then bound the white kilt around his waist. With quick strokes, he fingerpainted his arms and legs. He lifted his chin, pressed a jar of black paint into my hand. "Make the *nakwatch* symbol on my neck, in the same place as Tonochpa has it."

"Now wait just one minute," I protested. "I've gone along with you this far because I want my cable placed in the dam. You start this mumbo jumbo and I'm out."

Mike whirled to me, but his face was calm. "You may lie to yourself, but you do not lie to me. Your magic tells you that the dam is threatened. You believe your magic."

He had me there. I'd been watching those jiggling recorder traces with my heart in my mouth, hoping one of them would cross a limit so I could justify recommending an evacuation. I could just see the dam crumbling with the men still crawling on it, releasing the water that had already begun to back up behind the lower section. He might have a hair of a chance of being right . . .

He touched the spot under his jaw. I painted. I put

streaks on his face and spots on his body to make him resemble a desert wildcat, then drew back as he began to chant and stamp.

The rope jerked, began to move again. Mike danced harder, chanted louder. Again it stopped. I wondered what in hell was happening to Tonochpa. If she got stuck, she'd die in there. There'd be no way to get her out.

Mike had been dancing with his eyes half-closed, his face lifted dreamily toward the sky. His head snapped down, his eyes opened as if someone had slapped him. Still stamping in rhythm, he beckoned to me.

"Take your shirt off," he panted. He took the paints I was still holding while I peeled out of my shirt and undershirt. Even as I was still wrestling my arms out of the sleeves, he began painting my chest in brown and white, adding spots. Then he did my face, adding the *nakwatch* sign in the same place under my chin. I must have looked a sight, capering about bare from the waist up with a paint-streaked face capped with a hard hat.

"Dance," the Indian commanded, and I did my best to imitate his powerful stamp-shuffle. Suddenly I found myself face to face with him. Without hesitation, he reached out and placed two fingers firmly on my neck where the *nakwatch* sign was drawn. It happened to coincide with my carotid pulse. He pressed so hard it hurt and I began to feel dizzy, with white flashes starting before my eyes.

He told me to press his mark in the same manner and so we stood, arms crossing, fingers pressing each other's throats. I looked into his eyes and saw that the pupils were reshaping themselves into vertical slits. I felt dizzy, light-headed, as if I were losing control of my body. My legs buckled. I sagged. I felt him go down with me, gradually sinking.

It was not earth I came to rest on but a viscous black nothingness that gave beneath me and surrounded me. Mike was there, too, for my fingers remained on his neck as if glued there and I felt the ever increasing beat of his pulse along with mine. The beats changed in cadence and character as they blended together. Now it was the pace of a heart much faster and wilder than a man's, a thrumming that seemed to echo off curved walls of steel that imprisoned the creature Mike and I had become.

Yet Mike and I no longer existed as separate beings. We had fused to become the bobcat—I was the bobcat. I never questioned that I had ever been anything else. I felt my whisker ends brush the walls of the pipe, felt ice-cold steel beneath my pads as I inched my way along in darkness. I strained my muscles against the drag of the rope tied to my harness. And then I stopped.

Now I could hear the rustling and squealing and the patter of feet transmitted to me by the faintly ringing metal walls of the tunnel. The musky smell grew in my nostrils, first making me lick my chops, then making me shiver as it became strong, then overwhelming.

A wave of rats and mice poured down the pipe, running between my paws, along my sides, even over my head. My hunger for prey possessed me. I caught a rat in my jaws and shook it, then remembered. I had been sent on this journey by one who trusted me. I could not take time now to kill.

More rodents spilled down the pipe until I could hardly avoid treading on them. As if they resented my ignoring them, the mice and rats nipped and bit. I swatted them aside, dug away mounds of gray-furred bodies that threatened to block the way, scratched, scrabbled and butted my way through, dragging the weight my companion had fastened on me.

Several long-tailed stragglers scurried beneath my paws and then suddenly, I was free of the pests. I crawled on.

I felt the curved wall bump my back and wondered if the tunnel had become smaller. My paws seemed to slip and slither in the narrowing gutter in which I walked. There came a strange wrenching sound and the pipe itself gave a spasmodic jerk, as if someone had twisted its two ends in opposite directions. I heard the deformed metal groan aloud. I fought to drag forward one forepaw after another, feeling the tunnel grow tight about my shoulders. At last I could only let my forepaws slide before me as I pushed myself onward with my rear paws and still the tunnel constricted as if I were in the coils of some great snake.

And at last, I could only lie at full length, the shivering metal binding me tightly. My heart fluttered and I felt the chilling weakness of fear. Why had my companion sent me here to die of terror fighting a thing I knew nothing about? Then a voice seemed to speak within my head. The pipe was made of metal, the voice said. Alloy steel has a strong bending resistance. It would never twist like a wrung-out towel no matter how much force was applied to the ends. That was impossible, therefore it wasn't happening. I did not need to understand the details, only to believe I was no longer trapped. And I heard the voice of the one who sent me into this darkness telling me to believe that the pipe could not hold me.

I buried my nose in my forelegs. Some part of me knew those words were true, but the animal part of me was afraid. I could only try to convince myself that the way would open again and I could resume my journey. I thought of my companion and the other voice that spoke with him. That voice knew. That voice understood. And so I believed in what it said, though I understood little.

The walls withdrew from around me. I stood up, shook myself and went on.

I felt as though I had crawled forever in a world of darkness and inward-curving walls when I heard something that made me freeze in mid-step. It was a whispering sound with a hard edge that reverberated within the pipe. I listened again, swiveling my ears backward, feeling the sound vibrate the hairs of my ear tufts. It came from behind me, a sibilant buzz I knew well. I had heard it once when I startled a big diamondback sunning on a rock. Now the musty snake-smell drifted to my nostrils and sweat from my paw pads slicked the pipe's interior.

The rattler was behind me; I quickened my pace to

gain distance. A dry sound, half crackle, half buzz, sounded again close to my tail. I scrambled and wiggled down the pipe in a frantic attempt to get away from the snake. And then I felt a change in the thick line that was fastened to my harness. Its surface seemed to change as it moved against my flank, becoming rough, like bark and then scaly.

No longer were its motions the results of my pulling. The thing seemed to writhe with its own life. Had I been able to turn my head in the pipe, I would have bitten away the lashings that bound it to me. But I had no room, so I could only scuttle as fast as I could lay down my paws.

The lashings and my harness changed and thickened. Through my fur I could feel scales emerging on the straps that rubbed against my body. I screamed in dread as they began to crawl, shifting and coiling about me as I ran. I felt the snake's chin glide through the fur on my side, then up over my back. I threw myself about in a frenzy, trying to smash the rattler's head against the walls of the pipe.

The snake came on, undulating over my shoulders and down around my neck, the smell and feel of it driving me into maddened thrashing. I ripped scales off with my claws, tried to sink my teeth into the thing, but it only kept coming. A faint part of my mind wondered why it hadn't struck me with its fangs.

And then I knew. I felt the snake's wedge-shaped head probing in my fur beneath my jaw, searching for the thong that tied the pouch of blue cornmeal around my neck. It slipped beneath the thong and twisted to break it. The pouch fell away and the snake with it.

When the rattler's coils loosed, I gathered myself for a leap that would shoot me down the pipe. I could see a slight circle of daylight in the distance. My journey was nearly over. But I knew, with a certainty that was not mine, that if I abandoned the pouch of cornmeal, I would leave my task unfinished.

I was shuddering so hard I could barely keep my footing. A part of me screamed in consuming panic, begging me to run toward the light. But I remembered the one who had sent me and knew I could not fail him.

Instead of springing ahead, I backed up until I felt the rattler's coils against my hind legs. Scrabbling about with all four paws, I snagged something leathery, wrenched it away from the snake.

A blow knocked me against the sides of the pipe and two fierce stabs of fire penetrated my flank. The rattler had struck. The poison burned outward from my hip, swelling and stiffening my hind leg. I grabbed the neck of the cornmeal pouch and fought my way toward the light, which wavered now before my eyes as my body became heavier and heavier. The snake kept its grip, pumping venom into me as I dragged it along. But I thought only of moving my three leaden feet and dragging the useless fourth as I kept my jaws clenched about the neck of the medicine pouch.

And then, as I struggled toward it, the light seemed to flare, then dim. My yowl of dismay echoed down the pipe, but just as suddenly, the surface dropped from beneath my feet and I tumbled, still entangled in the snake's coils, its poison in my blood and nothing but black emptiness around me. . . .

I came to with a sudden start. The band of the hard hat still encircling my head felt so strange I wanted to claw it off. What were the wrappings about my waist and legs?

I felt a hand shaking me. My head wobbled. "Dale!" Mike's voice hissed in my ear. "She's through! Hurry"

Still discarding shreds of bobcat thoughts, I staggered to my feet. Mike had thrown aside the plywood and gone sprinting along the wooden catwalk that led to the other end of the dam. I pelted after him, wiping the black paint from my face as I ran. I didn't even try to make sense of what was happening, I just followed the Indian in his flapping white kilt.

I saw him leap down into a nest of plywood forms and steel bars that awaited the next pour. That's where the coolant pipe emerged. When my boots hit the concrete near where Mike had dropped, I saw him stooping over the body of the bobcat. She had used her remaining strength to drag herself out of the pipe. I could see the trail of blue cornmeal grains running from the pouch around her neck back into the pipe and disappearing down its depths.

At first I thought Tonochpa was dead, then I saw her rib cage tremble. With a curse, Mike wrenched something from her flank. It was the desiccated corpse of a huge Western diamondback, the fangs in its flattened head tipped with bobcat blood.

"Burn it," he said fiercely, as he gathered up Tonochpa and threw down the dried snakeskin. I bent, played the flame of my battered lighter under the long-dead rattlesnake. It startled me by catching fire like a piece of resin timber and crumbling into embers.

Mike put the limp cat in his lap, He massaged her rib cage with his thumbs, his face tight with worry. "Little one," he moaned, "the snake was never alive, no poison runs in your blood." I stood beside him, not knowing what to do. I'd heard that some wild creatures were so highly strung that they could die of shock.

Then he did something I didn't expect. Quickly he laid a piece of his woven kilt-sash across her face, covered her muzzle with his lips and blew short shallow breaths through her nose and mouth. He did several cycles, each time pausing to pump her rib cage with his fingers and listening for signs that she would breathe on her own. The last time, I thought the moisture in his eyes would spill over into tears, but the wildcat gave a sudden jerk away from the cloth, opened her mouth in a huge gape, and inhaled.

She kept breathing. Her ears twitched, then her eyes opened, fixing me with a baleful glare as if she knew my part in setting up this crazy adventure. At Mike's request, I retrieved both our clothes and his knapsack. He wrapped Tonochpa in my shirt and fed her something medicinal from a clay jar in his pack. Gently he untied the rope from her harness, handing the end to me. I touched the rope hesitantly, fearing it might sprout scales and writhe in my hand, but it only hung stiffly. A bundle of twisted fiber tied to a cable I could now winch through the dam—that's all it was.

And I was an engineer again, someone whose realities consisted of hardware, measurements, and records. For an instant I wondered if the entire experience had just been some kind of hallucination. I certainly couldn't deny the presence of the rope in the conduit or the trail of blue cornmeal running out of the pipe's end.

Tonochpa had completed my task. I wondered what else she had done. Mike stood, cradling the recovering bobcat in his arms, his eyes fixed on the line of cornmeal. Then he turned to me. "Black Canyon Dam is safe. My partner did her work well." His smile turned ironic. "Perhaps too well."

I scratched my head under the hard hat meaning to ask him what the hell he meant by that, but he got in ahead of me. "Let's see if your white-man's magic agrees with mine," he said, holding Tonochpa in the crook of his elbow as he climbed out of the plywood bracings of the form. I followed, eager to see what my recorder tracings revealed.

I stared at the charts with my mouth gaping. For the last hour, every trace looked like the output of a seismograph during an earthquake. But in the short interval following, the pens returned to the same solid baseline values I had seen before the changes of the last few weeks took place.

"My God," I said, looking at Mike. "Now I have to believe."

"The dam is whole. You are a medicine man, as I said. You and I and Tonochpa, we worked together to make the healing. We have done even more than that."

I paused, staring at him. "What?"

"The line of cornmeal that Tonochpa laid during her passage through the pipe will do more than ward off evil magic. It will bind the dam together against all attempts to destroy it." He paused. "In truth, I did not want this to happen, but it was the price I have paid to save my uncle and his family." He paused and looked at me steadily. "Black Canyon Dam will never fall."

It didn't matter whether I believed him or not. We had no way to undo what we had done, even if we wanted to. What mattered now was that I had my cable in place as the contract specified and I could hook up my instruments permanently and finish the job.

There isn't much more to say, I guess. A week or so later, Mike told me he was leaving the site. Now that the preparation for the inlet tower foundations was done, the company was laying off all the high-scalers. I thought that was a pretty mean reward for all Mike had done for the dam, but as he pointed out, no one would ever believe such a wild tale anyway.

"Things are happening as I said they would," he said philosophically the last time we met. "The dams provide work for me, nothing more. I'll go up to Washington, to that new Grand Coulee project."

I stroked Tonochpa. She seemed pretty well recovered from her experience; all that remained were two round scars in a bare patch on her flank. "You taking her with you?" I asked.

He grinned. "There are some fine big mountain wildcats up in Washington. Maybe Tonochpa will find herself a mate, hey?"

He opened his knapsack, the bobcat jumped in and he trudged off across the construction site, disappearing into the rolling dust. That was the last I saw of him.

Well, Black Canyon's holding up mighty well for a dam its age. Holding back more water and putting out more power than its designers ever thought it would. You know, I have a sneaky feeling that Mike was right. The lake might silt up, but the dam will never crumble. Perhaps in a few million years people will dig it up out of the sediments and asked how the hell a man-made thing lasted so long. Well, you and I will know, won't we?

BORROWING TROUBLE

by Elizabeth H. Boyer

"You are the sorriest excuse for an apprentice I've ever encountered!" roared the Meistari, blinking through the soot floating around him. "Imbecile! You nearly incinerated us all! I swear I can't tolerate another eighty-nine years of your presence in my school! The next traveling tradesman I see, I'm going to sell your articles of apprenticeship to him and be rid of you, Agnarr Henstromsson!"

Agnarr sneezed and commenced righting the blackened crucibles, spilling more of the materials inside as he did so. The brazier was still smoking and stinking, and sinister little orange flames lapped out hungrily for another taste of the Meistari's cloak.

"I can't fathom what went wrong," Agnarr said anxiously. "Perhaps a word in the wrong place, or it's possible those troll bones were still a bit damp—"

"It's nothing so small as a mistake!" the wizard snorted, and the rest of the apprentices all sniggered smugly and exchanged winks and nudges and grins. "It's general incompetence! It's a total lack of aptitude for magic! I'm sick of being blown up and set on fire! I'll never make a fire wizard of you, Agnarr! I rue the day I ever set eyes on you at that hiring fair! Your clan chieftain must have been ecstatic to get rid of you, and at an exorbitant price, at that. I never expected to be cheated by the Galdur clan!"

Agnarr drew himself up indignantly at this insult to the clan known for producing the most and best wizards in the Alfar realm. "You weren't cheated," he declared, pushing back the shreds of his charred hood. "I was born to be a wizard, and I'm going to be one. Let me try this experiment one more time. The third time is always lucky for me."

"By the remains of my beard, no!" bellowed Bjarnadr, his eyes bulging with rage. "You've had all the chances you're going to get! You're a failure! Get out! I don't want to lay eyes upon you again! I wash my hands of you!"

Agnarr measured the distance to the door in a quick glance and haughtily glared back at Bjarnadr. "Very well, but I think you're giving up much too soon," he declared. "One of these days you'll be sorry, when I'm a better wizard than you. I intend to join the Fire Wizards' Guild and fight the Dokkalfar, rather than teach a lot of boring, useless nonsense to a bunch of thick-headed, snotty-nosed little apprentices!"

He almost made it through the door before a sizzling dart of flame caught up with him, setting his breeches ablaze. Bjarnadr bellowed something after him, but he was halfway to the horse trough to extinguish his trousers and didn't catch all of it, but he supposed it was more words to the effect that his presence was no longer desired in Bjarnadr's magic school and what ill effects his return might have upon his person.

Agnarr sighed and heaved himself out of the horse trough. Sacked again, and he'd have to sew up the burn holes in his pants. Sacking Agnarr was getting to be a regular ritual with Bjarnadr, one which the other apprentices enjoyed immensely, especially the younger ones. Spoiled brats, all of them, bestowed with gifts and talents they had not earned or deserved, while he, Agnarr, had to struggle so desperately to control the smallest fire-raising spell.

Worse yet, a closer inspection revealed that his breeches weren't going to tolerate another scorching from Bjarnadr. There was nothing left to repair, so the only alternative was to visit the laundry-drying lawn and steal a pair from one of the other apprentices.

Already the bright side of the situation was occurring to Agnarr as he pulled on his stolen pants and contemplated his situation. Here he was, liberated in the middle of the day, out in the sunshine while the other seven scholars were grinding off their noses over tedious spells and smelly experiments. Another glorious holiday lay before him, while Bjarnadr's temper cooled. Usually it took only a day or two until the Meistari had regained his composure and was in the humor to try again. After all, Agnarr was a son of the clan Galdur, the wizards' clan. Somewhere in that unprepossessing and inept lump of potential, there was a magnificent talent waiting to be discovered and taught.

In the meantime, Agnarr would make himself scarce, lying low until he could waylay an apprentice and inquire into the condition of Bjarnadr's temper. It did give him a bit of uneasiness to note that with each sacking, Bjarnadr's temper seemed to take longer to recover. Next time, he told himself sternly, he would try harder to do exactly what the Meistari told him, no matter how ridiculous and elementary it seemed, instead of trying to find shortcuts. Shortcuts were his downfall in every case. He would begin to work a spell, with the appropriate words, gestures, and magical apparatus, but all of a sudden a brilliant idea would pop into his head. Sometimes it was a seemingly-ingenious shortcut; sometimes it was a hilarious practical joke obtained by twisting the words of the spell just slightly. Given his Galdur heritage and great latent talent, he had no choice except to give in to inspiration. Once or twice the results had indeed been spectacular successes and he had conjured wonderful elemental creatures of wind, fire, earth, and water, or he worked some witty shape-shifting spell upon one of his fellow apprentices that made everyone laugh. Unfortunately, the failures had outnumbered the successes far too many times and they were, of course, in the manner of all failures, absolutely dazzling in their awfulness, thereby eclipsing any good Agnarr had ever done in his entire lifetime, and thus raising Bjarnadr's doubts about Agnarr's future as a wizard.

In these times of duress, Agnarr departed Bjarnadr's moss-covered ruined fortress which housed the magic school and took up a temporary abode at Finn's inn, some five miles on the other side of Geltafell. Old Finn was always glad of more help and set him to work at scything hay or digging potatoes or putting up endlessly fallen stone fences or any one of the innumerable chores essential for the husbandry of creatures as troublesome and stupid as sheep.

Young Finn, however, hoisted one black eyebrow and grunted, "Sacked again? That's the fifth time, isn't it?"

"I haven't been keeping count," muttered Agnarr, pretending to be in a great hurry to go pick ticks off the sheep.

"You'd better buckle down, lad, or you'll be picking ticks off sheep's bellies for the rest of your life," went on Young Finn with an admonitory gleam in his eye. "And that would be a great waste now, wouldn't it?"

It was enough to make Agnarr think he might have to find some other place to lie up while Bjarnadr was in one of his foul humors.

Toward evening, during the long hours of northern twilight, when the trolls were roaring and grunting in the rough heights of Geltafell, a cart came rolling into the inn yard, drawn by a monstrous shaggy black ox with wicked curling horns. Agnarr went out reluctantly to stable the beast, while the two Finns rather warily made the traveler welcome. He was tall and lean and well-cloaked and hooded about, but in spite of his secretive manner, Agnarr sensed magical powers emanating from the stranger. Perhaps the stranger sensed something about Agnarr also; he glanced at him sharply and said, "Mind your step around that ox, or he'll hook you a good one. He kicks like a demon, too."

The stranger availed himself of the plentiful food and drink offered by Finn's wife, warmed himself briefly near the fire, then announced that he preferred to sleep in his wagon, which was enclosed against the weather and perfectly comfortable. Agnarr felt powerfully compelled to follow him outdoors, on the pretext of seeing if the stable was securely locked up for the

night. When he was well away from the house, the
stranger stopped and waited for Agnarr to approach
him.

"Well? What is it you wish?" the stranger asked.
"You're simply burning for something, aren't you? Is
it a necromancer's ring you want, to put under the
tongue of a corpse so it will tell you the future? Rune
sticks, with almost every spell you can imagine on
them, for summoning storms, trolls, giants, or for
finding treasure? Secret names of all elements and the
beasts of the earth, cloaks of invisibility, swords of
power, belts of strength, boots that will take you anywhere in a stride—a veritable enchanted wardrobe
awaits you in my wagon. And the philters, potions,
distillations, extracts, and liquors—"

Agnarr was shaking his head as the list went on,
until the stranger broke off sharply, "What's the matter? You haven't got any money to pay? Well, good
night then!"

"No, no, that's not it," Agnarr protested swiftly.
"It's just that I don't have the knowledge to use all
those things yet. I'm only an apprentice. And not
exactly the Meistari Bjarnadr's favorite, either."

"Oh, you're not any good, is that it? And you think
I might have something in my wagon to help you?"
The stranger rubbed his narrow chin, his eyes making
two shining points in the dark. "Perhaps there is.
Follow me and we'll see if we can come to terms."

The inside of the wagon reminded Agnarr of Bjarnadr's
forbidden storeroom, which he had only stolen fascinated glimpses into a few times. Shelves lined the
sides of the wagon, laden with alluring little boxes, all
carefully sealed with blobs of colored wax and strings,
dark, tightly-stoppered bottles, jars labeled in runic,
embroidered bags and pouches, bundles of herbs, dried
lizards, snakes, bats, and cages with live creatures
peering through the bars with bright, suspicious eyes.
The only ordinary thing here was a great orange and
white cat bulging over the sides of a basket, sleeping
curled half inside out, with one white paw clamped
over his face.

The smells alone made Agnarr's head feel like a cork bobbing lightly on the water. He inhaled rapturously, feeling recognition and wonder burning within him, knowing he was truly in the world where he belonged.

"It should be something small and unobtrusive," the stranger mused aloud, his gaze running over his inventory. "I'm thinking that what you need is a familiar." He raised one unsavory, withered finger to underscore the word.

"Of course! That's it exactly! It would know all the spells, and it would help me do them, and the Meistari would never know the difference! A rat would be ideal. I could keep him in my pocket." Agnarr peered into a cage, where a large black rat bared his teeth at him and took a savage nip at his fingers.

"No, old Rotta's not for you. You're too inexperienced. A familiar can take you over if you're not careful, and you'll be the servant. Let's see now, how about this little cricket? I think you could control him."

Agnarr's expectations of a familiar were not fulfilled by the cricket, or the mouse, or the finch, or the lizard the stranger showed him, although he did hesitate over the lizard. "Haven't you got something bigger?" he asked. "All these things are too cute."

"You can't control something bigger," the stranger said. "You've very much a novice at magic, and you might end up with a master far worse than old Bjarnadr."

Agnarr was gazing at the cat as he spoke, and one large green eye popped open suddenly, focusing on him with increasing interest. The cat unrolled himself, stood up suddenly on his toes and yawned ferociously, baring his yellowed fangs in a tortured grimace. Then he sat down heavily and squinted sleepily at Agnarr. Fanning out his whiskers, he started a rumbling purr, kneading his big white paws enticingly. Agnarr reached out and scratched the cat's wide skull, ridged with the scars of many fights, and the purring doubled in volume.

"Oh, no! Don't you even think about old Skuggi,"

the stranger said before Agnarr could speak. "He's too much for you. Too much for almost anyone. He only tolerates me because I feed him well and let him do exactly what he pleases."

"Skuggi? He doesn't fit his name. He's no shadow," Agnarr said. "He's the size of two cats in one skin."

"Don't insult him. He hears and understands every word you say and he holds a grudge forever. Now forget about him. He can get very rude and nasty, can't you, Skuggi?"

Skuggi smiled and rubbed his jowls on Agnarr's arm, still purring like mountain thunder. When Agnarr turned away reluctantly, Skuggi leaped down from his basket with a solid thud and followed him, rubbing himself on Agnarr's ankles at every step. When Agnarr sat down, Skuggi jumped into his lap and settled down possessively, digging in his claws gently whenever Agnarr stirred. His lazy green eyes fairly beamed with benevolence.

"I think he likes me," Agnarr said. "Why can't I have him? He won't do anything to me. I'm sure of it."

"I refuse to be responsible for what might happen. I'd lose the good faith of all the wizards I sell to. I simply can't allow you to take him." He reached out to lift Skuggi off Agnarr's knees, but Skuggi flattened his ears and uttered a deadly growl, followed by a hiss that sputtered with menace. His weight seemed to increase, augmented by his sheer determination not to be picked up.

Agnarr smoothed down Skuggi's fur, which was half-bristling, and Skuggi resumed his tuneful purring, keeping a wary eye turned upon the stranger. "I'm going to take him. How much do you want for him?"

The stranger sighed dismally and pressed his fingers to his temples. "I can't accept money for Skuggi without grave retributions befalling me. Does that give you an idea of his value? Take him if you dare, but one day perhaps I'll demand a favor of you—if you happen to live that long. All I ask for payment right now is a small surety. Nothing but a lock of your hair to seal our transaction."

That was easily and swiftly done, and Agnarr could hardly contain his impatience to get back to Bjarnadrshol to show off his prize. In the morning, and done with his assigned chores on time for breakfast for a change, he strolled into the sooty great hall which served as dining room, lecture hall, and sleeping quarters for the apprentices. Skuggi paced at his heels, waving his tail and sniffing the food smells approvingly. The other apprentices left off their empty-headed chattering and stared as Agnarr took his place at the table. Skuggi sat down expectantly on the table next to him. No one said a word when Agnarr appropriated Hrifa's sausages and oatmeal for Skuggi.

"Ho, Agnarr," Hrifa greeted him warily. As the apprentice next upward from Agnarr in status, Hrifa always viewed Agnarr as his most threatening rival. "What are you doing with that cat?"

"Having breakfast, you dolt," Agnarr answered.

"That's unusual in itself, and therefore suspect," Hrifa said. "Is this another of your hideously bungled attempts at working some spell, or just another absurd practical joke?"

Agnarr heaved an impatient sigh. "It's none of your business, but I suppose it makes no difference if I tell a bunch of lowly worms like this lot. He's a familiar."

Eyes rounded in astonishment and knives halted in midair, skewered with sausages and drippings. Hrifa scowled enviously and demanded, "Where'd you get him? I don't think that's fair. The Meistari will never put up with it. Apprentices aren't allowed familiars. How'd you ever pay for one? They're frightfully dear, I've heard. You practically have to ransom your soul to some wizard or demon to get one. but I can't figure out who would want your soul, Agnarr."

"You seem to forget," Agnarr replied in a bored tone. "I was born in clan Galdur of chosen parentage."

"Galdur isn't a real clan," Hrifa snorted. "It's only a sept. It's nothing so special as you'd like to believe.

There's just as many cowherders and wool-dyers in Galdur as any other subclan."

"Perhaps, but there are definitely more wizards," Agnarr shot back. "And far better wizards, one of which I hope and expect to become one day."

Hrifa glowered at him. "Give me back my breakfast. That's no familiar. Knowing you, it's just another joke."

"Take it back if you dare," Agnarr invited.

Hrifa reached out his hand, but Skuggi planted one clawed paw on the edge of the plate to defend his breakfast, and growled softly, watching Hrifa from the corner of his eye. Hrifa jerked his hand back, and the younger apprentices laughed jeeringly.

In a generous humor, Agnarr gave part of his own breakfast to Hrifa—a rather small part, though.

When the food was done away with, Bjarnadr swept into the hall, already spewing forth instructions, reprimands, and encouragements couched in threatening terms, as well as administering his knuckles to a few boyish skulls in passing.

"What is that?" He suddenly halted, stock-still, as his gaze fell upon Agnarr and Skuggi.

"A cat, Meistari," Agnarr replied respectfully.

Bjarnadr clasped his hands behind his back. "A cat, you say? Thank you for that information, Agnarr."

The apprentices sniggered. Skuggi was occupied with washing his immaculate white paws and did not deign to even glance at Bjarnadr.

"He's a familiar," Agnarr said as casually as he could.

"Indeed! And where did you get him?"

"At Finn's inn. From a traveling magic merchant."

"I see. And with what did you pay the merchant? I hadn't noticed you were so wealthy."

The apprentices began exchanging knowing glances and nudging each other. Agnarr ignored them, replying, "We agreed that I should pay him later, if I would give him a small surety now. All he wanted was a lock of my hair."

Bjarnadr inhaled a deep breath, raising his eyes to

the ceiling. He spoke gently, with admirable restraint. "Did it not occur to you that by giving a part of your person to this stranger that he will gain a certain degree of power over you, depending upon his skill? Perhaps he will someday sell that hair lock to one of your many enemies, when you are an adept wizard, enemies who will then be able to do you great harm."

"He seemed an honest fellow," Agnarr answered.

"And a trusting one, to have given a lowly apprentice such a valuable familiar," Bjarnadr went on. "Did he tell you the cat's name? Was it Boots or Mittens or Stripe?"

"I can't tell you his name," Agnarr said. "That's for me alone to know."

"A familiar tells you his true name—not something a traveling trash merchant tells you. Agnarr, this charlatan has sold you nothing but an ordinary cat in exchange for what could be your entire future as a wizard. You've been completely duped and made a fool of by that fellow, as well as this ridiculous, overfed, lascivious, hairy beast." He ended with a shattering sneeze and dabbed at his reddening eyes, while the other apprentices whooped with mirth. Hrifa grinned with wicked satisfaction, rubbing his knuckles, no doubt plotting where he would waylay Agnarr for his revenge.

Agnarr stole a sidewise glance at Skuggi, who was still washing himself. "He hears and understands you perfectly," he said. "You'd better not insult him."

Bjarnadr sneezed again. "He's nothing but a fur-bearing nuisance, and fat and stupid." Skuggi began washing his hind foot, seemingly oblivious, and the apprentices added their own epithets. All to no effect. Skuggi ignored them all with supreme contempt. For a moment Agnarr felt a small doubt nibbling at his confidence.

"There, you see, he didn't understand a bit of it," Bjarnadr declared triumphantly. "You've been cheated. Now I strongly suggest you get rid of him. Besides, he makes me sneeze." Two more rapid-fire sneezes followed.

"Supposing he were a familiar, how would one go about learning his name?" Agnarr pursued stubbornly.

"The names of all things are contained somewhere within them," Bjarnadr answered, quaking with suppressed sneezes. "You can discover his true name if you're diligent and observant. And if indeed he's got one. Now let's proceed with our experiments." He sneezed and stalked away, wiping his nose and glaring back at Skuggi. "Today we're summoning a minor fire elemental, and hopefully containing him while we stand safely within our rune rings. I hope you've all studied the procedures adequately." One final sneeze almost blew his hood off.

Agnarr eyed Skuggi suspiciously. It seemed to him that Skuggi uttered a little mutter for each sneeze, and he certainly smiled as if Bjarnadr's sneezing amused him. He rubbed his chin on Agnarr's hand and purred. With breakfast and bathing taken care of, he curled up on Agnarr's cloak amongst his magical apparatus on the table and went to sleep, exhausted by his heavy responsibilities.

The day went from bad to worse immediately. Agnarr scratched his rune ring on the floor around himself, reciting the proper words, but the elemental got to him anyway, buffeting him around and setting his clothes on fire. Bjarnadr banished the elemental, the other students laughed, and Skuggi watched from the safety of the rafters. In the uproar, Agnarr heard an unfamiliar voice croak some words, and suddenly the fire elemental returned. A huge, roaring ball of flame caught everyone defenseless, including Bjarnadr. The apprentices fled in terror while the master stood and hurled fire bolts and shouted spells. By the time the fire elemental was banished, the entire hall was blackened. Lessons were canceled for the day to clean up the mess, and Bjarnadr was in a frightful humor. He stalked around looking for Agnarr, snorting smoke.

"Is this your idea of a joke?" he roared. "A fire elemental is nothing to play games with! Someone might have been fired! Agnarr, I know you're responsible for this!"

Wisely, Agnarr took Skuggi and hid in the top of an abandoned tower. The old fortress was large enough to afford him several secret hiding places, where he went to escape the wrath of Bjarnadr or the idiocy of the other apprentices.

With a groan he threw himself down on the improvised bed of moldy hay. At once Skuggi made a mattress of Agnarr's stomach, turning around a few times before settling down to purring and flexing his claws.

"Why won't you speak to me?" Agnarr rubbed Skuggi's ears to awaken him. "If you had helped me, I wouldn't have conjured that elemental. It was some of my finest work, though. A pity I wasn't expecting it. Come on, Skuggi—or whatever your true name is—I need some help or I'll get sacked for good."

Skuggi bestowed one reassuring lick to Agnarr's hand and rose up to tromp out a more comfortable resting place on Agnarr's stomach. Curling himself up tightly, he went to sleep and refused to respond to Agnarr's questioning with anything but a sleepy grumble. A bar of warm sunlight soon made Agnarr too lazy to worry about any of his problems and he, too, went to sleep, with Skuggi coiled up in the middle of him like a large stone.

When he awakened around midday, hungry, Skuggi was stretched out full length beside him in the sun, sleeping with his orange-spotted white belly turned upward. It was a fascinating pattern of dots and bars. Agnarr ran his hand down Skuggi's belly, and Skuggi stretched luxuriously, making his belly-spots look even more like runic writing in fur. Suddenly remembering what the Meistari had said about names being found on the creature in question, Agnarr tried to stretch Skuggi out again to get another good look at the pattern, but Skuggi took umbrage at such liberties and writhed and kicked indignantly with both hind legs. His dignity much ruffled, he commenced grooming himself from head to toe with obvious exasperation, as if he had been disfigured almost beyond recognition.

Agnarr watched and smiled, congratulating himself.

His Galdur heritage assured him that his instincts were good, and his instincts told him that Skuggi's true name was written on his stomach. He was also certain he had recognized the middle two letters of the name.

The days that followed were not easy. Bjarnadr got over his temper as soon as the hall was cleaned up, but not for long. At mealtime, when Agnarr attempted a simple come-hither spell to slide the bread within his reach, the loaf flew into the air and landed with a splash in someone else's soup and the knife whirled in a deadly gleaming disk, straight toward Bjarnadr at the head of the table. He plucked it out of the air with a well-directed fire bolt, but he was not amused. Agnarr was sentenced to kitchen duty for a week. In addition to his regular lessons, kitchen duty added two hours onto each end of his day, besides doing away with the afternoon digestive period directly after the midday meal. Skuggi faithfully accompanied him in his disgrace, and thrashed any ordinary cats he saw and helped himself to the leftover scraps. By the end of the week he was so fat that the letters on his stomach were farther apart than ever.

Disaster seemed to stalk Agnarr. Simple spells that he had once mastered exploded in his face, and spells that he never dreamed of seemed to leap off his fingertips, and they always backfired in the most hideous way possible. Bjarnadr retained his temper with great and visible difficulty, even though it cost him two cloaks and a complete new gown and hood and sleeves. He hovered over Agnarr, watching him, which was borrowing trouble. The sneezing recurred at Bjarnadr's most important moments, when he was explaining a complicated concept, or scolding an apprentice, or working a spell, thus completely destroying the effect. Agnarr's errant magical powers attacked Bjarnadr when he was occupied with something else and caught completely off guard. Even Agnarr was frightened by the menace of his own sorcery, but try as he might to get it right, the words always came out wrong. He thought about the hair lock he had traded away, wondering who possessed it now.

The final straw was the day Agnarr's shape-shifting spell momentarily converted Bjarnadr to a skinny black goat. Luckily the spell did not stick, but it made the apprentices hilarious and Bjarnadr furious.

"It's that blasted cat!" he roared. "Nothing has gone right since you brought him here! If I see that beast one more time, Agnarr, there won't be enough of either of you to send to the rag and bone man!"

"But he's helping me," Agnarr protested. "I've just got to polish my skills a bit—"

"I'll polish your head with my staff!" Bjarnadr waved it, trailing clouds of ominous black smoke, and Agnarr grabbed Skuggi and fled to his tower retreat, with Skuggi yowling and kicking at such undignified treatment.

"Skuggi, I don't know what's going to happen to us if you don't tell me your name." Agnarr glared at Skuggi, who was stretching out in the sunshine for a nap. "But right now your name is Trouble and mine is Mud." He leaned on the window ledge to peer down at the mossy roof of the great hall below. If he were sent home to his clansmen in disgrace, it would be worse than having his articles of apprenticeship sold to some common tradesman. Gloomily he pictured himself apprenticed to a woodcutter, a shipbuilder, a slaughterer, or a blacksmith.

"Cheer up, it's not that bad," said a voice behind him, and he whirled around in outrage to see who had tracked him to his favorite secret place. All he saw was Skuggi, half-asleep and looking at him with one eye open. He plunged to the doorway and looked out, expecting another trick from some of the younger apprentices. The narrow winding stair was dark and empty.

"Skuggi?" he said, and Skuggi began to purr, rolling over to get a bit more comfortable. "I've guessed your secret name! It is Trouble, isn't it? Trufla, in the old tongue. I ought to have guessed it, from the way you've messed up my magic spells and playing tricks on Bjarnadr. All I can say is thanks a lot for ruining my life. Some familiar you turned out to be!"

Skuggi opened both eyes and sat up, with some

difficulty. His speaking voice was squeaky, a bit hoarse, like his meowing voice. "It wasn't my fault, old boy. It's that wizard you bought me from. You've heard of Mord Corpse-Eater in your lessons, I presume? One of the most powerful of the Dokkalfar wizards?"

Agnarr gaped in amazement. "That was Mord Corpse-Eater? He seemed an ordinary traveling merchant to me."

"He's an old enemy of Bjarnadr's. He's the one who has been sending your spells awry against Bjarnadr, and yes, he's been using me—and you—to do it, thanks to your generous gift of a hair lock. Unless you stop him, he'll kill your master, or put him into some shape he can't get out of for a long while."

"How can you tell me this? Doesn't Mord hear you?"

"No longer. Now that you've found my true name, I'm freed from him and bound to help you. He's not going to be pleased that you found out my name. He never expected you'd be able to, you know, and frankly, neither did I."

Agnarr struck an offended pose, still congratulating himself on his unexpected good fortune. "Didn't you, now? After all, I come from the Galdur clan." Nervously he added, "What do you think he'll do?"

"Oh, he's going to get ugly now. But don't worry, I'm going to help you. Right after I take a nap."

"Nap! Skuggi, not now! Or should I say Trufla?"

"All right, all right. We'll talk. There's little else to do until Bjarnadr cools off."

Agnarr avoided Bjarnadr for the rest of the day, but Bjarnadr still had not cooled down by the midday following. He peered down at the hall and cocked his ears. Too much black smoke and shouting still issued from the great hall, and the loud thwacks and yelps from the apprentices did not bode well for his return. So Agnarr practiced the spells he knew, and some new ones with Skuggi prompting him, and they came off flawlessly. Skuggi crouched beside him, filling in the proper words when his memory faltered and sternly forbidding any shortcuts or doubling up of ritual gestures.

"Learn the basics first," Skuggi reprimanded him. "Then you'll know for certain where you can trim the fat. You're terribly sloppy at summoning elementals. You've got to get better; elementals are a wizard's most valuable allies. I'll introduce you to Skotvopn, a nice little elemental who's looking for a wizard patron. He's young and inexperienced like you, but very eager. Those mossy old elementals Bjarnadr calls upon are used so often by so many wizards that they've gotten irritable about it."

On the following day Bjarnadr's temper had returned to normal, so Agnarr slipped unobtrusively into the hall, filled to bursting with anticipation. With nonchalance, and Skuggi's prompting, he summoned Skotvopn. It was a clear and bright-burning elemental, instead of the sullen red fireballs Bjarnadr summoned, and Skotvopn was willing to be molded into any form, from great bolts like lightning to a shower of small burning darts. When Agnarr had exhausted his limited commands, Skotvopn returned obligingly to hover over the brazier in a brilliant column until Agnarr banished him. There were no tricky explosions, no counterattacks, and no misguided sparks to burn holes in Bjarnadr's gown or beard. Agnarr stifled his urge to yell and jump up and down in elation, and maintained a modest demeanor even though the other apprentices were staring in awe and Bjarnadr was chortling and rubbing his hands with satisfaction. Hrifa's face was like a disappointed thundercloud, already sensing his inevitable decline into a dismally-distant second place behind Agnarr.

Agnarr gloried in the benevolence of Bjarnadr's approving glances, and reveled in every bit of additional advice the master singled him out for, and wondered why he had waited so long to discover the joys of being the favored scholar. His present satisfaction was far superior to the wicked glee of pulling pranks.

One evening when he had been released from his lessons early as a reward for doing so well, and he had returned to his tower to coax more advanced spells from Skuggi, Skuggi's keener ears caught the sound of wheels and hooves approaching Bjarnadrshol. He leaped to the window sill to sniff the night air, and his fur stood on end in a ridge from ear to tail tip.

"Follow me, quickly!" Skuggi hissed, his eyes suddenly blazing. "Swear you'll do exactly at I tell you!"

By now, Agnarr had learned not to question Skuggi's orders. "I swear," he muttered, wondering who was actually in charge in their familiar-apprentice relationship.

They crept into the hall unnoticed as Bjarnadr was welcoming his guest, the highly distinguished wizard Godvildr, who visited the school several times a year. Not only was he famous and powerful, he was kind to lowly apprentices, always speaking to each one by name and giving him a small tasty gift. Agnarr put himself at the end of the receiving line, his mouth watering. They never got cakes, and these were filled with fruit and oozing with sweet juice. As he received his, Skuggi twined around his ankles, yowling as if he were begging, but to Agnarr's ears the voice was perfectly plain.

"Throw it back in his face! If you take one bite of it, you'll fall fast asleep for two days!"

Agnarr hated himself, but he hurled the cake back at the genial Godvildr, and everyone in the hall gasped in horror. Bjarnadr glared, disappointed and angry, with smoke curling out of his ears.

"That's our Agnarr," he apologized stiffly. "He's going through a difficult stage right now. I fear it's only going to get worse for him." He hoisted one singed eyebrow significantly.

"I don't know what came over me," Agnarr said faintly. "At times, my power is too great to control."

Godvildr eyed Agnarr mildly and brushed the crumbs off his chin. "It's no matter," he said in a genial tone. "I was young once myself. Mischief seemed to come naturally."

At the table, Skuggi climbed onto Agnarr's lap beneath the table as he always did and hooked choice bits off his plate for himself.

"Skuggi!" he muttered. "You're ruining my entire life with these pranks! Don't make me do any more!"

"Hush!" said Skuggi. "This is going to be interesting. Just do as I tell you and nothing will go amiss. You swore an oath you'd do as I told you."

"I must've been mad," Agnarr growled. "Why abuse poor old Godvildr?"

"Agnarr!" Skuggi hissed, when the jug of mead was brought from the kitchen. "Don't let Bjarnadr drink that! It's poisoned!"

A come-hither spell directed amiss jerked the cup out of Bjarnadr's hand and spilled it over his gown. He glowered straight at Agnarr, his lips moving, but Skuggi hastily put the words in Agnarr's mouth to avert whatever spell it was, diverting the energy into the roasted fowls before Godvildr, which burst into flame and turned to cinders.

"A spirited youth, your Agnarr," Godvildr observed with a tolerant chuckle, starting to pour another cup of mead.

Skuggi whispered, Agnarr spoke, and all that came from the flask was sand. The silence in the room was awful, with everyone gazing at Agnarr, the apprentices in terrified admiration, and Bjarnadr in smoldering rage. Godvildr only smiled sadly and shook his head. "He's got to get it out of his system somehow," he said. Another jug was called for, but Skuggi allowed this one to be poured and swallowed.

As Skuggi predicted, the other apprentices all fell asleep soon after the sweet cakes were eaten at the end of the meal, leaving Agnarr and Skuggi to face the two wizards. They settled beside the fire to smoke their pipes. Godvildr leaned his staff against the wall, carved with runes and topped with a dark ruby knob.

"Off with you to bed, Agnarr," commanded Bjarnadr. "And be certain to take that wretched cat with you. I'm going to deal with both of you tomorrow."

"I believe I'll stay a bit longer," Agnarr said, and

sat down on a stool opposite Godvildr. Skuggi hunkered down watchfully, his eyes upon the two wizards.

"Let the lad stay," Godvildr said, amused. "I like
his spirit. Perhaps you've met your match, Bjarnadr."

"It's nothing I can't correct," Bjarnadr grunted,
turning back his sleeves and removing his long pipe
from his belt pouch. "Tomorrow, with a hazel switch."

"That's a fine cat," Godvildr went on, offering his
pouch to Bjarnadr to fill his pipe. "I had a cat much
like that myself once. A delightful companion he was,
but he came to a very bad end, I'm afraid. Cats often
do, it seems. Do try this leaf, Bjarnadr. It's the finest
you'll ever know."

Skuggi purred loudly and rubbed his chin on Agnarr's
clenched fists. "The pipe," he muttered. "Get rid of
it."

Obligingly, Agnarr incinerated the pipe before
Bjarnadr could draw one breath on it, blackening the
wizard's face and littering his clothes with hot little
embers and bits of shattered clay.

Bjarnadr hopped up with an inarticulate roar of
wrath and rapidly dusted away the fragments of his
beloved pipe, and Agnarr knew he was doomed. He
was about to flee for his life, but Skuggi tripped him
up, sending him sprawling.

"Well done, cat!" Bjarnadr seized Agnarr by the
collar and shook him, while Skuggi yowled. "Now I've
got you, Agnarr! Not one more ridiculous prank!"

"Now, Agnarr!" Skuggi shouted, leaping up to knock
Godvildr's staff out of his reach, just as he was reaching for it. A loud squall conveyed everything Agnarr
needed to know, and it left him gasping in terror.

Agnarr twisted around to face Godvildr, summoning a powerful voice from unknown depths. "Fara af
stad, birtu! I know your name to be Mord Corpse-
Eater! Now I command you to reveal yourself!"

Godvildr's patient smile twisted into a sour grimace.
With a smoky puff and a gust of ice-cold air, the
appearance of Godvildr melted away, revealing Mord
Corpse-Eater, clad in tattered black and bedecked
with the amulets and tokens of the necromancer's

trade. He flinched away, swatting at unseen darts of power released by Agnarr's words, trying to find his staff without taking his eyes off Bjarnadr and Agnarr.

"Curse that cat!" he sputtered, stung in a dozen places at once as he groped for his staff, but Skuggi pounced on it and rolled it away. "Blast you, Bjarnadr!"

"Gott kvold, draug-eater!" Agnarr shouted, and with a terrible shriek, Mord burst into flames. Bjarnadr belatedly bellowed spell words, raising his staff and blasting Mord with a force that threw him against the wall. He thrashed about, shriveling and shrinking, melting into a black pool of ichor, except for his cloak and staff and amulets, one of which was Agnarr's hair lock, tied up with colored threads. Bjarnadr lifted the magical objects carefully with the end of his staff and edged them into the fire, where they burned with crackling ferocity.

"Well, then, that's the end of your hair lock," he said to Agnarr gruffly when he was finished. "I thought it was all another of your hoaxes until it was almost too late. You've saved me from becoming another of Mord's trophies. Or was it merely another accident?"

Agnarr shrugged, his throat still dry as he looked at the puddle that had been Mord Corpse-Eater. Skuggi crouched at Agnarr's feet, protective even as his eyelids sagged toward a doze. "Skuggi told me. He's the one that saved you. Mord sent him here to work harm against you, but I learned his name and got control over him. Sort of."

Bjarnadr blinked and snorted, a smile breaking through the soot. He dropped a companionable hand on Agnarr's shoulder and squeezed it fondly. "Well, perhaps. If you say he's your familiar, then I shall do my best to believe you. I'm amazed that you saw through his glamour spell and I didn't. But I knew from the start that I'd make a wizard of you—with a little work and patience. I never doubted you a moment, my lad. Oh, perhaps I did, once or twice. I think it's time you moved on to more interesting spells, and rooms of your own, away from these common, chattering numbskulls. And whatever you like from the kitchen, of course. I foresee taking an assistant one of these days, a talented youth with a great talent for magic. But only upon one condition—no more mysterious accidents."

Agnarr glanced down at Skuggi, who blinked and said, "What, and spoil our fun?"

Agnarr scowled at him and said firmly, "Of course. I'm in charge of my skills now. No more accidents, Meistari. You don't mind Skuggi, then?"

"Of course not, my lad! Your cat is welcome anywhere!" declared Bjarnadr, bending down to thump Skuggi's back heartily, as if he were a dog, and followed this ill-conceived gesture with a gusty sneeze. "Perhaps he'll do something about the mice overrunning the scullery. Come along, we must have a serious talk about your future, now that you've just graduated from apprentice to assistant."

Agnarr soon found himself in the enviable position of assistant. In this exalted capacity he was called upon to assign the menial duties of the school—none of which devolved to himself—to invent tests of skills, to administer thwacks to laggard apprentices, to sit at the Meistari's right at meals, and other agreeable duties. His skills far surpassed Hrifa's, whose life became one of disappointment and envy.

Skuggi never again advised him to throw cakes in Godvildr's face, and his stripes and bars achieved even greater distances apart, rendering his runic belly completely indecipherable.

DAY OF DISCOVERY

by Blake Cahoon

There is a theory that cats are really aliens from outer space.

Lyssa Tyler wasn't sure if that was true or not, but the way the long-haired black cat stared at her from across the crowded room, she knew it was definitely a sentient being.

"David, do you see that cat over there? It keeps staring at me."

David Eisner tore his gaze from a nubile student, barely clothed in a red cocktail dress, to focus his attention on his professor's needs. "Cat?" He shoved the red-rimmed glasses up on his nose and gazed across the crowded room. "What cat?" He frowned, making his hawkish features appear even more birdlike. "Lyssa, you're being paranoid again," he scolded her. He glanced down at her hand, which clutched an empty martini glass. "You need a refill. I'll get it for you."

She let him pry the glass out of her hand without a word, and while he melted into the crowd, in search of further refreshment, she headed in the opposite direction, toward the cat.

She'd only gone two feet when Professor Drake literally bumped into her.

"Oh, my dear, you must be more careful," the old man chastised her. He paused to glance around the room with sad eyes. "This whole thing is so tragic. Doctor Belson was a good man. His theory of molecular transference was brilliant, if a bit farfetched. Are you planning to continue his work?"

The cat had disappeared, and Lyssa's concentration on the present was brought sharply into focus with

Drake's prattling. She drew herself up to all five feet four inches of her height, and drew back her shoulders, bringing Drake's gaze to momentarily rest several inches below her blazing blue eyes. "First of all, Dr. Drake, the theory of molecular transference wasn't Ted Belson's. It was mine," she sputtered. "And it isn't farfetched. Einstein proved that there are other dimensions to be explored, if we knew how. And as for Belson being a 'good man,' that question is still out with the jury." A flash of red caught her eye, it matched the high crimson in her cheeks. "Do you see that Julie Anderson? Is that an appropriate way to dress? For god's sake, this is a damn wake, not some stupid faculty cocktail party!"

Drake looked taken back; David was quick to intervene, as he came to the rescue, drinks in hand. "Sorry about that, Dr. Drake. You have to forgive Dr. Tyler. She's been under a lot of strain, with Dr. Belson's tragic accident and all. Here, have a martini." The graduate assistant shoved both glasses at the shorter man and took Lyssa by the arm. "Come on, Dr. Tyler. You've got a lot of work still to do on that project." He threw Drake an apologetic grin, and steered his red-faced, weaving professor out the door.

The high laughter of Julie Anderson, in her cheap red dress, rang in Lyssa's ears, as David drove through the rain.

"I suppose you slept with her, too," she accused David, breaking the silence. "I saw the way you looked at her at the party—I mean the wake." She laughed out loud. "Ha! Some wake! They all hated Ted. Because they were jealous. Because he was brilliant. They all hated him. All of them . . . except Julie."

"And you."

Lyssa glanced over at the young man, who would be handsome if he cut his longish blond hair and switched to contact lenses, instead of the peculiar-colored glasses. "Ted and I are history. I mean—were history. Ever since he stole *my* theory." She fell silent for a moment, staring out beyond the windshield where the gentle slap-slap of the wipers was driving off the rain.

Tall evergreens lined the lonely stretch of back road. "The police think *I* had something to do with the accident," her voice trailed off. "The car went over . . . the cliff . . . the brake lines . . ."

"They don't have any evidence to prove that ridiculous theory," David said.

"No . . ." she agreed. "Still, I suppose it doesn't look good that only three days after I publicly accused him of stealing my theory, the highly acclaimed physics professor, Theodore W. Belson, is sent over a cliff to his death." David glanced over at her, and caught her smiling. "Do you know what the 'W' stood for?"

"No, what?"

"Willard, like that movie about a rat. That's what Ted was—a rat."

"Willard was the name of the man, not the rat."

She turned to him, still smiling. David knew it was the smile of someone who'd had too much to drink; he should have known not to get her a fourth martini. "Are you sure?"

"As sure as I know, you didn't kill Ted. You were still in love with him."

The smile faded, Lyssa turned to gaze back out the windshield, uncomfortable with David staring at her so. Suddenly, her face turned to horror as she pointed, screaming, "Watch out!"

David turned and saw the flash of black streak in front of the car. He slammed on the brakes, throwing the car into a skid along the dangerous, wet road. The car screamed to a halt.

"Did you hit it?" Lyssa was already unfastening her seatbelt, now totally sober, in light of the surge of adrenaline.

"No, I don't think so. Where are you going?"

"To make sure it's all right." She threw open the car door, and scurried out into the rain, searching the roadway and the nearby bush.

"Lyssa, you're going to get soaked!" David yelled after her, as he climbed out. "What the hell was it, anyway?"

"I think it was a cat," Lyssa yelled back, as she

disappeared down the far embankment, slipping in the wet grass.

"A cat?" David yelled back. He remembered something Lyssa had said at the wake. " 'David, that cat's staring at me.' " And wasn't there a comment from her at the funeral. " 'David, do you see that black cat over there, by that headstone? It's just sitting there, in all this rain, and it's staring at . . . me.' "

"Lyssa," he yelled at her figure as it disappeared into the woods. "It's probably long gone by now."

He frowned, trying to decide if he should go after her.

Ted had a cat—a black cat, named Einstein. It had disappeared the day Ted was killed.

"Lyssa!" He called out again, without luck. He got back into the car and parked it off the road, then started to go after her. He didn't have far to roam; Lyssa reappeared, with a wet, frightened black cat in hand.

Her bright face smiled at him. "Look who I found—Einstein!"

David remained dubious. "It's a long-haired black cat, sure, but how can it be Einstein? We're miles away from campus."

The cat was shivering, its mud-coated fur ruining Lyssa's dress, but she didn't seem to notice. "I just know, that's all." She marched back to the car. "Come on, let's get back. Einstein needs a good meal and a bath."

David went along with her, shaking his head, and got them underway again. Lyssa cooed over the cat like a mother hen.

From the corner of his eye, David watched. "That cat is filthy. He's ruining your clothes."

But Lyssa paid no attention to him, continuing only to stroke the damp fur; the purr from the cat became loud and clear. The sound complemented the slap-slap of the windshield wipers and the murmur of the gentle rain on the car roof.

Fir trees whizzed past, Lyssa lay her head back a moment, closing her eyes.

"Are you okay?" David knew the reaction from the alcohol and adrenaline rush was probably making itself known.

She opened her eyes, her head came forward, as she gazed out at the swiftly passing evergreens. "Who was it that asked, 'If a tree falls in a forest, and no one is around to hear it fall, does it make a sound?' "

"Socrates?" David shrugged. "I don't know. Philosophy isn't my forte."

"Where do all those extra socks go when they become lost in the dryer?" Lyssa was still studing the trees, "And have you ever watched a cat just stare and stare at nothing, for hours and hours? It's as if they know something we don't."

" 'Ah! Cats are a mysterious kind of folk.' Now, that was Sir Walter Scott, that much I do know."

" 'It is their task to see everything, to hear everything,' " Lyssa said. "An old medieval saying." She stroked Einstein. "Isn't that right, boy?"

They were just pulling into campus when David said, "You know, that cat isn't going to bring Ted back."

"If this cat could talk, it might tell us who murdered Ted."

"I still say that can't be Einstein."

"Look, I know you saw the cat at the funeral and you saw the cat that was at the wake. And now, this cat shows up. Do you know what I think?"

"Wrong—I didn't see the cat at the wake, only at the funeral. And so what if they were all black cats, that cat is not Einstein."

"How do you know it's not? I knew Einstein, you didn't. Besides, you don't like cats."

"I do so like cats. I like all animals. I just find cats are—"

"Mysterious creatures of the night?" Lyssa smiled. "This *is* Einstein."

"Are you trying to say that all those cats are the same cat? Einstein, somehow teleported? How did the cat get from place to place?"

"Maybe using Tyler's theory of molecular transference," she smiled.

David found his gaze being drawn down to the cat, which stared up at him with luminous green eyes, the same smile that played on Lyssa's face, played on his. He raised an eyebrow at the animal. "They are still calling it Belson's theory."

"Not for long," Lyssa said, as David pulled in front of the physics lab. She quickly got out and headed for the building.

"Lyssa, why are you doing this? You should be home." David pleaded with her, as he caught up with her in the third floor corridor.

"Why? To mope? To grieve after a man who not only jilted me, but stole my theory as well?" Lyssa shook her head. "Oh, no, the time for that is past. Now, I have to go into action. To prove that Ted Belson was a fraud. That his theory was really my theory." She unlocked the lab door, as Einstein squirmed his way to the floor, dashing inside the darkness as the door cracked open.

Lyssa threw on the lights, revealing a modest laboratory, complete with long tables, test tubes, an assortment of electronic equipment, and several computers. She headed toward the back, behind several bookcases that were jammed with notebooks, stacks of papers, plus an assortment of books. A peculiar setup of what appeared to be a miniature jungle-gym, the kind found on children's playgrounds, was sitting on a table. To the side was an assortment of electronic monitoring devices, along with an array of laser equipment. The jungle-gym had a horizontal point of sorts which was aimed at a distant wall, where a large sheet of translucent plastic stood.

Einstein was currently nowhere to be seen. David wasn't worried about the cat, however; he was worried about Lyssa. David sat on a nearby stool, as she began turning on the various pieces of equipment. The silence of the room was soon shattered by a steady hum.

Lyssa was already studying her notes. She looked up long enough to note, "You could make yourself useful."

"I'm tired, it's been a long day."

"Well, no matter. I need to work. I want to work.

Phelps had us on a deadline. That deadline is next week. It's either get results or good-bye grant money. So I have to work."

David watched her, furiously scribbling, checking her devices. A soft meow caught his attention, and Einstein reappeared at his feet, indicating want of attention or food. He smiled gently, and patted his lap. The cat gave out an approving meow, and with a graceful leap, landed neatly in his lap, immediately settling down. David scratched the dry fur, amazed at how clean the cat was, and how loud his purr. "Well, fellow, I can't say if you're the old Einstein or not, but regardless, welcome to your home, new or otherwise," he told the cat gently. The cat's purr got louder, as huge green eyes cracked open enough to acknowledge the human, then squeezed shut, a smile on its whiskered lips.

"Dr. Tyler, not only have you broken the rules that the police laid down on this matter, worse, you've disregarded my rule of not becoming involved further in this matter," Dr. Perry Phelps, the departmental chairman, chastised her. No wonder the faculty called him "windbag" behind his huge back.

"Dr. Phelps, you know this project was mine to begin with, not Ted's. He stole my—"

"Young lady, we have been over this a thousand times already. Right now, I don't care whose theory it is, the whole thing is academic now anyway. The project is dead. It died the day Ted died."

"But it doesn't have to be that way! I am so close. I know I am. You've got to give me more time. You've got to let me into my lab."

Perry steepled his hands together on his desk, his usual hangdog expression even more so, as his frown became deeper. "Look, Lyssa, I know you and Ted were close—"

"Oh, hell, Perry," Lyssa shot back, now that the initial academic bull was over and they were back on a first name basis. "Ted and I were lovers for two years, everyone on the staff knows that. Maybe one day we might have gotten married, if he could have stopped chasing the skirts he was supposedly tutoring. Yes, I was mad when he finally said that portion of our relationship was over, but we've been working on this project for the last three years. We are so close. We—"

"Wrong, Lyssa. You were so close. Now, Ted is done and—"

"And now, you want to cancel the project? Why? Because the theory is—let me see, how did dear old Dr. Drake put it?—'farfetched'? I know it's farfetched, but, Perry, I am so damn close. All I need is the rest of the time allotted for this project—just another week— that's all, to get back into my lab, and I will prove that there are other dimensions out there."

Perry considered her. "It's just that this whole thing is so . . . controversial. And the media is blowing this whole thing out of proportion, with the murder and all. You *did* ridicule Ted in public at that dinner. And your accusations toward Julie Anderson—"

"My god, Perry, I had just found out Ted was dead, and she wandered in. I was in shock."

"Well, I understand that, but . . ." He was squirming in his chair.

"Please, Perry, just another week. That's all I ask."

Perry didn't look comfortable, but he relented. "Okay, but if in a week, when the deadline is up, you have nothing to show, then not only will that be your last day here, but I'll make sure you'll never do research anywhere ever again."

"I ask for nothing more," was her only reply, and she headed out the door.

"There is a theory that cats are truly aliens from outer space."

"And whose theory is that?" David asked, checking over his clipboard of data.

"Mine," Lyssa replied. She gave Einstein a gentle stroke, and the cat rolled over from its sitting position on the table, to fully stretched out, making accessible a long length of furry stomach to stroke. Lyssa obliged the request, and Einstein's purr rivaled the electronic humming. " 'When I play with my cat, who knows if I am not a pastime to her more than she is to me?' Montaigne, 1580."

"Interesting theory. I'd almost buy it, too."

"But?"

"But I have a more interesting theory."

"Oh, really? And what is that, Mr. Eisner?"

"Well, Dr. Tyler, it's based on your own theory, actually," David expounded in mock tone.

"Tell me your theory then."

"I believe cats are truly . . . pan-dimensional creatures."

Lyssa smiled. "Pan-dimensional, eh?" David nodded, a smile on his lips. "Now you wouldn't be mocking my dimensional theory, would you? Not after all this time working on it?"

"Not at all, my dear professor. Indeed, I believe your theory will prove my theory."

Lyssa studied him for a moment, and his eyes smiled at her in the same way Einstein's did when he stared at her, silent cat secrets swirling in his feline mind. "And here, all this time, I didn't think you liked cats."

David only smiled at her and beneath her hand, Einstein purred louder.

"Two more days and this project is over," Phelps warned her, when he stopped by the lab.

"Two more days is all I need," Lyssa answered, not bothering to acknowledge him further, her pert nose in her notes.

Phelps glanced around, noting the presence of several half-eaten hamburgers left cold in their cardboard trays, stacked up in a nearby trash can. In the corner, David Eisner, with several days' beard growth, looked up bleary-eyed from his computer terminal. A large black cat sat by his side. It looked at Phelps and yawned.

"What is that animal doing in here? It is against regulations—"

"It was Ted's cat," David announced, as if that was the only explanation needed. Lyssa glanced up, as if to defend the cat's presence, but David's pronouncement seemed to satisfy Phelps.

"Oh. Well, then . . ." he looked about uncertainly, noting the cat was now staring at him, a look of disdain in its large green eyes. Phelps decided to leave.

"Good boy," David told the cat. Einstein glanced up at him, as if to say, "Of course," and then settled back to its own thoughts.

"Now, if your calculations are right, and we've made the necessary adjustments to the matrix correctly, then . . ."

"Then when we throw the switch on the laser cannon, and if the matrix is correct, we should . . ." Even David was afraid to speak the words.

"Then we should open a door to another dimension," Lyssa finished for both of them. "The only problem is, what dimension? What type of rift will we cause? What will we find?" Her eyes glowed as brightly as Einstein's over the lid of her milkshake cup. She sucked on the straw briefly, then the features of her face became soft. "You know, David, if it hadn't been for you, putting in all this work, picking up where Ted left off . . . well, I just don't know how to say . . . thank you."

David glanced up from where he was feeding Einstein the last of his hamburger. "You know I believe in you, Lysa. I always have. That's why I wanted to work with you. I specifically requested to work for you."

"You did?" She smiled. "I never knew that." Studying his face, she found that she liked the beard. It seemed to suit him.

"That's probably because we never really talked like we have since . . . since Dr. Belson's . . . passing."

Lyssa wiped off the excess sweat from her paper cup, licking her lips slightly. "I guess I was sorta wrapped in . . ."

"Yeah, I know." He let out a sigh. "The police are no closer to finding his killer, either."

"Lt. McDonald called again yesterday, and warned

me not to leave town. If after tomorrow, the matrix doesn't work and the project is a bust, then I'll be the laughingstock of campus. Dr. Phelps has told me that I'm history. Here or anywhere else."

"Don't worry. The matrix will be correct. I know it." David told her optimistically. From the floor, a loud meow was heard. "See, Einstein agrees."

Lyssa smiled. "He does, does he?" She bent down and the cat deigned to let her rub its head. "You and Einstein have gotten close these last few days, I've noticed."

"He's been helping me," David said. "Actually, I think it's he who fed me those last figures."

"You mean the figures the matrix is based on?" Lyssa asked. "Is this somehow tied in with your pan-dimensional theory?"

"Maybe. You're the one that got me started though. I still want to know how, if this cat is really Ted's Einstein, and if it's the same cat that somehow got from this lab, to the grave site, to the wake and then out along that back road, how did it get from place to place?"

Lyssa smiled. "Your pan-dimensional theory? Or my molecular transference theory? How do you think I came up with the theory in the first place? My grandmother had a cat which I swore disappeared into some other dimension. I'd go into the bedroom where I saw the cat run, and not find it anywhere. And then I'd go downstairs, and there it would be, grooming itself by the fire. Now, I know I didn't see the cat pass me on the stairs."

"Which made you begin to realize that maybe the cat knew something that the rest of us didn't. I read your paper, remember?"

"Nobody took that paper seriously. Except Ted. He's the one that looked me up and said he could get us grant money if we pursued my theory." Lyssa rubbed Einstein's tummy. "Of course, he took all the credit, and I did all the work. I was blind, I was so in love with him. He was taking me for a fool."

"Careful, the walls have ears. Someone might think you really did the old boy in."

Lyssa looked up at him. "You don't believe that, do you?"

"Of course not." He stood over her, and slowly she rose to her feet, his hands on her small shoulders. His eyes, so green and gentle, gazed into hers. She found herself falling into those mesmerizing pools of green. Funny, she hadn't ever noticed how green his eyes were. Now, as his face drew closer to hers, she found herself thinking how very much like a cat's his eyes were.

His lips touched her lips, his strong arms held her tight, protecting her.

She withdrew, her cheeks felt hot. She turned away. "We . . . we have work to do." Her voice was barely a whisper.

"Of course," he said. He bent down to retrieve the empty cardboard container from Einstein, who now sat up on the computer table, licking his lips, and silently grooming himself, a self-satisfied look on his whiskered face.

The calculations were complete; all the elements of the jungle gym were in place. The laser cannon was ready to be fired.

David was making last minute adjustments. Lyssa was donning a pair of goggles. Einstein was dozing on a far counter, wedged between a computer and a microscope.

It was only when Lyssa threw the switch to the laser and a steady hum escaped from the machinery, that the long-haired black cat decided to wake from his nap. Long limbs stretched into the air, green eyes squinted, then opened wide at the red light beam that played within the matrix. He let out a yowl.

Lyssa didn't immediately notice, she was busy monitoring the situation. "Aim the beam at our intersection point," she ordered David, who nodded and made the appropriate adjustments through the computer terminal.

"It's almost there!" he shouted, over the increasing hum.

The red laser beam danced among the bars of the jungle gym, slowly aiming higher, to a small opening at the horizontal apex. It was aimed at the plastic screen, which was beginning to shimmer, and take on a life of its own.

Einstein's eyes grew wide, the cat yowled once more, more loudly than before. It jumped down from the counter, knocking over an empty test tube rack, which clattered and broke.

The sound drew Lyssa's attention, her eyes went wide as the cat began to run toward the screen, its fur standing on end, its gait weaving crazily.

"No, Einstein!" Her words fell, just as David made the last adjustment.

"Lyssa, look!" he shouted, as the laser fell into place.

The large screen, where the eerie glow had started out small and grown with each passing adjustment, now became a swirling vortex of luminous effervescent colors. The sight of this undulating mass was spell-binding; Lyssa momentarily forgot about the strange behavior of the cat, as she became mesmerized. The air in the room became heavy and still.

"Wow!" David said, "Will you look at—" his words were cut off as Einstein uttered a final yowl which broke the spell for Lyssa as she watched in horror. The cat dashed for the whirling vortex and suddenly disappeared inside the colorful mass.

"Einstein!" she shouted, and almost lunged in after the creature, but David was quick to grab her arm.

"No, Lyssa! We don't know enough yet to venture in!"

"But Einstein! Ted's cat!" she shouted.

"It's gone. Besides, we never really knew if that was Einstein or not," David argued.

"It was Einstein," Lyssa insisted. She relaxed her arm, and stared at the vortex. "I wonder where it goes? If Einstein is in some other space, place, or time?"

"We have to do this scientifically," David insisted. He began studying the computer data, which was on automatic printout.

Lyssa continued to stare. "We wanted to prove we could do it. Well, we did it. But now, the question is, how do we use it?"

"Wrong. The question is what is it?" David said. "And these numbers aren't telling me a thing."

Lyssa turned toward the computer, but as she did, a sudden flash of brilliant light from the vortex sprang at her. She screamed and fell backward. David sprang forward and caught her as a streak of black rushed past them both and landed in a small heap, near a bookcase.

The two scientists got to their feet, just as the vortex shut itself down, along with the laser equipment. The lab became engulfed in sudden silence, except for a small voice, saying, "My God, talk about your rough landings!"

Lyssa and David stared, their eyes wide, their mouths agape, at the small black creature which was, for all intents and purposes, grooming itself back into proper appearance. It was definitely feline, pure black, just like Einstein, with one noticeable exception: it had wings. Long, translucent, butterfly type wings.

And it talked.

It looked up at both of them, with cat eyes, summing them up. "Don't gawk. It isn't polite."

Lyssa found her voice first, although it cracked in the middle of the sentence. "Einstein? Is that you?"

"Do I look like Einstein?" the cat had a definite male voice. Its lips were slightly parted, but it was hard to tell if the sound they heard was being spoken, or simply thought-transferred. "No, I am not. He simply saw a way home and couldn't resist the temptation."

"Home? Is that what we've created?" Lyssa asked.

"Who or what are you?" David asked.

The cat seemed to smile at him. "I am a Pryliwyk."

"You look like a cat with wings," David said.

The Pryliwyk studied him, its eyes bright with secrets, a smile on its whiskered lips. Then it turned toward Lyssa. "You're a bright woman, Dr. Tyler. However, your calculations were misleading you, into a situation where you would have no control. The cat that you refer to as Einstein had to rectify those critical errors."

Lyssa still couldn't believe what she saw or what was happening. "You know my name?"

"Of course. 'It is their task to see everything, to hear everything,' that's what you told Mr. Eisner in the car, didn't you?"

"Well, yes . . . but—"

"But Einstein was in your lap, remember?" the Pryliwyk said.

"Yes. Was Einstein a Perli . . . ?" Lyssa asked. David had found himself a stool to sit on.

"Yes. Actually, just over a third of your cat population are Pryliwyks."

"They are? But they don't have wings!"

The Pryliwyk groomed himself, as he said, "Take off your glasses."

"Huh?" Lyssa said, but removed the protective goggles from her face. Immediately, the Pryliwyk's wings disappeared from sight, leaving him looking like a normal black housecat, grooming itself, a smug look on its face. It looked up at her, and meowed. "Your wings are gone," she announced. She held the goggles back up. The wings reappeared.

"It's your glasses. They were polarized by the energy bolt when the rift occurred between the two dimensions. Put them back on and you'll see the wings."

Lyssa slowly nodded, in comprehension. "Yes. But why didn't I feel them when I petted Einstein."

"The human mind doesn't acknowledge easily what it doesn't see or accept." This statement came from David.

The Pryliwyk glanced over at him. "I suppose that's a simplistic way of looking at it." He looked back over at Lyssa. "Your instincts were right—there are dimensions other than your own. Every now and then, an opening to another world will appear, by one of several ways. Either man-made or by natural circumstance. For the most part, we can control the results of those occasional rifts in space and time and right the worlds again. That is our job. Pryliwyks are guardians;

indeed, their task is to see everything, to hear every-thing. Actually, it was a wise wizard named Ambrose who said that originally," the Pryliwyk explained. "But when humans choose to interfere in the natural order of things, then it is our task to set things straight. This is what happened to your Dr. Belson. His calculations were leading him straight into danger. He had to be stopped."

"You killed Ted?"

"No. Actually, we saved him. The police were right, his brake line was cut, and his brakes were out. He was trying to steer his car, so it wouldn't go off that cliff, when one of our agents ran in front of the car. In order not to hit the cat, Dr. Belson veered, sending himself over the cliff, exactly as we planned."

Lyssa eyes opened wide. "Then you did—"

"No, Dr. Tyler, we didn't kill him. There was an opening along the route that car took, which we pulled Dr. Belson through. He survived, the car didn't."

"Then Ted's alive?" It was too much to hope for; Lyssa's eyes grew bright.

"Dr. Tyler, Dr. Belson used you. He stole your theory, he jilted you, and besides, those broken brake lines were meant for you, not him. Dr. Belson's favor-ite student, Julie Anderson, saw to that."

"What?"

"Think back, Dr. Tyler. You ridiculed Dr. Belson at that dinner party, and did not have very many pleasant things to say about Miss Anderson. She wanted to get rid of you, so she had the brake line in your car cut. She had no way of knowing that Ted would take your car instead of his that day. She didn't know about the flat tire."

"With you out of the way," David said, "Ted would become a rich man with his discovery. Of course, Ted had no intention of ever becoming permanently in-volved with Julie. But she didn't know that. He was only playing with her."

Lyssa looked over at David. "What do you know about this?"

David smiled and looked over at the Pryliwyk. He

got off his stool and crossed over to her, taking off his glasses. "Here," he said, "Put these on." Puzzled, she took them from him, and tried them on. "They weren't polarized," he told her gently.

What she saw were wings, wings on the Pryliwyk, and when she looked at David, her mouth dropped open. "David, your eyes!"

David's eyes were green, a cat eye green, but more than that, they were cat eyes. David Eisner had cat eyes.

"The glasses hide the reality," he explained.

"I don't understand. Who—what are you?" Lyssa asked.

"A graduate student, who saw that the lady scientist who was going to discover for herself where cats disappear to, got himself assigned to her, so he could help her find the way from her world into mine," he said, slipping the peculiar red-framed glasses off her nose, and then putting them back on his own. Immediately, human eyes looked back at her, with warmth and gentleness. "But he never reckoned on falling in love with her, at the same time."

Lyssa stared up at him, confused and bewildered at all that was happening. "David, I . . ."

"Then don't say a word," he finished for her. "Ted is alive and safe, in another world, where he can chase all the females he wants. You were right when you said he was a rat. But you were so in love with him, you were letting him destroy you."

"But . . . who are you?"

He smiled down at her. "My real name is Ambrose," he told her. "And once upon a time, I was a wizard who opened a rift . . ." he started, and then he kissed her.

WART

by Jayge Carr

Wart hunkered down, scarcely breathing, only the cream-colored tail with its black tip swishing impatiently high.

"Wart's stalking something again." Human-tom sounded amused. (Wart wished Human-tom would be more careful. That big booming growl of his had scared off more delicious prey—)

Human-mommy laughed. "Probably a scrap of printout."

"Are you criticizing my housecleaning," Human-tom teased. Even Wart could hear the amusement rollicking through the deep human growl.

"Well—" Human-mommy sounded as though she were growling reflexively while concentrating on something else, the way Wart twitched his tail while stalking prey. "Better that than worrying about picking up pests on that last landfall."

A smacking sound, as Human-tom did that funny noisy mouth-lick humans seems to use instead of proper tonguing. (Though they did that, too. Wart had seen them several times. But oddly, only when they were in the bunk together.)

Then he growled, "I'm sure you deconned thoroughly, love."

"Uh-oh," said Human-mommy.

"Picked up another transmission?" Human-tom was staring at the funny-window.

"Jere—" Human-mommy's voice had that significant note in it; Wart swung his head around. "Jere, it was *your* turn to deconn last landing."

Silence. Wart swung his head around, verrrry slowly

stretched out a paw. Almost he had it, almost, just another little bit, just anoth—

"Devi!" Human-tom almost shouted. Wart flinched at the noise, and his own motion swirled the dust bunny away. Wart froze again, as Human-tom went on, "Miri! It was your turn to deconn. I know it was."

Silence, except for the click of Human-mommy's claws against the funny toy she called "keys."

"It *was* your turn, Miri."

More clicks.

In a different tone: "Devi—" (Wart turned and saw Human-tom's gaze fixed on the funny-window.) "Devi, but I'm sorry Miri. I was so sure I didn't even bother to check the roster."

A sigh. "It's all right, Jere, that's what we have the cats for, after all. Last resort against pests." Breath. "I just wish the computer would hurry up with the translation."

Shrug in the voice. "In this sector of space—" Wart moved toward the dust-bunny again.

"I know." Worry in Human-mommy's voice. She repeated Human-tom's words, somehow giving them a completely different meaning, loaded with significance. "In this sector of space . . ." A swallow. "But the transmission was so strong, although the sweeps show nothing, and nothing unusual in the scoops we've pulled in and dumped into the cargo hold. It—I—I just have this crawly feeling, Jere. I—I want to pull in the rest of the scoops and lie doggo."

Sputtering from Human-tom. Wart ignored it. In just one little—

"I know, Jere. I know what it'll cost us, in wasted fuel for the scoops, to say nothing of this ship's stopping and restarting, in time, in everything. But—we'll be much harder to spot, doggo; and I—I'll feel safer."

Human-tom made the bird sound called a whistle. "And I'm supposed to be the gypsy fortuneteller of the pair of us, Miri. Well, my gorgio, supposed unesper love, if you feel that strongly about this, let's do it. Now."

"Thank you, Jere."

Human-tom lip-smacked her cheek again, then: "Gotta take care of all three of us. Shall I sit copilot."

"You sit pilot and do it all, if you will, Jere. I want my console to concentrate on the translation."

"All right." Sounds of large body plumping into seat. Wart ignored it. Snap! Triumph! Chomp. He he he, neither of them noticed. The last time he had caught a dust bunny, Human-mommy had grabbed at it, snapping, "Winston Churchill IV—" which he knew meant she was *really* angry, "—give me that, it's bad for you."

Wart licked his chops in contented satisfaction. The mighty hunter had—

"Mrrrrr—" demanded another feline voice.

Wart shrank into himself.

Majestic as always, Grimalkin—Grey for short— stalked regally into the small control room.

"Mrrrrrrr—"

"Here, Grey." Human-tom patted his lap. "Don't jump on Miri—"

But Grimalkin knew whose orders she obeyed and whose she didn't; and whose lap—even in its present distended state—she preferred.

"Devi—" Human-tom swore, rising out of his seat, but instinctively keeping his hands on his controls.

"It's all right, Jere." Small giggle. "There's still room."

Human-tom muttered something that made Wart shrink himself even smaller.

Then Wart noticed that Grimalkin's tail was swinging over the side of the lap, as she tried to accommodate her full sized Persian self into a decreasing area of lap.

Swish swish, the tail moved hypnotically back and forth. Swish swish. Swish swish. Bushy and supplely-moving and oh . . . so . . . attractive. Wart crouched again. Swish. Moved forward a step. Swish. Another step. Swish.

There was just the slightest change in the almost subsonic mutter of the ship, that Wart thought of as the giant ship-monster breathing. Wart hesitated.

"I'm going to reverse power on us gradually, love, and cut power on the scoops but leave them out on a random drift pattern. Slowing us down that way'll take a couple of hours, but I want to conserve fuel as much as I can. We'll restart the scoops and collect them later."

"Thanks, Jere." Human-mommy shifted slightly, and the tail—Wart had his gaze fixed on that fluffy gray eminence—picked up its rhythm slightly.

"Wart!" Human-tom had spotted the stalk. "Don't you dare!" It was a Must-Be-Obeyed tone. Wart immediately sat up on his haunches, and began industriously cleaning between his toes, all innocence and ignorance. Who me? Doing what?

Human-tom choked off a laugh, but Wart could feel the human gaze fixed on him. He spread his paw luxuriously and continued to clean.

"Oh my God!" The sick horror in those tones froze all three of the listeners. Even Grimalkin's tail stopped moving.

"What is it?" Human-tom broke out of his paralysis to fling himself out of his chair. "Love? Miri? Is it time."

He bent down, slid his arms under her knees and shoulders as though to pick her up.

"No, Jere. Look! *Fredessers!*"

Wart didn't know what fredessers were, but he had heard the humans mention them before several times, always in a tone that he himself used for sneaky stinging scorpions or those little slimy things that burned your mouth if you bit them, or maybe a swarm of buzz-divers.

"Devi take them!" he breathed. "Where do you think they're hiding—"

Sounding sick: "I don't know. I've been scanning all along at full range—"

Thump as he landed back in the other chair again. "I'm reprogramming all doggo—"

"Quickly—" Her voice rose on the last syllable.

"Keep yours trying for a full translation," he gritted between his teeth.

"I am. Do you want to switch chores?"

"No. You've better intuit than I do. You keep with the translating. Engine work is practically automatic for either of us. Soon as I finish this, I'll send out an all-alert."

"Oh, yes. If there's a fredesser armada in this sector—"

"Aleko protect them!"

"Jere! I have a partial translation! Ambush! A larger vessel ambushed *them*!"

"Good! Give the rotten sneaks some of their own back!"

"Wonder why we can't see any of it. With the transmission so strong—"

"Just out of range. Devi! No telling what direction we're getting it from either."

Wart decided that Human-tom was sufficiently distracted, i.e., attention off IMPORTANT matters, i.e., **Wart**, that he could make another try for that marvelous swinging tail . . .

"Devi take them," Human-tom was muttering. "If only we knew where their home world is."

Wart slid into his very best crouch.

"Or home bases. Or *anything*." Human-mommy, despite large cat and equally large protuberance, was bending over her funny-window, her claws clicking frantically against the keys. Then she giggled. "If a computer generated translation of a nonverbal transmission could sound furious, this one does. They been had."

Grim: "Serves 'em right." Wart waited his chance, tail a-twitch.

Another giggle, as Human-mommy shifted slightly, and Grimalkin's tail stopped—and restarted its slow rhythm. "The other vessel was doggo and then just turned on and tractored them—like a giant scoop clearing its filter and restarting. Sluuurp."

"Giant scoops? Don't be silly, love." All business: "I have the slowdown programmed. I'm recording the alert message, now. I'll send it—" Wart oozed closer to the flicking, twitching temptation.

"Everywhere in this sector."

"Don't teach grandma how to suck eggs," he muttered. Somehow, without taking his gaze from his own funny-window: "*Don't*, Wart."

Wart decided that as long as Grimalkin was in here—and the humans alert to a tail attack—he would do much better elsewhere. Casually, he got onto all fours and began strolling out.

"MrrrrrRRRR—" Grimalkin sneered at his retreat.

Wart ignored her, his tail high and swishing.

Once out of the control room, he had to decide what he wanted to do. Explore some more, follow a scent trail, just find a long corridor and do some dashing—

This new ship was so much smaller than the place he had been a kitten on. But he liked Human-mommy and Human-tom here. There he had been one of many cats, with many humans. Here it was only two humans and two cats. Loads of smells, too, ground-in, years-old faint smells, and newer, fresher ones, including the fascination of what Human-tom called his "herbgarden." So many things to like here, like the jingle and shiny-brights on Human-tom's jacket made when Wart pawed at them or when the human moved, Human-mommy's warmth—when Grimalkin wasn't hogging it . . . 'course, that was the stinger . . . Grimalkin . . .

If only Grimalkin wasn't so—so—

What had Human-tom meant when he said something about, "Just be patient, little buddy. When you're old enough, instinct 'll put her right where you want her . . ."

Wart stopped, wondering. Sniffed. Wrinkled his aristocratic nose. What was different? Then he knew. The rumble had changed—that was it. It was much quieter!

Much much quieter!

And . . . he felt funny. Almost as if—

A tiny dust fluff floated by. As he had many times before, Wart lunged for it. But this time, instead of rising perhaps three or four times his own height, he sailed up and up—

WheeeeeeEEEEEE!

Wart landed with a light crouch. When he had been allowed out off-ship once, he had watched the flutterers going by in the air, jumped for them, wishing he, too, could float up as they could. Now he was!

He took another jump, and *mrrrr*ed in displeasure when he slammed against the ceiling. There was more to this floating bit than he had thought!

Another jump.

Wheeeeee!

Another. He had the knack now. He just had to turn in mid leap, and land Up, as if he were landing down, using his legs and—whooops! He "landed" on the ceiling, but when his legs crouched, he found himself launched off again—

"MMRRRRRRR!" From the sound, Grimalkin was close behind him and didn't like the new strangeness at all. Wart sniggered to himself. Let'r suffer!

Another launch—now that's the ticket. Don't aim up, aim forward! Look at that leap! Wart! King of the cats! Stalwart defender—

He continued his leapings, traveling much farther then he usually did. He didn't even think to worry how he was going to find his way back, because he was leaving scent marks much much farther apart than normal walking, or even leaping after a prey.

Something small was flying slowly down the corridor, humming. Wart stared at it, head cocked. It was about his own size, but dark and with the funniest shaped head he had ever seen. Winged, too, like the flutterers. PFEUGH! It smelled AWFUL. What a *stench*! He didn't even want to try to identify it!

"Mrrr?" He issued a tentative challenge.

Pff*fut*! At the noise, Wart launched himself. He had meant to go backward, but with his new lightness, he went up and sideways instead, bouncing off a wall and caroming in another direction again.

BLAM! A section of the wall exploded outward. Wart, in midair again, looked amazed at the pieces of debris raining outward from the site of where the wall had been.

One of the chunks hit the flying awful-smell (worse

than a buzz-diver it was! . . . or had the creature hit the wall hard enough to break it?) and instead of flying steadily, it, too, seemed broken, was careering clumsily, randomly about.

Wart cowered back. It was tumbling through the air, hit a wall and bounced as he had, and slammed off again.

It came close to him, and he batted automatically. Both he and the awful-smell spun off.

Ha! New game. Wart turned, got his feet under him, and launched again.

Wham BOUNCE! The SMELL collided with his paws, and hit a wall and spun off. Wart twisted and launched again.

OWWWWW— Something bit his paw. Wart ran, howling. It hurt. Every step hurt. He ran, leaving a trail of blood behind him.

But if he ever saw that thing again, or anything that smelled like it—

It was a long, long time before he found a scent trail that led back to Human-mommy and Human-tom. He was tired and hungry and his paw felt dreadful.

He had stopped and cleaned it twice, there was a small hole on one of his pads, and a tear, too.

He didn't even notice when he crossed through an open doorway, and got his weight back. Though less than he was used to when the ship's engines were giving close to normal G.

Wart entered sleeping quarters complaining at the top of his lungs.

Nobody was there.

He headed for the control room.

Yes, there they were.

Grimalkin was licking her chops, too.

Wart ran over to Human-mommy and rubbed against her.

She didn't even scratch behind his ears!

"MmmRRRRRR!" Wart complained. He could smell fish on Grimalkin's breath. She belched more fish in him smugly.

"MMMMMRRRR!" He jumped up onto Human-mommy's lap.

"Not now, Wart," she said absentmindedly. "I have to get this translated.

"I'll take care of him." Human-tom stood up. "You keep working." He bent over Human-mommy's lap and scooped up Wart, heading out of the control room.

Wart purred. He knew he was going to be fed and that now!

"Here you go, pal." Human-tom popped him on the shelf that came in and out in the eating room, and put a bowl in front of him. "Jus' a sec now—" Then he was scooping FISH into the bowl.

Wart dug in.

"Milk for a growing boy," Human-tom added. "Not that the diagnos says you're going to grow any more, Wart my runty little man. But we can always hope, can't we."

Wart didn't pay any attention to Human-tom's growl. He was EATING.

"Small-bred, my foot," Human-tom continued, a genuine growl in his voice. "Runt is more like it. They saw us coming, Wart my little man. They saw us coming." A sigh. "I wonder if you're really pure bred, too. Though you look it, right enough. I admit, it seemed a neat cross for when you were grown, Siamese and Persian. Besides, Miri thought those two different colored eyes of yours were adorable." A sigh. "I wanted her to have what she wanted, even as little a thing as a kitten with mismatched eyes." A snort. "But I fixed that fakir when he tried to up the price for it, being so unusual. Humph. It isn't. Damn him. But you're a good kid, aren't you, Wart, you can't help being made out of spare parts, and not all working right, either—"

His hand rubbed just the right way and Wart stretched under the caress, but didn't miss a movement in his almost frantic eating.

"Devi, but you eat. I don't understand. We've run you through the diagnos twice, no problems, and you eat like you were starving, but you don't grow." A sigh. "You know what I'm doing, Wart my little friend, don't you. I'm talking so I don't have to think about what's going on in the control room, how close we are to those murderous fredessers—I saw what was left of a world after they got through with it once, Wart. It was a cinder. Not a living thing on it. Yet nobody even knows why, much less how they do it."

Another caress. Wart stopped eating long enough for a short appreciative chirrup.

"The best anybody can come up with, is that they have a scorched earth policy. Whenever they find somebody settling on a world in what they consider their territory, they burn them off. Totally. No mercy, no survivors. The trouble is, nobody knows what they consider their territory, so nobody knows where they'll show up next. Nobody's ever even seen a fredesser, just picked up occasional transmissions and seen the results. They burn worlds, Wart, my man, whole worlds." An amused chuckle. "More? Where do you put it, Wart." But he scooped another serving into the dish, and Wart took care of that, too.

"Nobody's ever seen them to survive and tell the tale, no ambassadors we sent with armed convoys or in unarmed ships came back, no NOTHING. Devi only knows how many indies like us who have disappeared, ran into a fredesser. Nobody knows. Though we all know the risks, and there's dangers enough out here in the boonies without counting on a fredesser armada." A laugh with no humor in it. "Though we may be small enough to ignore. If that's what's out there, I only hope so!"

Wart burped politely.

"Enough, little man. If we did take on a pest or two last landing, I only hope you're still hungry enough to take care of it."

Wart wondered where the wounded flying awful-smell creature was. If he found it, it wouldn't have a chance to bite him again. This time, he'd be smelling for it. This time—

Human-tom turned and strode out of the eating room. Wart debated following, and decided to. Maybe he could get up on Human-mommy's lap and get a little petting—

"Anything new, Miri?"

"Message from the nearest naval base." Her growl sounded strained. "Acknowledging the alert, warning us to be careful, asking us to keep them posted—"

"The usual."

"Except for one item. They ran a computer analysis on indies in this sector. They say that there's an abnormally high percent of indies who haven't checked in recently. Of course, it's hard to keep track of indies, I could hear the sneer in that one, but—"

"Devi!"

"I've had a second transmission, too. The translation's faster, now that we have the base to work from, if you can call what little we think we have a base. It's incomplete, of course, like the first one, but the ship's almost certainly a scout, and there was a second ambush, smaller single vessel, and they've had to abandon ship. But they—or maybe it's a single survivor—are going to try to take the larger vessels, I can't tell which one, maybe both of them. It's a rough translation, of course, with no equivalent of a rosetta stone, all the translations are guesses at best."

"I know." Human-tom was scowling. Wart decided he would be better off exploring again. He trotted out.

Nothing (he sniffed in disdain) interesting anywhere near quarters, though he did find a scrap of printout and played with it a while.

Then he decided to explore again.

Sniff sniff. Most of the scent trails were obvious. His, or Grimalkin's, or the humans'. Nothing interesting.

Again he crossed an invisible line, and found his weight going. Wheeee! It was fun bouncing around . . .

Sniff? Was that the faintest hint of awful-smelling flyer?

He stopped his caroling and took a deep breath. Sniiiiif.

It was—and it wasn't.

Another sniff.

It ran along here—

Was it stronger this way or that? Wart galloped along a straight corridor, decided it was getting weaker this way, and turned and retraced his path.

Yes. *This* way! It was getting stronger. He slid to a crouch, and began moving as stealthily as he knew how.

Unfortunately, with his weight almost nothing (though mass normal) this wasn't very stealthy; he still hadn't adjusted to being able to practically throw himself on the ceiling with every step. But if he just *ooooooozed* along—

Whatever you wanted to call it, when he was above the floor and not touching it most of the time.

The smell was getting stronger. YUCK!

Wart slithered along as best he could. He must be getting close—yes! Something was scuttling along ahead of him. It had more legs than he and Grimalkin and maybe both humans put together. It was a lot smaller than the other creature, too. He wasn't sure if he could get the whole thing in his mouth, but he thought he could if he tore the legs off first.

But you had to be careful with scuttlers. Some of them had stings and bites that could be painful.

Wart tried to get a little closer, bring the thing into focus.

It moved too fast. All he could be sure of was that it was a smells-AWFUL many legged scuttler, heading along a wall.

Maybe it wouldn't even be good to eat. Nonetheless, it was in HIS territory, and HE was going to show it its mistake!

Besides, it might be fun to play with.

Before he ate it—or decided not to.

Wart edged forward, as stealthily as he could.

The thing stopped.

Wart froze, only the tip of his tail up and swishing impatiently.

Wart could hear his own heart pounding loudly, the "breathing" of the ship-monster—and nothing else.

Beat beat.

Beat beat.

The scuttler moved on.

Wart moved on.

The scuttler *crapped* on *WART's* Wall!

Wart leaped.

One slam of his paw sent the scuttler in one direction and its garbage, breaking up into tiny pieces, in another.

OoooWWWWWWW— This time the bite was in his shoulder AND the paw he had smashed the crap with. GrrrrrrrRRRRRRR! Wart launched and again the scuttler went spinning.

Ooo*WWWWWW*— This bite was his leg, but Wart's feline pride was outraged. No paw-sized scuttler was going to foul HIS territory and send HIM running off, tail drooping!

The trouble was, he wasn't used to this funny flying. Cats hadn't the ability to fly, though they could leap. Wart soared and heard a funny buzz. Then he saw. The scuttler had jumped, too.

—and come down—WHERE WAS HE?

Wart sniffed—and started to swing his head around—

There was a bright light reflected off the walls, and it made him blink. Had he been facing it directly, or with his good eye, it would probably have blinded him momentarily—or long enough. He whirled. There it came. He leaped, and this time his paw connected, but not a catch as he intended. The scuttler went flying— and landed with an odd crunch.

Wart stared, but it didn't move. He stalked closer— and almost fell. Between one step and the next, weight—the humans could have told him he had crossed over into the art-grav section—gripped him. As it had the scuttler. Hard. The scuttler had fallen from a considerable (to its smallness) height. It wasn't moving.

Wart batted it against a wall, as hard as he could.

It bounced and then lay. Still. Very still.

Wart stalked grandly up, and gave it a small bat.

Nothing.

A bigger bat.

Nothing.

No fun.

But maybe—he tugged a leg. Hard outside. The inside might be good enough, despite the smell.

Ugh, it was tough. Wart struggled and worked, finally he got the trick of it. You gripped one leg between your teeth, and put your paw on the body and worked and worried until the leg came off. Or partly off.

YWEWWWWW! The inside stank even worse than the outside! He spat the end of the leg out of his mouth, and then spat again, just to get the remembrance of that awful STENCH out of his mouth.

Where the leg was half torn off the body leaked some sort of fluid. DISgusting. Awful. NASTY-stink.

Wart automatically went through bury-it motions, kicking dirt over it.

Trouble was, there wasn't any dirt there. It still stank.

Wart didn't even want to put it in the litter box. After all, HE had to use that.

But where could he get rid of the awful thing?

Wart gave the body a kick, and it skittered down the corridor.

If only it didn't stink so, it might be fun to play with. He gave it another kick. It went farther.

Now his paws stank of it. Ugh. But maybe— He kept batting until he was opposite the sleeping room. In the sleeping room was a large potted plant . . .

Wart got the dead scuttler up against the pot. Checked in. Yep. Plenty of dirt there. The humans had spanked him enough to keep him from using the plant's dirt for his own toilet needs, but this was different. He leaped up onto the rim of the pot, dug a neat hole, leaped back down, carefully picked up the scuttler by a leg and made another leap. Dropped it in. Covered it back up. Tramped all around to pound the dirt back down.

Smelled his feet. Tramped some more, until good honest dirt smell replaced the awful stench.

Only when there was no smell left on his feet at all did he condescend to clean them, complaining and spitting, as even the memory of that smell lingered.

He hadn't quite finished cleaning his paws when he started feeling sick.

He ran for human-smell, feeling sicker and sicker. He just made it inside the door when the first surge came.

"What the—" Human-tom turned around.

Wart spewed.

"Wart's throwing up," Human-tom announced the obvious, in tones of acute disgust.

"You overfeed him." Human-mommy was still concentrated on the funny window.

"He still looks like a kitten who needs to eat—I'll clean it up, you keep working on those translations."

"I may never have it any better than I do now."

But Human-tom had gotten out of his chair, and was getting a sheet of paper out from the printer, and using it to clean up the worst of the mess.

Wart wanted to help bury it, but he felt dreadful.

Human-tom walked out of the room with the paper full of Wart's upchuck, came back a minute or two later with a couple of wet disposables and a spray bottle. He finished getting up Wart's spew in the disposables, and then sprayed carefully over the whole area with the cleanser disinfectant.

Wart appreciated that. Somewhat. He didn't much like the smell Human-tom used, but he liked the sour smell of his own upchuck even less.

Then Human-tom put his cleaning equipment on a tabletop; and swooped on Wart and started out the room.

"What, Jere—" Human-mommy asked.

"You keep working on those translations. I'm going to put our boy through the diagnos again."

"I told you—" But he was gone.

Wart recognized the door to the diagnos, which he hated.

The less said about the next few minutes, the better.

Human-tom was putting antiseptic on his scratches as he went back into the room where Human-mommy was.

Wart stayed out in the corridor and glared. But he was still feeling too rotten to go too far away.

Grimalkin had come in during the altercation, and added her own sneers to his misery. Now she was back in Human-mommy's lap, but Wart felt too awful to be as much as slightly tempted by the swishing tail.

"Food-poisoning." Human-tom flopped into his own chair. "Odd. Maybe we did pick up an alien pest."

"I think I have all the translations." Human-mommy

was paying no attention to Wart's misery or its possible causes.

"As soon as this is over, I'll run a deconn—" Then what Human-mommy had said sunk in, and Human-tom stood straight up. "Let's have them!"

"We'll never have the whole thing, but what I have boils down to this. A larger vessel, huge, used some sneaky new weapon they'd never encountered before, ambushed their ship; the fredesser managed to—I think camouflage itself. Then another, smaller vessel attacked, only one of the crew was able to abandon ship. Destroyed it, I think. He intended to plant a small—it comes out as fusion-starter—maybe that's what they use on planets, too, I don't know—anyway, he was going to plant that, only it was a portable, all he could carry, and it had to be close to the ship's own reactor to do the job. The last transmission says he'd actually planted or was about to plant the fusion-starter, and he ran into the smaller vessel again. His weapons were limited, but he planned to use a broad-beam laser to burn out their visors, and then—I haven't heard any more."

"And nothing on our screens." It wasn't a question.

"Zip."

Wart decided it was time he made a pathetic little moan.

"We'll never know how it came out," Human-tom sighed.

"Unless we run into either the scout or the armada it was probably working for or the human (if they are human) vessels. Or hear about them later when they come in and report."

"Them's the breaks," Human-tom said. "If the fredesser manages to plant his little bomb, we'll never hear, they'll never make it."

Wart, hunkered down and miserable, made another, slightly more plaintive (but imperative) moan.

"Poor little man." Human-tom made a gesture, but Wart didn't see it. "Oh, poor kid. I forgot. That's your blind side, isn't it. Here—" Human-tom stood up, walked over, and gently picked up Wart, petting him softly, while grumbling under his breath, "My own people. Not saying a word about two colored eyes and what they mean in some breeds. Blind in one eye. My own people. N'mind, Wart, little buddy. You're home with us now. We'll take care of you. And—" grin in his voice, "—we'll let you take care of us."

He sat, Wart on his lap.

"I wish we knew," Human-mommy said softly.

Wart purred as Human-tom patted him. He knew he had saved his own small universe once again; and the next time a scrap of paper, a dust bunny, a pest, or anything else threatened, he would be there.

"How much simpler to be Wart, eh," Human-tom said, with a small laugh. "Not to have to worry about berserker killers like fredessers."

Human-mommy laughed, too, and gave Grimalkin a pat. "Oh, I imagine feline folk have their own problems," she said.

Wart burped, and went to sleep. Grimalkin, the only other being in the room with a good enough sense of smell to catch the awful-tang sneered. Neither of the humans could smell something that faint.

But neither of them could have recognized very diluted fredesser anyway.

Just as Human-tom thought the tiny fragments of the fusion starter were only bits of dirt tracked about by the cats when he swept it up a few ship-days later. (Luckily the only radioactive part was encased in shielding until it was activated.)

Evil things can sometimes come in amazingly small packages.

But as Wart, patrolling the ship, could have said, good things come in small packages, too.

Even runt-small packages.

Even Warts.

YELLOW EYES

by Marylois Dunn

Cat entered the castle through the cat door built into the wall near the kitchen. The dogs also used the door as did an assortment of mice, when there were no cats passing through. Scenting the various passers-through as he entered, Cat thought to himself that it would be better for the entire castle had they made the opening too small for the great hounds. A few cats in the house would have kept the varmint population to nothing. With the dogs coming and going, bringing their fleas and their filth and their aging bones with them, there was no way to control the intruders.

He turned into the kitchen and sat under a table waiting for a handout. The cooks were like the dogs. They came and went. He did not know why or where and, frankly, did not care. There were usually one or two who would toss something under the table for him. Occasionally, he found a cook who would take time to discover his preferences, but at the present time, he did well to get a biscuit that was not too tough to chew.

The alternative was to make his way to the top turret of the castle where the white cat ruled. She had cream for dinner every night. She had the best of the meat, liver, kidneys, and sweetbreads, chopped fine or sometimes lightly braised with butter. Other times, raw. Always tasty.

The white cat was fond of him and generous. It rather hurt his pride, though, to make his way up those long stairs too often. He did not like to seem a beggar.

Of course, he could always hunt, but rats and mice

were such filthy things. More often than not, those which lived in the castle lived with or near the dogs and smelled like dogs. When he hunted, he went outside the walls of the keep where there were rabbits, and fat, sweet field mice.

Today, however, the weather had turned foul; cold and wet and his rabbit hunting had gone sour. He came into the castle grumbling to himself and stopped off in the kitchen to see what might be offered. While he waited to be noticed, he attended to his toilet. He began at his shoulders and worked his way down, tonguing carefully until he had all four paws clean and was nearing the tip of his tail. He did this by turning himself almost double and putting one forepaw on his tail to hold it in place while he licked.

An armored warrior came clanking into the kitchen, accompanied by four hounds who slavered and shook water all over the floor. They acknowledged Cat's presence but did not attempt to come under the table where he sat. None of them were fools.

One small female lay down beside the table, watching Cat with her yellow eyes. *Have they fed you?* she asked.

Not yet, Cat replied. *How was your hunting?*

The hound picked at the burrs between her toes with her small front teeth. *Not very good,* she said. *When the rain began, it was hard to pick up a scent. Some of those stupid males went off after a wee little bunny. I knew it was useless, and I had a better trail. For which, I caught a lash across my flanks. If he were not the master, I would think him as stupid as those males.*

What were you hunting?

Deer is what he said we were after. We came across some old tracks but nothing fresh. We have hunted too much too close to the castle. The game moves out. We should as well.

I would have settled for a wee rabbit, Cat said.

The yellow eyes looked at him mildly. *Come with me sometime. I will chase one your way.*

Cat did not answer but thought he would have to be starving to hunt with a hound.

The hound opened her mouth and panted with her tongue curled upward. Cat knew she was laughing at him.

A scullery maid trotted past, kicked at the hound and said "Ho, there, Cat. Is that hound pestering you?" She gave the hound another boot and Cat saw it disappear into the great hall after the others. Strange, he thought. The hounds usually do not acknowledge more than my presence. This one seems almost feline. She does not look like the others either. Smaller. Lighter color. Leaner. Yellow eyes. Cat's eyes. Strange.

Then he did not have time to think about the hound. The scullery maid had brought a saucer of fresh milk and some tidbits of meat. They were cutting the roasted haunch for the dinner table and she had sneaked a few scraps for Cat's supper.

After he had eaten and washed his whiskers, Cat made his way into the great hall where a fire burned fiercely on the large hearth. The sun was down and there was no light coming through the windows, but Cat leaped up on his favorite resting place anyway. Enough heat from the fire came across the room to keep him comfortable on the window ledge. He enjoyed curling on his pillow, paws tucked under his chest, watching the proceedings in the room from slitted eyes. No one noticed him there. He was as much a fixture as the window itself.

The warrior, who ruled under the woman, was speaking. "There is something abroad these nights that I do not like. Have you not felt it, Claire?"

"I feel the winter's approach. Nothing more."

"Perhaps you should light your herbal fires and consult your crystals. Something is abroad. I feel it. The hounds feel it. Something unnatural."

The woman laughed. "Unnatural? What seems unnatural to you, Ruger?"

"The game has all left the vicinity. The dogs feel it. They do not turn their noses after the harts because there are none to find. If I do not take a party out to find what is creating this disturbance, we may eat rabbit for the rest of the winter. It is not a prospect I relish."

"Nor I, my dear. I should have known it was your stomach which was disturbed. The weather is terrible right now. Allow me to consult my resources. Rest yourself and your men until the weather clears and, perhaps, by then I will be able to tell you what you are looking for."

He took her hand and kissed it lightly.

There were many people in the room; listening to the conversation between the master and mistress had kept most of them silent. When it was done, the chatter and laughter began again. Knights seeking ladies. Knights entertaining each other with lies of valorous deeds. Cat wondered what one of them would do if he actually saw a live dragon. His whiskers flattened against his cheeks in amusement.

A moist nose came over the window sill and touched his own nose. Cat opened his eyes and sat up quickly. *Oh,* he said, seeing the yellow-eyed hound looking up at him. *What do you want?*

That looks like a good place to watch without being noticed. Is there room enough for me?

Certainly not. The ledge is little wider than I am. In fact, Cat craned his neck and studied the hound's size, *I doubt you could fit up here alone.*

Too bad, the hound sighed and lay down below the window sill. *The hounds are over there by the fire scratching fleas. Eating bones I would not bother to bury. They stink, you know.*

I know, Cat murmured not quite sure if the hound meant the bones or the other hounds. After a long silence Cat said, *Why are you talking to me? Dogs never talk to me.*

Their loss, I expect. I don't know why. You seem like a sensible fellow. In my village dogs and cats were companions, not enemies. I do miss my home.

I thought you looked different from the others. Where is your home?

The hound sighed again. *The village name was Timbaca, but I know that means nothing to you. It was*

*a warm, sunny country and the game differed greatly
from game here. I came over much water in more than
one boat. It was a long journey. The master bought me
at a fair. He called me a leopard dog and said I would
be a good breeder. So far, I have not taken one of those
idiots to mate. If I have my choice, I won't, either.
Ever.*

Cat, who had never seen more water than the stream
which ran through the keep and who did not know
what a boat was, found the hound's story interesting.
A leopard hound. He had heard of leopards. They
were giant cats with spots. Legends, really, like drag-
ons; but he had heard the legends. No wonder the
beast was different. If she were part leopard and part
hound, no wonder she seemed brighter than the rest.

*Since you are not native to our countryside, I don't
suppose you noticed anything strange. The master said
it was "unnatural." Have you noticed anything "unnatural."*

Yellow Eyes panted thoughtfully. *It is hard to say.
Perhaps.*

Cat lay back down and tucked his paws.

Yellow Eyes said, *I've been here for several months.
I'm familiar with most of the game the master hunts.
While the other hounds were rabbit hunting, I cut a trail
I recognized but not from around here. It reminded me
of my home.*

A creature like yourself? Cat asked.

Yellow Eyes sat up to look into Cat's eyes. *Oh, no.
We called it "the leaf-ear." The humans called them
"tembo." Did I not know there are none here, I would
have thought the track I found belongs to a leaf-ear.*

I do not know leaf-ear or tembo. Cat said. *Can you
eat it?*

Not in ten years, Yellow Eyes panted, laughing. *The
leaf-ears are huge. Tall as the beams in this room.
Taller than the keep's gate. It is so tall and wide it could
not pass through the Horse Door in the donjon.*

Cat's eyes widened. It was hard to imagine anything
so large it could not pass through those tall, massive
double doors. *An animal?* Cat questioned.

There were herds of them in my homeland, like herds of cattle or deer here. It has a distinctive paw print and its scent is unmistakable. At first I thought I was only wishing, but the track was clear, pad after pad. I was beginning to course it when the master called me back and lashed me for not following with the hounds.

He did not see the track?

It was a grassy flat. Humans seem neither to see nor scent as well as we do.

No, Cat agreed. *They have many weaknesses. Those are two of the obvious ones.*

Both of them were absorbed in conversation and did not notice that the woman, Claire, was coming their way. "Get out. Get away from my cat, you filthy hound." She struck at the dog and Yellow Eyes slunk away and hid herself in the pack near the fireplace.

The woman stroked Cat and murmured nonsense words to him, while he preened and purred under her touch. It was, he thought, a small price to pay for comfort. If only the woman considered his stomach as thoughtfully as she did that of White Cat. Him, she left to hunt for himself. Ah, well. He raised and rubbed his head against her.

"Oh, you are such a love," she said.

"Would you fondled me as warmly as you do that beast," Ruger's voice was brittle and cold. "Come, I have a gift for you."

"This cat is a favorite of mine. Do keep your hounds away from him." She gave Cat a last pat and put her hand on the man's arm, allowing him to lead her from the room.

Cat sank back onto the pillow and began to wash. The woman's hands smelled of stale grease and sour wine. Another failing of humans was that they seldom washed.

When he was clean enough, Cat leaped down, making his way around the edges of the room to the hearth near the pack of hounds. They were gnawing at the bones tossed from the table and gave him little more than a glance and a snarl. Yellow Eyes came close and Cat asked, *Do you know where the tower room is?*

Where the woman makes her spells?

Yes.

I know.

Meet me there when all is quiet. I want you to tell someone else about the beast that is larger than the Horse Doors.

Remember. I did not see it. What if I was mistaken about the track? I have no reason to believe there are any leaf-ears in this part of the world.

This one is wise in all things. She will know if it is wishing only, or a real thing. Cat looked around at the dogs to see that there were none paying attention to them before he stood and slowly strolled away.

He spent some time in the kitchen where it was warm and full of good smells. Cat allowed the house to quiet down before he made his way up to the tower room. The door was open a crack and he slipped in and looked around.

White Cat watched him from her fur covered bed, which she sometimes shared with the mistress. *Ho, Cat. What brings you up to the tower to see me? What scheme are you hatching now?*

He leaped up on the bed and greeted her with a lick. *You know perfectly well it has not been that long since I have been up here to see you. It seems to me that I brought a live field mouse for your entertainment and a snack. Was that a scheme?*

Her whiskers flattened against her cheeks and she gave him a lick. *You are right, of course. You know I have a suspicious nature.*

They talked of inconsequential things until Cat heard Yellow Eyes' toenails on the stone steps outside the room. She stuck her head in the door and White Cat sat up, every hair on end. *How dare you come in here? Be gone!*

Cat said, *Now, now. This is a new friend of mine who has a strange story to tell. The master feels there are unnatural forces working around the castle and this hound may have something to say about them. Will you listen?*

White Cat sat down, but her fur did not entirely

smooth down. *Cat, you do make strange friends. Come in then, hound. Tell your tale.*

Yellow Eyes told again about the village to the south and about the great herds of leaf-ears there. She told about finding the track where none should have been. *Cat said you were wise. You would know whether this was a true thing or only a wish of my mind.* She sat down beside the bed and waited for White Cat to speak.

I am flattered by Cat's confidence. I cannot know, from what little you tell, whether or not this is a true thing. How would a leaf-ear come here? What do they do? Are they good for anything? Do men ride them, or plow them or use them for beasts of burden?

On, no. They are too fierce for that. I have never seen a tame one. They are wild and they break down the village walls, sometimes the very houses. Occasionally, one is killed. The meat is good to eat. That is the only use I know.

It seems unlikely then that anyone would bring one here by boat or by magic. What would be the purpose?

Could an enemy have brought one here to break down the castle walls? Cat asked.

There are easier ways to make war than with strange animals. It seems to me that you need more information. Dog, could you find the track again and, perhaps, follow it?

Yellow Eyes licked her front paws thoughtfully. *I think so. The track seemed fresh, and the dampness of the night will make the scent stronger. If I go now, will the master be angry?*

Cat said, *If you go now, who will know? Are you afraid to go alone?*

The dog sat up. *No. I am faster than anything in these woods. I have nothing to fear except the master, and if I go now and return before dawn, he will not know.*

Yellow Eyes trotted quickly to the door, looked back over her shoulder at the two cats, and then without another word, slipped out of their sight.

The White Cat asked, *Will she really go?*

I think so, Cat said. *She seems different from most hounds. Braver.*

They heard footsteps on the stairs and Cat jumped quickly from the bed and slipped under it to watch without being seen.

Claire came into the room. She cooed over White Cat for a minute or two and then went to the table where she worked her spells. She pulled a large stone bowl to the edge of the table and filled it with herbs from leather bags and wooden boxes. With a stone and flint, she struck a spark and breathed on it until a small flame set the dried weeds to flame. Aromatic smoke filled the room, turning its air to blue haze.

Cat watched while she pulled a white leather pouch from her sleeve. From it she took a red crystal the size of a hen's egg and held it to the light, turning it slowly to study its facets.

"Power," she said. "I feel your power. Where do you come from? What is your story? Such beauty! Such power! How could anyone trade you for a horse, even a good horse? They must not have known what they had."

The red crystal seemed to glow with inner fire. As she turned it, flashes of red light, bright as fresh blood, stabbed the dark corners of the room.

Cat drew back deeper into the darkness under the bed. He knew it was a spell, and he wished White Cat was under the bed with him so she could explain the process and, perhaps, tell him what has happening.

As the fire burned itself out, the woman put the crystal away and came over to the bed, which creaked as she lay down. Cat could hear her talking to White Cat. "How much of what you see do you understand, my pretty Puss? What could you tell me if you could talk? I wish I knew. There is so much mystery in your eyes. I know there is intelligence there as well. Could you tell me about the giant I see stalking about our castle? Perhaps it is a dragon. I have never seen one and I'm not eager to see one now, but there is something out there. It is from the east. The crystals tell me that much. Come here by magic so strong, I do not

know if I can counter it. I wish I could talk to my
Sisters to the south. They could tell me what to do.
We must think, Puss. We must think."

The room grew silent. After awhile, Cat slipped out
and down the stairs to wait by the door for Yellow
Eyes' return.

The kitchen came to life early. Fires were lit. The
morning meal was being distributed to the people of
the castle as they made their way to the great hall. Cat
wished someone would put one of those bowls under
the table for him.

He was considering his own emptiness when Yellow
Eyes dragged through the cat door, saw him and
dropped down beside him, panting with weariness.

Well? Cat said, impatient at her silence.

Yellow Eyes said, *When I can make the climb, let's
go to the tower. I don't want to tell it twice."*

Cat switched his tail irritably. After all, it was he,
not White Cat, who had waited the long night in the
cold, drafty hall for Yellow Eyes' return. *Quite all
right,* Cat said. *I don't care to hear it twice. You'd best
find yourself a good hiding place to rest. You look
terrible. I'll go up now. Follow when you can.*

Cat stalked off, grumbling to himself. He did not
even know if she found the track or saw the leaf-ear.
She could have told him that much. He avoided the
feet of people coming down the stairs as he made his
way up. People tended to become very angry when
they clumsily stepped on an innocent cat moving on
the stairs.

Outside the tower room, Cat waited until the mistress was no longer there before he nosed open the
door.

White Cat was sitting on the work table, lapping at
a bowl of mush. As Cat leaped onto the table, she
moved over and indicated he was to share with her.
She sat back and washed while he finished the bowl. It
was better than he usually had, cream had been added
and something to sweeten it. White Cat waited patiently until he finished eating and had time to groom
himself.

Did the hound return? she asked.

She did, muddy and covered with burrs. She must have gone a long way because she was too tired to climb the stairs.

Did she find the beast?

She did not want to tell it twice, Cat said primly.

White Cat licked her paw and washed her ears. *She could have told you something. Unfeeling. Just like a dog.*

I suppose she can't help that. Did the woman tell you anything about her vision? Cat asked.

Nothing useful. She did seem frightened by the red crystal. White Cat sniffed the white leather bag. *I didn't see anything unusual about it other than the color.*

Do you ever see the visions?

I don't think so. Not the same thing she sees.

Cat looked at the white leather bag. He wished he could see the red crystal for himself; it had made such frightening flashes of red light in the firelight. Perhaps it was wise to leave it covered.

They heard the slow click of toenails on the stairs and Yellow Eyes slipped into the room. She looked better. The mud had dried and had been shaken off. Some of the burrs had been picked from her coat and there was a slight bulge in her lean belly which told Cat she had found something to eat.

Both cats jumped down from the table and made themselves comfortable on a braided rug facing Yellow Eyes. *Well?* Cat said again.

Did you find the leaf-ear? White Cat asked.

Yellow Eyes stretched out on her belly, paws before her neatly, facing the cats. *It was not easy. I found the track, but the rain had washed away more of the scent than I thought it would.* She licked her paws alternately. *The leaf-ear makes one step to my ten. I followed up the mountain and down into the next valley. In a small swale with a heavy canopy of trees, I saw a faint light, a fire. When I crept close, I saw a master and the beast. Strange, though. It was a leaf-ear all right. It smelled like a leaf-ear, but it did not quite look like the ones*

*from my home. It is smaller, its horns are shorter, and
its ears are smaller. It is friendly with the human and
that is unlike the leaf-ears I know.*

White Cat was less interested in descriptions than in
facts. *Could you communicate with it? Where did it
come from? How did it get here? You did ask, didn't
you?*

*Better. The human called to me and invited me to
share their fire. It is the first human I have known to
communicate directly with me. Understand me, that is.*

Cat hummed to himself. He remembered one such
but did not want to interrupt Yellow Eyes' story so he
stayed silent.

*He is from a far eastern country sent here to seek a
jewel of great price. It was stolen from his homeland
and traded and sold many times before he traced it to
this land. He has a green stone which is the companion
to the red one which was stolen. The green stone glows
when it is near its companion and he showed it to me. It
is glowing now in its leather sack.*

A white leather sack? White Cat asked.

Yellow Eyes looked at her in surprise. *How did you
know?*

White Cat looked at Cat and closed her eyes. *I have
my ways*, she said.

Cat looked away to hide his smile.

Does he think it is in the castle? White Cat asked.

*He asked if I had seen or heard of such a stone. I
have not, of course.*

Of course, murmured White Cat.

When he learns where it is, how will he get it back?
Cat asked.

*He did not tell me, but he is weary of searching, and
he has strong magic. I think he could take it by magic
or, perhaps, he will use the leaf-ear to tear down the
gates and come in and get it. It could, you know.*
Yellow Eyes stretched her eyes to make them rounder
and nodded her head wisely. She had seen the leaf-
ears in action. She believed it could breach the castle
walls easily. Certainly, it could crash the gate.

Suppose he got it back. What would he do to the

ones who have it now? Cat asked. *Would he reward
them or punish them?*

*He didn't say. He did tell me that he understood my
longing to see my homeland again. He feels the same
way and would like to go home. I suspect he would
take the stone and go.*

How would he go? White Cat asked.

*I don't know how he got here. I suspect magic. I
suppose he would go home the same way he came.*

A sensible answer to a needless question, Cat thought.
He said, *Friend, be not offended. White Cat and I need
to discuss something outside your hearing. Rest yourself here until we return.* He stood up and nudged
White Cat.

She glared at him, but after an appropriate wait she
stood and followed him into a small anteroom where,
speaking softly, they could not be heard by the hound.

*The mistress' new crystal is the red jewel the Easterner
seeks, is it not?* Cat asked.

*I feel sure it is. What will happen if he does not get it
back?*

Cat nibbled his back toes and looked thoughtful.
*There is only one man and one leaf-ear. I tend to think
our castle can defend itself. But we have seen powerful
magic, you and I. If he works magic against us, there is
no way to guess how much harm can befall the castle
and all its inhabitants, including us.*

*You are becoming most wise, Cat. I agree with you.
Perhaps we should return the jewel to this man. First, I
would want to be sure it was truly his. How can we
know?*

Cat spat out a burr. *Yellow Eyes seems sure there is
a red jewel. We only suspect this is the same one. I see
no way except to go to the Easterner and talk with him.
We could carry the jewel with us but hide it before we
reach his camp. If we are convinced it is his and he will
leave peacefully if he has it, we could give it to him. I
think it a small price to pay for peace.*

It isn't your stone, White Cat said. *And I am not
going outside the castle.* The way she emphasized the *I*

Cat knew she meant it. She had never been outside the castle walls and had no wish to go now.

What will the Mistress say when her new crystal disappears.

Explain that to the Easterner. He may offer a solution.

Good thinking. Let's tell Yellow Eyes and see what she thinks.

She thought the journey was too far to make again so soon, the stone was probably not the right one, the master would beat her severely if he found her gone too long, there was less danger from the Easterner than from the master. In all, Cat got the feeling she did not want to go again.

Would it make a difference if I go with you? Cat said finally, tired of the arguments.

Yellow Eyes thought for a bit. *It would be a good thing to have it settled. I cannot believe there is danger to the castle, but if I am wrong . . .* She left the question open. *All right. But not before tonight.*

The two cats agreed that it would be a good idea to go after the evening meal had been served. The master was not as likely to look for his hounds then. They were fortunate he had not left the castle this day.

Cat remained with White Cat most of the day, leaving only after he had shared the evening meal she was served.

Yellow Eyes was waiting at the cat door. *It's about time.*

Cat, who had hauled the white pouch with its crystal contents down the stairs in his mouth, stepped under a wide table and sat down in its shadow. *I got this thing down the stairs, but I cannot carry it through the forest. It's hard enough for me to travel by myself such long distances. Can you carry it?*

The hound moved under the table with Cat and picked the pouch up in his mouth. *It would be awkward. Look. It has long strings on it tied with a knot. Could you pull them up over my head if I can get my nose into the loop?*

Good idea. Here, I can hold the knot up while you get your nose through.

Yellow Eyes worked with Cat until the loop was over her head. *Careful. Don't pull my ears off. There. It's a bit tight, but not uncomfortable. I don't think we can get it off though. Is it noticeable?*

Cat agreed that it was, indeed, noticeable. His whiskers flattened against his cheeks and his eyes sparkled. *Wait here until you hear a commotion in the great hall. Then slip outside and out of the gate. I will meet you there shortly.*

Yellow Eyes watched Cat swagger toward the great hall with his tail held high. In moments, he heard a dog yelp. A great uproar of dogs barking, chasing, fighting each other sent the kitchen help rushing to the hall to see what caused the ruckus. She slipped out the door as Cat had instructed and made her way through the shadows to the gate and out through the narrow slots at its base.

Cat arrived a few moments later, out of breath and all of his fur still on end. *You know the black male who thinks he is king of the pack? I slashed his tail end and hid under a table. He jumped the nearest dog. They fought all around the hall and, the humans were running around and trying to quiet things down. Food spilled. Wine went all over the floor. It was a fine brawl.*

It sounded so. I can't stand that arrogant beast. Come. We'd best be off. It's a long way, but I'll go slowly.

Quite all right, Cat said. *Go at your own pace. I'll keep up.*

After quite a long way at a hard run, Cat had to call out to Yellow Eyes. *Ho. You are right. My legs are not as long as yours. Please slow down.*

The hound stopped and allowed Cat to catch up and rest. *Sorry. It is a long way.*

Yellow Eyes slowed and allowed Cat to set the pace. It was full dark and the moon was high in the sky when she said, *Shuu, now. Just beyond this brook is where they were camped last night. Perhaps they have remained there because of the rain. I'll stay back in the shadows with the crystal while you go into the camp. I think he will greet you kindly.*

Does the leaf-ear like cats? Cat asked.

It did not seem to notice me. I doubt it will notice you either.

Good! Cat muttered. *I'm not sure I want to meet a creature as large as a castle gate.*

They saw the fire as they came up from the bed of the brook and made their way quietly into the brush nearby. They could see the man stirring a pot, which hung over the fire.

I wish it was a pot of fat field mice, Cat said.

I EAT NO MEAT. The man had caught Cat's remark, and he looked at the brush where they hid. I WILL SHARE WHAT I HAVE WITH YOU. COME TO ME.

Cat stepped out into the firelight with his tail held upright in a friendly gesture. He walked over to the man and sat down facing him. *How is it you understand me and can speak directly to my mind? Few humans can do that.*

IN MY CULTURE THERE ARE MANY WHO HAVE THE ABILITY TO COMMUNICATE WITH OUR FELLOW CREATURES. The man held out a bowl, which he had filled from the pot over the fire. Light curls of steam rose from the stew and its fragrance was inviting.

Cat smelled it politely and felt his mouth water. *Thank you. Let it cool a bit. Where is this miraculous place where humans have some respect for us?*

DO YOU KNOW THE OCEANS?

What are "oceans?" Are they the great waters my friend the hound crossed to come to this place? Did you come on a "boat?"

IF YOU DO NOT KNOW THE OCEANS, IT IS HARD TO DESCRIBE WHERE MY COUNTRY IS. DOES IT HELP TO SAY IT IS BEYOND WHERE THE SUN ARISES?

Cat curled his tail around his front paws. The fire felt very good on his back. *That tells me that it lies to the East and is very far away. Can the leaf-ear ride on a boat?*

MY COMPANION AND I CAME SOMETIMES

*BY BOAT AND SOMETIMES BY MORE MIRAC-
ULOUS MEANS. THE DOG TELLS ME THAT
THERE IS MUCH MAGIC IN THIS LAND. COULD
SHE NOT COME BACK?*

His eyes fixed on the copse of brush where Yellow
Eyes lay as he spoke and Cat suspected that he knew
she was there. *Yes. She led me here. She will come in
later. A Wise One has told me to ask you about the
jewel you seek.*

I TOLD THE HOUND. IT IS A STONE OF
POWER. SISTER TO THIS ONE. He took a white
pouch from his pocket exactly like the one Yellow
Eyes carried, spilling the green stone into his hand. It
began at once to glow as if it had fire within. THEY
CAME FROM A TEMPLE, A PLACE OF WOR-
SHIP, IN MY HOMELAND. THE PRIESTS USED
THEM TO CONTROL THE WEATHER CONDI-
TIONS THERE. WITHOUT BOTH STONES, THEIR
MAGIC IS EMPTY. OUR CROPS DIE FROM
LACK OF RAIN. THE PEOPLE GO HUNGRY. I
WAS SENT TO SEEK THE LOST STONE AND
RETURN IT TO ITS PROPER PLACE. CAN YOU
HELP?

At what cost?

COST?

You are not here to punish those who took the stone?

I HAVE ALREADY DONE THAT. BUT THE
STONE HAD BEEN PASSED INTO HANDS IN-
NOCENT OF ITS THEFT. I FOLLOW TO TAKE
IT BACK AND RESTORE IT.

I sense that you do magic.

YOU ARE PERCEPTIVE.

Cat lifted his right paw and licked the pads. *Of
course. Why did you not take the stone by magic?*

IF YOU KNOW MAGIC, YOU KNOW THAT
YOU CANNOT USE MAGIC AGAINST A STONE
OF POWER WITHOUT DANGER OF LOSING ITS
POWER ENTIRELY. I CANNOT RISK THAT. I
MUST TAKE THE STONE BY HUMAN MEANS.
TRADE, PERHAPS.

You mean no harm to the castle or its inhabitants?

NONE.

I believe you, Cat said. *We brought the stone. We have heard that our master traded a horse for it at the fair. Our mistress has much magic. She took the stone out last night and it flashed light like blood around the room. She knows it is a power stone but does not know the use of it yet. She is going to be very angry when she finds it is missing. If we give it to you, we will displease our mistress.*

MAY I SUGGEST A SOLUTION?

Please do. We would be glad to hear it. Cat called to Yellow Eyes who came out of the brush, tongue hanging, tail wagging. They sat down side by side. The man made no move to take the stone though the pouch hung in plain sight.

He reached back and pulled a large bag forward, rummaged in its contents and brought out a pouch that looked much like the other two except that it was brocaded in silver. He poured its contents into his hand, another large red stone. This one lay glistening in the reflected firelight, but no flashes of crimson light lashed the area about them.

THIS STONE HAS POWER OF ITS OWN, BUT IT IS NOT A SISTER STONE TO THE EMERALD. IT IS CUT MUCH LIKE THE OTHER AND WEIGHTS ALMOST AS MUCH. DO YOU THINK SHE WOULD NOTICE THE DIFFERENCE?

The two animals looked at each other. Cat widened his eyes slightly. *Looks the same to me. She has only seen it a couple of times. I think it could pass. How about you?* He looked at Yellow Eyes.

I think so, too. I'm willing to trade. She stood and allowed him to take the pouch from around her neck. He patted her kindly. I AM NOT HERE TO PUNISH, BUT I WILL REWARD MOST GENEROUSLY. He took the stone from its pouch and the green and red fires from both stones made both Cat and Yellow Eyes lie down and cover their eyes. He put the stones back in pouches, but he put his stone into the brocaded pouch and the stone he was going to give them into the pouch the dog had carried. Before he slipped it back over her neck, he lengthened the strings so she could pull back out of them easily when they arrived home. I HOPE THIS WILL BE ALL RIGHT. I WOULD NOT LIKE FOR YOU TO SUFFER ON MY ACCOUNT. HOW MAY I REWARD YOU?

Cat switched his tail. *A cat needs nothing but a good meal every day, a dry place to sleep and a little respect. I have all of these already. You could reward me with a ride back to the castle on your beast. It is a long walk.*

A SIMPLE REQUEST WHICH WILL BE GRANT-ED. HOUND, WHAT MAY I DO FOR YOU?

Yellow Eyes looked at Cat sadly. *I hate to leave you, Cat. You are a good friend and I think we would have good times together, but I miss my home. I would like to go home more than any other thing.*

The man smiled. I KNOW THE FEELING. CAT, IF I TAKE BOTH OF YOU ON THE BACK OF MY BEAST AND RIDE YOU TO THE CASTLE, CAN YOU CARRY THE STONE BACK TO WHERE IT BELONGS?

Of course, Cat said.

THEN LET US GO. I AM AS ANXIOUS TO BE HOME AS THE HOUND IS. SO IS MY BEAST. REST HERE. EAT. I WILL PACK AND MAKE READY.

Cat would never forget the journey back through the woods to the castle. Small trees crashed down before them and every once in a while the great beast lifted her long nose and blew a trumpet call that threatened to shatter his eardrums. They rode in a little house trimmed in fine silks and cushoned in golden brocades. The beast moved in a swaying motion, making Cat dig in his claws to hold his place. The man held Yellow Eyes before him to keep her from falling. Cat was beginning to wish he had not helped the dog finish the bowl of stew the man had given him as they reached the edge of the woods in sight of the castle.

There is something I would like to ask for, but I don't know if it is possible, Cat said as they stopped within the woods.

ASK, the man said.

The master has said the game is gone from our forest. Is there something you could do to bring it back so we do not go hungry?

I DO NOT EAT MEAT, the man repeated, BUT IF THAT IS WHAT YOU WISH, IT IS DONE. I HAVE TIED THE POUCH AROUND YOUR NECK. CAN YOU MAKE YOUR WAY FROM HERE?

Easily, Cat said. He leaped and landed on all four paws. He looked around to say good-bye and saw only the forest. Cat felt a chill go through him and his hair stood on end. He could see plainly the tracks of the leaf-ear, but there was no trace of the beast anywhere. Rat's Eyes, he said to himself, I have never seen magic like that.

The dawn was beginning to show on the eastern horizon as he slipped through the gate and into the cat door. The kitchen was busy, but on the stairs, few feet stirred. He made his way unseen to the tower room. The door stood partly open as it usually did. The mistress was walking about as she dressed, looking in drawers and under things, muttering to herself.

"I know I left it on the table. Now, where has it gone?"

Cat waited until her back was turned before he raced silently for the safety of the bed. White Cat saw him and, when she could, jumped off the bed and came under. *Did you do it? Was it his stone? Is he going to harm the castle?*

We found him. It was his stone. He is a kind man, who will harm no one. He is gone. Is she looking for the stone?

Yes, since last night. Where did he go?

I don't know. Vanished. He said he had magic so I suppose he took Yellow Eyes to her home and then went on to his homeland in the east.

Yellow Eyes is gone, too?

Poof. Gone. As soon as I jumped down from the leaf-ear, they all vanished.

Cat, you are so clever. You have saved the castle, sent the danger away and come back safely. If only we could find some way to satisfy her. There is no way to tell her what happened.

And no need to. The man thought of that. Here, pull this bag off my neck and push it over to the edge of the bed where it just shows under the coverlet. She will find it sooner or later and be happy. It is a stone much like the other but not the same. He had a green sister stone to the red. Together they make fire that makes you hide your eyes. I was glad to see it go. This is a much calmer jewel.

White Cat moved close to him, purring, and licked his ears. *Cat, you are truly a marvel.*

He had never been so sleepy in his life and this seemed as good a place as any to take a nap. *I know,* he said and closed his eyes. Tomorrow would take care of itself. He had had his adventure for today.

IT MUST BE SOME PLACE

by Donna Farley

At a quarter of midnight, I sat with my tail curled around my paws, perched on a dryer in the deserted laundromat—deserted, that is, except for myself and the wizard's apprentice.

All around us, several dryers and the one unbroken washer hummed and clattered like a herd of mechanical cows chewing on some particularly indigestible cud. What they were actually chewing on was the laundry Jack had been saving up for the last three weeks while his uncle and master Hugh was away at a wizards' convention.

"There you go, cat," said Jack, tipping an anchovy quite delicately into my mouth. The boy had enough sense not to try to get me to stand up and dance on my hind paws like a circus dog, as my "owner," Miss Parke, sometimes does. I licked in the salty tidbit and bolted it down with my tongue-spines, then fixed my eyes expectantly on his face as he bit into his pizza.

He was a slightly pudgy teenager, who, if he'd been a cat, would have been called "Ginger" because of his hair color. Similarly, my "owner" had named me "Butterfly" because of my attractive coat, orange, cream and black in color, a pattern cat fanciers call tortoiseshell. However, I'm not an ordinary tortoiseshell cat; I'm a tortoiseshell tom. Which means I'm impossible.

Oh, very well, I'm exaggerating. Cats do that habitually. However, I *am* a rare animal, to say the least.

You see, in the scheme of things feline, tricolor coats are for ladies only. There is no such thing as a tortoiseshell tom. But once in a blue moon (such as the one I was born under) the impossible happens.

Tortoiseshell toms are magical.

You think I'm exaggerating again. Well, you needn't believe my story or even listen to it; it doesn't singe my whiskers. Cats, especially tortoiseshell toms, are not interested in human opinions about felinity, except for a good laugh now and then. Back fence clubs often have a howl or two over the quaint and bizarre ideas humans hold about cats. Oh, Eliot did see something through a glass darkly—"jellicle" is a genuine Feline word, though where he managed to find it is a real mystery. But other than Eliot, the only human to ever come up with a real cat tale was Lewis Carroll. What he and his illustrators never realized was that the so-called Cheshire cat was really a tortoiseshell tom.

Wizards know, and therefore we tortoiseshell toms avoid wizards like the plague. I, however, had had the bad luck to have one move in upstairs.

Master Hugh was fat, balding, and beetle-browed, and very bad-tempered, even for the wizard. If, for instance, Jack were to tiptoe up the stairs a little too loudly on his return from school, waking his master perhaps ten minutes earlier than he preferred, it would not be unthinkable that Hugh would turn the boy temporarily into a mouse for his familiar, Samantha, to practice on. Fortunately for Jack, Hugh's repertoire did not include any spells much more deadly than this one. But if any doubt remains as to Hugh's character, let me merely remark what I have observed with my own eye (the blue one, which perceives psychic phenomena): his aura was the approximate color of ancient motor oil in a commuter car, with tinges of Chinese restaurant grease that only gets changed every six months, and a few overtones of red the shade of a bargain basement hooker's lipstick.

They say that familiars reflect the personalities of their masters. Samantha, Hugh's black cat, was a form of life lower than a kicked dog's ego. She was also quite untalented magically, and I had no difficulty placing a lock-spell on her mouth when Hugh and Jack first moved into Miss Parke's upstairs, so that the wizard remained unaware of my true nature. After

that, I stayed far from both his path and Samantha's
(some black cats really are bad luck) but Jack was
another matter. It was a mistake, of course, but I have
a weakness for anchovies.

Jack saw me watching him eat and smiled—he has a
grin like the Cheshire cat's himself—and tossed me
another anchovy.

"How'd you like to be my familiar, cat, when I
finish my apprenticeship?"

I nearly choked, and he patted me on the back. I
looked at him suspiciously, curling my tail tighter around
my toes.

He took another bite of pizza. "Uncle Hugh says
cats gotta be black to be smart enough to be familiars.
Personally, I think if they're all like Samantha, then
it's their low morals and not their brains they got in
common." He tendered me another anchovy, and I
took it, purring approval. He was a very good judge of
character, however naïve he was in other respects.
And unlike his master, he had an interspecies rapport
gift; in other words, animals liked him, even Samantha.
Naturally it had no effect on a tortoiseshell tom; I was
only there for the anchovies and the warm clothes
dryer under my backside.

"Lemme show you something, pal," Jack said, and
pulled out a pair of baby-blue socks with black em-
broidery from the gamy basket that was still waiting its
turn for the washer. He took off his own shoes and
socks and put the blue ones on, then stood up with a
flourish. "Ta-da! Whataya think of that, cat?"

I blinked. His figure had faded to a pale ghost of
itself. Obviously they were magic socks which made
the wearer invisible. I, of course, was still able to see
him faintly, but I was betting he was completely invisible
to humans, and probably to most other animals as well.

I decided to play along, because it gave me an
opportunity for free anchovies. As he stood there in
silence with folded arms, I rose to all fours and pretended to be puzzled, searching the room for him.
Then I made a quick spring to the bench where the
pizza box sat, and calmly helped myself.

"Hey!" He snatched the box away, and I leaped back to the dryer, keeping my eyes glued to the food while he pulled off the socks and tossed them in the basket again.

When his form regained its solidity, I looked expectantly from him to the pizza box and back. He rolled his eyes, then gave me the slice of pizza I had stuck my paw into.

"I guess the master's invisible socks don't impress you much, huh?"

I ignored him, catfully working away at picking the anchovies out of the mozzarella. Of course I wasn't impressed—I can turn invisible without the aid of any idiotic socks.

Jack sighed and picked up the basket, taking it to the washer as it shuddered to a stop. He pulled out the wet clothes and dumped them on top of the dryer beside me, then emptied the basket into the washer, adding the detergent and setting the machine.

I picked away happily at my pizza while he put the machines through their cycles, until at last he had the final batch loaded into the oversized, heavy-duty dryer beneath me. I smacked my lips and curled up, savoring the warm vibrations of the machine. Now the clock read midnight.

Jack leaned on the machine with one elbow and scratched me in the perfect spot behind the left ear. "If I didn't know better, Butterfly, I'd say you were a magic cat," he said.

I kept cool, but I didn't like the sound of it. Sooner or later, Jack was going to find me out. When that happened, his uncle would want me. I would have to stay on my toes, or I would end up like that snake-bellied Samantha. I sniffed indignantly at the thought. I'd run away from home before I let them catch me!

"You know, Butterfly, I'm thinking of running away from home," Jack said.

I couldn't help flashing my eyes open. Did he have telepathy, too? If so, he seemed no more aware of it than of his talent with animals. But a second later something else set my sixth sense jangling like an emergency phone. I leaped up on my paws, twitching my whiskers and ears, and made a slow radar sweep with my tail.

"Hey, what's up, cat?"

The dryer rumbled to a stop and I leaped to the bench, landing beside the empty pizza box, and turned to face the dryer door.

"Oh, the laundry's done," he said, as if that explained my behavior, and proceeded to unload it into the basket.

I watched intently as he pulled out star-spangled underwear (Hugh's) and Woolco sweaters (his own) and socks in large clumps, tossing them into the basket without regard. Last out of the dryer was a lone baby-blue sock. Jack frowned and started rummaging through the basket.

You're got to understand that laundromats are some of the few places on earth where you'll find randomly appearing interdimensional doors these days. Go ahead, laugh. Even the wizards don't believe it. They're too prejudiced against modern technology to consider the evidence. But just try to demonstrate scientifically the whereabouts of all the lost socks.

Jack's expression was getting frantic. "Uh-oh," he said, and stuck his head in the dryer for a look. Then he tried the washer. Then the other machines. And behind the machines. I twitched my tail impatiently.

"Will you do something!" he implored me.

"Like what?" Ooops.

He stared at me (and they call cats saucer-eyed!) then suddenly his face was transformed by that Cheshire cat grin, his green eyes glowing. I don't know—maybe he *had* been a cat, in some other life.

"Aha! I knew you were a magic cat."

I proceeded to wash my face.

"Butterfly, old buddy, old girl, you have got to help me find that sock! Please, girl? C'mon, I'll buy you an extra-large anchovy pizza."

I yawned at him. I'm not sure why I had spoken to him, but now that I thought of it, if I wanted to keep the wizard's claws off of me, enlisting his apprentice as an ally might not be a bad idea.

"Butterfly, baby, girl—"

"I am not a girl," I said tartly, and stood up and made a pirouette with my tail high, so he could see for himself.

"Geez—I thought all calico cats were female—"

"Tortoiseshell," I retorted. What abysmal ignorance—and from a boy of his particular talent! Obviously Hugh was not only nasty, he was a hopelessly incompetent teacher. "Tortoiseshell cats are all female. Except that once in a blue moon, you'll get a male like me. We're magical."

"Right." He straddled the bench and leaned down so that his face was level with mine, which I continued to wash. After a minute he burst out, "Will you quit with the primping already— Uncle Hugh will have my ears if I don't find that sock!"

I riveted my blue eye on him, observing the bright true blue and nature green of his psychic aura, and said, "I doubt he'd have any use for your ears. Your heart, maybe, or your entrails, but not your ears."

He grimaced, shuddering, and the aura took on a yellowish tinge about the blue and green. Of course the idea of Hugh actually extracting his own nephew's entrails was just a bit of feline exaggeration. I think.

"I may be able to help you," I said, "for a price."

"A price! Hey, I thought we were buddies!"

I gave him a disdainful look. "Cats—especially tortoiseshell toms—do not have 'buddies!' "

Jack moaned and ran his fingers through his gingery hair. "Okay. What do you want?"

"To make sure your uncle never finds out that I'm a tortoiseshell tom."

"But how can I do that? I wouldn't ever tell him of course, but—"

"But my 'owner' might let it slip, or Samantha may find a way to break the silence spell I've put on her."

"I don't see how we can prevent any of that. Why do you stay around? You'd be safer if you just ran away from home—heck, so would I," he added glumly.

I twitched my whiskers. Why Jack was considering leaving was not my concern, but if he did go I would lose my ally. "I was here first, before that wizard moved in. I don't intend to desert my territory without a fight."

Jack nodded slowly. "I don't blame you. But how can I help?"

"Well, for now you can warn me if there's any sign that he's beginning to be suspicious of me. I'll come up with a plan soon."

"Great. And now that that's settled, what the heck happened to that sock?"

"It's gone down the rabbit hole," I said, stretching a little.

"Where?"

"Well, through the dryer, actually, but it's ended up the same place it would if it went down the rabbit hole."

"Uh-huh. How does—"

"Look. If you want it back, you'll have to follow it. It's that simple."

"You want me to get in there?" He jerked a thumb at the dryer.

I turned a critical eye on him. Although he was a little flabby, he wasn't big, as adolescent humans go, and the dryer was a large-capacity one. "We should just make it."

"I suppose you know what you're doing," he said doubtfully.

"That's more than I can say for you," I growled. "Imagine tossing a pair of magic socks straight through a dimensional doorway!"

"I still have one of them," he said defensively, holding up the remaining blue sock.

I sniffed at him. "What good is it being half invisible?"

"Oh, you win," he said glumly, and stuffed the sock in the pocket of his jeans. He opened the dryer door and took a deep breath. "Geez. Uncle Hugh has had me doing some pretty weird magical stuff, but this takes the cake. Do I have to start it?"

"Just get in. My own magic will get us moving."

He crawled in, and when he got settled he looked

about as comfortable as a Great Dane in a Chihuahua cage. I pounced in and found a spot in the nook made by his contorted body.

"Ow! Watch where you put those claws!"

"Here we go!" I said, and with a wave of my tail, I started us spinning.

I'm afraid Jack found it a bumpy ride, though I was quite comfortable, curled up in his lap. He made a good shock absorber.

The interdimensional transition was great fun, like being inside a kaleidoscope going five hundred miles an hour. We landed very gently, however, under a pink sky amid a vast, rolling plain of woolly texture and infinitely varied hue. It was so comfortable I was tempted to lie down and have a catnap, but instead I watched Jack, who was hunched over as if he were chucking up a furball.

He lifted his face, which was rather green. "Never," he advised me, "eat anchovy pizza before taking a ride in a dryer."

He sat up and gazed around, and for a minute I thought he was feeling better, but then I saw his jaw dropping, as slowly and surely as a hydraulic lift. His eyes swelled almost out of their sockets as he turned his head from side to side, surveying the scenery. He lowered his eyes again to the ground beneath him and suddenly fell on his knees, clutching at the multicolored tubes of yarn, coming up with two handfuls.

"AUGH! There must be a million socks in this place!" He tossed them in the air and stood up, sinking to his knees in the myriad variety of style, size and color of the little human foot-warmers.

I had found a more solidly packed pile, which I proceeded to knead with my claws into the most comfortable contours, before settling down with my tail curled up. "Billions, I would say."

"Oh my God," he said and dropped to the ground again, his head in his hands. "Maybe I'll just give up wizarding altogether and join a circus somewhere." He groaned and looked around again. "What is this place?"

"The Valley of Lost Socks," I was almost purring because it was so cozy. "You won't find a single matched pair among them, either."

"A whole world full of nothing but lost socks?"

"Oh, no. That's just this section of it. Elsewhere you'll find the Beaches of Lost Buttons, the Forest of Lost Ways, the Marshes of Lost Marbles, and the Caverns of Lost Voices, to name a few."

"Lost Voices? Come on!"

"They tend to come and go," I admitted, "more than the more solid items that end up in this dimension."

"Which is where? Uncle Hugh never told me anything about this place!"

"Oh, I'm sure he did,' I purred, really feeling comfortable now. "Hasn't he ever said to you, when you've lost something, 'Well, Jack, it must be someplace?' *This* is Some Place."

He stared at me. "Oh, gimme a break!"

But I merely watched him through slitted eyes. I thought I saw something moving in the mountain of argyles and ski socks behind him.

Suddenly I went on an all-six-senses alert, and a shiver of pure excitement ran along my spine.

Heaven! My nose twitched at the unmistakable scent, and I eased slowly to my feet and began to stalk toward the argyle socks, noting at the same time that all angles of my vision showed tiny rustlings all around us. Jack, meanwhile, was as still as a human can make himself, watching me silently.

I approached within a cat-length of the movement, waiting for it to betray itself again. Suddenly a green-checked sock slid from the top of the pile, and I sprang, diving into the heap with every nerve and muscle intent on the prey. My jaws clamped on a furry morsel, and I leaped triumphantly up with my prize, ready to display it to Jack.

"Ooh—eek! Let me go! I'm the queen of the mice, and you'll be sorry!" squeaked the little rodent.

"Butterfly!" Jack leaped over and grabbed for the mouse. "Leggo! It talks!"

I held on, fuming.

"Shriek!" cried the mouse. "Oh, mighty master of animals, I implore you, save me from the jaws of your familiar!"

I spit her out, right into Jack's hands, which closed protectively about the little brown body. "I am *not* his familiar," I said indignantly, and then gave Jack's forearm a swipe of my claws for good measure. I had lost my temper—I suppose it had flown to some other quarter of Some Place.

"Ouch!" said Jack, but didn't let go of the mouse. "Hey, Butterfly, look—she's got a little gold crown on! She really is the queen of the mice!"

I eyed the creature coldly, licking the mouse hairs from my lips. "It's some woman's lost wedding ring," I said, with all the contempt I could muster.

"Oh, most gracious, wonderful, merciful master of animals!" said the disgusting little beast, fawning all over Jack's hand, caressing his fingers with her little bitty paws and kissing his palm over and over. Jack put on his Cheshire cat grin. It positively made my fur stand on end.

"What a pretty little thing!" said Jack, stroking her fur with one finger.

"Oh, blessed wizard and beastlord! My people are your grateful and loving slaves forever!"

"Uh, thank you very much," said Jack, "but don't you think they might object to that?"

"Oh, no," the mouse queen squeaked, straightening her ring-crown. "Not when they've seen you! They'll know what you are!"

"Mice have a very low magic-resistance threshold," I pointed out.

"What do you mean, Butterfly? I'm not using any spells—heck, I hardly know any yet."

"Oh, beautiful king of all that moves! What need has one like you for spells?" said the mouse, bowing and scraping on Jack's palm again; then she scuttled quickly up his arm and perched on his shoulder, nuzzling his ear.

"What?" Jack laughed.

I coughed. "You're an empath, dolt."

"I'm what? I thought I was a wizard's apprentice and part-time high-school student."

"You have a natural magic talent that surpasses any of the spells your uncle could teach you. You evoke sympathy, affection, even obedience in animals."

"Holy cow! he said, then winced, scrunching his shoulder; the mouse-queen was tickling his ear. "You mean all I have to do it say jump and they'll ask how high?"

"It's hardly that simple," I said, twitching one ear. "Obviously, the less intelligent the animal, the more profound the effect." I fixed my pupils on the simpering mouse, who was, of course, unaware that she had been insulted. "Why don't you see if she can be any use in finding the sock?"

"Hey! Great idea," said Jack. He pulled the one blue sock out of his pocket and held it up. "Queenie! I have to find the mate to this sock! First, we'll start by having all your people carry all the blue socks here and make a big pile, then you can all help me go through them until we find the right one. Whaddaya say?"

He plucked her from his shoulder and held her in his hands allowing her to sniff over the sock. She looked mighty puzzled, and I knew why. For a fellow who was an animal empath, Jack knew appallingly little about his field.

"What a clever idea, Jack," I purred sarcastically, "but mice are color blind."

"Uh-oh." He scooped up the mouse and put her back on his shoulder and gazed despairingly around at the wide Valley of Lost Socks. He stuffed the magic sock back in his jeans, sat down again, and then suddenly put his fists to his head. "Think, Butterfly—is there anyone else here in your weird Some Place who could help us? Some animal in huge numbers, like the mice, but with color vision?"

I blinked. The boy did have a head on his shoulders after all. "Songbirds," I said. "On the Mountain of Lost Notes." I licked my lips. Winged prey was more challenging than the four-footed kind.

"Great! Let's go. And don't forget, Butterfly, when we get there, don't chase the birds!"

I glared at him, but he didn't notice, and I wondered again just what were the limits of his talent.

"Chirpy-birds place is that way," the mouse chittered. "I will show you, dear master!" She nudged Jack's chin and peered at me saucily from her perch on his collar. I bared my fangs at her, and she disappeared behind his neck.

"Listen!" Jack said as he puffed along. Wading through several miles of knee-deep sock piles was taxing for one slightly out-of-shape wizard's apprentice, and boring for a tortoiseshell tom.

"I've heard them for quite a while," I said with my nose in the air. Unpleasant, thin chirping noises— anyone who calls bird sounds music has never heard a really good caterwaul chorus.

Before us loomed a forbidding gray mountain, like a great mound of concrete formed in the shape of scoop on scoop of slate-gray ice cream. Poking up from its surface like hedgehog spines were numerous tall, black poles, between which were strung five black lines that snaked their way from pole to pole like telegraph wires all the way to the mountain top. The birds in their profusion of colors, scarlet, blue and yellow, flitted from line to line, pecking off the musical notes that hung there like ripe black cherries. As we approached the mountain, I watched a small sapphire-colored bird pluck and swallow four notes in succession, then open his mouth and give forth with the opening notes of Beethoven's Fifth. Well, who can expect originality from a birdbrain?

Mindful, in my benevolence, of Jack's plea not to chase the birds, I decided to amuse myself otherwise. I leaped to the top of the nearest pole and launched myself out onto the top line like a tightrope artist, then with one paw began knocking the notes to the ground with a flourish, delighting in the jazzy sounds that resulted as they hit the rocky surface of the mountain. This was better than a back fence jam session!

"Butterfly!" Jack shouted, and my reflexes took over, landing me at his feet. He gave me a really insolent look—as if he were a cat himself and my equal!—and turned his attention to the sapphire blue bird. Sticking two fingers in his mouth, he gave a shrill whistle and cried, "Here, birdie!"

The bird flew at once to his shoulder, and he raised a finger to give it a perch. "Fantastic! Butterfly, how come I never got this kind of response before? I mean, animals have always liked me, even old Samantha— but this!"

My eyes were glued to the bird, who was repeating the Beethoven again. I slowly switched my tail. "Some Place is a magical realm. I think you'll have to work very hard to develop your talent to the point where you'll get such results in the mundane world."

The bird exhibited only slightly more dignity than the mouse had done. It flew in delighted circles about Jack's head, serenading him with the annoying Beethoven repetition. Fortunately this was only a prelude to the business for which we had come; to Jack's inquiries it replied excitedly that it and its fellows would be thrilled to aid us in our search. Only moments later the entire flock lifted into the pink air and headed for the valley, where, the blue bird assured us, the job would be virtually completed by the time we walked back.

The creature kept its word, amazingly enough (you can never tell with birds; their little minds fly in a thousand directions at once.) Long before we reached it, we saw a baby-blue mountain looming in the center of the valley. I flicked a whisker and looked at Jack for his reaction, but he seemed undaunted, tramping cheerfully along through the socks and whistling Beethoven. When we came to the base of the battle-cruiser-sized pile of blue socks, Jack waved happily to the cloud of birds clustered above, and called out confidently as the last few blue socks were added to the summit.

"Thanks, fellas!" he said, and they flew off to their

mountain again, with the exception of the little blue bird, who swooped to a perch on one of Jack's shoulders, the other still being occupied by the mouse, to whom he now displayed the magic sock again. He pointed out the sigils of invisibility woven into the side.

"Take it from the bottom up, Queenie—you and the rest of the mice."

The mountain of socks began to vibrate as the hosts of mice swarmed round its base, pulling out socks one by one, examining them quickly and scampering away to lay them in reject piles all around. My whiskers began to twitch as I watched their activity; it was so unbearably boring to merely watch and not chase. Jack sat down and stroked my back as we waited.

The pile grew smaller, and Jack grew less confident.

"Mrrrff," I growled, annoyed because his distraction had made him less attentive about stroking my fur. He scratched under my chin.

At last the ground lay bare, the socks redistributed to form something resembling the rim of a baby blue moon crater. As Jack slowly stood up, the blue bird whistled a rather halfhearted rendition of the Beethoven.

"Oh, master!" the mouse queen said tearfully, "What poor servants my people have been to you! Oh, great beastlord, pray forgive us!"

Jack spewed out a long series of curses, such as "Beelzebub's belly blubber!" which, having been learned from his wizard uncle, would be considered quite picturesque by human standards, but which were unimpressive to the feline ear. The mouse wept, and the bird sang his dirgelike phrase again.

Revolted by the lot of them, I turned my bored gaze outward to the horizon, and was startled to see an approaching clamor of birds, who seemed to be harrying some earthbound creature toward us through the foot-deep layer of socks. I focused all six senses on the approaching thing, and soon reached an unpleasant conclusion.

"Oh, Bastet save us! It's a *dog*," I said disgustedly.

Still pursued by the birds, the ugly canine stumbled

along as best it could through the socks, pitching forward frequently onto its nose, and falling at last in a dirty-yellow heap at Jack's feet. In its mouth was a blue sock.

"Is that it?" Jack cried, his hopeful expression suddenly rekindled.

The dog dropped the sock and leaped up barking, "Yessir! Nosir! Threebagsfullsir!" and hurled himself with joyous slobbering at Jack's face.

The mouse shrieked, and the bird gave out shrill, quick repetitions of the Beethoven phrase, making it sound like a stuck phonograph.

"Geddown!" Jack yelled, and scooped up the sock.

The dog fell back whimpering, and Jack patted its ugly head as he examined the sock. "Good boy."

"Butterfly!" he cried, "this is it—but just look at it!"

I peered at the sock, and it was immediately apparent what had happened; the dumb mutt had chewed on it till the invisibility sigils had become almost unrecognizable.

Jack pulled off one shoe and sock and tried the magical one; there was no doubt. The spell on the sock was ruined.

"Well, that does it," said Jack. "Know any good circuses I can run away and join, Butterfly?"

"How easily you humans are discouraged," I said. "The sock has *lost* its magical properties, has it not?"

"Yeah, exactly, and I'm gonna *lose* my head when Uncle Hugh finds out!"

"The point is," I said patiently, "everything that is lost eventually ends up Some Place. If we look long enough, we're bound to find the invisible power which the sigils had previously bound to the sock."

"Butterfly," Jack said slowly, "are you telling me that we have to look for invisibility?"

"I believe I said that," I sniffed.

"Butterfly, how can you possibly find something invisible? Invisibility itself?"

"Look here," I said, "if you're ever going to be more than the amateur wizard that your uncle is, then you'd better learn to free yourself from the habit of rigid thinking. After all, he didn't even tell you about the existence of Some Place, did he?"

"Yeah, well, I've been thinking of looking for a new master—and that's not the only reason."

I twitched my tail in annoyance. "One thing at a time."

Jack sighed and said, "Okay, I'll bite. How do we look for what we can't see?"

"First, let's see the sigils on the other sock," I suggested.

He laid the pair out together so we could look at the line of mystic characters running from cuff to ankle. "They were both the same?"

He nodded. "He commissioned them. Socks were cheaper than a cloak, though I hear they wear out faster."

I sniffed. One can only pity those who have neither their own magic nor their own fur and must manufacture substitutes for both.

"So you know nothing of the spell for their making, I take it. Well, there's always more than one way to skin a mouse," I said, and glanced at the little rodent perched on Jack's collar. She ducked quickly inside his shirt. "First we've got to repair the fabric of the sigils; then we'll see about recapturing the invisibility spell itself."

We waded through the socks again, but this time in the opposite direction, toward the Plain of Lost Civilizations. We had reached the outskirts of the marbled splendor of the Ancient Greek quarter, where I planned to lead the party (alas, the dog, bird and mouse were still with us) into the Religion and Mythology section, when Jack sat down for a rest.

"Butterfly," he said with a yawn, "I don't think we're going to make it back in time to put all that laundry away before Uncle Hugh gets home in the morning."

"Don't be absurd," I said. "What do you think it is that people lose more of than anything else?"

"I dunno—socks, from the look of the valley."

"*Time*, you rodent-brain," I said. "There's enough lost time floating around in the clouds up there to last you a lifetime. We'll simply recover some on our way home."

"Wow!" his green eyes went wide.

"However, I suggest we move on now."

"Okay," he said, "Heel, Yeller," he added to the ugly yellow mutt, which it did, just as if Jack had trained it from a pup. I shuddered. The talent manifest in my naive young human neighbor was of greater proportions than I had imagined.

I managed to drag Jack through the streets of Lost Greek Civilization without stopping to talk with every Tom, Dick and Herodotus, for, as Jack had discovered to his delight, language barriers do not exist in Some Place, the air being saturated with the lost pre-Babel universal mutual comprehension. Eventually we arrived at our destination, a modest house in the Origins street of the Mythological section, where I instructed Jack to knock and enter.

"Don't go blundering ahead before your eyes adjust," I advised him. My own more versatile vision revealed a mazelike array of shimmering webbing draped about the interior, and the walls hung with unbelievably lifelike tapestries. Amid all the gossamer stood a large and dusty loom, and a similarly disused spinning wheel.

"Oh, now who is it?" a creaky voice complained. "Don't you wizard tourists ever get tired of gawking at poor unfortunate people who happen to have incurred the wrath of the gods?"

"How do you do, Miss Arachne?" I purred, and a line descended quickly from the ceiling, suspending a large black spider at Jack's eye level.

"Well, what have we here? You're a good-looking young fellow."

"Uh, thanks," Jack gulped.

"I suppose you think I'm ugly just because I'm a spider," she said bitterly.

"Oh, hey, I—"

"Well, you're right," sobbed the spider. "You have no idea what a pretty girl I was before Athena did this to me!"

"If you don't recall the story, Jack," I said, "Arachne here challenged the goddess Athena to a weaving contest. It seems Athena is a sore loser."

"Gosh, I'm sorry, Arachne," he said, and stuck out his palm. The spider just hung there for a moment.

"People don't usually like spiders to crawl on them," she said suspiciously.

"But Arachne, you're not really a spider," he said.

"Well," she said, opening and closing her mandibles, "that's true. But what about that bird?"

"Huh? Oh, Blue Boy won't hurt you. Don't touch the spider, birdie, she's a lady."

"Tweet tweet tweet tweeeee!" said the bird, and the spider crawled cautiously onto Jack's thumb.

"We have a problem only your skills can solve, Arachne," I said. "Show her the sock, Jack."

The spider scuttled around and peered down at me from Jack's thumb. "Well, look at that—a tortoise-shell tom! Is he your familiar, Wizard Jack?"

I opened my mouth for a hiss, but Jack quickly said, "He's just a friend. And I'm afraid I'm just an apprentice." He pulled out the socks and explained the situation.

"Oh, that's easy," said Arachne. "I can have it done in two shakes of a cat's tail." My whiskers twitched, but I said nothing. "But drat it—I was hoping you were a wizard and could help me get back my true form."

"From Athena?" I said skeptically. "Not even a master magician can compete with a goddess."

"Well, she's only a retired goddess nowadays—I thought there might be a chance," Arachne pouted.

"Of course we'll help you—won't we, Butterfly?" said Jack.

I stared at him, my pupils dilating in astonishment, but for some reason I couldn't think of an appropriately catty reply. Before I knew it, the spider was working away at the sock, and we were back in the street.

"Which way to Athena's place?" asked Jack, gawking about in all directions, until he caught sight of the Acropolis. All the lost glory of the Parthenon sparkled from its heights—the ruins that exist in the here-and-now mundane world are less than a mere shadow of it.

My tail was swishing as furiously as a fly swatter.

"All right, Jack," I said. "This is what we'll have to do. In half an hour we walk back into Arachne's, reclaim the sock, and tell her all she has to do is get herself up to the Parthenon and she'll be disenchanted. Then we snag ourselves a bit of lost time and beat it."

"Butterfly!" I winced at the outrage in his voice. "Now, what's our best bet? Do we try to strike some kind of bargain with Athena, or do we try to trick her into turning Arachne back?"

"Our best bet is to cut our losses and run," I said dryly.

"Oh, come on, Butterfly, she can't be all that bad. It seems to me that I remember Athena was one of the better Olympians."

"That's not saying much," I snorted, then put on my radar. If any local deities had heard me, we would really be up to our ears in damp kitty litter.

"But we owe Arachne *something* for fixing the sock," Jack said.

"Your trouble, Jack, is that you haven't learned to think like a cat. Try it—you'll see, things work out much better when you look out for number one."

He gaped at me, then got angry, if you can imagine. It's astounding how such insignificant creatures as humans (and such a poor specimen of the race as a pudgy teenage sorcerer's apprentice!) can muster such amazing delusions about their own moral stature.

"You know, Butterfly, for all that you're a tortoiseshell tom, you really aren't any better than Samantha!"

"I beg your pardon?" I sat up straight. "What could a mouse-brained biped like you possibly know about the comparative worth of felines?"

"Oh, well, I suppose I can't expect morality from you, can I? But I did think you had as much pride as an ordinary alley cat. I didn't think you would back down from a challenge—much less be scared of a mere goddess."

My tail went lashing around like helicopter blades. "If you think, just because you're an animal empath, a tortoiseshell tom will let you get away with a cheap trick like insulting his pride, then think again! So long, Jack!" I spat, and disappeared—not from the plane of Some Place, but from Jack's view. It was only with difficulty that I suppressed the satisfied grin which, like the Cheshire cat's, could betray the presence of my otherwise invisible form.

"Butterfly!" Jack looked about frantically. "Come back here, you louse of a cat!" He heaped a number of curses on my name, but of course as it was only my ordinary, everyday name and not my secret name, the curses were entirely ineffectual. "Shoot! How do I get home now?" he asked the dog.

"Track!" the beast responded, and demonstrated by sticking his nose to the ground and starting to follow our trail back toward Arachne's place. I levitated and sat hovering in the air several feet above his head, and suddenly he started running in a confused circle. Even Jack couldn't help being disgusted at this display of idiocy.

"Oh, bother," he said. "All right, gang, the first thing is to try and help Arachne. Maybe she can tell me how to get home afterward. I guess without Butterfly we'll have to try the direct approach—we'll go beg for Athena's mercy."

And with that the whole idiotic group set off for the Parthenon. I could scarcely believe my eyes.

I followed them closely, still invisible—not, you understand that I had given up on the Feline First Law of Self-Preservation; it was just that I was indulging in another common mode of cat behavior: curiosity. Don't say it—I know. It kills cats with alarming frequency.

"Hello?" Jack called into the empty temple—empty save for the goddess' gigantic ivory and gilt statue. "Athena? Are you here?"

"Of course I am," said a gently reproachful feminine voice. "But who else is?"

Jack's eyes swiveled from side to side in his frozen head. I could see his Adam's apple bobbing up and down in his throat like mercury in a thermometer, and thought maybe he didn't have any cat in him after all. "UHHHH—um, your majesty? Uh, your divinity, I mean?" he said, sweeping an awkward bow. "My name's Jack. Hope I haven't disturbed you." He was still looking around for the source of the voice.

"Look at the statue, twerp," I hissed, before I remembered that I wanted to let Jack worry a bit longer. Oh, well.

"Butterfly!" he said, looking about hopefully, but I kept my invisibility anyway.

"Did you come here to speak to me, mortal, or to the air?"

"Uh—oh, excuse me, to you of course, ma'am," said Jack, finally realizing that the voice did indeed come from the nevertheless immobile lips of the statue, which, with his slow-adjusting (definitely nonfeline) eyes he was now regarding with wonder. "Wow! Is the statue really you?"

"Merely the palest shadow of my true divine glory, which vision I am sure you could not withstand, mortal," she assured him.

Suddenly there was a tremendous swooping and fluttering, and Jack gulped as a fifteen-foot owl alighted in front of him and hunched its head toward him with dinner-plate sized eyes. The mouse queen (as usual) gave a shriek and dove into his clothing, while the Beethoven-chirping bird clung tightly to his collar and the dog yammered.

"Shut up, you guys," he said, and they did.

"From the Prime Material Plane, aren't you, young man?" said the owl, swiveling its head as it scrutinized Jack's features. "I think I like you, though I don't know why."

"It's a sort of talent I have," Jack admitted, and I could have clawed his legs off. It certainly proved he had no cat in him after all. Imagine laying your cards down like that before the game's begun!

" 'Zat so?" said the owl, who still appeared well-disposed toward Jack. "Honest, too, hmmmm?"

Jack blushed. "Uh, I guess so. I might as well tell you I'm here on behalf of a friend."

"Come back, Poopsie, dear!" the goddess called, and the owl winced, trying to clear his throat.

"But, milady—"

"Now, darling. I want to talk to the little fellow myself."

"Yes'm," said the owl, and flew dejectedly back to some shadowy niche in the top of the temple.

"Poopsie likes you," the goddess observed.

"Yes, ma'am. I was just saying I have a talent with animals."

"Delightful," said Athena, "Python wants to meet you, too."

"Python? Ulp!" said Jack, as an immense golden snake slithered out of the shadow of the statue's Gorgon shield and curled itself amiably around Jack.

"Keep cool, team," he said to his nervous menagerie. The creature's girth was almost equal to the boy's height.

Python's tongue flicked out and in again, and he said in a sizzling voice, "SSShe likesss me to fffrighten blasssssphemersss, but you are not afffraid of me, are you?"

"N-not much," Jack gulped.

"Enough, Python dear," the goddess said sweetly, and the serpent slunk back beside the shield.

"Snakes and owls are the wisest creatures in the world, you know, and being the goddess of wisdom myself—even if I am retired—I value their opinions. I can't remember either of them taking to a mortal so. So what can I do for you?"

"Well, ma'am, it's to do with Arachne."

"Arachne. Oh, that's so sad," said the goddess.

" 'Scuse me?" said Jack.

"Yes. She was really quite a favorite of mine, or I would never have made her such a successful artist in the first place. But she really couldn't bear to admit I was better at the loom than she was. She was so mortified at her failure after that silly contest she turned herself into a spider."

"What? That's not how I heard the story—"

Athena sighed. "Well, if there's anything you mortals lose more easily than time, it's the truth. The metamorphosis was the direct result of Arachne's own humiliation. I've simply let her stew in her own juices."

"Then you could turn her back?" Jack said hopefully.

"I'm afraid that wouldn't be good for her. She hasn't learned humility yet, you see."

Jack's face fell. "But I promised her," he said, and proceeded to explain his agreement with Arachne. "Couldn't we work something out? Maybe she's never going to learn humility as a spider—maybe what she needs is to get back to being herself before she can learn anything. Maybe if she had to learn to do something else she wasn't so talented at. . . ." Jack's brow was puckered with his effort to find a solution.

The goddess laughed softly. "Young man, if I hadn't retired, I think I would want to be your patron, even if wizards are more properly under Artemis' protection. Suppose I put Arachne in your hands, and let you teach her humility?"

"Me? But how? I'm only an apprentice."

Again the golden laugh. "Well, to begin with, you'd be a good example. But I'll tell you. Take Arachne back to the Prime Material Plane with you, where I will allow her to recover her human form in the daytime, while she reverts to a spider at night. When and if she attains humility, you will bring her back here to report to me and apologize for her previous behavior. Then I will lift the rest of the curse. Now, isn't that a wise plan from the goddess of wisdom?"

"Uh, yes, it sure is. But your goddess-ship, could you please tell me how I can find the magic sock's lost invisibility before I leave?"

"Oh, that's easy. You want the Sea of Lost Spells, beyond the Beaches of Lost Buttons, on the other side of the Valley of Lost Socks. Poopsie dear, take Jack to pick up Arachne and then drop him and his critters at the Sea, would you? I think you can carry the dog in your claws, but do be careful. Oh, and be nice to Jack's little invisible feline familiar, however tempting his little fat body looks."

"I am *not* his familiar!" I flashed into indignant visibility. I should have known a goddess would be able to see me. "And I am not fat—just a bit longhaired."

"Spare me," she said coldly. "If you're lucky, I'll put in a good word for you with Bastet at the Retired Goddesses Club meeting this afternoon. Ta-ta, Jack!" she said, and the owl swooped down and escorted us outside.

" 'Poopsie.' Cute name for an owl," I meowed as we made our way down the Acropolis.

"Poplios to you, cat!" the big bird squawked.

Jack said, "Cut it out, and let's get to Arachne's," which we did quite quickly, the denizens of Lost Greece clearing the streets as Athena's owl approached. When we arrived, we found the spider had indeed finished her work.

"Humility!" Arachne shrieked when Jack told her the goddess' plan. "Athena wouldn't know humility if it bit her!"

"She's not supposed to. She's a goddess," Jack said reasonably. "Come on, Arachne, isn't it better to be human half the time than not at all?"

Arachne reluctantly acquiesced, and crawled to a perch in Jack's hair.

Outside, Jack got himself mounted on the owl's back, and I jumped up in front of him, settling my claws into Poplios' back like grappling hooks. The owl reared up and flapped its wings like a hawk bating.

"Watch it, Poplios!" cried Jack, clutching at the feathers.

"Sorry, Master Jack," said the owl, as he swiveled his head around one hundred and eighty degrees to glare at me.

"Wait, I can make sure we don't fall off," said Arachne, and quickly spun a seatbelt. When all was secure for takeoff, Poplios beat his wings and launched into the air, making one quick circle before diving to snatch up the dog, who yelped in terror (of which he dropped a token or two on the heads of some unfortunate Greek citizens as they observed our departure.)

The Valley of Lost Socks passed quickly below us, and soon we had landed on the beach. It stretched along into the distance in two directions, as vast a collection of buttons as the valley had been of socks. Near the water they were well packed down, but still slippery to walk on, and the dog went racing about among the little plastic chips and mushroom shapes with all the grace of a Clydesdale in a gravel pit.

When we'd untangled Arachne's threads and alighted, I began to scratch at the beach; buttons weren't kitty litter, but they would have to do.

Jack was staring out at the Sea of Lost Spells as it rolled in. As each wave broke, instead of sea foam, a host of transparent scrolls was deposited on the shore and lay on top of the gleaming buttons, just waiting to be picked up.

"Those are the spells," said Poplios.

Jack stared at the incredible wealth of magic that lay at his feet, then reached for one of the scrolls. "Butterfly! How come all the wizards in the world aren't here trying to pick up these free scrolls?"

"Well," I said, grooming my chest fur, "I suppose it's because—"

There was the sound of an immense rush of water as the sea serpent lifted its head from the waves, and I was caught in the splash on the beach, and shot about ten feet straight into the air with a yowl. (I didn't mind the sea monster, of course—it was just the getting wet.)

The dog broke and ran yelping away from the water, while the owl stood frozen, without even giving a hoot. The mouse was already in hiding, and the blue bird's refrain was (for once) silenced. Arachne screamed and crawled into Jack's ear.

"Get outta there," he said in an annoyed tone, as he focused on the sea serpent.

Its head was about the size of an apartment building, and each eye looked like a fluorescent purple domed stadium. Raised nostrils like twin subway tunnels were set on a pink scaly snout, and the creature opened an awful maw full of Volkswagen-sized teeth to speak.

"Thay, withard, thoth're my thcrollth, tho handth off!"

"Uh—sure," said Jack, dropping the scroll.

"Thankth. Tho long," said the serpent, and began to sink back into the ocean.

"Wait!" Jack called.

"Yeth?" said the beast, with a bat of one purple eyelash.

"Uh, I just came for one spell, one that I lost. Couldn't you spare just one? I mean, what do you do with them, anyway?"

The monster's head lurched forward, and its chin landed on the beach with a chinking of buttons against scales, directly in front of Jack.

"I eat them," said the sea serpent. "I altho eat withardth who try to thteal them from me. It'th nothing perthonal," it added apologetically, "but if I didn't, pretty thoon there'd be hundredth of withardth here thtealing my thcrollth, and then I'd thtarve."

"Oh, I understand," Jack said sympathetically.

"You do?" said the monster, a light in its great violet eye. "Thay! You're pretty nithe, for a withard."

"I'm only an apprentice," Jack said modestly. "Gosh, look at the size of you!" he added, with pure admiration. I heard a little gurgle of horror in the owl's throat as we watched Jack reach out and scratch the monster's purple-bearded chin. Arachne crawled back to the crown of Jack's head to get a better view.

"Thay! That'th fantathtic!" said the sea monster, and closed his eyelids with a sigh like a jet engine winding down.

"Tell you what," it said, opening one eye again, "for you, I'll make an ekthepthion."

"Really?" Jack beamed. "Hey, thanks!"

"Hmm," I said, as I went on washing my paws, not really watching the monster any more, except out of the tiniest corner of one eye, "Now all we have to do is find the right spell."

"We need the spell that makes this a sock of invisibility," said Jack, holding up the newly-mended sock to the monster.

"Pardon me, sir, may I be of assistance, sir?" said a small voice at Jack's feet. My ears perked up, and I slunk nonchalantly over to investigate. The voice was that of a fiddler crab, who saluted Jack smartly with his large pincer.

"Cap'n Crusty of the beach patrol at your service, sir. Noticed your aura when you arrived. Volunteering for any aid we can give you, sir."

My whiskers quivered. All those exciting moving parts—

"Don't even think about it, Butterfly," Jack warned me. I glared at him and licked my lips, curling my tail up as I sat down.

The crab and numerous other denizens of the beach made short work of the search. Within minutes, Jack held the necessary scroll in his hand. It was transparent as plastic, and nothing could be seen upon it—not by human eyes.

"Open it," I told Jack, and as he did so I fixed my left eye—the amber one, which can see into the infrared spectrum—on the document. "The sigils on the sock will answer to the vocal component of the spell, and merely putting the sock on serves as the somatic. The material components must be woven into the sock to complete the spell."

"What are they?"

"An eyelash, and some gum arabic."

"Uh-oh," said Jack. "Uncle Hugh's all out of gum arabic at home. He was planning on picking some up at the wizards' convention. Where does gum arabic come from, anyway?"

One of my whiskers quirked. Hugh was obviously useless as an instructor for Jack; I would have to do something about it when we got home. But first things first. "It comes from a desert tree, the acacia."

"I suppose there's a desert here in Some Place?"

"Oh, yes." I switched my tail, watching the sea monster, who was still gazing moonily at Jack. The boy's talent was beginning to alarm me.

Suddenly the fiddler crab, who had joined the zoo on Jack's shoulders, pinched the mouse's tail, and this led to a mad chase in and out of Jack's shirt. "Okay, that's it!" Jack yelled. "Listen up, gang. From here on in, any animal on or around my person is under truce as regards all other such animals—indefinitely!"

I went on washing my face, and gave the dog a dirty look, but Jack didn't take up the challenge.

"All aboard Poplios for the desert, folks," he said.

"With I could go," sighed the sea serpent.

"The Desert of Lost What?" Jack said, as Poplios came in for a landing.

"Lost Minds," I said, leaping lightly down to the hard, dry ground. To one side was a cliff, populated by yellow-blossoming trees, while to the other was the pleasant rush of a seasonal river. "Don't worry, there aren't many of them."

"You should fit right in with lost minds, cat," said the owl.

I bared my fangs at him, then turned to the cliff, where the fifteen-foot acacias grew from clefts in the rock.

"Now, we're going to need a month to collect the gum," I purred.

"A month!" Jack yelled. "What are we going to do all that time? Now that I think of it, it's been quite a while since that anchovy pizza. And what—"

"Oh, don't go shedding your fur," I said in annoyance. "We won't have to do anything. Poplios here can just fly up to the clouds and collect a month's worth of lost time—which will put him a month into the past, you see, at which time he will make a nice, neat incision in one of these trees with one talon, and then, voila! We'll be able to collect one month's exudate of gum arabic from it here in the present." I licked my lips, satisfied with my plan.

"Do you really want me to do that, Master Jack?" asked the owl.

"Uh—I'd really appreciate it, Poplios," Jack said, with a quite sincerely winsome look.

"Right. I'm off, then. Been nice meeting you!"

Jack waved the giant owl off, and I started for the nearest tree. "We shouldn't have to wait any longer than it takes him to reach the clouds," I said.

Jack sat down at the foot of the tree and started pulling at the dog's ears. I leaped into his lap; truce or no truce, I wanted it made clear just who was top cat around here. Jack shoved the dog gently aside with a sigh, and I gave the mutt my best slitted-eye look of triumph, but he was too dumb to understand and sat watching with his tongue lolling as Jack stroked my fur.

"Butterfly, how does Poplios get back to the present?"

"The hard way," I said, as I settled myself. "He waits a month."

Jack frowned. "But can't he get some more time and—"

"It only works backward, Jack. Don't bother your head about it—time travel is an advanced subject, hardly of a level for an apprentice at your stage."

"Yeah? Look, Butterfly, I've been thinking. Since Uncle Hugh seems to have neglected to teach me such a lot, how about if I become your apprentice instead?"

I had to start washing my face in order to think of an appropriate reply for such an absurd suggestion. I was interrupted, however, by Arachne, who cried out, "Jack! The tree!"

Sure enough, a great gash had opened in the bark, and along its edges were a number of pale yellowish, walnut-sized lumps.

"There you go," I said. "Now, pluck out an eyelash, roll it in the gum, and have Arachne weave it into the sock."

There was a tense moment when Arachne, having completed her task, seemed to be stuck to the inside of the sock, but Jack pulled her free without harming a hair on her little spidery head, and reinstalled her behind his ear.

"Okay, this is it," he said, as he pulled on the first sock, the undamaged one. Even the blue bird held its breath as he rolled up the second sock, the newly repaired one, and slipped it over his toes.

"Itworks itworks itworks works worf!" barked the dog, and the rest of Jack's menagerie—concealed on his person and so sharing his invisibility—joined in with their various cheers.

Jack took off the magic socks and stowed them safely in his shirt. "Well, gang, I guess that finally wraps—"

I felt the tingling of my sixth sense too late. Jack pitched forward as if struck by a hard blow and landed flat on the ground, sending his menagerie scattering in alarm.

I squinted my amber eye closed, so I could watch with my blue one. There was a tremendous upset in Jack's aura, blue and green light flashing about and then suddenly dissipating and being replaced by an unhealthy glow rather like radioactive gangrene in color. By the time he was on his feet again even his face had a different look about it.

I began to wash my paws with studied nonchalance. I needed time to figure out the details. What had happened, of course, was that Jack had been possessed by one of the Lost Minds that wandered about in the desert; the question was, whose mind? And what exactly did he or she intend to do? And was Jack still in his body, dominated by the invader to the point where his aura was no longer recognizable, or had he been ousted to the desert?

I cursed many mental Feline curses—I won't shock you with them just now. I should never have brought him here—as the incompetent Hugh's apprentice, he had never learned any psychic self-defense. The whole wild-goose chase through Some Place had gone much too easily up to now, but this was a situation where Jack's animal talent was useless. It was up to me to right things now.

"Jack" was dusting himself off, but his miniature zoo showed no inclination to return to their perches upon his person, and the dog whined, obviously uneasy but not understanding it all. "Jack" did not seem to notice.

"Well," I said, pretending not to have noticed anything, "if you're through being clumsy, Jack, what do we do next?"

"I want to go to the Sea of Lost Spells."

He was eyeing me carefully, obviously uncertain. He could not know we had just come from the Sea, but whoever he was, he knew of the Sea's existence, and wanted the power and wealth of the scrolls. That fit with the unpleasant overtones I observed in his muddy aura. That aura bothered me; not only was it hostile, but it seemed familiar.

"But, Jack," I purred, "we've just come from there."

"Well, I decided I want to go back. I'm not leaving here without some of those scrolls."

I twitched my whiskers, and felt an itch behind my ear.

"Don't scratch me off!" Arachne whispered. Jack's other animals, no longer attracted by his unique charisma, had wandered off in various directions.

"Well, unless Poplios the owl happens to come back, we'll have a rather long walk there," I said to "Jack."

"Oh, Beelzebub's belly blubber!" he cursed.

My eyes dilated repeatedly. No wonder the aura seemed familiar—it belonged to Jack's uncle! But how had he lost his mind? Then I remembered; of course, he had gone to a wizards' convention, and most likely was drunk out of his mind at a party. Eventually, his mind would have to leave Jack's body in order to return to his own, when it sobered up, at which time anything he might remember about Some Place would seem to be an alcoholic delusion.

"I know who you are," I said, now that I knew all I had to do was wait him out.

"You do, eh? And I know who *you* are—my land-lady's supposed pet. Blast that Jack—some apprentice! While I'm away, he steals my socks and takes up with a tortoiseshell tom! Well, the joke's on the two of you, because I'm not going back to my body. Jack's is a good deal younger than mine, and I can use a long life to study the scrolls I'm going to take from that legend-ary sea. And don't think of deserting me—I'm holding Jack's body hostage. I can toss it off a cliff and go

back to my own body and he'll be stuck in this desert
indefinitely, while I won't be any worse off than when
I started.''

I froze. Even my tail stopped twitching. Could he
really do it? "All right," I said, "you win. But it's still
a long way to the sea. We'll have to walk along the
river bank.''

The wizard grumbled, but off we went, and as we
went I tried to think of a plan. I turned on my telepathic radar, and, as I had hoped, I detected a presence hovering behind us as we walked and knew it
must be Jack's mind. He was following us, but I knew
he didn't have the telepathic training or experience to
reenter his body and kick his uncle out. By the time
the wizard was ready to sit down and rest I had a plan
worked out.

"Don't try anything," he said, watching me suspiciously as he settled back after a drink from the stream.

"Me? I'm for a catnap," I said, and folded my paws
under me, closing my eyes. I had already told Arachne
in whispers just what I intended; she would wait for
my signal. Now came the hard part.

I began purring my cat mantra, quickly dropping
into the meditative state of consciousness which is
preparatory to feline "paranormal" activity. All cats
can do at least a little in this line, but tortoiseshell
toms are experts. I reached outward with my mind,
carefully so as not to attract the wizard's attention.
But the psychic wall he had built to prevent Jack
reentering his body had also effectively "blinded" him
telepathically and he didn't even notice when I reached
past him to net Jack's mind and draw it into my own.

—Listen carefully, Jack— I told him, as we sat in the
safe refuge of my brain. *—I'm going to breach the wall
he's built around your body and pull you in on my tail,
so to speak. But once we get in, it'll be up to you to
overpower him and toss him out.—*

—Just say when— Jack said grimly.

I sneezed, which was Arachne's signal. She hopped
off my shoulder and I watched through slitted eyes as
she scuttled across the ground and around behind the

wizard. For a moment all was quiet, and then I saw her, climbing up "Jack's" shoulder to her former perch above his ear. She flexed her mandibles—

—This is it, Jack—

—and I twitched a whisker at her. Arachne bit the ear.

"Yow!" The wizard jumped up and brushed at his ear, sending the spider flying, and while he was distracted I drove my mental force straight between his eyes like a battering ram. The psychic walls shattered, and I slung Jack's consciousness in where it belonged.

—Hit him while he's down, Jack!— I said, and retreated to my own body, in case Hugh tried to flee there when Jack ejected him.

I watched the rather bizarre spectacle of a body being fought over by two separate minds. He kept trying to get up, moaning in pain, holding his head in his hands. More spectacular was the flickering clash of auras, twined in combat around the body. There was nothing more I could do, now. It was strictly a contest of wills between Jack and his uncle. I was placing my bets on that (admittedly hypothetical) feline spark in Jack's nature, and when suddenly the struggle subsided and the aura shone emerald and sapphire around his body, I knew I was (as usual) right. I leaped at once to his side, scanning around in a wide circle, and detected a mere bedraggled wisp of a mind retreating along the stream.

"Sweet Bastet!" I hissed. "What in a cat's nine lives did you do to him, Jack?"

"I turned him inside out. He's had it coming for a long time!" he said fiercely.

I looked at him in astonishment. Seeing this sentimental animal-lover trounce his own uncle with such a very feline viciousness gave me a whole new opinion of him.

I licked my lips. "Well. I don't think you'll need much more psychic training to protect yourself from him in the future."

"'He won't get another chance. He was stealing my power for his own use. If I had not found this way to break free, I would soon have been completely enslaved by his sorcery."

Though she did not know what we were talking about, Arachne was concerned for Jack.

"Are you all right now, Jack?" she asked timidly as she crawled up his sleeve, marvelously uninjured from her "flight."

"Thanks for helping, Arachne," he said. "I'm fine now except my mind—tastes foul."

"It should pass," I said. "Meanwhile, your uncle's mind will soon return to his body on the mundane plane. I suspect he got here via the bar at the convention. Which means in fact that he's still there, so we won't even have to stop on the way back for some lost time."

Jack blanched. "I have to face him again when he gets home?"

"Not exactly," I said. "People who lose their minds through chemical means don't usually remember having been here when they sober up. Now let's get going—you owe me an anchovy pizza."

We materialized in the laundromat, just before sunup, where, miraculously, no one had stolen Jack's three weeks' worth of laundry. Jack was moaning as he contemplated the job of putting it away, when a shriek of delight came from behind him.

"Jack! Look! I'm human again!"

I am no judge of human beauty; I can only observe that Jack's jaw hit his chest when he caught sight of the new Arachne, who looked about his age and height. I rather disliked her sleek black hair myself, but then humans are not cats, so I am sure it was nonsignificant. Her body, Jack informed me later, was "built," and apparently (so he thought) showed to advantage under the ancient Grecian-style costume she wore.

Arachne wanted a mirror, but the best thing available was the glass door of a laundry machine. "I'm more beautiful than ever!" she squealed.

I sniffed, and Jack nudged me. "Uh, Butterfly, what's she saying?"

I realized then that of course she was speaking Greek, which I knew, but Jack did not. It was one of the many things Hugh should have taught him but did not. It was also apparent, from the way Jack's eyes followed Arachne, that he wasn't going to be much use at teaching her anything about humility. I sighed; with one thing and another, there was nothing for it. As soon as we could work it out, Jack would have to become my apprentice. (You may think I decided this because I happened to like the boy, or because his empathic talent was influencing me; to which I will reply that, on the contrary, it was merely a case of ordinary feline whim.)

"Let's get Arachne some better clothes," I suggested, "and get this laundry put away."

The problem of what to do about Jack's uncle, as well as Arachne's disenchantment still loomed before us. But for now everything was organized. Arachne had been introduced to Miss Parke as a recent immigrant from Greece, looking for domestic work, and the ideal tenant for Miss Parke's spare room on the ground floor, where Arachne was now safely installed. The socks of invisibility, along with the rest of the laundry, were safely put away. And the scent of anchovy pizza lingered in the empty box on the front steps in the morning sun. I leaped to a perch on Jack's knees and checked for the most comfortable spot.

Jack yawned, then scratched the back of my right ear. "Say, Butterfly, old buddy, do you like me at all? Just a little bit?"

I gave him an appropriately aloof feline stare, then started kneading my claws on his lap, finally finding the perfect position to curl up in.

"What a perfectly ridiculous question," I said.

THE DREAMING KIND

by C. S. Friedman

1

There was a time between sunset and evening when the wall between the worlds grew thin; when, if one was watching—if one knew how to watch—the dark little creatures of the dreamworld could be seen slithering through.

The one called Hunter-In-Darkness knew how to watch.

The time would come just before true darkness fell, in that moment when Night and Day were most precariously balanced. It would last for just a few seconds (but they were long enough) and then the way would be closed again, and the things which had come from *there* to *here* must now remain *here* forever.

He never hunted until after it was over. Never failed to watch it happen, once he had learned how. The shadowy dream-creatures fascinated him, as did their presence in his world. He had seen such things in the dreamlands, of course, and had hunted them there; to do so was a cat-custom as old as the worlds themselves. But here they seemed . . . wrong, somehow. As if passage between the worlds had weakened them. Their inner light was dim, often flickering, and their edges dissolved as the wind brushed against them, trailing off into thin wisps of fog. They came in a thousand shapes, no two alike: from tapering worms of amber-gray mist to the deep carmine crabs that scuttled over unseen pebbles and stones in their path to an invisible sea. And all seemed wrong to him.

He had hunted them once, in his kittenhood, but

172

had quickly learned the futility of such action. In the world of dreams these creatures had substance and might be hunted, slain, and eaten, but in the waking lands they were wraithlike and could not be grasped, either by claws or in the teeth. One was left with only a foul tasting residue wherever contact had supposedly been made, a bitter reminder that *something* had not been caught. It was better to leave such things to one's shadow-self, and devote one's waking hours to the capture of more solid prey.

Tonight he would hunt in the manlands. The moonless night was perfect for it, the darkness so thick that he could feel it brush against his coat, black against black in the chill autumn wind. There was the fence to deal with, of course, but that was no real obstacle. Like a neuter's spray it lacked any scent of authority; his people had scratched their way under it or climbed across the branches that crossed over it so often that it looked—and smelled—like a thoroughfare. He found a channel that cut under the wirework and crawled through it easily, into the home turf of the same two-footed creatures who had once tried to kill him.

And there he found prey. He saw it first, a point of light against the ebony darkness. Mouse? He was already downwind, and began a careful approach. Soon the scent came to him, cool and promising: Mouse. He put one paw forward onto the carpet of dying leaves, shifted his weight slowly to follow. *Careful. No noise.* It couldn't smell him, couldn't possibly see him; only the sound of his presence might warn it in time.

It pricked up its tiny ears, wary. He froze. Time passed. The wind shifted, but didn't fully reverse itself; it would no longer serve him, but nor would it warn his prey. *Be still. Be still.* The field mouse looked about, moved two steps closer to a patch of ivy. *Be still, Hunter.* And then it relaxed at last, and began nosing down among the fallen leaves for food. He dared a slow step forward, then another one. The scent was unclear, but the mouse was in plain view, and the wisps of bodylight that clung to its coat played foolishly across the brown fur, heedless of danger.

It would hear him when he leaped, he knew, and would probably dart for cover. He guessed that it would run off in *that* direction, prepared himself to compensate. . . .

And: flight. Strong hind legs propelled him into the air, straight as an arrow shot toward his prey. It ran, in just the manner he had anticipated . . . and he had it, his claws dug firmly into its shoulder, his teeth closing joyously about the tiny neck. Its bodylight played into his nostrils as he subdued it, and—when he tired of its struggles—killed it. He knew from experience that such light took time to fade, that not until dawn would the last of it drift off. He ate the mouse where he had caught it and then left the scraps, faintly glowing, upon a pile of gold-edged leaves. A good meal. To be followed by a good washing, after which—

It was then that he became aware that something was watching him.

He turned quickly. Ears flattened, claws unsheathed, he was ready for whatever battle the intrusion required. But all he saw was a dream-creature, its form glowing brightly against the contrasting darkness. An unwholesome shape, half fish and half slug, with a gaping, toothless mouth at the forward end. He jumped out of its way, no longer certain that such things were harmless. His fur was on end, and although he made a token effort to smooth a bit of it with his tongue, his soul was on edge as well; the ugly thing had *frightened* him.

But it had no interest in feline company. It floated past him, against the breeze, until it came to the place of his recent meal. And then it paused, as though thinking. He felt himself growl, in loathing and in fear. Though the thing had no scent, its aura was decidedly threatening; it took all his self-control not to turn and run, nor to attack it outright.

It hovered over the mouse carcass for a long while, its foggy flesh pulsing. And then it settled itself upon the body, leechlike, its round mouth fastened to what was left of the head. Horrified, Hunter-In-Darkness watched it feed. No flesh passed into the dream-creature, but the light contained within the carrion slowly began to fade. Flickers of radiance shivered above the flesh, then extinguished; within a short time there was only the light of the leech-thing—and Hunter himself—to see by.

Fear outweighed curiosity at last, and Hunter-in-Darkness turned and ran.

2

The house, Miles noted, was just as he had expected it to be, no more and no less. A small farmhouse which had withstood the force of the northern winters for nearly two centuries, which his friend and old college roommate had decided to renovate; it stood as a monument to Wesley McGillis' unique personality. Half renovated, and it would probably remain that way forever; Wes had a tendency to grow bored with any project once he had mastered the skills necessary to complete it, and this house was no exception. A pity, Miles thought. The building had promise. Maybe Wes' daughter, who had recently moved in with him, would motivate him to finish the project.

He bounced down a dirt road with thick grass growing down its center, into a yard long overgrown with weeds. Wesley was waiting on the porch—and damn him, he hadn't changed a day since last they met! Nearly ten years now, Miles realized. *He* had changed, that was certain.

"How do you like it?" his old roommate asked, with a gesture that encompassed the house, the grounds, and even the gleaming white citadel of Bell & Hammond's primary research facility, some miles in the distance. "Nice, eh?"

"Cold." He had left his coat in the trunk in Maryland, and he quickly retrieved it and put it on before pulling out his suitcase. "Give me the southlands, any day."

"Here, I'll take that." Wes reached for the suitcase, finally had to take it forcibly out of his hand. "You're sounding like them, you know that?"

"Who?"

"Southerners. Never thought you would." He led him up the stairs of weatherworn porch, to a screen door that was obviously new. "Elsa sends her love, wishes she could be here. Some business down at NMHI, I'll tell you all about it when you're settled in. Odd stuff, really." Opening the door, he waved Miles through. "Watch the cats," he warned.

As if on cue, a gray tabby bolted for the door. With practiced grace Wes blocked its way, pushing Miles into the primitive kitchen as he pulled the screen door shut behind them. The cat yowled once—a token effort—and then disappeared into a nearby shadow.

Adjoining the kitchen was a common room, in which a central fireplace managed to drive back the worst of the chill. Wesley indicated a calico-covered rocker and then nodded toward the stairs at the far end of the room. "Make yourself comfortable while I put this away. There's hot water on for coffee or tea, your choice. Be back in a minute."

Miles had just had time to notice that the legs of the rocker were scarred, and its cover fringed by the repeated application of animal claws, when a cry of "Downstairs, damn you!" resonated down the staircase, and a small ball of fur followed. Black from head to tail with white socks on three of its feet, the small cat leaped to the center of the room and then stopped there, suddenly, as if considering its actions. Hesitantly Miles extended one finger toward it; he was a dog man himself, awkward around felines, but if the cat was Wes' pet he would at least make an attempt to be friendly.

The cat turned suddenly, facing him, and its eyes grew wide. Hissing, it drew back. Its long, thick fur was standing on end, an effect that was at once ludicrous and frightening. The tiny throat seemed to spasm, and a roaring sound issued from the tiny cat's mouth that was certain proof of its kinship to lions.

Shaken, Miles withdrew his hand. Any sound or quick movement seemed to irritate the beast even more, so he made himself very quiet—and very, very still—and waited for Wes to return and save him.

From the top of the stairs came the sound of footsteps, then the rhythm of a man descending. "I've given you the front room; it's somewhat small, but the most restored. I think . . ."

He stopped as his head cleared the landing and took in the tableau—*cat vs. professor of philosophy*—in one measured glance. "Calm down, Miles." His tone betrayed his amusement. "He isn't going to attack you. He isn't even interested in you."

"But when I moved toward it—"

"Yes, but take a look. At his eyes, I mean. He isn't even looking at you."

He looked at the cat again, more closely this time, and realized that Wes was right. Its eyes were fixed on some point slightly to the left of him, closer to the center of the room. "Then what the hell is its problem?"

Wes sighed. "Not an easy question to answer. I suppose I should tell you about Elsa's project—since you're going to be living with the results of it for a while. We haven't got it all worked out just yet, but that's why she's gone to talk to the people at Mental Health.

"Because of a cat?"

"Four cats. And two litters before that, which were destroyed soon after birth. These are the first we've allowed to grow—and I'm not sure we should have. Coffee?"

"Please."

"With cream?"

"Black." Concern for his health had weaned him from such additives; he had a tendency to put on weight. As Wes left to make the coffee, he asked nervously, "It's not dangerous, is it?"

"What, the coffee?" He laughed. "No, they're too small to do us any damage. I imagine mice feel differently, though."

The cat was still on edge, though its roar had quieted somewhat. *I didn't know they could make noises like that.* "What's it looking at? What's it afraid of?"

To him it seemed that there was nothing else in the room, yet the cat was obviously tracking something. By watching it closely he could tell where the *something* was, but he had no clue as to its nature.

Wes returned with two cups of steaming coffee, and was about to speak when the cat suddenly leaped straight up into the air. As though it had been clawed by something, Miles thought. Or burned. It bolted for the dark space under an easy chair and dove into it, its whole body shivering with terror. A moment later its eyes were visible, two amber points in shadow, and they scanned the room anxiously.

"I guess I'd better explain," Wes offered, and Miles nodded. It was an understatement.

Sloan-Kettering's research department had been working with cats for some time now (Wes explained) in connection with their studies of vision development in premature infants. When genetic recombination became a reliable science, they imported a number of specialists in that field to produce feline specimens with specific visual handicaps. Elsa had joined them in the mid-nineties. One of her projects involved splicing a litter for improved chromatic sensitivity—a routine operation, which should have had routine results. Instead it produced a set of four kittens which, from the moment they opened their eyes, exhibited all the symptoms of human schizophrenia.

"They were put to sleep," Wes told him. "And she tried again. Same results. By then she had checked and double-checked every genetic factor, and had an autopsy run on every corpse. To no avail. Both theory and autopsy insisted that all she had done was improve the sensitivity of the cat's visual apparatus with regard to color; there was no indication of any change in the brain itself, or in the chemical balance of the body, to explain such drastic behavior."

"So they let the last litter live."

Wes nodded. "And you see the results. She had them sterilized so they could live to adulthood, but not until the last possible minute. She wanted to see if the change in hormone balance would affect their madness. It didn't. That was after she talked me into letting them live here, so they could have some kind of 'normal' upbringing."

"It didn't help?"

"See for yourself." A black-tailed tabby was slinking into the room, stalking something that none of them could see. A moment later it hissed and ran out again. "Not that some cats don't have imaginary playmates . . . but not to this extent, and rarely do they inspire such fear. So Elsa got in touch with the people at the Mental Health institute and discussed the problem, and they asked her to come see them. To discuss possible human analogs for their condition, and uses they could be put to. Meanwhile. . . ." He shrugged toward the small black cat, which was only just now extricating itself from its shadowy fortress. "I've got three of these to contend with, and that's no bargain."

"Three? I thought you said—"

"There *were* four," he said quickly. "But one got out of the house before we'd had them neutered, and . . . We had no choice, Miles. We couldn't lure it back, and the FDGA is fanatically strict when it comes to gene-spliced specimens. If he hadn't been fertile, we could have let him go."

"As it was?"

"We hunted him down." He sipped his coffee pensively. "A friend of Elsa's did it, actually. Shot him right in the head. The poor thing had only been out for two days and nights, so the odds that he had found a mate were minimal. He was still really a kitten . . . so we didn't report it. Didn't want to risk Elsa's license, you understand? So it's a litter of three, now, as far as the records are concerned. Always has been."

The small black cat walked with leisurely grace to the nearest chair, climbed into it, and proceeded to wash. As if nothing had happened. Just like a real cat, Miles thought. Only it wasn't. Science had altered it. *Non-cat. Anti-cat.* He had never approved of splicing the larger animals, and now he knew why. Too much DNA, and far too little knowledge. Of course, you could probably splice dogs safely. Dogs were predictable. Comprehensible. Cats were . . .

He looked at the small black feline and shivered.

. . . *alien.*

3

They were gathering in the manlands. Dozens of them, moon-bright against the evening sky. Not the dreamerlies he had hunted as a kitten, his small paws passing through their flesh as they fluttered through the walls of the manhouse, unresponsive to his efforts. These were large ones, grotesque ones. Like the dream-creature which had claimed his prey, they stank of *wrongness,* of decay; they frightened him, and only as he watched them gather about the gleaming white manhouse did he finally admit that there were more of them every night, and that they seemed to be gathering for some purpose.

That the nights were growing colder didn't help matters. He was heavily armed against the winter's chill with a coat of fur that grew thicker each night, but his paws were unaccustomed to treading frozen ground and the scar which cut across his face, marking the place where a bullet had once struck him, ached painfully when the temperature dropped too low. Both played havoc with his temper. When the dream-creatures approached he often swung at them, claws extended, even though he knew in the back of his mind that no waking creature could hurt them. He tried anyway, giving vent to his irritation and discomfort, and only snarled in frustration when his paw passed through them. He had hunted them in the dreamlands and never understood why here, in the waking world, they were intangible; now the situation was becoming intolerable, as they followed him during his hunt and claimed his kill and he was powerless to drive them away.

The answer was in the manlands, and he was determined to find it. But out there, in the empty fields, where man's will had cropped the grass to indecent

shortness and torn free every last bit of cover, he
would have to be wary. He knew the power of man all
too well, and was not anxious to test it. Once, in his
kittenhood, he had come across stream bed and brush
root in response to a familiar voice . . . and it had
answered him with thunder and a searing pain that
blinded him, until his head struck rock and the shadowlands claimed him. No, he was not one to seek out
man's company, but the manlands must be braved.

The dreamerlies were there. And they must be driven
away. That was simple fact.

Carefully he slid between the grasses, his body low
to the ground, inching his way slowly forward. The tall
white manhouse was his destination, and carefully he
approached it. Like the smaller manhouse it had a
fence surrounding it, and its appearance seemed to be
much the same. There were no trees here to offer a
convenient overhang, nor any visible pathway scratched
beneath. He decided to climb the fence itself, and
took a running leap to gain as much height as possible—

—and his paws were burned as they struck the wire,
a searing pain that sent waves of hot terror through his
entire body, that made his legs spasm so that he lost
his hold and went crashing down to the distant ground,
with no sense of balance left to save himself. He
yowled as he hit the frozen earth and lay there, stunned,
his paws on fire, his body paralyzed from shock.

Not like the other fence, no. This one had man's
magic in it, and like the voice of thunder which had
struck him down before, it was his enemy, armed to
kill. If he had clung to it, he realized, he might have
died; only his fall had saved him.

Humbled, he pulled himself onto his feet. His paws
were numb and his legs weak and trembling, but he
made them carry him westward, to the nearest patch
of brush. There, with the trees for shelter, he could
examine and cleanse his wounds. Not here, where
man could find him.

He passed a scent-mark but ignored it; he lacked
the strength to return to his own territory, and so must
risk the sin of trespass. Not until the brush was deep

about him did he pause and look for cover; incapable of climbing, fighting new pain with every step, he finally collapsed into a clump of ivy, hoping that whatever cat had marked this place was someplace far away, patrolling some other border of its territory. He had no strength to fight.

He was slipping into dreaming when the rustling noise awoke him. The shadowlands faded away like smoke and he found himself standing knee-deep in ivy, with pain shooting up through all his paws but ready for battle—yes he was!—and woe betide the cat that picked a fight with him, even when he was wounded.

Then the rustling grew louder, and a head peeked out from between two branches. A tiny head, all eyes and whiskers. Then a second, equally small. The wind brought him kitten-scent, and its warning: *keep your distance.*

And then the third face appeared, and he forgot all else in his wonder. For the green flame that burned in its eyes was like his own bodylight, and he knew by the way it picked its path through the brush that it could see in the darkness as well as he. Green fire played along its black fur as it sauntered up to him, playful and curious. He was about to try to take its scent when a dream-creature came into view; with a yelp the tiny kitten leaped after it, crashing into dying branches as it fell to the ground again and again in its attempts. It could see them in the waking world! Hunter-in-Darkness was stunned. In all his time in the woods, he had never met another cat who hunted the dream-creatures as he did.

He was preparing to follow the youngster when another scent came to him, this one adult—and hostile. He turned, and found himself facing an enraged female. A paw swipe mere inches from his face drove him back a step; he found himself loath to do battle with an angry mother, and stepped back yet again as she lunged at him. Finally, with no thought for pain or dignity, he turned and ran. There was no other choice.

And the fire burned in his paws until at last he could

run no longer, and he dared to stop and turn and look behind him. She was no longer there. Off collecting her kittens, no doubt. Thankful for her maternal instinct, he fell to the ground and started licking his wounds anew.

That kitten . . . and its mother. What was it that seemed so familiar about her? Not her scent, he thought. Not quite. He had known another female once, in the time of warmth and rain, but that scent had been different. More welcoming. Hadn't it?

Warmed by the memory of his consort in season, he dragged himself into a comfortable position—or a reasonable semblance of one—and let the shadowlands carry him away, so that his body could do its healing in peace.

4

Miles looked up at the gleaming white building, the cold blue light of morning playing across its upper ramparts, and nodded. "So this is It?"

"This is It," Wes agreed. "Home of my pet project. And thank God for Bell & Hammond because I couldn't have covered the cost of this through the standard grants. Not with an estimated decade or two before any promised results."

"You tried?"

He showed his passes to the guards, clear plastic strips that they passed through a reader and then returned to him. They clipped something to Miles' lapel that looked like a credit card.

"Of course I tried. But I couldn't get the guarantees I needed, and so . . . private sector, last bastion of scientific curiosity. This way," he said, using his security card to open a windowless door.

The corridors of the Bell & Hammond facility were as clean and sterile as the outside. Miles wondered how his friend, who tended toward a cluttered lifestyle, could stand the place. That he managed it at all was a measure of this project's importance to him.

At last the final door, and a separate key card to

open it. "Welcome to Eden," Wes announced, throwing open the door with a flourish.

For paradise, it was remarkably unimpressive. True, there were computers everywhere, along all four walls and a shoulder-high island in the room's center—but they had the same sleek facade which marked the entire complex. There was no way of telling why they were here, or what they were doing. He waited.

"The Eden project, that is. My brainchild, start to finish. Well? What do you think?"

"You have a lot of hardware," he allowed. "More than that will wait on an explanation."

"Of course. But where do I start?" He looked proudly about the room; it was his brainchild, all right, in every sense of the word. "About five billion years ago the first life appeared on Earth. Here, in this room, I mean to repeat the process. How's that?"

"A little more detail might help," Miles offered. Then what he had just said sank in. "Are you serious? In this room?"

"Just so. Think about it. We know that some set of conditions initiated a biological process we call *life*, about that time. Maybe never more than once. Maybe the conditions were only right for it one single time, or the odds so astronomically small that they were never repeated . . . we never have understood it, for all that we've come close. We've made our own viruses, fashioned bacteria, played God with some of the higher animals . . . but always there's a seed of life that we start with, some bit of a living thing that we use to get it all going. I propose starting from scratch. Is that crazy enough for you, Miles? Will you write it all off as another eccentricity of mine—God knows, I have enough—or do you want the details?"

It did sound crazy, but . . . "If you can convince a company like Bell & Hammond that you're not insane, I can certainly listen. Do go on."

He placed a loving hand on the central island, and static crackled as he touched the screen. "Here's my reasoning. We know, approximately, the period in which life first appeared. Give or take a billion years.

We know the condition of the Earth during that time, from its composition to its surface temperature, and can work out all the other relevant details, such as gravity, orbit, magnetism, etcetera. Somewhere in all that data is the set of conditions that permitted a combination of amino acids to become self-replicating— which is the bottom-line definition of life, as I see it. Now: we've tried to find some formula that will reveal these conditions to us, and failed. We've tried to logic our way backward to it six ways from Sunday and had no success whatsoever. All I propose is letting computers do what they do best: go through the data bit by bit until they find something promising, and then test it in all its permutations. These machines," and he indicated the wall-to-wall computer banks with a sweep of one hand, "mathematically reproduce the conditions of the Earth during that period. Every possible factor is allowed for. Sunspots, volcanic activity, meteoric impact . . . you think the project immense? It is. That's why only machines can handle it. And why it may take decades before we have any kind of an answer."

"I'm not surprised you had trouble financing it."

"I'm surprised B&H agreed to do so," he admitted, "but not sorry. The answer could come in decades—or tomorrow. It's a structured trial-and-error system with an almost infinite data base. I tried not to prejudice it with any human expectations, since the human systems have failed. In here," and he patted the central island lovingly, "the practical tests will be run. As soon as it comes up with a situation that makes the right chemical binding possible, the system will initiate a testing program that will reproduce those exact conditions. First mathematically, of course. That part is automatic." His eyes were gleaming, his voice more full of life than Miles ever remembered it. "I dream of coming in here and discovering that the testing sequence has already started. The odds are against it, of course."

It was just beginning to sink in as Miles looked around the room in amazement. "So one might say—in a mathematical sense—that the process of creating life has already begun."

"I like to think that."

He shook his head in amazement, trying to absorb it all. "It's a good thing you're not a religious man, Wes. Or a philosopher."

"Why? Do you think I would have done things differently, in that case?"

"If there is such a thing as a soul, and if all living creatures have them . . ." He came up to the central island, and touched a hand to its surface. Cold. It surprised him, though it shouldn't have. Had he unconsciously equated life with warmth? "Where will your new soul come from, when you create this living thing? Do you create that, too? Or is there some kind of consciousness, not yet alive, that would bond with your creation? Move in and take up housekeeping, as it were? A religious man might worry about that—and about its possible source."

"You're getting morbid in your old age, Miles. The world is filled with souls, old and new. Or so say our high priests."

"But once it wasn't. And your machines are reproducing those very conditions." He shrugged. "It's food for thought, anyway."

"You're free to write a paper on it."

"Be a long time before I could publish."

"Will it?" He hesitated, and his voice grew lower. Almost whispering, he said "I can feel it happening, sometimes. I stand in here and I feel like I can sense the process, like something is *almost*—but not quite— right. Like it will start any minute now, maybe while I'm standing right here . . . am I crazy, Miles?"

"Always have been."

"Can you *feel* it, I mean. The incipient . . . the *incipience* of it. If, as you say, the process has already begun—"

"All I feel is tired. And a bit of a headache." He touched his forehead with a chilled hand, wondered at the weakness which had suddenly come over him. "I'm afraid you've quite overwhelmed me, Wes. I need some time to absorb it all, before I can glory in wild speculation."

"You all right?" he asked, concerned.

"Just tired, I think. It was a long drive. And this really is quite overwhelming." He rubbed his forehead, where the worst of the tiredness seemed to be centered. "The philosophical implications really are staggering. Give me time, Wes. And breakfast."

His ex-roomate smiled as he led the way out. "Then a short nap, eh? You never were a morning man."

"Took you thirty years to notice . . ."

Hunter-in-Darkness watched from the forest's edge as the two men came back, keeping to the shadows so that they wouldn't see him. The sunlight was blinding, but not so much so that he failed to notice the crablike shape which sat atop the shorter man's head. A dreamerly, dark fog against the morning sunlight; it had tentacles pressed to the man's upper face, and now and then the man swatted at it as though he could sense its presence. But his hand passed right through.

Chilled despite the morning's warmth, Hunter-in-Darkness crept back to the shadows.

He needed to think.

5

Dear Dad—

Well, I'll be staying longer than I originally planned, but didn't we think that might happen? There's so much to tell you that I hardly know where to start; suffice it to say that we've come up with some interesting hypotheses to explain those little monsters' behavior.

So far, the most promising theories involve some manner of dream disturbance. Dr. Langsdon pulled a tape for me, of cats who had been treated so that while they dreamed their motor activity was not inhibited, as it usually is during sleep. The result was that they acted out their dreams, and—

*you guessed it—the resulting behavior was very
similar to that of our little houseguests. More in
that line . . . but I really should wait until I get
home, to tell you in person. It's all so very exciting!*

   *The upshot of all this is that I won't be leaving
until next Sunday at the earliest. Does this mean I
miss seeing Miles? Tell him to stop off in Maryland
if he drives home earlier than that, I'll take him to
lunch. Or dinner.*

*Pet the monsters for me,
Elsa.*

6

The shadowlands were unusually dark this sleeptime,
which made the glitterlings even more dramatic than
usual. And therefore more distracting. Hunter-in-
Darkness stopped for a moment in the dreamland
forest, watching the tiny firesprites burst into life and
dart across the leafless branches, trying to sense their
rhythm so that he might anticipate them. Sometimes it
was possible. Overhead, the cold, dead trees of the
shadowlands wove a spiderweb canopy of jagged black
branches, and the brilliant glitterlings played like squir-
rels between them: darting down the length of one
branch, doubling back to sizzle the bark of another,
leaping across open space—and then suddenly, inevitably, disappearing into darkness. There were many of
them tonight, and as they played across the skyscape
their light danced into the shadows, making the darkness shiver. Not a good sleeptime for hunting, he
decided. Even the trees seemed blacker than usual,
and their branches, like cracks in the sky, made ominous patterns overhead. And there was a smell in the
air that was not of the shadowlands, nor of the waking
world: a hint of foulness that the wind carried to him,
that made his lips draw back from his teeth and brought
a hiss of disgust to his throat. He turned around to
escape it, to find his prey elsewhere.

   And remembered . . .

What?

He shook his head, confused. The smell urged him to go away, to *run* away, to be anywhere but where he was at that moment . . . but something he didn't quite remember urged him to stay, and its call was slightly stronger. Something from the

(he struggled to place it)

waking world?

Suddenly he was *aware*, and memory came to him so suddenly that it nearly knocked him off his feet. True, he had been trying to remember—for how many sleeps now?—but each time he passed into dreaming and walked the shadowlands anew, all memory of his waking intentions had left him. Not so this time. A trickle still remained, and he held onto it with all four paws, trying to grasp what it was barely within his nature to understand.

Like all cats, he dreamed. Like all cats, he hunted in the perpetual twilight of the shadowlands, perfecting his skills in a world that demanded the utmost in timing and concentration. And like all cats—until this night—he had passed from one world to the other without thought, rising from the shadowlands to awaken and smooth his fur and then passing back into the dreamworld once more, in and out again in a rhythm as ancient and as natural as sleep itself.

But tonight was different. Tonight he knew—he *understood*—that while he hunted in this place, beneath these jagged trees, he was also asleep in a leaf-cushioned hollow. For the first time in his life, without words or experience to guide him, he struggled to comprehend the nature of *dreaming*. And understood at last why this double awareness had come, the reason why he had gone to sleep with a special image fixed in his conscious mind.

He turned toward the source of the foul wind. No longer was its fear-message dominant in his mind. He took time to savor it, to measure its taste upon his tongue. Images of dreamerlies came to him, clumps of fog that left just such a foulness in one's mouth; it was the stink of danger, and he growled deeply as he recognized it.

Under normal circumstances he would have fled, but he was more than mere shadowself now and was twice as angry as he was afraid. Prompted by memories of misshapen dreamerlies, he turned toward the source of the odor. Outside of the dreamworld he was powerless to hunt such creatures, but here, in the land of their birth . . . he hissed his fear as he began to move, and his fur pricked upright, but there was no question of turning back. Those things had fouled his territory, ignored his spray, and despoiled his kill; either his waking self must abandon its terrain, or he must deal with these enemies on their own home ground.

With the stealth of a hunter who has marked his prey he crept slowly toward the source of the odor, placing each paw as though his life depended on silence. All about him new glitterlings burst to life, danced in fiery zigzags, and were consumed by darkness; by their light he picked his way across the lifeless roots, letting his sense of smell guide him. Gradually the smell grew stronger, and its message more clear. *Turn away. Go back. This place is not for you.* He had to fight his survival instinct to ignore it, but memory drove him on.

How long it was before he heard the cry he couldn't say; he was consumed by his greater purpose, and was not wholly cognizant of the world which surrounded him. But it broke through his awareness at last, a plaintive mewing that stopped him dead in his tracks. A kitten-cry, rich with pain and terror.

He knew the voice. But it belonged to the waking world.

How was that possible?

For a moment he stood still, frozen by indecision. Then the cry came again, a terrible yowling of pain and need that made going on impossible. He began to trot—to run—toward the source of its distress. In his mind's eye a tiny black kitten beckoned, its greenfire eyes sparkling like glitterlings in the shadowlands twilight. What was it doing here, this cat from the waking world? Didn't each hunter come to the shadowlands alone?

He ran. Over twisted roots, between glitterlings and dreamerlies and floating pods of luminous seeds that settled to earth in his wake. The sound was growing fainter by the minute, he had to reach it before it was extinguished, must hurry if he was to—

He came upon the clearing suddenly, had to use all his claws to brake to a stop.

It was there. The kitten. The same one he had met in the waking lands, whose fiery gaze had so impressed him.

So were they. The dreamerlies. The foul ones, with the teeth and the bloated bodies and the unwholesome odor, who had followed him to his kill and then claimed it.

They had downed it, and were feeding. Suckers and teeth were affixed to its trembling body, and strangely shaped forms glowed brightly as they fed. Their light was bright enough that Hunter-in-Darkness could see the kitten's blood where it had soaked the ground, and the carmine glitter of wounds across its jet black fur.

Rage consumed him. He abandoned thought, became a creature of blind action. One leap and he was upon the nearest, a fishlike thing with claws for fins and a spiked tail half his length. Here such creatures had substance, and he tore into this one with relish. So quickly did he dispatch it that the others were just beginning to react as he chose his next victim. This was not hunting but killing, plain and simple, and he took no pleasure in it. A snakelike dreamerly with silver spines drew itself up to fight; he clawed at its face before it got a chance to position itself effectively, was rewarded with a gush of hot blood across his paw and chest. Teeth bit into his hind leg, but he kicked out savagely and they were gone. There were more dreamerlies than he could count, but he was a whirlwind of teeth and claws and at last, hissing their displeasure, those that had survived his initial attack withdrew from the scene of battle.

He took no time to lick his wounds, but looked for the injured kitten; it had crawled off during the battle, leaving a thin trail of blood behind it. So dim was its bodylight that he nearly lost the little creature, but he let his sense of smell guide him and finally found the shivering infant, a tiny wet ball of fur that hissed weakly as he approached it. It was badly injured, and clearly terrified. And no wonder! One of the advantages of hunting dreamerlies was that they didn't fight back; one could stalk them—or the glitterlings or the floating pods—with no fear of injury, practicing one's skills in safety against the day when the waking world would require them. That they would do this was . . . unthinkable. That they *could* do it was terrifying.

Gently he nuzzled the youngster, and began to lick its wounds clean of blood and dirt. At first it didn't respond, and he thought it might be past saving. But then, after a time, a tiny tremor of sound began in its throat, which rose and fell with the rhythm of his cleaning.

He did what he could for the purring youngster, marveling at its recuperative powers. At last he sat back, content that it would survive, and tended to his own wounds. In the wake of his indignant rage his greater purpose was calling to him again, and he knew he would have to move on. The kitten could take care of itself, he decided. It would have to.

He turned to leave, took three steps—and stopped. And looked behind him. The kitten was on its feet, standing right behind him. Ready to follow. He growled a warning, but the sound lacked sincerity—and like most kittens, this one ignored adult hostility. Twisting his head back to watch the small cat, Hunter-in-Darkness moved forward again . . . and watched in amazement as it trotted along behind him, a brief chirp indicating that its legs *did* hurt but, yes, it was coming along, it would manage to keep up with him somehow.

With a snort of disbelief he began to trot toward his destination. Wondering why he was pleased that the tiny thing—too young to be prudent, too damaged to be helpful—was still alongside him.

It was there, in the distance. Faint, almost ghostly, its outline uncertain in the shadowland darkness . . . but clearly *there*, despite the fact that it shouldn't be.

The white manhouse.

He crept to the edge of the forest, head low, suspicious. The wall between the worlds must be thin indeed, if such things could cross it. For some reason the thought made him cold inside, and he looked back at the kitten to see if it was still beside him. It was. And strangely, that comforted him.

All about the building were dreamerlies. Mutant dreamerlies, even more unwholesome than the ones which had attacked the kitten. As before, they seemed to be waiting for something . . . but what?

The kitten was the first to move. Too young to be inhibited by fear, he slipped between two heavy roots, out into the open. Against the dark grass his small black body slithered like a shadow, its inner light almost dim enough to pass for reflected glitterglow. Cautiously, Hunter-in-Darkness followed. He was a larger cat and a brighter one, and the lack of cover made him uneasy; nevertheless he followed, and not until they got to the fence did the two cats stop to consider their situation.

Cautiously, prepared for the worst, Hunter-in-Darkness eased one paw forward, and quickly touched it to the wires. Man's magic had guarded this place before, but that was in the waking lands; here, where no man existed, the fence might be passable. And indeed, his paw passed through the wires as though through an illusion; the manfence had no solidity in this world, and no power to harm.

He went through the fence; the kitten followed. A few dreamerlies passed overhead, and perhaps they saw them. If so, they showed no interest. Like any hunting cat they preferred the small and the weak for prey; perhaps they were wary of Hunter-in-Darkness' size, and would avoid the kitten because of it.

It was when they were halfway to the building that the Change began.

At first he failed to recognize it. The shimmer in the air, the distortion of all outlines beyond it, the feeling of bodily tension which accompanied its appearance . . . at first these things were unfamiliar, and he sank down into the grass in wary silence. But then he realized what it was, and what he could accomplish if he got to it in time—and in an instant he was on his feet and running, heedless of the dreamerlies and the kitten and any other shadowland concern, trying to reach the wall between the worlds before it healed itself and became impassable once more.

Crossing it was like diving into a snowbank. For an instant there was cold, so chilling that he could hardly move his body, so all-pervading that he lost all memory of ever having been warm. And darkness. For a moment he feared being trapped within the barrier, sandwiched between the worlds without access to either. Then the fear—and the cold—were left behind him, and he stumbled out onto a man-made floor, skidding to an undignified halt as he slammed into the base of a wall that had become, all too suddenly, solid.

He was inside the man-structure—inside!—and back in the waking world. He had crossed the same way the dreamerlies crossed, and if his reasoning was correct. . . . He leaped up and clawed at an overhead dreamerly, and felt his talons tear flesh before he fell back to the floor. Yes! He could hunt them now, in his own world. On his own terms. Hunter-in-Darkness, who had passed through the shadowlands and beyond!

A thudding sound reminded him of his kitten ally, and he turned to find the small cat bundled tail over head at the base of the same wall. He pushed it back onto its feet, noting that the impact had reopened a gash along its shoulder. A faint carmine smear marked the spot where it had struck the wall, and it left red footprints as it came to Hunter's side. The larger cat shrugged; there was nothing more he could do for it.

But he was relieved that it had managed the crossing, and licked its flank once to welcome it.

Then a low humming sound caught his attention, and his skin crawled as he realized just what it was.

The sound of dreamerlies.

The kitten had stiffened, its ears pricked upright; it heard it also, then, and knew it for what it was. No matter that they had never heard a dream-creature make the slightest noise before; the sound was fixed in their instinct, and identification was instant. Something about this place, or the opening between the worlds, had given these creatures a voice. And they hungered. That was clear in the tone of their call, and fear surged through Hunter's heart when he heard it. For a moment instinct got the better of him, and he nearly turned to flee. But then he remembered: he was Hunter-in-Darkness, Crosser-Between-Worlds; the identity gave him courage.

Legs stiff, fur erect, he looked about for a way to reach the source of the sound. There was no direct route available, but an open door in a corner of the room offered access to that general direction. He could circle back later. Clinging to shadows as he went, he skirted beams of moonlight that fell across the manfloor from small, barred windows set high in one of the walls. Not much light, but he needed none; his bodylight was bright with anticipation, and the kitten beside him was regaining luminescence with every passing minute. With care he slipped between the door and its frame, a space hardly wide enough to admit him.

Beyond it lay a man.

His first reaction was to back away. Men had hurt him badly, once; he had no intention of waiting here while they tried to do it again. But then he picked up the man's scent, and tasted its wrongness. And touched his nose to the cooling flesh, wondering at how such a powerful creature could have been struck down without any wound. There was no scent of blood or fear or illness to point to a cause of death, merely the fact of stillness and a growing darkness of its flesh to witness that yes, it had died.

If the dreamerlies could bring down one such as this
. . . How could he, a single cat, hope to fight them?

As if in answer, the kitten chirped beside him. Two
cats, then. It would have to do; they weren't pack
animals by nature, and had no way of summoning
more claws to their aid.

He stepped over the body, leaving footprints of
bodyfire in its newly dead flesh, and followed the sound
of the dreamerly-call into the depths of the building.
Now that they were in the waking world the walls
were solid to their touch, and it took time for them
to find enough shafts and windows and half-open doors
to get them to the place where the dreamerlies were
gathering. But at last they came a place where the
dreamerly-call was so loud, and its followers so
numerous, that Hunter-in-Darkness was certain they
had reached their destination. One last door . . .
They could hear the sound clearly now, could feel it
resonating in their bones, a low hum that reminded
Hunter of manthings, that brought back memories of
his kittenhood with sudden, unwelcome clarity. How
small the dreamerlies had been, then, how harmless
and playful! Without a doubt, they had been been
changing . . . and this place, this *thing* beyond the
door, was responsible.

With sudden courage he pushed against the final
door, forcing it to swing aside. The kitten was beside
him, nose to nose as they braced themselves for attack. But there was none. Slowly the hinged panel
moved out of their way, and they had a clear view into
the heart of the dreamerly rebellion.

There were hundreds of them. Thousands! Stable
dream-creatures, whose shapes were like those Hunter-
in-Darkness had sported with in his youth; massive,
distorted forms, which flickered in and out of existence as though some vital force was not yet fully
stabilized; dreamerlies which were unlike any the cat
had ever seen, bits of black fog which would brush
against others, leave behind dark splotches of midnight fungus that grew and grew and at last fully
consumed their victims. There was a manshape lying

in the far corner, newly expired; a dozen of the most distorted dreamerlies were clinging to its body like leeches, feeding on the last of its bodylight. Perhaps they had killed it, as they would have killed the kitten.

And in the center of the room . . . *there* was the manthing that had summoned them all, that sang of feeding and hunger and death in a low humming sound which made all the dreamerlies quiver with excitement. It was made of cold, sleek metal, and the light of a thousand glitterlings was fixed upon its forward face. From its rear end trailed thick black cords, manroots to anchor it. Upon its face of mirrored glass green glitterlings danced in measured patterns, tracing words and phrases which no cat or dreamerly could read.

CAUTION

APPLIED TESTS BEGUN 19:53:01

FIRST SEQUENCE IN PROGRESS

DO NOT INTERRUPT

Hunter-in-Darkness hated it. He had never hated before, not in this way. But then, he had never before killed for any reason other than hunger or the pleasure of the hunt. Now the kitten was beside him, and the killing rage that its plight had awakened in him began to resurface. If such deformed creatures were allowed to keep growing, to feed—to *breed*—the shadowlands would soon become filled with them. Then how long would it be before the dreamerlies attacked older cats, skilled hunters who were deft with tooth and claw but who couldn't hope to stand up to a pack of dozens of parasites—or of hundreds? How long before cats dared not dream at all, and therefore dared not sleep? Then *these* creatures, which had managed to enter the waking world, would take advantage of their weakness, and dispatch them as easily as they had done with the two men. No, they must be killed here and now, and Hunter-in-Darkness must do it.

But how?

He kept to the walls, began slowly circling the room. Watching them. They hardly seemed to notice him, but focused all their attention on the manthing and its song. Good. The kitten was still with him, and he was pleased to see that it hadn't given in to its fear. It would make a fine hunter someday, he thought. If it survived this confrontation.

The feeding ones were leaving their kill, now, to float about the manthing with their fellows. Periodically one of them would butt into it. Trying to hurt it, or move it? Or trying to get inside? What could be inside the man-made shell? A ripe female, perhaps? The mother of these creatures? Some dreamerly equivalent of catnip?

One thing was certain: he had to kill the manthing, and soon. More and more dreamerlies were arriving every minute, and they pulsed in rhythm with the others as they settled in beside them, circling. Whatever the dreamerlies were waiting for was about to happen—and when it did, the full power of the manthing would be loosed. The power to bridge worlds; the power to kill cats. He had to do something, fast.

Memories from kittenhood: playing with his brothers and sisters in the great wooden manhouse, stalking dish towels and rolling pencils and the ultimate Great Enemy, the black cords which were man's most precious possession. They coiled about the base of every magical manthing, and stretched across the floor like rivers of ink. Dish towels the cats might shred to bits, furniture they might destroy, pencils might be hunted and subdued, but no cat ever dared to touch the black cords. That was absolutely forbidden, and the cats in the manhouse quickly learned it. The black roots were beloved of man, and vital to his magic.

Hardly daring to move, Hunter-in-Darkness crouched down against the cold manfloor, preparing to spring. A flick of his tail kept the tension from freezing his hindquarters as he gauged his distance, considered his chances . . . and leaped. Into the midst of them, the clawed ones and the flickering ones and even the black foggy ones. They were solid to him now, and he slashed out to thrust them aside as they came between him and his objective. Dreamerly gore clogged his claws and spattered his fur as he fell to the ground some feet short of where he needed to be; he had done considerable damage in his flight, but not nearly enough.

They turned on him now, in numbers too vast to count. A thousand foul clawing creatures that stank of *wrongness*, armed with tooth and stinger and a pawful of weapons that Hunter-in-Darkness had never seen before. He fought them bravely, gaining ground inch by inch as he did so; but the numbers against him were too overwhelming, and the enemy too well armed.

A paralyzing sting disabled one hind leg, forcing him to drag it. A spiked tail swung directly at his eyes, forcing him backward a step. Then two. He was losing. He would never reach the mancords now, would never cut short their magic. The shadowlands would be overrun, and the waking lands would soon follow. He tried to leap forward, desperately trying to gain some ground, but he struck a clump of dreamerlies head-on and fell to the manfloor, stunned. One of the smaller ones sank its twisted fangs into his good hind leg, and he dared not turn to claw at it. He was losing blood, could not last much longer.

A screech split the air, like the cry of an enraged mother cat—only much, much harsher. Something which was not a dreamerly bumped into Hunter's hind leg. And then, suddenly, the fangs which had been fastened about his leg broke loose; dreamerly blood joined his own on the floor. The kitten had caught up with him, and it nudged him once in the flank, urging him with silent insistence: *Go on! Go on!* Another dreamerly attacked Hunter-in-Darkness, and was struck from behind; the tiny cat was wreaking havoc from a direction none of the creatures had thought to guard. *Go on!* The older cat dragged himself forward, digging his front claws into the manfloor as the kitten danced about his head, protecting him from harm. His hind-

quarters were nearly useless, but soon that wouldn't
matter; he was a catslength away from the black cords,
now, and closing. Only inches . . .

His teeth closed about the nearest one, and he pulled.
Yanked. Tore with his claws at the soft, yielding surface, knowing he must break through quickly or die.
The air was full of dreamerlies, and his eyes were
filled with blood; he could hardly see, was maneuvering by feel through a thicket of black manthing roots.
Tearing at them, wildly. One of them fought back,
and burned him. But the pain only served to increase
his determination. He had been right; the magic was
here.

Now more and more of the cords tried to defend
themselves, and even the dreamerlies backed away. In
the back of his mind he noticed that the song had
stopped, and he sensed that the dream-creatures were
directionless in consequence. Good; the kitten might
be safe. He slashed at a cord and searing pain lanced
through his paw, but the cord seemed to die in consequence and was safe to touch thereafter. There were
very few of them left to hurt him now, most had lost
the strength to defend themselves. Besides, there were
so few places on him left to be burned. . . .

He slid into the shadowlands, but never knew when.
Fell into something that was not quite sleep, but deeper;
not quite a dream, but just as compelling.

His last thoughts were of the kitten.

7

The call came at 10:30. By 10:32 he was out of the
house, and by 10:46—Miles firmly in tow—he had
arrived at the facility, a whirlwind of anxious inquiry.

"What the hell's going on here? What did Davis
mean, a *power failure?* Eden has its own generator
. . . Who are all these people, and what are they doing
here?" There were at least a dozen unknown faces
gathered about the main entrance to the building,
some uniformed and others not. One, a woman, was
in tears. Haskell's wife? *What the hell—*

"This way, sir." A security guard—not one he knew—took him firmly by the arm and led him into the depths of the building. Not his usual route. That was blocked, by a crowd of guards and medics and the sprawling, lifeless body of a technical assistant from the night shift. Jerry Haskell?

"What happened?" he demanded.

"Heart failure, as I understand it."

But he was in perfect health . . .

He almost stopped, to ask more questions. But whatever had happened to Haskell, it was over and done with; there was nothing he could do now to save him. The Eden project, on the other hand, might still be salvaged.

He broke into a run, with no concern for whether his two companions could keep up with him; when he reached the proper sector he burst through the door of the project with a question on his lips and fear, like an icy serpent, in his heart.

"What—oh my God . . ."

Blood had been spattered across one section of the floor, and up and down two whole sides of the central island. Human blood . . . or animal? Was that a cat down there, tangled in the smoldering wires?

"What on earth—Davis, what's going on?"

His assistant left the small group of guards that had converged at the far side of the room. Was that Casey's body at their feet? "We don't know," he said bluntly. "Power was interrupted at approximately 8:15. I came to investigate and found . . . this." He indicated the room, the blood, the body. "I would have called you earlier, but they wanted the police in here first."

"That is Casey, isn't it? How did he die?" He nodded toward the body, but his eyes were fixed upon the island. Damn that cat! What on earth had caused it to get tangled in the power cables?

"Cardiac arrest, they say."

"Which means they don't know. All right, we'll have to wait for an autopsy." He hesitated, afraid to ask the question that most concerned him.

At last he dared it. "How much was lost?"

"Nearly an hour of program time, and some supporting data. A lot depends on whether the power went off cleanly, or there was erratic activity preceding total loss. We could be clearing out glitches for days. Richard is on line now, trying to save the series, but some data will be irrecoverable. She says we've lost this test sequence for sure."

Damn! But it could have been worse. The program would eventually pick up where it left off . . . and what were the odds, realistically speaking, that the one set of conditions they were searching for was being run through the program at the exact time that the system crashed?

He walked over to where the cat's body lay, and squatted by its side. Yes, no question about it, this was what had done the damage. Damn the animal! Just like those nuisances at home, who never knew when to leave things alone—

And then he saw the mark across its forehead, and the single white toe on one forward paw, and he knew.

"Dr. McGillis?"

"Go help the medics," he told Davis. He was pleased that his voice was still steady. "See if they need anything."

When he was gone, he whispered, "Look, Miles. Do you recognize it?"

"You mean, does it look like one of your cats? Yes."

He pulled out a pencil and used the point to turn the animal's head aside. The scar from a bullet wound was clearly apparent, surrounded by charred flesh and bits of torn fur.

"It's the fourth of that litter. But how did it survive? My God, the implications . . ." He reached out a hand to steady himself against the island console; his knuckles, Miles noted, were white. "Fertile, genetically altered . . . and free in the woods for months now. If the FDGA ever gets hold of this . . . Elsa will lose her license, that's for a start, and as for this project . . ." He shut his eyes. "It'll set applied genetics back a decade if the fundamentalists get hold of it; all the old fears will come out again. Christ!"

"Do they have to know?" his old friend asked quietly.

Wes looked up at him, a flicker of hope in his eyes. "No. Of course not." His grip on the console eased, and slowly he stood. "They'll have enough problems figuring out how it got here in the first place. No one will think to ask about its background."

And his eyes, red-rimmed, said it all: *Destroy the cat as soon as possible. Salvage the program. Deal with the rest as it comes.*

He walked slowly back toward the group of guards surrounding the body, fielding questions as he approached. No, he'd heard nothing of the incident until a mere half hour ago. No, there was nothing connected with the project that could cause such a disaster. Nothing at all. It was all quite beyond him. . . .

Miles looked down at the floor again—and then quickly away. And decided to say nothing about what he saw. Let Wes think, for now, that it was over. He had enough to deal with as it was.

There'd be time enough later, when things had calmed down a bit, to tell his friend about the kitten tracks.

TROUBLE

by P. M. Griffin

Trouble purred loudly to tell Dory that he was content and to let her know that she was doing well.

She deserved the praise. She also needed it. These humans were sad creatures. They seemed to have so little innate belief in themselves, most of them, even those of high inner quality and real, strong talent like this kitten of their kind.

Well, that could hardly be counted a fault in his Dory. Those around her had either actively striven to strip her of confidence and stunt her rightful development or else had lacked the courage to do anything very positive in her cause. Her strength of soul had sustained her thus far, keeping her spirit unbroken and her basic fineness intact, but even that would not suffice forever.

The purring stopped. He had realized for some time that this abuse must cease. It was fortunate all this had occurred, disruptive as it was. She had been forced to act at once, without the agonizing and indecision which would have preceded a planned move. That was another area in which humans differed from felines. They did not seem to know their own minds, and even when the correct, the only reasonable, course was plain before them, they had great difficulty in acting upon it if it involved any degree of significant change whatsoever.

Trouble began to purr again, more loudly this time as affection swelled within him. That was not fair to Dory. No kitten left his home readily, however wretched it was. Cat and human alike, all youngsters needed the care and instruction provided by the adults of their species.

For an instant so fleeting as almost not to have been, he growled. It was little of either that she had enjoyed in her life! Even her body was ignored, and the neglect of such a mind, such a gift, was worse than that which kept her so wan and thin.

The wind whipped up, and the big cat allowed Dory to press him closer to her. He did not require the additional warmth she was striving to give him. It was she who was cold in her threadbare jacket; his thick coat gave no passage at all to the brisk autumn breeze. No matter. She was offering love and care, which were not to be rejected, and, in truth, it felt good to have her arms around him in the midst of all the uncertainty and confusion surrounding their lives at present.

Shouts, the bellowing of many voices sounding together, shattered the early morning stillness.

Trouble yawned and, wriggling free of the girl's hold, stretched himself. Stupid human herd! Did they imagine she would come to them when they summoned and threatened in the same breath?

The girl, however, was terrified. She leaped to her feet. "Oh, Trouble! They're sure to find us! They're on the street, and there's no other way out of this alley!"

The fence, foolish one. That is why I brought you to sleep here in the first place.

She could not hear him, of course. That would not come for another few months, not until the attainment of her physical womanhood opened her inner ears and voice, but for the moment, that was just as well. Humans were trying, all of them, and he sometimes found it difficult to restrain his sarcasm when dealing with them. She did not need that right now, poor kitten.

Dory looked about her in despair. Three-story buildings towered on either side, and a fifteen-foot brick fence walling off some comfortably fixed man's court-yard was in front of her. Behind was the only exit, and that was blocked by the presence of Jocko and his cronies.

She had to do something! The communal voice of

the mob was getting distinctly louder, and those comprising it were indeed searching every possible hiding place for her.

The fence had to be it. Trouble was already sitting upon it, patiently waiting for her.

It was too high for her to reach its top unaided, but there was plenty of debris scattered about including a number of big wooden crates, empty, fortunately, but sturdy enough to support her not terribly crushing weight.

With fear to drive her, she soon had the biggest of them, that in which she had slept, dragged over to the fence and a second, smaller one placed on that. By standing on them and stretching herself to the full, she was able to get her hands over the top.

Voices! Those hunting her would be on her in a moment! She half scrambled, half hauled herself up the rough-set bricks and hoisted herself over the narrow top. Without pausing even to look, she dropped down the other side, first lowering herself on her arms as far as she could to make the actual fall as short as possible.

Dory sat up. Her hand flew to her mouth in horror. She had escaped one firepot, temporarily at least, but it was only to leap headfirst into a second. She had landed in a garden, in a bed of alternating yellow and white flowering shrubs, and the gardener was standing not twenty feet from her.

Trouble was sitting regally at the edge of the flower bed, watching her in that silent amusement which only a cat can experience or display. Before his charge could either ruin everything by screaming or trying to flee, he got up and casually walked over to the man, rubbed against his leg, and raised his head, demanding to have it scratched.

The human complied, but his amazement at having a scrawny girl-child and a superb black-and-white tomcat suddenly and quite literally drop into his sanctuary did not lessen.

It was a measure of the man that he saw with very

nearly the first glance that the child was terrified and, submerging his astonishment, gave her a friendly, natural smile.

"Are you all right?" he asked with unmistakably real concern.

"I-I think so," she stammered.

"Stay where you are, then, and I'll lift you out. You've created enough havoc with your surroundings."

"I am sorry about that, sir," Dory told him earnestly.

"Doubtless. You don't look particularly malicious. Actually you were quite considerate in your choice of a landing place. Mums are hardy enough to take some abuse. Now, my roses over there would be in a lot sorrier state had you come down on them even though they're done flowering." He smiled again. "So would you. I seem to prefer varieties blessed with strong and plentiful thorns to match the quantity and color of their blooms."

He took one long, carefully placed step into the bed. It brought him close enough to reach his unexpected visitor whom he picked up without apparent effort and carried out onto the walk where he set her on her feet once more.

"There, that's better. Now I believe an explanation is rather in order."

Over a meal, donkey tail. She is hungry. So am I.

That was a demand. Trouble knew from Jasmine that this man's inner ears and voice were both fully open. That fact and the tabby's other reports had induced him to bring Dory's in her need. He should have done it sooner, but, of course, he was a very young cat himself. . . .

In good time. Kindness coming too fast can frighten as much as brutality, the human answered in kind, giving no outward indication that anything had passed between them.

He held out his hand to the girl. "I'm Martin."

She took it gingerly. "Dory." Bending, she brushed her friend's head with her fingers. "This is Trouble."

Martin's gray eyes sparkled as they rested on the cat. *That I can well believe.*

Trouble did not reply. It was beneath his dignity to do so. Besides, it was a merited revenge after his donkey tail remark of a few moments before.

"And is he?" the man asked smoothly.

"Oh, no! No cat could be more wonderful! It's just that he was in a lot of it when we first met."

All the while, Martin had been studying Dory. Her age was hard to judge. She was painfully thin, and she had a very young looking little face, now remarkably smudged, but he imagined she would be about twelve. She was pale complexioned, too pale at the moment, with stringy light auburn hair which would have been attractive had it been styled at all. Her eyes were truly lovely, blue-green, large, and fringed with long, thick lashes the same color as her hair.

Her clothes were unremarkable: well-faded blue trousers, checked shirt, also faded, and a jacket that was nearing the end of its useful life. The nearly universal brogs of the region covered what appeared to be quite small feet.

She looked to be what he expected she was, a badly used little apprentice or servant. The like were common enough, too common, even in this none-too-affluent neighborhood. He normally paid small heed to any of them, but this one he did know, if only by sight.

"I've seen you before," he remarked. "You're always talking to Jasmine when she's out in the fore-garden."

As he spoke, he pointed to a delicately boned tabby who had glided into the yard and was sniffing curiously and without fear at Trouble, who was not slow to return her attentions.

"Whenever I see her. She's such a friendly little thing. I think she's prettier than any flower there!"

The girl stopped herself, embarrassed.

Martin sighed. She had probably learned early in her life not to reveal too much enthusiasm for anything.

"It's good to meet another full-blown cat lover," he said casually, then inclined his head toward the big house forming the opposite boundary of the well-planted courtyard. "Why don't we go inside? It's just about time for breakfast. You can tell me about yourselves while we're attending to that." There was no mistaking her look of interest. Trouble was right; the child was hungry. "Good. I'll make a quick run in to arrange everything and then come back to show you the way."

He would arrange things, all right, Trouble thought. A lot of people would be astonished at the means by which the promised meal was produced, but he did not object. Cats are practical beings, not narrow-minded fools. The food would be good to taste, wholesome, and quite real. What more could one ask? *Excellent thought. Do not take too long.*

I won't, Sir Trouble. As my little lady has probably already told you, I don't mistreat my guests.

As promised, Martin returned quickly, and soon all four of them, humans and felines alike, were sitting comfortably in a small, sunlit eating room.

There was no talk during the meal. Dory's attention was fully centered on her plate. Her host watched in good-natured amazement at the speed with which she put its contents away. She might not have eaten for a month the way she was going at it.

A day! That is long enough.

Too long. Someone should have a bit of a talk with her master.

More than that. You will hear.

The girl handled her cutlery well for all her eagerness, and when she at last finished eating, she set the ware aside in the correct manner and politely thanked him.

Trouble, too, did full justice to his meal. After clearing his well-filled dish, he carefully washed himself and rubbed against Martin's leg, purring loudly. Manners were not demeaning, and good service such as this deserved a reward.

"Well, Dory," the man said as he settled back in his chair, "tell me about yourself."

"What would you like to know, sir?"

"Everything. Where you live would be a good start, I suppose."

"I don't live anywhere now," she responded frankly. "I used to stay at Jocko the Farrier's, three squares north of here. Imelde, his wife, is my mother's cousin. That makes her mine, too, I suppose."

"Your parents?"

"They died when I was three. Quick plague. It missed me somehow."

"And that was the last kindness you knew," he muttered.

"I don't know," she replied seriously. "Imelde made a fuss over Trouble and claimed she loved him even though she really didn't, just so I could keep him. That was a kindness, wasn't it?"

"It was," he agreed slowly.

"Also," Dory added, trying to be fair—and not wanting to entirely blacken her kin before this stranger, "I may not be fat, but I get enough to eat that I'm never sick. And I've always had a good dress for church even though I do have to work like this."

Worked hard, he thought, to judge by the state of her hands. That was not right for a child.

Trouble sighed. These humans! They seemed to have no instinct whatsoever for digging out a story properly. Now Martin was going to ask why she left, and by the time she answered and went back to explain how the situation had come about in the first place, they would have spent triple the time needed to tell a simple tale.

Ask how she met me, he instructed patiently. *That is the beginning of it.*

Very well, Sir Trouble. Thank you for the hint. "At least you were able to bring Trouble away with you when you did go," he remarked. "When did you two get together?"

"About a year ago." She smiled and again began to caress the cat. "He's the best thing that's ever happened to me."

Her expression clouded. "There's a well in back of Jocko's house. He won't cover it even though there are some big families in our square. Says it's up to the parents to watch their brats, and he doesn't want any of them on his place anyway. He doesn't worry about garbage falling in since it's my job to fish it out. It was my job, that is. He'll have to do it himself now."

"A considerate neighbor as well as kindly kin, I see," he muttered dryly. "Your mother's cousin showed poor taste in her choice of a husband, girl, or her father chose badly for her. But please continue. Trouble managed to get into the well?"

She nodded. "He did. I don't know where he came from since he was too tiny to have been away from his mother for long, but there are a lot of dogs around. One of them must've scared him into bolting down there.

"Anyway, I was going for water when I heard him crying. I couldn't see anything at first when I looked in, but then I spotted the white stripe on his nose. He was clinging to this ledge that goes most of the way around the well down almost as far as the water. It used to snag the bucket on me if I wasn't careful. I couldn't think of any other way to get him up, so I took the bucket off and tied the rope around myself."

Martin frowned. "You lowered yourself down that hole?"

She hardly flew! Do you doubt that my kitten has spirit?

Your kitten should have had help, he said sharply. *That was an adult's job.*

Dory's eyes darkened. She took his seeming silence for disapproval, and her chin lifted. "What else could I have done? I couldn't very well have left him down there."

"No, not and remained human yourself. I was just wishing someone like me had been there to give you a bit of a hand, that's all."

"Oh, I mostly have to do everything myself. I'm used to that."

Martin sighed. "I know. You're to be admired, but I can't say I like the idea all the same."

Dory saw the speculative look her host was bending

on her, and her eyes fell. She had done it again, she thought miserably, but she really could not help that she sometimes sounded more forty than twelve as Imelde put it, and like a schooled forty at that. She certainly could not help her thoughts. She had learned to read before that accursed plague had taken her parents, and she had continued to read, everything she could lay her hands on that was worth the effort, thereby rendering her life at least bearable. Unfortunately, she had somehow modeled her speech more after those formal writings than after the example of those around her. Jocko hated that—how he hated it!—and his friends hated it, and she had learned to say very little around any of them, but her tale was long, and already, even before it had rightly begun, she had given herself away.

The hard, sick knot of fear and unhappiness loosened in her stomach when she raised her eyes again. Martin was a different man entirely. She saw no resentment, no rejection in him, only mild surprise, guarded interest, and, she thought, excitement.

The man's pulse had quickened, though reason insisted that he check his hope for the moment. A highly intelligent, sensitive child like this could be expected to lose her loneliness in books, assuming she possessed the basic skill to read them, and it certainly was not unknown for some in that situation to develop an astonishingly mature manner of thought and the vocabulary to express it. Dory could be no more than an example of that.

It was also just possible that she was many times more. Verbal and mental precocity almost inevitably accompanied strong talent, and he thrilled with anticipation at the thought of watching and helping such a gift develop again. It had been so long since he had last been privileged to share in that blossoming.

For the moment, he put that dream out of his thoughts. This storm-tossed pebble might indeed be a true diamond, but they did not have the leisure to explore that possibility now. Besides, he believed she had detected his awareness and was frightened, a natural enough reaction in face of the upbringing she had received. Bullies like this Jocko the Farrier rarely cared for any sign of superiority in the weak little things they terrorized.

He smiled encouragingly. "Go on, child. I want to hear the rest of this tale. Did you have any problem getting him out?"

"Not from Trouble. He let me pick him up and just snuggled close to me, like I was the only safety in all the world."

Anger flashed suddenly into her eyes, making her appear both older and stronger. "That was when the rope dropped. Jocko was above and had loosed it. He shouted that he'd lower another but that he wasn't going to lift two loads and that I'd have to leave the cat behind."

"He what?" Martin hissed.

Both the girl and Trouble looked swiftly at him, startled by the cold, controlled fury in this seemingly mild man.

"It was a false threat," she told him quickly, not wanting to provoke an outburst of anger, even one not directed at her. She was trying to escape such storms. "It's a busy square like I said, and someone would've hauled us out in no time. Jocko knew that, too, and anyway, he didn't want me dead. I did too much work for him. He just thought I'd panic and not figure all that out."

Her hands clenched. "I wasn't scared. I was furious. I'd never been angry like that before in my whole life. He actually tried to make me leave that poor, terrified, trusting little creature to die alone and cold and wet, to make me choose to do it."

She gripped herself before she could either fly into a rage herself or burst into tears.

"I don't know what came over me, except that I was so mad and couldn't do anything else, but I glared at the rope, which was still sort of floating in the water below us, and I shouted at it to go back up, tie itself again, and pull us out." She swallowed hard. "It did. It did just that."

The man drew a long, sharp breath. He glanced at the cat, who was purring softly, seemingly unmoved by his human's emotion, then his eyes returned to the girl.

"Had anything like that ever happened to you before?"

"No, of course not! I didn't even know such things were possible except in books."

Trouble, was it you?

It was not, the cat replied half contemptuously. *It was the kitten. Listen to her.*

"A great many things stranger than that are possible, child," he said softly. "What was Jocko's reaction?"

"Oh, I believe that he was mad, but that came later. Right then, he was raw scared that someone might have seen what had happened."

"Did anyone?"

She shook her head. "Not as far as I know. He was lucky there. He'd have been in big trouble if they had. He's in the Antimagic League, you see. President of the local cell, in fact . . ."

"That bunch! Well, from the sound of it, he fits right in with the rest of them."

"They're hard cases most of them," she agreed. "Anyway, he dragged me into the house and started whaling me. I think he'd have half killed me, but Imelde told him to let me be, that I'd had a fright enough and that I'd brought her the kitten, which she was going to keep." Her voice softened. "She'd seen, from the way I had been holding him, I suppose, that I loved him. She was sorry for him, too. She said later that we were both orphans and should stick together, but we'd have to keep him out of Jocko's way, which we did between us.

"After that, things sort of went back to normal, except that Jocko started asking me questions. I was always good at guessing things like what the weather would be or that someone would be coming to the house and maybe even why. Now Jocko wanted to know who'd win a race or fight or something like that, and he'd bet on the name I'd pick. Never much, mind you—I'd often be wrong—but there'd be peace around the house when he did win. I'd get a knock when he lost, of course, but not too hard as such go. He did know I couldn't control that part of it."

She rubbed her ear, and her eyes brightened momentarily. "He might even have done me some good. I don't make nearly as many mistakes now as I did at first."

"The practice did you good. Knocks do nothing, or they hinder. Talent can't be forced by abuse."

"Talent? It's not much of one, sir."

He smiled. "Big things often start out small." Martin's expression darkened again. "You didn't have ideal living conditions, but it was nothing worse than you'd always known. What caused the break?"

"Imelde, I guess, though she didn't mean to," the girl answered promptly. "You see, she's the one with the money. Her father thought he had done well binding her to a tradesman, but when he saw what he'd really gotten for a son-in-law, fair enough to him, he moved to protect her since she didn't want to leave Jocko."

"Some people don't, no matter how bad their partners are," he explained in response to the lack of comprehension in her tone. "What did he do for her?"

"He set up something called a trust. She gets money out of it every three months, but no one can touch the whole lot as long as she's alive. Jocko's the laziest man you could meet, sir. He's a farrier like I said, but he'd much rather sit in the local and talk bull with his friends than work at it. That's why she's always been able to keep some control over what goes on in the house, provided she doesn't try to push him too far. He knows full well that she can manage very nicely without him and that he'd lose a comfortable lifeway if she upped and left.

"He's always had his fancy ladies, though," she continued contemptuously, "either stupid little things he can brag to until they see through him or else those who put up with him for pay, but his latest's something different. She's young and pretty and too smart not to know she could do a lot better than Jocko. He knows that as well, and he does want to hold onto her. He's not so young anymore, and he's not going to attract anything like her again. Sure, he never could before.

"Well, Imelde's no fool either. She saw what was going on—the whole square did—and she belted off to her father. Imelde told him her story and said that she didn't want to be worth more dead than alive to anyone. By the time she got back two days later, she had it arranged that the money would all go back to her father if she died without a babe, as seems likely now, or be handled by him or her older brother if she went after having a child. Jocko'd have no part of it at all without her."

She shivered. "I thought he'd gone stark mad when he heard. That's how bad his rage was. He shouted and cursed and slammed his fist against the wall so hard that I hoped he had busted his knuckles, but Imelde didn't blanch or blink. I've never seen her face him better. She just let him rave on, always keeping out of reach, of course. When he'd tired himself out with yelling, before he could start with his fists, she calmly told him that they could either go on as in the past, or she could return to her father. The choice was his. If he kept on cheating, that was her answer right there. She was still packed and would just turn around and leave again, and this time, she would not be coming back." Dory grinned. "He just shut his mouth like it was a trap, and out he went. That was the night before last."

She shuddered, and her whole body tensed as if in anticipation of a death blow.

Trouble left off grooming Jasmine and leaped onto the girl's lap. He licked her hand and looked up into her face. As he had known she would, she smiled tremulously at the rasping caress and almost unconsciously began stroking him.

"He didn't come back until morning," she continued in a small voice. "He was drunk. Jocko always gets mean when he drinks, and this was about the worst he ever was.

"I spotted him coming in, and you can lay money down that I stayed up in the attic where I sleep until I thought he'd either gone to bed or dropped off in the kitchen." Her hand trembled on the black fur. "I guessed wrong. He was waiting for me."

Jasmine picked up her horror and responded with a soft, inquisitive meow, but the male cat only gave a loud, rumbling purr.

Go on, Kitten, he encouraged although she could not hear him. *You are doing well.*

Martin, too, read her terror. He reached over and covered her bony hand with his. His grasp was firm, reassuring. Only Trouble, whose back the long fingers also touched, was aware of the strength in them, a power surprising in a scholar who spent his life amongst books, as this human represented himself to be. That could even be true—his mind was that of a seeker—but it was obvious he respected his body as well and knew enough to keep it sound.

"It's all right, Little One," the man said gently. "Take your time and tell it in your own way."

He felt sick inside. Was this Jocko the Farrier monster enough to brutalize her sexually as well as with his hands?

No. Soon perhaps, but not yet.

His head bowed in relief. *Praise the Most High for that.*

Dory had used the brief silence to collect her thoughts. "He wanted revenge, but he's a coward. He didn't dare take it directly. He thought Imelde loved Trouble, and he'd often heard her say how beautiful and dignified he is, so he ordered me to put a pair of donkey's ears on him. I told him I couldn't, that I didn't know what had happened with the rope and that I didn't know how to do such things, but he wouldn't listen. He said that if I refused, he'd beat me until I did do it or until I was a pulp, and he meant it, sir. He meant every word of it."

"Imelde . . ."

She shook her head. "She knows better than to come near Jocko when he's drunk. So does everyone else, and it's well known that he's never done permanent hurt before. By the time anyone'd realize this was different and could interfere, it would've been too late for me."

"One thing I don't understand. If he believed you could do that to Trouble, where did he get the nerve to tangle with you himself? You've said the man's a coward."

"I don't know. Maybe he was too potted to think of it."

Trouble growled low in his throat and yawned. Humans! Who cared what moved the beast, anyway?

Bullies never think that what they dish out can happen to them.

That's just as well in this case. He'd have killed her after that rope business if he felt threatened in any way.

Once more, he squeezed the girl's hand. "No matter now. What did you do? Run or stall?"

"I couldn't do much of either. I didn't have time. The door was shut, and he was between me and the window, so escape was out unless I could get him to move, or forget how fast I could run. I planned to say I'd try and then start jumping around and saying strange things and maybe distracting him enough for me to be able to make a dash for the window, but straight away I knew it wouldn't work. Trouble was still somewhere inside, you see, and I couldn't leave him. Jocko'd be sure to kill him outright or do something even worse if I did.

"I was scared, shaking scared, but I was angry, too, when I thought of him. Look at Trouble, sir. He's a prince, more a prince than any human man wearing a crown, and he'd never done Jocko or anyone else harm. All he did was love me and trust me, and I was supposed to do something like that to him in return!"

"He'd still have been a prince, Dory," Martin told her. "Nothing can take that from him."

"I know, but I wasn't going to hurt him. I wouldn't even pretend to agree to hurt him. I—I just hoped it wouldn't hurt for too long, that I'd pass out or something."

Tears sprang to her eyes but she blinked them back. Her voice changed as confusion melded with her former fear and anger.

"All of a sudden, I started thinking about those ears, big, hairy, floppy ears. I could really see them there in my mind. I could almost reach out and scratch them. The next thing I knew . . ." She began to sob for a fact, and this time, she was powerless to check herself.

Even before the cat could do anything, Martin had her in his arms.

"Easy, child. Take it easy, Dory. It was only an illusion. Talent can't be forced to work against the real will of its wielder. Look at Trouble. He's fine, and he certainly puts no blame on you."

The tomcat's green eyes fixed him. *The ears were real. She did not set them on me.*

Martin's lips parted They curved into the beginnings of a smile. He released the girl.

"Dory, just where did you put those ears?" he asked, already knowing what she would say but waiting with delicious pleasure to hear her confirm it.

"On—on Jocko," she whispered.

The man laughed. He laughed until he fell back in his chair and his cheeks were wet with tears. When he finally regained control over himself again, he caught her hand and kissed it in delight.

"Well done, Little Sorceress! That was the finest and most fitting bit of magic I've heard about in a long, long time!"

So you will help her?

A frown touched the human's thoughts.

I'd have helped her without this. You knew that, or you wouldn't have brought her here.

Calm down! She is laughing. Do not spoil it.

Martin's merriment was contagious, and Dory did laugh as memory of that moment of realization returned to her.

"They aren't proper donkey ears. They're floppy, just like I pictured them." She giggled. "They bent down over his eyes. You should've seen his face when he saw them hanging there. He gave them a tug, then another, real hard one. What a yowl he let out! He sure as anything knew they were real after that!''

Her host shared her laughter, but then they both sobered.

"That was when you made your break?" he asked.

"Seconds later. Trouble appeared at that point. It was like he was watching the whole thing and knew just when to show up. He jumped onto Jocko's back and really gave him reason to scream. He caught hold of those ears and went to work on them with his claws. Trouble kept at it, whatever Jocko did to try to catch hold of him. Even sober, he's not as good as my cat. Drunk, and with Trouble on his shoulders, he had no chance at all!

"Only when I made it through the window did Trouble let go. He sprang out after me, and the two of us took to our heels.

"We knew we'd be done if we went back, so we just kept going." She sighed. "I was lucky I'd been going out for water, or I wouldn't even have this jacket."

"You didn't get far."

"I—I needed time to think, to figure out somewhere to go, or even just a direction, and I was hoping to pick up a little food after the market today. There're usually a lot of leavings when the farmers go home if one's not too fussy.

"I came this far to put some distance between me and my old haunts, figuring Jocko'd probably know those and search them out after he bound up his ears. He had to do that first; they were dropping blood all over the place.

"It took time to get here. Everyone knows us, and we didn't want to be seen, so we had to sneak from spot to spot. Then it was threatening to rain, and I was tired. I wanted to find a place to hole up. Trouble led me to your alley. There was this nice, dry box just big enough for both of us, and we spent the night in it. See, not a drop touched us, though it poured the whole time."

She bit her lip. "Everything was fine, apart from

being hungry, until we heard the mob a little while ago and knew we were trapped. We had no choice then but to go over the fence. We wouldn't have done it otherwise, sir."

"Forget that, child. It was fate and the will of the Most High that sent you to me." And Trouble's plotting, he added mentally, to the cat's satisfaction. When credit or partial credit was due him, Trouble liked, and expected, to receive it.

The girl's fingers twisted together. "I thought we had the time. I truly didn't believe he'd call in the League, not . . ." her voice trailed off.

"He has no choice but to hunt you down and try to force you to undo your magic. Failing that, he'll at least want the satisfaction of killing you."

"He'll kill me anyway now," she said dully.

"Probably. If he takes you. Cheer up, Little Sorceress. That's not going to happen, and you've had some payment for all he's put you through. He'll be a laughingstock from now on, whether he regains his old form or not."

"That'll just make it the worse for us, she said glumly.

Dory took a deep breath. This was the hardest thing she had ever been forced to do, but she could not fail Trouble.

"You like cats, sir. Please keep Trouble with you. I—I'll be happy just knowing he's safe and well fed."

Martin stared at her. Most High, but she had courage! That tomcat was her only friend, the only one who had loved her since the day her parents had died, and yet she was willing to part with him in order to spare him the perils and hardships she knew she faced. But, then, her entire tale was testimony to that strength.

Of course the Kitten has courage.

The man looked at him. A prince Dory had called him, and a prince he was, a fitting companion for such a queen.

"Do not worry on that score, Dory," he said with frigid certainty. "No one in that mob will do a thing to any of us or to my property that I do not choose to permit."

Her head cocked to one side. "There are so many of them. How . . ."

Martin raised his hand to silence her. "How old do you think I am?" he asked.

She shook her head. She was still young enough that all adults seemed old to her, but she knew enough and was sensitive enough of others' feelings not to say that.

Trouble, too, looked at him curiously. His body's appearance and smell were that of a man in his prime years, but his inner scent did not reflect that, and Jasmine could give him no information or explanation. She was a young cat herself, only a little older than him, and she was timid by nature. She had not learned as much as she might have about her companion, as much as he, Trouble, would assuredly have uncovered.

"I don't know, sir," Dory responded.

"I was already old, ancient even, when the Antimagic League was first formed."

She looked at him as if he were mad. "That was over five hundred years ago!"

"There are some benefits in possessing talent and knowing how to use it," he replied mildly, his gray eyes turning almost silver with amusement.

"Then you are . . ."

"A sorcerer? Oh, yes. I'm head of our Great Circle, as a matter of fact. Have been since my youth."

"So the League didn't get you all like they claim," she mused. "I'm so glad!" She had little sympathy with any of the organization's aims, considering what she knew of its members.

Martin laughed without humor. "Those curs couldn't get their great-grandmothers if the old ladies set their backs against them! They eliminated a lot of charlatans, true, and they made life pretty miserable for minor, unschooled talents until we quietly stepped in and took the pressure off them, but face down a sorcerer of the first water? Hardly! Look what happened when one of them clashed with you, and you've had no training at all.

"We eliminated our own evil members. The League

did accomplish that much good. It forced us to police ourselves. Before that, we were lax, lazy and cowardly both, I suppose. An adept can always recognize a person who walks the dark path, and so we were never threatened. As a result, we contented ourselves with keeping an eye on those of our number who did turn sour, making sure none of them made a grab for too much control over the untalented and did not go too far in other ways, but that was all. The formation of the League pushed us into action. It was a vigilante organization, and we dearly wanted to keep it that, to remove its cause before it could have real laws pushed through against us. We reasoned, rightly as it turned out, that if we did, the movement would soon stagnate into a social organization for bullyboys. We succeeded so well that most of its members don't even believe that magic really exists now." He smiled faintly. "Except your friend Jocko, of course."

He was silent a moment as his thoughts drifted back through time. "It was not an easy fight we waged. A number of us died, and some of us still bear scars. Painful scars . . ."

The sorcerer recalled himself to the present. "That's neither here nor there at the moment."

Dory shook her head. "I'm glad you all survived." She paused. "There must be hundreds, thousands of you if you all live for centuries."

"On the contrary. We are very few. Major talent is rare and many a century passes without giving us even a single recruit. Of those who are born with the gift, some fall victim to accident or illness or violence, and there are always the few who turn to the dark and so are lost to us."

The gray eyes met hers. "That's why you're so precious, Dory, and also so dangerous."

She stared at him a moment, uncomprehending, then her eyes widened. "You think I have talent?" she gasped half in protest.

"I believe you are a major talent, possibly one of the strongest I have ever encountered," he replied seriously.

"And I'm . . . dangerous?"

He nodded. "Yes, unfortunately. Your power is just stirring in you now. It will awaken fully when your body settles down to assume its biological adult role. You will not be able to suppress its manifestations entirely unless you are properly trained to handle it, and the outcome may not always be beneficial to yourself or those around you. What has happened already is proof enough of that."

"Where can I get that training?" she demanded. "Who can teach such things? I can't stay here with you, even if you'd want me. I'm too well known in this area. Someone'd be sure to see me, and Jocko'd get me thrown in jail or something, and maybe you with me."

He leaned forward. "I'd be proud to have such an apprentice, and I can protect you so that no one would recognize you, but the price of working with me would be very high. I'll fully understand if you choose not to pay it and will arrange to send you to another very nearly as knowledgeable as I who will be equally delighted to have both you and Trouble."

Dory stiffened. Price? Imelde had warned her that some men . . . And there were the old stories, too, those about the payment anyone trafficking in sorcery was supposed to have to pay.

Martin read both thoughts easily enough without recourse to any special abilities of his calling.

"Your virtue's safe enough, girl. I like women as well as any man, but they do have to be adults and neither victims nor purchases. Your soul's equally secure. That can be won or lost only by your own choices, not by a mere commercial transaction."

"What, then?" she asked, puzzled. Surely he realized she had no fortune, nothing valuable to give. If not, she did not want him for a teacher anyway!

Patience, Kitten, Trouble thought wearily. Why must her species always leap to ridiculous conclusions, and in matters of such importance, too? It would be a tragedy if she reared up and ruined her chances with the sorcerer before they had even begun to work together.

Martin sighed. "Your youth, Little One. What's left of your childhood and your adolescence. No one will take a grown woman for a twelve-year-old girl."

Dory started to ask if he could really do that but bit the question back in time. If he was what he said and proposed this, then he could accomplish it.

"My childhood hasn't been very happy," she said after several minutes' deep thought.

"No, but the rest would be. Consider this carefully. I would teach you well and treat you well, but the step's irrevocable once taken. You will appreciate the loss as an adult, Dory, and regret it. That's why I'm not pressuring you now, much as I want to have you with me."

"What about Trouble?" she asked slowly after a moment. "You can't make him old, too."

"No. He'll have to spend the next two or three years as an all black cat. After that, we'll be moving anyway. Those of us who don't age must change our bases periodically to avoid arousing comment. Once we do, it'll be safe for him to resume his natural coat again. I, for one, will welcome that. He's beautifully marked. Do you agree to that course, Trouble?" he concluded in both verbal and inner speech.

The cat slowly inclined his head. *I prefer my true coloring, but this is necessary.* Dory's eyes widened.

"It's like he really understood and answered you!"

"For shame, child! These animals comprehend a great deal. You'll soon realize how much, whether you accept my offer or not."

His offer. Her mouth felt dry. She had to give Martin his answer and give it soon. As matters now stood, she was a danger to all of them. One way or another, she had to escape her enemies and learn how to manage this unwanted but apparently unavoidable power of hers.

Indecision tore her. Stay, and she must trust herself to this stranger's magic. Flee . . . She would have to trust him still, him and some other as well, maybe someone who would use her as hard as Jocko had or harder.

The girl looked frantically to Trouble, but the cat sat motionless and unblinking on her lap, more warm statue than living being for all the response he gave her. Never had he been so cold to her need . . .

"He won't tell you what to do," the sorcerer said gently. "He can't. He knows that only you can make a decision this important to you."

There was no contradiction or comment from the cat, just understanding, respect, and the hope that his comrade would choose well.

Thank you, friend, Martin whispered.

Dory's head raised. Both courses seemed equal in their potential for good and for ill. Her heart and instinct had to be the deciding factors.

"I've never had any chance at real schooling," she said. "If I'm going to start now, it might as well be with the best. That seems to be you."

"Are you certain, child?" he asked with a strangely sharp pang of regret. He would not be calling her that again.

"I am," she responded with surprisingly mature firmness. Now that her decision was made, she found she had no qualm about standing by it.

Trouble gave a half purr, half meow of delight. He rasped his tongue once along her cheek to emphasize his happiness and approval.

She held him close to her.

"I'm not wrong about this. Trouble wants it, too, and he likes you. That's all I need to tell me it's right, really right for all of us."

SKITTY

by Mercedes Lackey

:Nasty,: SKitty complained in Dick's head. She wrapped herself a little closer around his shoulders and licked drops of oily fog from her fur with a faint mew of distaste. *:Smelly.:*

Dick White had to agree. The portside district of Lacu'un was pretty unsavory; the dismal, foggy weather made it look even worse. Shabby, cheap, and ill-used.

Every building here—all twenty of them!—was offworld design; shoddy prefab, mostly painted in shades of peeling gray and industrial green, with garish neon-bright holosigns that were (thank the Spirits of Space!) mostly tuned down to faintly colored ghosts in the daytime. There were six bars, two gambling joints, one chapel run by the neo-Jesuits, one flophouse run by the Reformed Salvation Army, five government buildings, four stores, and once place better left unnamed. They had all sprung up, like diseased fungus, in the year since the planet and people of Lacu'un had been declared Open for trade. There was nothing native here; for that you had to go outside the Fence—

And to go outside the Fence, Dick reminded himself, *you have to get permits signed by everybody and his dog.*

:Cat,: corrected SKitty.

Okay, okay, he thought back with wry amusement. *Everybody and his cat. Except they don't have cats here, except on the ships.*

SKitty sniffed disdainfully. *:Fools,:* she replied, smoothing down an errant bit of damp fur with her tongue, thus dismissing an entire culture that currently had most of the Companies on their collective knees begging for trading concessions.

Well, we've seen about everything there is to see, Dick thought back at SKitty, reaching up to scratch her ears as she purred in contentment. *Are you quite satisfied?*

:Hunt now?: she countered hopefully.

No, you can't hunt. You know that very well. This is a Class Four world; you have to have permission from the local sapients to hunt, and they haven't given us permission to even sneeze outside the Fence. And inside the Fence you are valuable merchandise subject to catnapping, as you very well know. I played shining knight for you once, furball, and I don't want to repeat the experience.

SKitty sniffed again. *:Not love me.:*

Love you too much, pest. Don't want you ending up in the hold of some tramp freighter.

SKitty turned up the volume on her purr, and rearranged her coil on Dick's shoulders until she resembled a lumpy black fur collar on his gray shipsuit. When she left the ship—and often when she was in the ship—that was SKitty's perch of choice. Dick had finally prevailed on the purser to put shoulderpads on all his shipsuits—sometimes SKitty got a little careless with her claws.

When man had gone to space, cats had followed; they were quickly proven to be a necessity. For not only did man's old pests, rats and mice, accompany his trade—there seemed to be equivalent pests on every new world. But the shipscats were considerably different from their Earth-bound ancestors. The cold reality was that a spacer couldn't afford a pet that had to be cared for—he needed something closer to a partner.

Hence SKitty and her kind; gene-tailored into something more than animals. SKitty was BioTech Type F-021; forepaws like that of a raccoon, more like stubby little hands than paws. Smooth, short hair with no undercoat to shed and clog up air filters. Hunter second to none. Middle-ear tuning so that she not only was not bothered by hyperspace shifts and free-fall, she actually enjoyed them. And last, but by no means least, the enlarged head showing the boosting of her intelligence.

BioTech released the shipscats for adoption when they reached about six months old; when they'd not only been weaned, but trained. Training included maneuvering in free-fall, use of the same sanitary facilities as the crew, and emergency procedures. SKitty had her vacuum suit, just like any other crew member; a transparent hard plex ball rather like a tiny lifeship, with a simple panel of controls inside to seal and pressurize it. She was positively paranoid about having it *with* her; she'd haul it along on its tether, if need be, so that it was always in the same compartment that she was. Dick respected her paranoia; any good spacer would.

Officially she was "Lady Sundancer of Greenfields"; Greenfields being BioTech Station NA-73. In actuality, she was SKitty to the entire crew, and only Dick remembered her real name.

Dick had signed on to the CatsEye Company ship *Brightwing* just after they'd retired their last shipscat to spend his final days with other creaky retirees from the spacetrade in the Tau Epsilon Old Spacers Station. As junior officer, Dick had been sent off to pick up the replacement. SOP was for a BioTech technician to give you two or three candidates to choose among—in actuality, Dick hadn't had any choice. "Lady Sundancer" had taken one look at him and launched herself like a little black rocket from the arms of the tech straight for him; she'd landed on his shoulders, purring at the top of her lungs. When they couldn't pry her off, not without injuring her, the "choice" became moot. And Dick was elevated to the position of Designated Handler.

For the first few days she was "Dick White's Kitty" —the rest of his fellow crewmembers being vastly amused that she had so thoroughly attached herself to him. After a time that was shortened first to "Dick's Kitty" and then to "SKitty," which name finally stuck.

Since telepathy was *not* one of the traits BioTech was supposedly breeding and gene-splicing for, Dick had been more than a little startled when she'd started speaking to him. And since none of the others ever mentioned hearing her, he had long ago come to the conclusion that he was the only one who could. He kept that a secret; at the least, should BioTech come to hear of it, it would mean losing her. BioTech would want to know where *that* particular mutation came from, for fair.

"Pretty gamy," he told Erica Makumba, Legal and Security Officer, who was the current on-watch at the air lock. The dusky woman lounged in her jumpseat with deceptive casualness, both hands behind her curly head—but there was a stun-bracelet on one wrist, and Erica just happened to be the *Brightwing*'s current karate champ.

"Eyeah," she replied with a grimace. "had a look out there last night. Talk about your low-class dives! I'm not real surprised the Lacu'un threw the Fence up around it. Damned if *I'd* want that for neighbors! Hey, we may be getting a break, though; invitation's gone out to about three cap'ns to come make trade-talk. Seems the Lacu'un got themselves a lawyer—"

"So much for the 'unsophisticated primitives,' " Dick laughed. "I thought TriStar was riding for a fall, taking that line."

Erica grinned; a former TriStar employee, she had no great love for her previous employer. "Eyeah. So, lawyer goes and calls up the records on every Company making bids, goes over 'em with a fine-tooth. Seems only three of us came up clean; us, SolarQuest, and UVN. We got invites, rest got bye-byes. Be hearing a buncha ships clearing for space in the next few hours."

"My heart bleeds," Dick replied. "Any chance they can fight it?"

"Ha! Didn't tell you *who* they got for their mouthpiece. Lan Ventris."

Dick whistled. "*Somebody's* been looking out for them!"

"Terran Consul; she was the scout that made first contact. They wouldn't have anybody else, adopted her into the ruling sept, keep her at the palace. Nice lady, shared a beer or three with her. She likes these people, obviously, takes their welfare real personal. Now—you want the quick lowdown on the invites?"

Dick leaned up against the bulkhead, arms folded, taking care not to disturb SKitty. "Say on."

"One—" she held up a solemn finger. "Vena—that's the Consul—says that these folk have a long martial tradition; they're warriors, and admire warriors—but they admire honor and honesty even more. The trappings of primitivism are there, but it's a veneer for considerable sophistication. So whoever goes needs to walk a line between pride and honorable behavior that will be a *lot* like the old Japanese courts of Terra. Two, they are very serious about religion—they give us a certain amount of leeway for being ignorant outlanders, but if you transgress too far, Vena's not sure what the penalties may be. So you want to watch for signals, body language from the priest-caste; that could warn you that you're on dangerous ground. Three—and this is what may give us an edge over the other two—they are very big on their totem animals; the sept totems are actually an important part of sept pride and the religion. So the Cap'n intends to make you and Her Highness there part of the delegation. Vena says that the Lacu'un intend to issue three contracts, so we're all gonna get one, but the folks that impress them the most will be getting first choice."

If Dick hadn't been leaning against the metal of the bulkhead, he might well have staggered. As most junior on the crew, the likelihood that he was going to even go beyond the Fence had been staggeringly low—but that he would be included in the first trade delegation was mind-melting!

SKitty caroled her own excitement all the way back to his cabin, launching herself from his shoulder to land in her own little shock-bunk, bolted to the wall above his.

Dick began digging through his catch-all bin for his dress-insignia; the half-lidded topaz eye for CatsEye Company, the gold wings of the ship's insignia that went beneath it, the three tiny stars signifying the three missions he'd been on so far. . . .

He caught flickers of SKitty's private thoughts then; thoughts of pleasure, thoughts of nesting—

Nesting!

Oh, *no!*

He spun around to meet her wide yellow eyes, to see her treading out her shock-bunk.

Skitty, he pleaded, *please don't tell me you're pregnant—*

:Kittens,: she affirmed, very pleased with herself.

You swore to me that you weren't in heat when I let you out to hunt!

She gave the equivalent of a mental shrug. *:I lie.:*

He sat heavily down on his own bunk, all his earlier excitement evaporated. BioTech shipscats were supposed to be sterile—about one in a hundred weren't. And you had to sign an agreement with Biotech that you wouldn't neuter yours if it proved out fertile; they wanted the kittens, wanted the results that came from outbreeding. Or you could sell the kittens to other ships yourself, or keep them; provided a BioTech station wasn't within your ship's current itinerary. But, of course, only BioTech would take them before they were six months old and trained. . . .

That was the rub. Dick sighed. SKitty had already had one litter on him—only two, but it had seemed like twenty-two. There was this problem with kittens in a spaceship; there was a period of time between when they were mobile and when they were about four months old that they had exactly two neurons in those cute, fluffy little heads. One neuron to keep the body moving at warp speed, and one neuron to pick out the situation guaranteed to cause the most trouble.

Everyone in the crew was willing to play with them—but no one was willing to keep them out of trouble. And since SKitty was Dick's responsibility, it was *Dick* who got to clean up the messes, and *Dick* who got to fish the little fluffbrains out of the bridge console, and *Dick* who got to have the anachronistic litter pan in his cabin until SKitty got her babies properly toilet trained.

Securing a litter pan for free-fall was not something he had wanted to have to do again. Ever.

"How could you *do* this to me?" he asked SKitty

reproachfully. She just curled her head over the edge of her bunk and trilled prettily.

He sighed. Too late to do anything about it now.

". . . and you can see the carvings adorn every flat surface," Vena Ferducci, the small, dark-haired woman who was the Terran Consul, said, waving her hand gracefully at the walls. Dick wanted to stand and gawk; this was *incredible!*

The Fence was actually an opaque forcefield, and only *one* of the reasons the Companies wanted to trade with the Lacu'un. Though they did not have spaceflight, there were certain applications of forcefield technologies they *did* have that seemed to be beyond the Terrans' abilities. On the other side of the Fence was literally another world.

These people built to last, in limestone, alabaster, and marble, in the wealthy district, and in cast stone in the outer city. The streets were carefully poured sections of concrete, cleverly given stress-joints to avoid temperature-cracking, and kept clean enough to eat from by a small army of street sweepers. No animals were allowed on the streets themselves, except for housetrained pets. The only vehicles permitted were single or double-being electric carts, that could move no faster than a man could walk. The Lacu'un dressed either in filmy, silken robes, or in more practical, shorter versions of the same garments. They were a handsome race, upright bipeds, skin tones in varying shades of browns and dark golds, faces vaguely avian, with a frill like an iguana's running from the base of the neck to a point between and just above the eyes.

As Vena had pointed out, every wall within sight was heavily carved, the carvings all having to do with the Lacu'un religion.

Most of the carvings were depictions of various processions or ceremonies, and no two were exactly alike.

"That's the Harvest-Gladness," Vena said, pointing, as they walked, to one elaborate wall that ran for yards. "It's particularly appropriate for Kla'dera; he made all his money in agriculture. Most Lacu'un try to have something carved that reflects on their gratitude for 'favors granted.' "

"I think I can guess that one," the Captain, Reginald Singh, said with a smile that showed startlingly white teeth in his dark face. The carving he nodded to was a series of panels; first a celebration involving a veritable kindergarten full of children, then those children—now sex-differentiated and seen to be all female—worshiping at the altar of a very fecund-looking Lacu'un female, and finally the now-maidens looking sweet and demure, each holding various religious objects.

Vena laughed, her brown eyes sparkling with amusement. "No, that one isn't hard. There's a saying, 'as fertile as Gel'vadera's wife.' Every child was a female, too, that made it even better. Between the bride-price he got for the ones that wanted to wed, and the officer's price he got for the ones that went into the armed services, Gel'vadera was a rich man. His FirstDaughter owns the house now."

"Ah—that brings up a question," Captain Singh replied. "Would you explain exactly who and what we'll be meeting? I read the briefing, but I still don't quite understand who fits in where with the government."

"It will help if you think of it as a kind of unholy mating of the British Parlimentary system and the medieval Japanese Shogunates," Vena replied. "You'll be meeting with the 'king'— that's the Lacu'ara—his consort, who has equal powers and represents the priesthood—that's the Lacu'teveras—and his three advisers, who are elected. The advisers represent the military, the bureaucracy, and the economic sector. The military adviser is always female; all officers in the military are female, because the Lacu'un believe that females will not seek glory for themselves, and so will not issue reckless orders. The other two can be either sex. 'Adviser' is not altogether an accurate term to use for them; the Lacu'ara and Lacu'teveras rarely act counter to their advice."

Dick was paying scant attention to this monologue; he'd already picked all this up from the faxes he'd called out of the local library after he'd read the briefing. He was more interested in the carvings, for there was something about them that puzzled him.

All of them featured strange little six-legged creatures scampering about under the feet of the carved Lacu'un. They were about the size of a large mouse, and seemed to Dick to be wearing very smug expressions . . . though, of course, he was surely misinterpreting.

"Excuse me, Consul," he said, when Vena had finished explaining the intricacies of Lacu'un government to Captain Singh's satisfaction. "I can't help wondering what those little lizardlike things are."

"Kreshta," she said, "*I* would call them pests; you don't see them out on the streets much, but they are the reason the streets are kept so clean. You'll see them soon enough once we get inside. They're like mice, only worse; fast as lightning—they'll steal food right off your plate. The Lacu'un either can't or won't get rid of them, I can't tell you which. When I asked about them once, my host just rolled his eyes heavenward and said what translates to 'it's the will of the gods.' "

"Insh'allah?" Captain Singh asked.

"Very like that, yes. I can't tell if they tolerate the pests because it is the gods' will that they must, or if they tolerate them because the gods favor the little monsters. Inside the Fence we have to close the government buildings down once a month, seal them up, and fumigate. We're just lucky they don't breed very fast."

:Hunt?: SKitty asked hopefully from her perch on Dick's shoulders.

No! Dick replied hastily. *Just look, don't hunt!*

The cat was gaining startled—and Dick thought, appreciative—looks from passersby.

"Just what is the status value of a totemic animal?" Erica asked curiously.

"It's the fact that the animal can be tamed at all. Aside from a handful of domestic herbivores, most animal life on Lacu'un has never been tamed. To be able to take a carnivore and train it to the hand implies that the gods are with you in a very powerful way." Vena dimpled. "I'll let you in on a big secret; frankly, Lan and I preferred the record of the *Brightwing* over the other two ships; you seemed to be more sympathetic to the Lacu'un. That's why we told you about the totemic animals, and why we left you until last."

"It wouldn't have worked without Dick," Captain Singh told her. "SKitty has really bonded to him in a remarkable way; I don't think this presentation would come off half so impressively if he had to keep her on a lead."

"It wouldn't," Vena replied, directing them around a corner. At the end of a short street was a fifteen-foot wall—carved, of course—pierced by an arching entranceway.

"The palace," she said, rather unnecessarily.

Vena had been right. The kreshta were *everywhere*.

Dick could feel SKitty trembling with the eagerness to hunt, but she was managing to keep herself under control. Only the lashing of her tail betrayed her agitation.

He waited at parade rest, trying not to give in to the temptation to stare, as the Captain and the Negotiator, Grace Vixen, were presented to the five rulers of the Lacu'un in an elaborate ceremony that resembled a stately dance. Behind the low platform holding the five dignitaries in their iridescent robes were five soberly clad retainers, each with one of the "totemic animals." Dick could see now what Vena had meant; the handlers had their creatures under control, but only barely. There was something like a bird; something resembling a small crocodile; something like a snake, but with six very tiny legs; a creature vaguely catlike, but with a feathery coat; and a beast resembling a teddy bear with scales. None of the handlers was actually holding his beast, except the bird-handler. All of the animals were on short chains, and all of them punctuated the ceremony with soft growls and hisses.

So SKitty, perched freely on Dick's shoulders, had

drawn no few murmurs of awe from the crowd of Lacu'un in the Audience Hall.

The presentation glided to a conclusion, and the Lacu'teveras whispered something to Vena behind her fan.

"With your permission, Captain, the Lacu'teveras would like to know if your totemic beast is actually as tame as she appears?"

"She is," the Captain replied, speaking directly to the consort, and bowing, exhibiting a charm that had crossed species barriers many times before this.

It worked its magic again. The Lacu'teveras fluttered her fan and trilled something else at Vena. The audience of courtiers gasped.

"Would it be possible, she asks, for her to touch it?"

SKitty? Dick asked quickly, knowing that she was getting the sense of what was going on from his thoughts.

:*Nice,*: the cat replied, her attention momentarily distracted from the scurrying hints of movement that were all that could be seen of the kreshta. :*Nice lady. Feels good in head, like Dick.*:

Feels good in head? he thought, startled.

"I don't think that there will be any problem, Captain," Dick murmured to Singh, deciding that he could worry about it later. "SKitty seems to like the Lacu'un. Maybe they smell right."

SKitty flowed down off his shoulder and into his arms as he stepped forward to present the cat to the Lacu'teveras. He showed the Lacu'un the cat's favorite spot to be scratched, under the chin. The long talons sported by all Lacu'un were admirably suited to the job of cat-scratching.

The Lacu'teveras reached forward with one lilac-tipped finger, and hesitantly followed Dick's example. The Audience Hall was utterly silent as she did so, as if the entire assemblage was holding its breath, waiting for disaster to strike. The courtiers gasped at her temerity when the cat stretched out her neck—then gasped again, this time with delight, as SKitty's rumbling purr became audible.

SKitty's eyes were almost completely closed in sensual delight; Dick glanced up to see that the Lacu'teveras' amber, slit-pupiled eyes were widened with what he judged was an equal delight. She let her other six fingers join the first, tentative one beneath the cat's chin.

"Such soft—" she said shyly, in musically-accented Standard. "—such nice!"

"Thank you, High Lady," Dick replied with a smile. "We think so."

:Verrrry nice,: SKitty seconded. *:Not head-talk like Dick, but feel good in head, like Dick. Nice lady have kitten soon, too.:*

The Lacu'teveras took her hand away with some reluctance, and signed that Dick should return to his place. SKitty slid back up onto his shoulders and started to settle herself.

It was then that everything fell apart.

The next stage in the ceremony called for the rulers to take their seats in their five thrones, and the Captain, Vena, and Grace to assume theirs on stools before the thrones so that each party could present what it wanted out of a possible relationship.

But the Lacu'teveras, her eyes still wistfully on SKitty, was not looking where she placed her hand. And on the armrest of the throne was a kreshta, frozen into an atypical immobility.

The Lacu'teveras put her hand—with all of her weight on it—right on top of the kreshta. The evil-looking thing squealed, squirmed, and bit her as hard as it could.

The Lacu'teveras cried out in pain—the courtiers gasped, the Advisers made warding gestures—and SKitty, roused to sudden and protective rage at this attack by *vermin* on the nice lady who was *with kitten*—leaped.

The kreshta saw her coming, and blurred with speed—but it was not fast enough to evade SKitty, gene-tailored product of one of BioTech's finest labs. Before it could cover even half of the distance between it and safety, SKitty had it. There was a crunch audible all over the Audience Chamber, and the ugly little thing was hanging limp from SKitty's jaws.

Tail high, in a silence that could have been cut up into bricks and used to build a wall, she carried her prize to the feet of the injured Lacu'un and laid it there.

:Fix him!: Dick heard in his mind. *:Not hurt nice-one-with-kitten!:*

The Lacu'ara stepped forward, face rigid, every muscle tense.

Spirits of Space! Dick thought, steeling himself for the worst, *that's bloody well torn it—*

But the Lacu'ara, instead of ordering the guards to seize the Terrans, went to one knee and picked up the broken-backed kreshta as if it were a fine jewel.

Then he brandished it over his head while the entire assemblage of Lacu'un burst into cheers—and the Terrans looked at one another in bewilderment.

SKitty preened, accepting the caresses of every Lacu'un that could reach her with the air of one to whom adulation is long due. Whenever an unfortunate kreshta happened to attempt to skitter by, she would turn into a bolt of black lightning, reenacting her kill to the redoubled applause of the Lacu'un.

Vena was translating as fast as she could, with the three Advisers all speaking at once. The Lacu'ara was tenderly bandaging the hand of his consort, but occasionally one or the other of them would put in a word, too.

"Apparently they've never been able to exterminate the kreshta; the natural predators on them *can't* be domesticated and generally take pieces out of anyone trying, traps and poisoned baits don't work because the kreshta won't take them. The only thing they've *ever* been able to do is what we were doing behind the Fence: close up the building and fumigate periodically. And even that has problems—the Lacu'teveras, for instance, is violently allergic to the residue left when the fumigation is done."

Vena paused for breath.

"I take it they'd like to have Skitty around on a permanent basis?" the Captain said, with heavy irony.

"Spirits of Space, Captain—they think SKitty is a sign from the gods, incarnate! I'm not sure they'll let her leave!"

Dick heard that with alarm—in a lot of ways, SKitty was the best friend he had—

To leave her—the thought wasn't bearable!

SKitty whipped about with alarm when she picked up what he was thinking. With an anguished yowl, she scampered across the slippery stone floor and flung herself through the air to land on Dick's shoulders. There she clung, howling her objections at the idea of being separated at top of her lungs.

"What in—" Captain Singh exclaimed, turning to see what could be screaming like a damned soul.

"She doesn't want to leave me, Captain," Dick said defiantly. "And I don't think you're going to be able to get her off my shoulder without breaking her legs or tranking her."

Captain Singh looked stormy. "Damn it then, get a trank—"

"I'm afraid I'll have to veto that one, Captain," Erica interrupted apologetically. "The contract with BioTech clearly states that only the designated handler— and that's Dick—or a BioTech representative can treat a shipscat. And furthermore," she continued, halting the Captain before he could interrupt, "it also states that to leave a shipscat without its designated handler will force BioTech to refuse any more shipscats to *Brightwing* for as long as you are the Captain. Now I don't want to sound like a troublemaker, Captain, but I, for one, will flatly refuse to serve on a ship with no cat. Periodic vacuum purges to kill the vermin do *not* appeal to me."

"Well then, I'll order the boy to—"

"Sir, I *am* the *Brightwing's* legal adviser—I hate to say this, but to order Dick to ground is a clear violation of *his* contract. He hasn't got enough hours spacing yet to qualify him for a ground position."

The Lacu'teveras had taken Vena aside, Dick saw,

and was chattering at her at top speed, waving her bandaged hand in the air.

"Captain Singh," she said, turning away from the Lacu'un and tugging at his sleeve, "The Lacu'teveras has figured out that something you said or did is upsetting the cat, and she's not very happy with that—"

Captain Singh looked just about ready to swallow a bucket of heated nails. "Spacer, *will* you get that feline calmed down before they throw me in the local brig?"

"I'll—try, sir—"

Come on, old girl—they won't take you away. Erica and the nice lady won't let them, he coaxed. *You're making the nice lady unhappy, and that might hurt her kitten—*

SKitty subsided, slowly, but continued to cling to Dick's shoulder as if he was the only rock in a flood. :*Not take Dick.:*

Erica won't let them.

:*Nice Erica.:*

A sudden thought occurred to him. *SKitty-love, how long would it take before you had your new kittens trained to hunt?*

She pondered the question. :*From wean? Three heats,:* she said finally.

About a year, then, from birth to full hunter. "Captain, I may have a solution for you—"

"I would be overjoyed to hear one," the Captain replied dryly.

"SKitty's pregnant again—I'm sorry, sir, I just found out today and I didn't have time to report it—but, sir, this is going to be to our advantage! If the Lacu'un insisted, *we* could handle the whole trade deal, couldn't we, Erica? And it should take something like a year to get everything negotiated and set up, shouldn't it?"

"Up to a year and a half, standard, yes," she confirmed. "And basically, whatever the Lacu'un want, they get, so far as the Company is concerned."

"Once the kittens are a year old, they'll be hunters just as good as SKitty is—so if you could see your way clear to doing all the setup—and sort of wait around for us to get done rearing the kittens—"

Captain Singh burst into laughter. "Boy, do you have any notion just how *many* credits handling the entire trade negotiations would put in *Brightwing*'s account? Do you have any idea what that would do for *my* status?"

"No, sir," he admitted.

"Suffice it to say I *could* retire if I chose. And—Spirits of Space—kittens? Kittens we *could* legally sell to the Lacu'un? I don't suppose you have any notion of how many kittens we can expect this time?"

He sent an inquiring tendril of thought to SKitty. "Uh—I think four, sir."

"Four! And they were offering us *what* for just her?" the Captain asked Vena.

"A more-than-considerable amount," she said dryly. "Exclusive contract on the forcefield applications."

"How would they feel about bargaining for four to be turned over in about a year?"

Vena turned to the rulers and translated. The excited answer she got left no doubts in anyone's mind that the Lacu'un were overjoyed at the prospect.

"Basically, Captain, you've just convinced the Lacu'un that you hung the moon."

"Well—why don't we settle down to a little serious negotiation, hmm?" the Captain said, nobly refraining from rubbing his hands together with glee. "I think that all our problems for the future are about to be solved in one fell swoop! Get over here, spacer. You and that cat have just received a promotion to Junior Negotiator."

:Okay?: SKitty asked anxiously.

Yes, love, Dick replied, taking Erica's place on a negotiator's stool. *Very okay!*

THE GAME OF
CAT AND RABBIT

by *Patricia Shaw Mathews*

There is a wrong smell by the ship. We are docked at
Luna City Spaceport; the mass-driver *Lady Day*, her
captain, and her crew. That's me, Smitty, Human
Morale Officer and Pest Control Officer. Tail high, I
prowl the pressurized backstage area, and sniff suspiciously about the ships and dockers, machines and
cargo. I stop to renew my acquaintance with the old
tom who runs the spaceport; a sad case. He washed
out because he couldn't handle zero-gee. Not every
cat can. But he and I have a kitten aboard the *Outward Bound*; enough to make anyone purr.

Herself comes and scoops me up into a duffel bag,
saying "Sorry, Smitty, old girl" as she lopes along the
ramp. Nose to the vents, I yowl my outrage. Doesn't
she remember how I hate the cat-bag? She puts the
bag in its holder on the crash couch and fastens it
down. I know what happens when she does that! Our
auxiliary rocket boosters shake and make a loud noise
that makes my teeth and bones ache. I feel crushed as
if Herself had rolled over me. Then the noise and the
heavy feeling stops slowly, Herself zips open the bag,
and I sail out into our cabin, as light and fluffy as a
kitten in one-tenth gee. That's fun.

Herself comes to pick me up, as brazenly as if she
had never made a loud noise and locked me in a duffel
bag and made me feel crushed. Well, one more time. I
show her my claws. "Poor Smitty," she agrees. "Liftoff is awfully hard on a little cat, isn't it?"

That's better. With a haughty sniff to let her know I

243

have my pride, I let her tickle me under the chin and along the jawbone where it feels so good.

Herself is talking again, more to herself than to me. " 'Luna to Ceres in an economy orbit, cheap on fuel, risky on micrometeorites and radiation, what can *possibly* go wrong, Miss Weaver?' *Captain* Weaver to those landlubbing idiot groundhogs! Well, three circuit failures in eight hours is what!" If she were a cat, her back would be arched and the fur standing up on it.

I start thinking of the litter box. Liftoff always makes me do that. I wiggle out of her arms and over to the place on the back bulkhead. Something smells wrong, very badly wrong. Herself is still bouncing off first one bulkhead and then the other, very careful not to hit any of the many fine hiding places and exploring places stacked along them. "Another hiss-spit-yowl-meow short circuit!" Herself yowls again. "And not a Great Cat Blasted trace that shows up on any of my instruments."

This is human business. My business is with the wrong smell that hops around the *Lady Day* from here to there but never makes itself known.

My litter box is not real sand. It's a sort of plastic that gives under your paws but doesn't scatter when you dig in. I use it and leave; a little door under the box starts humming and sucks the thing away. It's too small for a cat to explore, and Not A Cat Place anyway. Herself stops to scratch my ears. "Good Smitty," she says. The wrong smell is hopping around under her very own chair, and I have to stop it. Narrow-eyed, I watch for a while, catching the faintest of movements out of the corner of my eyes. I raise my hindquarters and wind them up, then let spring. I am right on top of the wrong smell, but oddly enough, I miss. Oh, well, it happens. Vectors are hard to judge when you change gravities so much.

Daintily I push off one bulkhead, hook a claw into a hammock's webbing, and settle down for a good wash. Pest Control Officer on a vacuum-hopper like the *Lady Day* is a soft berth. There were no pests imported to either Luna, the Habitats, or the Belt, only pets; and any varmints that sneak aboard are easily

dealt with. We space the rats. Without pressure suits.
And now I am a pest control cat. A-hunting we will
go! Tally ho!

Herself is annoyed, and spits and yowls some more.
She's been poking into the control and instrument
boards that line the bulkheads with some odd human
detachable claws, and muttering under her breath like
an upset cat. I wish I could bring her a nice fat fresh
mouse to make her feel better. Whatever she's trying
to catch, I can't smell it. Unless she's also trying to
catch the wrong smell? But anyone with a nose can tell
it's nowhere around where she is now.

She picks me up by the midsection and dumps me
halfway across the cabin. "Not now, Smitty. Go play
somewhere else!" she snarls, and mutters "preferably
in the depressurized hold."

That place is not for cats either, unless the blinking
light by the air lock is on and the humans are coming
and going without pressure suits. Herself is only in a
tight coat of artificial fur that covers all but her paws.
(She is holding people-things in her back paws and is
playing with the instrumentation and the control board
with her front paws. She can change her claws and her
fur, but she doesn't have any of her own, nor any tail.
But the things she changes are a lot of fun to watch.)

She is upset. It is human business. My business is
finding the wrong smell, and I wouldn't be a cat if I let
a little thing like Herself's moods get in my way. I sniff
and prowl until Herself straightens up, gives one more
growl, and says, "All right, Smitty, all right! I'll feed
you!"

Well, hunting means food and food means hunting
to my ancestors. With another sniff, I follow her to the
food bag. The wrong smell is very strong around there,
but it is not a bad-food smell. It is a strange-prey
smell. The food bag has been chewed. Herself looks
angry at me, but I do not chew the bag. Plastic tastes
nasty.

The food is almost too sticky to eat, and it gets in
my whiskers, but it is totally delicious. Strange things
happen to your sense of smell in no-weight, but

humans—clever beings!—mix food with sharp-smelling things called *spices* to make it smell right. I go for another wash, and then I see a Thing out of the corner of my eye, over by my food bowl. The Thing smells like what I am smelling all day! Once again, I pounce.

Then Herself starts to laugh. "Oh, Smitty," she says, picking me up, "I'm sorry I snapped at you. You're just having fun, aren't you? I wish I were a little cat and could take things as easily as you do." And while she is cuddling me, the bad-smell-thing finishes my cat food, goes over to the control board and starts nibbling at the long strings between the lights.

It is cold in the ship. The lights are nice and dim, but they flicker and get strange and flicker again. The air is stuffy and the water tastes nasty. Herself is very worried. She keeps poking at all the buzzing and flickering things, taking off large sections of bulkhead and looking at the long strings behind them. She makes no more snarls and growls; she sits on the back bulkhead and howls, with water on her face the way humans do.

I love her and want to help, but the wrong-smell thing is being very busy. It is always at the long things. I try to catch it, but it is very fast. Sometimes it does not move at all, and then I cannot see it. When I do, it runs away.

It is eating all my food. I cry to Herself. She picks me up and wrinkles her face. "I don't know where all that cat food is going, Smitty. You must be growing a new coat of fur," she says, sounding very confused. The bag is not very full. She shakes her head. "Looks like half rations for you until we hit Ceres," she says. "*If* we ever get there!" She pours out a very small amount, gives me a little from her own squeeze bag, then gets back to work. I eat, catnap, then go back to work myself.

The bad-smell thing is poking around the place where she has the bulkhead open. Taking careful aim, I spring. I am between Herself and the string the bad thing has. I land. A hit! I have a mouthful of soft fur and loose skin, and my claws feel the tip of a long, long ear. I sniff deep.

In Luna City there are rabbits. Humans keep them for meat, fur, and leather. This is not a rabbit smell. But it is a rabbit feel under my paws. O-KAY! Now I've got you, you son of a rodent! Gleefully I stalk this long-eared varmint, following it everywhere. I know where it is being before it is being there, and go there first. I head it off at the bulkhead and I head it off at the food bowl. Herself wipes her face with a long piece of artificial fur and closes up the bulkhead. The rabbit-thing is in there. I pounce!

"Smitty!" she screams. "Look out!"

I hear a sizzle, a snap, a crackle, and a pop! It goes right through my fur and into my body, making it snap and sizzle, too. I jerk two or three times while the smell of singed fur reeks in my nose. I am hurt!

But so is the thing. I see it crawl feebly into the main cabin and over to Herself's pressure suit. It starts chewing again. I never know why it chews everything so much, but I see a dim glow around the string it chews. I see this glow when I am hurt. I hurt too much to chase the thing now. I lie on the bulkhead and mew. Herself brings me a bulb of water and squirts it into my mouth. In space you drink from the bulb like a kitten with its mother. Herself is my mother in space, I think; and I try to purr. She smiles, which is a human purr, and pets me. Then she sighs and sets me on the crash couch and gets up again.

She is going to the pressure suit! The bad-smell-thing is there. The string it chewed has that glow that means it will hurt. With one last effort I spring for the suit and sit on it. I growl. Herself sighs again and tries to pick me up. She must not touch this suit! It will hurt her, and the bad thing will get away! I show her my claws.

She says, "Oh, stop this nonsense, Smitty; this is an emergency." She tries to set me aside.

Now I spring at her! All my claws are out, and I bite her, too. She stares at me and starts to howl. Water comes from her face. "Smitty, that's too much! I hate to do this to you, but I have to lock you up. You've gone space-nuts from the strain. And the bad water and the bad air and the fear and the cold. . . ." she shakes. "They'll make me put you to sleep, Smitty. You don't want that!"

She means "kill." Humans are prissy about that. I do not want her to kill me. But I have a job to do, too. I growl and show her my claws again and sit on the suit. I do not let her near it. She draws a stun-gun. I stare at her. She will not touch this suit! It is Not For Humans until I take care of the bad rabbit-thing! I stare and stare. She looks at me, puzzled, and says, "I think you're trying to tell me something, Smitty. I always heard cats were a little bit psychic, but to tell you the truth, I don't have the least idea what's going on here."

Then the rabbit thing moves and I see it again. I pounce. This time I have it! I shake it back and forth until it squeals like a rabbit in the jaws of a cat. Herself is staring at me, gun dangling from one paw. "Maybe I've gone space-nuts?" she asks me. But I know better.

I shake it and shake it and play with it until I see drops of blood come out of it and fly across the cabin. Several hit the bulkhead. Herself drops the gun, breathes deeply, and straightens up. "All right, Smitty, I'll take it from here," she says. She takes the thing in her hands and her eyes get very big. She goes over to the cat-bag and zips it in. It will eat the bag. I hope it does! But that will be a big job even for that chewy rabbit.

She picks up the blood in a little squeeze-dropper and hurries over to her lab bench. She puts it in one of the machines and stares and stares. Then she starts to laugh.

"A rabbit! I do not believe this!" She goes over to the cat bag again and very carefully feels inside. She yelps. I could tell her the thing bites. She feels inside again. She gets a flashlight and looks inside. "I don't see him," she says, puzzled. "But I feel him." She zips up the cat bag again and goes back to the lab. I am on the crash couch having a good wash.

Then she makes a very loud and happy noise. She jumps and twirls around, making loud human happy sounds. I understand some of it. She is singing, "You caught me a wabbit, caught me a wabbit, caught me a wabbit, a wabbit you caught!" I hear those sounds when she listens to the Luna City Opera, but it is not about rabbits. I like her song better. She picks me up and hugs me to her. "And, Smitty, you're a little feline hero, you know that? And the scientists are going to love you to bits and pieces. I wonder what that critter's secret is?"

Then she goes to her own food and brings out a nice fat juicy fish steak and gives me half, and cuddles me until I get tired of it and jump down. Me for a good nap!

The people at Ceres never do find out what the bunny's secret is. They think he is a Luna City rabbit that got away, started living in the spaceport, and changed color fur to match whatever he was near at the time. I think he goes into the Otherworld but not the one cats look at. I am sure there is an Otherworld for rabbits as well as one for cats. Even humans have one, though they don't look at it much.

I say we go back to Luna City and catch a few and find out. Tally-ho! A-hunting I will go!

FROM THE DIARY
OF HERMIONE

by Ardath Mayhar

It is with great Hesitancy that I take Pen in Paw to recount this latest Incident. Indeed, I find it most difficult to criticize my Human in any way, and particularly when it involves, as does this, his seeming Ineptitude at working within his own Field of Endeavor.

However, if this is to be an accurate Account of the life I led in the House of Harlow Biddington, Sorcerer and Adept, I must, I fear, neglect my finer Feelings in the interest of Truthfulness. I do not, however, allude to anything of this Nature when speaking to my Kits, as they must be trained from Infancy in Respect and Admiration for Those who are in our Charge.

As I am a Graduate of the Coven of Familiars, it is, of course, my Responsibility to oversee and to Correct any Error of Judgment or of Practice that I note in the usages of my Associate. This has never, until now, posed a Problem for me, for Harlow Biddington, with all his Faults, and even considering that he is merely a Human, has been a most skilled and devoted Practitioner of the arcane Arts. His Studies have continued over the Span of many Years, and his Efforts have, more than once, been crowned with Success.

The dish from which my Kits drank their Milk was proof of this. His short Foray into Alchemy resulted in the transmutation of every metallic Object in the House. While the Result was a bit ostentatious for my Taste, it was nevertheless impressive when one considers the Many who have labored for Years without achieving any similar Effect.

His Explorations into the Nature of the Universe

resulted in a Volume of great thickness and complexity, filled with Mathematical Formulae of most esoteric Nature. This Work rebounded both to his Credit among Men and to Mine in my own somewhat more subtle Field. It is generally considered that the Atmosphere created by a Familiar can do Much to Stimulate the creative Processes of those involved in the Occult Sciences, and I pride myself that I am not lacking in that Area.

With such a formidable Array of Matters accomplished, it would seem that my Sorcerer should be one who would be content to rest upon his Achievements, except for minor Attempts to refine his former Work. Biddington, however, had never known Contentment in all his Life.

After his Triumph over both Mathematics and Nature, he determined that he must summon up a Demon. Although I found myself most Doubtful of this Project, I lent my small Skills and Efforts to his Objective. Any who has ever experienced such a Phenomenon will understand why I do not describe the Fulfillment of his Efforts. Some things are not suitable for the Perusal of decent Beings, and I will draw a veil over That. However, he did succeed, which set him Afire to attain Further Achievements.

At this Time I remonstrated gently with him, pointing out to the Man that he had gone more Deeply into Forbidden Matters than most are ever privileged to Go. "Be happy with what you have done!" I conveyed to him, through my most seductive Purrings and Twinings about his Ankles.

He understood my Message. Of that I am certain, for he was no Fool or Dullard, no matter how Simple he might sometimes appear. He reached down to pat my Head, stroking my Fur backward, which is always most Disconcerting. I placed my Paw firmly upon his besocked Ankle and let him feel my Claws, but he did not desist from his Researches.

At this Point, many of my Confreres might well have felt their Duty to be satisfied. However, I am made of sterner Stuff. I leaped into his Lap and put my Head on the edge of the Table, my Eyes being level with a large Book, at which he was staring as if Mesmerized.

Imagine my Horror when I read the illuminated Words writ in red Ink upon those musty Pages!

The incautious Man was studying a Spell for changing the Shape. I recognized the Ritual as being similar to one studied at my Alma Mater, and I almost Gasped with Astonishment and Fear. Of all Spells used by Sorcerers and Witches and their Sort, this is the most often subject to Error, to Misuse, and to most uncomfortable Accident.

I turned about in his Lap and thrust my Head beneath his Chin, mewing in my most pitiful and moving Voice. He scratched my Ears (which, though undignified in the extreme, is yet most Gratifying as a Sensation), and turned another Page.

Suffice it to say that he was in no way deterred from his Intention, no matter how I pleaded with him. At last I gave it up and went to suckle my Kits, musing sadly all the while upon the strongheadedness of Mankind.

When I returned to the Study, the Sorcerer was assembling the various Elements necessary to the Spell. I watched with growing Unease as he mixed the Chemicals, added the . . . organic Parts . . . and spoke those terrible Words that I had never before heard uttered by human Lips.

At the end of the chant, he lifted the Vial and sipped its unsavory Contents. There was a hissing Sound, and the fire in the Grate burned blue for a long Moment. The Shape of the Sorcerer who was in my Charge seemed to shiver about the Edges. Biddington groaned deeply, his Voice becoming lighter, higher, more like a Squeaking every Moment.

He shrank rapidly, his Clothing falling into untidy Heaps on the Carpet. For a moment I wondered if he had succeeded in totally Obliterating himself. Yet there was Motion among the displaced Garments. As I watched, Something moved in the Clutter, wriggling its Way out into the Firelight.

It stood on four frail Legs, looking about the Room from its suddenly altered Altitude. The Whiskers twitched frantically, and the long, slender Tail jerked in a spasm.

I could feel Pity for the unhappy Sorcerer. He had, according to the Spell he used, been trying to assume the Shape of a Bear, and what he had achieved was the tiny Body of a Mouse.

I could see in those beads of Eyes the desperate Plea for Help that he turned toward me. I sighed and washed my paws, which usually can soothe my Spirits while my Mind wrestles with heavy Problems.

The Situation was a difficult one. He had sent away his Housekeeper for a Fortnight Holiday, so as to be alone when his Plan went into Effect. There was no Human Aid to be had for many days. He did not associate with Others of his Kind, for there is none so jealously Solitary as a Sorcerer.

I washed again, Tail to Nose, for this was a Difficulty greater than Any I had encountered before. At last the only Course that I could determine was one involving much Risk and not a little Danger.

I must seek out Tabitha, with whom I had attended my training Institution. Her own Sorcerer lived on a nearby Estate, and though he was an Archrival of my own dear Biddington, I felt some Hope that he might come to the Aid of a fellow Human, whatever his personal Prejudices. Before leaving upon such a doubtful and desperate Mission, however, I must suckle my Kits again, for they must not be allowed to suffer through the Inattention of their Mother.

And there I made a fatal Error of Judgment.

The Kits had grown hungry while waiting for me to finish my Plan. All three, now moving quite well upon their strong little Legs, sought me out in the Study, as they had done before. Unfortunately, in former Visits, they had found me in the Company of a Human Being of large Size and forbidding Aspect.

I was now attending upon a Mouse.

As with other beings of sensible Nature, my Kind does not censure the Young for their Ignorance and

Enthusiasm. I had taught those Kits from their Birth that one of their major Roles in Life would be the Catching and Dispatching of Mice, whenever and wherever found.

My Peers, upon Consideration, agreed that Horatio, my only Son of this Litter, was not at Fault for following the teachings of his Mother. I must admit, however, that in my Heart I feel that it was very harsh Treatment for my erstwhile Sorcerer, no matter how Wrong-headed his Behavior might have been.

We have, of course, moved away from the Site of the Disaster. A Situation became available upon the untimely Death of another of my fellow Graduates when Hortense ran afoul of a Hansom Cab. We have been placed with her Charge, a most pleasant Gentleman who is interested solely in the Motions of the Stars and Planets.

Though I think often of Harlow Biddington, I feel that the Atmosphere here is far more Healthful for my Litter, who now have arrived at the playful Age, during which all too many of our Kind come to Grief. The Arrival of those of demonic Nature in the Home is never, I feel, a useful Matter when one is rearing Young.

So I must begin a fresh Diary, setting aside this Account of the years of my Youth and my first Sorcerer. Yet before I lift Paw from Pen, I will affirm a new Vow, freshly made in case of Accident;

Never again will I teach my Kits to catch a Mouse and eat it immediately. First, they must show their Prey to Me, so that I may determine that it is not Someone I may know.

> signed:
> Hermione, The Grange
> Oxbridge
> 1882

IT'S A BIRD,
IT'S A PLANE,
IT'S . . . SUPERCAT!

by Ann Miller
and Karen Elizabeth Rigley

Locals spotted a giant bird.

Simultaneously, UFO sightings started up again. Okay, fine. This time I planned to totally ignore the whole thing. If a flying saucer landed in my yard or an alien fell out of a tree on me, then *maybe* I'd mention it. Other than that, forget it.

Do you know how much credibility a science fiction writer— especially a *female* science fiction writer—who claims to spot UFOs receives? Zip. Zero. I saw one once, yet all I got were sage nods and knowing smirks. "Oh, sure," they all said. "Crazy Jackie Carlson is trying out a new plot, ha ha."

I was not amused.

I'd moved down here to the Rio Grande Valley from Houston when my writing finally started buying the beans, and bought a small cottage on several acres at the edge of town. Perfect for writing. It apparently came with a cat who appeared the morning after I moved in; a large cat, light gray with dark gray markings. His pale green-gold eyes, encircled by dark lines, gave him the appearance of wearing spectacles. That, along with his neutral coloring and timid personality, inspired me to call him Clark Kent.

He came to me now, settling in my lap with a contented purr while I sat staring at a blank piece of paper, wondering where my muse had flown. I heaved a sigh and leaned back in my chair. My new story refused to come to life. No matter what I tried to do with it, it just lay there, a flat old . . . tater. A day-old french fry. Soggy.

Stroking Clark's silky coat, I looked out the window. Light from a waxing moon filtered down through leaves of the orange tree that stood just beside the house, casting lacy patterns as a breeze stirred the branches. Odd, how the light flickered, almost changed colors. . . .

OH, NO!

I scrambled from the chair, dumping a surprised Clark, and rushed to the window to peer through the foliage of the orange tree, every cell in my body denying what I saw. A glowing saucer-shaped object hovered a few feet off the ground at the edge of my backyard. Two bands of changing colors, moving in opposite directions, flowed around the midsection of the craft. It hung there immobile while I gaped at it for several minutes until it dawned on me proof hovered just outside my window!

Springing for my camera, I quickly slunk out the back door and dashed from tree to tree, trying to get as close as possible to the UFO without being seen. I didn't relish the idea of becoming an abductee. There's a limit to what I'll do for a story—especially one that nobody would believe. I took several shots, then grew aware of an increasing hum that hurt my ears, but felt good at the same time. The rotating color bands sped up and the saucer shot upward. Just like that. Poof. I gazed at the spot where it disappeared, wondering if my pictures would turn out or if they got zapped by anti-picture rays.

That's what old Jim Trammell said happened to the photos he took during the previous rash of sightings that showed an empty meadow instead of the flying saucer he claimed had been there. Jim didn't carry any more credibility than I did, maybe less, due to the pickling process he had subjected his brain to for all those years. Except old Jim quit drinking after that night, even started going to church. UFOs have a way of changing your life, all right.

I hurried back inside to my darkroom, Clark sticking close beside me, determined not to be left outside alone at night.

Some brave cat.

Well, sure enough, my photos showed everything but the saucer. I could see a strange "pull" where the saucer had been, and figured they had a cloaking device. So much for proof of my sanity.

"Why can't you talk?" I asked Clark. "Act as my witness?"

"Meow," he replied delicately.

I put my writing away for the night, my muse having packed up and probably hitched a ride on that saucer. The next morning I drove into West Grove to the newspaper office and spent several hours writing up local stories about weddings and charity cake sales. I didn't mention my little excitement of the night before. Ed would have wanted me to write it up and I didn't intend to. My dear boss didn't mind me making a fool of myself on the front page of the *West Grove News* if it brought him publicity and more readers, thus increasing his advertisers. After that first flurry of UFO and big bird sightings, even people over in Harlingen and McAllen were buying our little weekly paper just to see what I'd say next. Ed Watson, esteemed publisher and editor of the *News*, cackled all the way to the bank. *He* didn't care if I was writing Chapter Seven or dabbling in controlled substances, as long as my articles increased circulation.

Perhaps later, if others reported sightings, I'd write up *their* stories, but not mine. And if Ed didn't know, then he couldn't badger me about it.

When I got home that afternoon, I walked out into the backyard to look around where I'd seen the saucer hovering the night before. Clark trotted at my heels, making little trilling sounds, probably advising caution. The big sissy. I didn't see a mark anywhere on the ground underneath the saucer, so I went back over to the tree I'd hid under the night before and leaned against it, thinking. I was carrying my camera, hoping I'd find something—some sign—I could photograph. Nothing.

Clark stretched and sharpened his claws on the tree, then started climbing it. He disappeared into the foliage. Presently, I heard rustling above me and peered up through the branches, trying to see what Clark was doing. At that moment something large—giant—flapped monstrous black wings and flew away. I heard a muffled cry, then Clark and something else fell out of the tree on me, knocking me down with a whump. Trying to protect my camera, I managed to avoid getting crushed, but in the process I tumbled across the fallen object.

Clark, atop the victim, let out a squall and scrambled behind me. I gazed at the prone form and thought, what's this kid doing here? Then I realized the wizened creature I lay upon was no kid. I moved off it and looked it over. It had a grayish complexion, narrow, four-digited hands, and a hairless, slightly oversized head. Large, half-closed eyes revealed dark irises that nearly filled the entire sockets. The nose was only a small bump and the mouth a slit, almost invisible when closed. It wore a garment that looked like a faintly iridescent bodystocking and a bumpy belt around its middle.

Still alive, it made a hissy-moany sound and I wondered how much I'd hurt it. It wasn't big, only about the size of a skinny ten-year-old.

Now what?

Clark crept forward to sniff at one slender gray hand and the huge sparkling eyes opened, the lids sliding up almost like a doll's eyes.

"Are you hurt?" I asked, not expecting a reply.

"Oooh, ooooh," it moaned, like crying, drawing away from Clark's inquisitive nose.

"Take it easy," I soothed. "He won't hurt you." My mind hit overdrive trying to believe all this. Obviously, the little creature was an alien. Extraterrestrial. It came from outer space. I glanced off in the direction the big bird had disappeared, then looked back at the alien. It was gazing wistfully in the same direction.

"Does that bird belong to you?" I asked sympathetically, wishing we could actually communicate.

"Shess," it sighed, startling me.

"Did you understand me?" I asked incredulously.

"A liddle bit. Hef you talk to me, I hunnerstand you bedder."

Still looking at it I said, "My name is Jackie. I write science fiction stories and also articles for a newspaper. Some people think they're one and the same. This animal is my pet cat, Clark Kent. Ah, several people in the area have seen the giant bird and even some flying saucers. I saw one, but nobody wants to believe a science fiction writer. I took pictures of a craft that hovered here last night, but they didn't turn out. Did you arrive in it?"

"Shess. I em come here to bring back the ba k'rah."

"The ba k'rah—is that the giant bird?" The alien nodded and I asked, "What's your name?"

"Worl."

"Worl," I repeated, not quite getting the sound right.

"En you, Shockie, you are not afred when you see the craft?"

I shook my head. "I told you I'm a science fiction writer. I write stories about those things. That's acceptable. But when I started writing true articles about them I got some skeptical looks to say the least. Are you understanding this?"

"Much bedder. Pliss continue spicking. Does Clairk Kendt also spick?"

"Meow," Clark replied, giving Worl another curious sniff.

"I do not hunnerstand his spicking."

"Cats don't really talk, Worl. They're animals. Does the ba k'rah talk?"

"No. Hit es stupid. But much trouble. And much expensive. I *must* get the ba k'rah back." He put a hand to his head and winced and I noticed he had a good-sized bump.

"Let's go into the house," I suggested. "We can get something to drink. The sunshine is growing warm."

Worl agreed to come inside with me. I believe he felt rather befuddled from the fall and conk on the head or he wouldn't have been so cooperative. I rested my hand on his thin shoulder, steering him toward the house and he walked beside me, one hand on the bump on his head. Inside, he gazed around at everything as I guided him to the kitchen table. Clark leaped into his own chair and stared across the table at Worl. I'd never seen old sissy act so friendly and open before with a stranger. And you couldn't get much stranger than Worl.

"Cola? Iced tea? What would you like?" I asked.

"I don' know. I not hef thiss things before."

I dropped ice cubes into two glasses and poured out some Coca-Cola. "Welcome to Earth," I said, setting down the drink.

He grasped the glass in one long-fingered hand and raised it to his mouth, watching me to make sure he was doing the right thing.

"Woo!" he said, blinking rapidly at the fizzy bubbles tickling his flat little nose. Not put off, he drank again. "Hit test preddy good. Thiss es a pleasure drink?"

"Yes, but nonalcoholic. It won't make you drunk. At least, it doesn't make humans drunk. I don't know about you. What are you? Where do you come from?"

"I come from Pra. I am Prael. And I am in a lot of trouble." He morosely dropped his head into his hands.

"What kind of trouble? And how come you speak English so well?"

"I will explen," he said, uncovering his face and reaching for his drink again. "The Prael hef a talent for learning languages. We hef a device to enhance thiss talent. I used it before coming here to find the ba k'rah. I was to observe and monitor your electronic entertainment to bedder learn your language. However, I hef not had time. Thus you spicking to me serves thiss purpose."

"That's nice. But what's your trouble?"

He had to search for the right words, but adequately explained he served as manifest officer aboard a starship that collected animals across the galaxy for zoos. These animals were ordered and half paid for in advance. A starship transporting animals needs water. They'd just come from a world called Igroon and the Prael didn't care for Igroonian water, so they stopped by Earth to take some on. A young assistant decided the ba k'rah needed exercise and the ba k'rah flew the coop.

"You mean," I prompted when Worl fell silent, "your assistant let the ba k'rah out of the ship?"

"No, no. But the ba k'rah es very large. If not confined, hit goes where hit wishes. We cannot harm thiss expensive animal. With our mistakes linked together, the ba k'rah escaped the ship."

I suddenly had a vision of a bunch of frantic little gray aliens chasing after the giant bird with a net.

"Hit es my responsibility. My assistant failed in his duty. The purchasers of the ba k'rah want their specimen. The ship will deliver remaining animals, then return here. My commander leaf me behind to capture the ba k'rah." He sighed, staring into his glass as if hoping to read answers in the melting ice cubes. "More trouble. Now I hef spoke to you. Many violations of laws. And the ba k'rah flew away, perhaps far, when Clairk Kendt frightened hit." He turned an accusing gaze on Clark who calmly continued washing his face, not at all contrite.

"Let me get this straight," I said, studying the little alien. "You must recapture the bird and keep your identity a secret." I punctuated the last words with a wistful sigh—here was solid proof to show the world. . . .

Worl blinked innocently at me. "You help?"

"Yes." I let my dream fade and squared my shoulders. "Of course, I'll help. Do you have any idea where the bird might go?"

"Eat." He shook his head sadly, his manner so pathetic, it made me want to comfort him. "Ba k'rah find food first."

"What kind of food?" I asked, hoping humans weren't on the menu.

"Here on your planet, citrus. More trouble."

Clark perked his ears up as if listening intently and I noticed Worl spoke both to me and the cat. I smiled, realizing the little alien assumed Clark could understand the conversation. Clark meowed at me as if he could read my thoughts. Startled, I concentrated on Worl who began talking again and rubbing the bump on his head at the same time.

"I hef to find the ba k'rah. Must go now." He stood and swayed.

I caught him. He felt very cold in my arms and certainly didn't weigh much. "You're not going anywhere yet," I said, compassion for the poor unfortunate creature welling inside me. Maybe a bit of guilt, too. After all, I fell on the little guy. "It's nearly dark and you're injured. Rest for a while and then we can decide how to catch the ba k'rah. Okay?"

He didn't agree or disagree. He just collapsed in my arms. I carried him into my bedroom and laid him down on my bed. He looked strange; yet so vulnerable lying there with those luminous eyes closed. He moaned softly. Clark leaped upon the bed to put his nose against the bump on Worl's head. In some way it must have helped, because Worl quieted and turned sideways, snuggling against my cat. Clark purred in a hypnotic rhythm that nearly lured me down beside them. I shook off drowsiness and forced myself into the kitchen, where I tossed a salad to chill in the fridge. If Worl got hungry, natural foods might be kinder to his alien digestive track.

A sudden knock echoed through the house. Don't panic, my mind screamed. I ran to the bedroom where Worl and Clark lay sleeping and shut the door, then rushed into the living room to reach the front door before my unexpected visitor began ringing the doorbell.

Opening the door a crack, my breath caught as I recognized Mike Harris, the blond hunky deputy sheriff whom I'd been hoping to meet since I moved here. But not now. Was harboring an alien a crime?

"Hello," I said, attempting to keep my voice from squeaking.

"Howdy. Sorry to disturb you, ma'am, but we've had reports of strange activities in this area. Could I come in for a few minutes?"

He looked great in his uniform and filled it out exactly like a woman wants a man to. I never dreamed

I could resist inviting him into my home, but I heard myself whisper, "This really isn't a good time, officer."

He placed one suntanned hand against the door-frame, his gaze hardening and his voice deepening. "I think you ought to let me inside, ma'am."

I nodded, swung open the door and decided to take my chances rather than rile the deputy sheriff. He relaxed and grinned as he entered my living room. What a grin! It made my heart dance, until I remembered my "other" guest.

"I'm Mike Harris," he said, taking my hand into his firm, warm grasp.

"Please sit down, Mike," I responded with my best smile, wishing I'd combed my hair after the tumble with Clark and Worl. He stared briefly at my auburn curls and I hoped no leaves or grass clung there. "I'm Jackie Carlson."

"I know." He grinned again, flashing pearly teeth. "The writer lady." He sat on my sofa, his long legs stretched out in front of him, quite at ease. "Miss Carlson, last night our switchboard lit up with calls from across the Valley, people reporting everything from flying saucers to monster birds. Most of the sightings came from this way. You see anything?"

Now, I don't make a habit of lying to lawmen, but when he cocked his handsome head, those keen blue eyes of his assessing my credibility as a witness before I even opened my mouth, all I could do was mutely shake my head no.

Part of me wanted to grab his hand and drag him into the bedroom to show him my little alien friend; most of me resisted.

Scratch, scratch. The bedroom door. I had to let Clark out before he woke Worl. "Excuse me," I said before dashing off to carefully open the bedroom door. Clark streaked by me, straight into the living room. I peeked at Worl, sleeping peacefully, and closed the door softly.

Clark stopped several feet from the sofa, staring warily through those green-gold eyes at Mike. Mike bent down, wiggled a finger and cooed softly, "Here, kitty, kitty.'"

"Clark's pretty shy," I said, seating myself in my recliner. Clark circled around, then jumped into my lap.

"Clark? Crazy name for a cat," Mike said, appearing a bit embarrassed that my pet had snubbed him.

"Clark Kent, actually," I replied, stroking the cat's silky fur obediently. Clark had trained me in a very short time.

Mike started to laugh. A nice deep laugh. "I see why—he looks like he wears glasses, right?"

Clark stuck his pink nose up disdainfully. "One of the reasons," I answered. "Do you have any more questions for me? If not, I do have a deadline on my story. . . ."

Mike got the hint and stood. "No, guess that's it. Unless you heard something last night?" he added hopefully.

"Sorry." I picked Clark up, then walked Mike to the door. Reluctant to completely blow my first meeting with this appealing man, I smiled and said, "It was a pleasure meeting you and I hope we see each other again soon." Just not *too* soon, I finished to myself.

Mike's blue eyes targeted mine. "I'd like that, Miss Carlson." He grinned and I felt tempted to ask him to stay. Clark sprang from my arms, reminding me of our situation.

"Please call me Jackie," I said, consoling myself with that much. Again, Mike shook my hand and even held it a bit longer than necessary before bidding me good night and departing.

Clark shot out the door as Mike left. Out of character for that cat. He rarely ventured out at night alone, but I let him go, confident he'd return shortly. Very shortly.

I grabbed a bowl of salad and settled down on the sofa to watch the late news. I clicked on the remote just as a newscaster announced last night's UFO sighting had been classified as ball lightning. "Oh, sure," I grumbled. Next came the big bird story, explained away as a runaway kite, since its huge size ruled out hawks, falcons or even eagles.

Clark scratched at the door, so I let him inside and

together we watched a newswoman interview old Sheriff Tuffy of West Grove.

"Warren Baily claims one of his competitors stripped his orange groves. Do you have any evidence?"

"Nope," Sheriff Tuffy replied, puffing out his plump cheeks and staring directly into the camera.

"What?" the reporter asked, looking surprised. "No tire tracks, footprints, witnesses?"

"Nope," Tuffy responded, teetering toe to heel, heel to toe in his cowboy boots, his hands stuffed in his pockets as he still stared into the camera.

"You're saying that Baily's Better Oranges lost a whole crop of nearly ripe fruit, two hundred trees stripped bare, and no one even left a clue?"

"Yep," said the sheriff, scowling at the camera.

"Uh, thank you, Sheriff," said the flustered reporter. "Back to you, Bob." I turned off the television and stroked Clark, who was acting strangely quiet since arriving back home.

"Citrus? Well, Clark, we better drive out to Baily's groves with Worl in the morning."

"Meow, meeow," Clark replied. I took it to mean he agreed.

I must have dozed off, because the next thing I knew I woke up to see the little gray alien holding Clark and both of them staring down at me while sunshine filtered through the front window.

"Shockie, you wake now. Help find the ba k'rah," Worl said. Clark wiggled free and jumped down.

I rubbed the sleep from my eyes as memories of yesterday crashed over my mind, waves of a receding dream. Clark poked his furry head under my free hand and I absently patted him.

"Okay, I'm getting up, but before we leave the house we need to disguise you, Worl. Even *I* can't run around the Valley with a little gray spaceman."

"Meow, meeoow," Clark chimed in, then darted off into the bedroom. I followed quite willingly, though my head felt woozy and my mouth full of cotton. I detoured into the bath to freshen up. When I came back out, Clark was sitting upon a big box wrapped in bright birthday paper. He waved his tail and stretched.

"Get down, Clark. You'll ruin the bow on Sue's present," I scolded, scooping the cat off his perch. He kneaded my arm with his claws, not enough to hurt, but enough to halt my action. "Oh, yes!" I cried, as Worl stepped inside the room. "The boots and jeans I bought my niece might work—Sue is just about Worl's size." I hugged Clark tightly. He squirmed in protest, so I let him go as I whispered, "Clark, you're the smartest cat on Earth!"

I changed my own clothes, then helped Worl into Sue's birthday blue jeans and tooled leather boots. Not too bad. I found an old blue workshirt of mine and Worl put it on. We rolled the sleeves up and it still looked big, but that's the fashion for kids, anyway. Worl's large head fit fine in a worn Stetson hat I'd stashed in a corner of my closet. I added a pair of sunglasses and stepped back to view the alien.

"You'll do from a distance. We just can't let anyone see you up close. Okay?"

"Okay, Shockie," Worl replied, playing with his hat, tipping the brim up and down in front of the dresser mirror. Clark brushed against my legs and me-owed at us. "Yes, Clairk Kendt," Worl added. "We go find the ba k'rah now."

Worl, Clark, and I piled into my car. I showed Worl how to fasten his seatbelt and he held Clark on his lap. Usually Clark preferred to cringe on the floorboard while riding, but this morning he acted eager to sit up and look out. Worl had insisted on wearing his bulky belt under the shirt I loaned him. Now he shifted Clark off his lap so he could reach a cone-shaped metallic object and pull it out from his belt. He pressed the top of the cone and it started bleeping softly, glowing red to pink.

"What's that?" I asked, starting the car.

"Finder. Hit will tell us where to seek the ba k'rah." Clark pressed his nose against the finder, then jerked back as if burned. "Naughty, Clairk Kendt," Worl said, shaking his head, looking rather comical in his

Stetson and sunglasses. The alien spun his cone in a circle, pointing north, and cried, "That-a-way, Shockie!" The finder throbbed lavender. I hit the gas pedal as we turned north on the highway. We sped past citrus groves and mesquite scrub and I noticed the finder deepen in color, the lavender now closer to purple. Suddenly it started screaming.

I wanted to cover my ears but kept my hands on the wheel while I pulled the car off to the side of the road. Worl bounced excitedly, his free hand dancing over the seatbelt until it clicked open to release him.

"Turn that finder off," I cried. He obeyed. I think even Clark looked relieved. I hope I never hear such a noise again.

"There, there!" Worl squealed, pointing to an orange grove on our right. "The ba k'rah! Flying! See?"

A giant bird, shimmering black except for a blood-red curved beak, hovered above the trees. "Look at that wingspan," I gasped, wondering if I'd been transported into some Japanese horror movie. "It's a monster." I gazed down at little Worl. "How can you capture that huge creature?"

He patted his belt. "My tanglefield. I hef hit inside here." He tugged one large bump and off came a fabric cylinder. "Jest let me out of you ship and I use hit."

I leaned over and opened his door for him. He hopped out, Clark following. I got out my side and rushed around to them.

Worl muttered something, grasped the tanglefield in his right hand, rotating his entire arm until I heard a bzz-bzz-bzzing. A pale lavender energy field ballooned up before collapsing back into its source. "Big trouble, big trouble!" Worl yelled, banging the tanglefield against his other hand. Another try brought the same result. With dire alien mutterings, Worl removed a tool pack from his belt and set to work on the malfunctioning tanglefield. Just then Clark began meowing loudly and in the distance I noticed the gleam of an approaching vehicle. An engine roared closer as a patrol car zoomed into sight.

"Quick, Worl, get into the car. Stay down and don't

speak. "We'll try to pass you off as my nephew." The little alien, still fumbling with his equipment, climbed back into my car and bent intently over his task. Clark stayed by me, weaving between my legs as if he, too, felt nervous.

The patrol car slowed and my heart gave a sudden leap as I recognized Mike Harris, the blond deputy. "Howdy, Miss Carlson." He climbed out and scanned the roadside. My gaze followed his. With mixed emotions I noticed the bird was no longer in sight. "Trouble, ma'am?"

"No," I said, shaking my head. "Mike, please call me Jackie."

He grinned. I smiled back but he soon turned toward my car. "What're you doing out here, Jackie?"

"Just taking my nephew for a drive. He's, ah, visiting from Houston." Mike walked over to my car and I managed to squeeze between him and the window. "Er, Willy is real shy. Maybe you'd better talk to him another time—after he's been around here longer. Okay, Mike?"

Mike stared at me funny, but at least he moved away from my car and back toward his own vehicle. I walked along with him. He stopped and turned to me, his blue gaze raking over me, as if sizing up a robbery suspect. I could feel a blush burning my cheeks, but returned his stare the best I could.

"Jackie, I've got to talk to somebody and you ought to understand. I mean, writing science fiction stories and all . . ." He hushed and gazed helplessly at me.

"What is it, Mike?" I asked, aware of Clark standing guard duty beside my car and hoping Worl would stay quiet.

"I saw something last night. I can't say anything—I might lose my job. Nobody would believe me. They'd think I was drunk. But after I met you last night, I started thinking that maybe you'd understand. You'd believe me if I told you I saw a flying saucer, wouldn't you?" he pleaded.

I blinked up at him in surprise. "Why didn't you tell me this last night?"

He shrugged his broad shoulders. "Do you believe I saw a UFO, Jackie?"

"Yes. Of course." Clark meowed and I hastily added, "Mike, I've got things to do. Can we talk later?" Just then Worl let out a yelp, Clark growled and a huge dark shadow glided over us. I glanced up to see the ba k'rah swoop above the orchard, orange-laden branches clutched in gigantic talons.

Worl scrambled out of the car, Mike drew his gun and took aim at the ba k'rah as Clark leaped up into the air, latching claws against Mike's upraised arm just as he fired. The shot went wild, hitting a tree trunk to the right of us with a sharp crack.

Mike swore. Clark landed with a thunk, meowing as if struck, and Worl hopped around chattering in his alien language until his hat bounced off. Mike paled, his mouth dropping open, as he gaped at Worl's gray alien head. Then the tall, strong deputy sheriff of West Grove swayed back to lean against his patrol car in a swoon.

"Worl, put your hat on!" I ordered, half-crazed myself. "The bird's getting away. Now what do we do?"

Clark jumped into my car and meowed at Worl. Worl climbed through the open door beside my cat, saying, "Shockie, Clairk Kendt is right, we must go in you ship after the ba k'rah."

"What about the deputy?" I asked, certain Mike was in shock.

The cat meowed and Worl said, "Clark thinks your lawman es hokay, but we hef to go before the ba k'rah makes a nest."

"Nest?" I repeated, wondering where in this part of Texas could a bird that big build a nest. "But I can't leave Mike like this."

"Go now!" Worl pressed his lipless mouth shut so tightly it disappeared. Then he added, "A ba k'rah alone desires to procreate. No need for mate. Hurry!"

I drove half a mile before I saw Mike's patrol car in the rearview mirror, lights flashing. Well, at least he wasn't still frozen in shock, I decided, ignoring him as we swerved off the highway onto a dirt track leading to a water tower. It stood, graffitti-scrawled silver, looking like a flying saucer perched upon spindly tall legs. Settled magnificently atop the tower loomed the giant, shiny black bird.

I braked the car and we spilled out, Mike's patrol car skidding to a halt beside us. "You *didn't* call for reinforcements, I hope?" I snapped at him.

"Heck, no," he drawled. "What would I say? Come help me chase down a girl, her cat, and a spaceman dressed like Roy Rogers?"

"All I want is to get that bird back for Worl," I said, trying to calm my breathing. "It escaped his ship and he must recapture it."

"Shess!" Worl cried, bobbing his large gray head. "Hef to capture the ba k'rah before eggs hatch. Then *big* trouble. Lots of baby ba k'rah eat all the citrus."

"Eggs?" I gazed up at the huge flapping monster. "Why, they'd wipe out all the groves in the Rio Grande Valley."

"On Earth," Worl added seriously. "What to do? My tanglefield not extend high enough. Not working right. Big trouble!"

Clark meowed, brushed against my legs, then darted off toward the tower. "Claairk Kendt," Worl called, trotting after the cat. He stooped, resting one thin hand on Clark's back, murmured a few moments, then trotted back to us.

"What, does the spaceman talk to your cat?" Mike asked me.

"I guess so. At first I thought it was silly, but look!" I pointed to the tower as my cat scaled it, climbing steadily higher, using the rungs and bracings to work his way around to the rear of the tower as he climbed. Just as if he'd been instructed. "Clark must be planning something," I said.

"Cats don't plan things," Mike scoffed.

"Not usually," I retorted. "But aliens don't usually fall out of trees on me and UFOs don't usually land in my yard, either."

"What's the cat going to do?" Mike asked Worl, a

bit of awe in his deep voice as he spoke to the little alien.

"Try to get the ba k'rah down low, so I can snare it in my tanglefield. Must fly almost to ground. Clairk can do hit."

Mike wiped his forehead. "Nobody's ever gonna believe this."

"So we won't tell. Right?" I wouldn't mind sharing a secret with the handsome deputy. Besides, this could write up into a great plot for my next novel.

My heart in my throat, I watched Clark climb the rungs leading to the top of the tower. If he fell. . . .

Clark wailed a harsh meow, giant wings flapped like thunder, then the bird dived off the tower as if devils were chasing it. There on the bird's back with claws dug into glistening black feathers, perched Clark Kent, supercat himself, driving the ba k'rah within range of Worl's damaged field. Worl aimed just as Clark leaped free, letting the field capture the huge bird. Clark landed on his feet in a pile of weeds and grass with a soft thump.

I ran to my cat, scooping him into my arms, cooing into his ear and stroking his silky fur. "You did it," I whispered, filled with awed pride.

"What a cat!" rumbled Mike, rushing to my side. "Who'd have thought it?"

Worl squirted a spray into the bird's face and it staggered forward, then fell still. "Thiss mek ba k'rah sleep."

"How will we get the ba k'rah back to my place?" I asked in dismay, realizing we couldn't take it anywhere in my small hatchback.

"Hit stay here. I stay also. The ship come here after dark to take us, the nest, and eggs. Clairk Kendt says many eggs are up there." Worl gestured at the top of the water tower. "Will sell eggs. Make lots of credit. No trouble."

Clark purred, adjusting his head so I could scratch his ears. "Do you really communicate with Clark?" I asked Worl.

"Shess." Worl took off the dark sunglasses to expose his big luminious eyes. "I want to take Clairk home with me to Pra."

Mike just stood staring at Worl, studying the newly revealed eyes. Clark stopped purring. I felt very sad, abandoned, and thought about how empty my house would be without him. "It's—it's Clark's decision," I stammered.

Worl took Clark from my arms and spoke to him in clicks, hisses, and what sounded like meows instead of words. Clark meowed several times as if responding. I wished I understood cat language.

"Clairk Kendt will stay with you, Shockie," Worl replied, handing my cat back to me. Clark pressed his nose against my chin and suddenly I began to laugh to hide a rush of tears filling my eyes. "Maybe I should change my name to Lois Lane?" I giggled into Clark's fur.

Mike leaned his head back and roared with laughter. We laughed until we both had tears spilling down our cheeks and the alien shook his head in wonderment at us.

"You must go," he said. "If the ship comes, my commander will see I hef break many rules. Big trouble. Go home now, and make Worl happy, too."

I kissed my little alien friend good-bye and Clark let Worl pet him. Then Clark and I got into my car, Mike got in his and we drove home caravan style.

That night, Mike sat on my back porch next to me and Clark curled up on my lap. Together we watched the sky. Spinning bands of colored light hovered in the distance above the water tower, then zoomed off into space, disappearing among the stars, leaving us with memories and a secret to share forevermore.

"Meow meow," said Clark.

"You're right, we *will* miss Worl," I replied in agreement.

Clark closed his dark-ringed green-gold eyes and purred with throaty contentment.

"What a super cat!" Mike said with pride. He slid an arm around my shoulder, pulling me close, as I kept stroking my cat and felt like purring myself.

NOBLE WARRIOR

by Andre Norton

Emmy squinted at the stitch she had just put in the handkerchief. Ivy had curtained almost half of the window, to leave the room in greenish gloom. Too long, she would have to pick it out. On such a grayish day she wanted a candle. Only even to think of that must be a sin. Miss Wyker was very quick to sniff out sins. Emmy squinted harder. It was awfully easy to sin when one was around Miss Wyker.

Not for the first or not even the hundredth time she puzzled as to why Great-Aunt Amelie had asked Miss Wyker to Hob's Green. Who could be ill without feeling worse to see about that long narrow face with the closed buttonhole of a mouth, and mean little eyes on either side of a long, long nose. Elephant nose! Emmy's hands were still while she thought of elephants, big as Jasper's cottage. Father said that they had great seats large enough to hold several men strapped on their backs and one rode them so to go tiger hunting.

She rubbed her hand across her aching forehead as she thought of father. If he were here, he would send old Wyker packing.

Emmy ran a tongue tip over her lips. She was thirsty—but to leave her task to even get a drink of water might get her into trouble. She gave an impatient jerk and her thread broke. Before she could worry about that, sounds from the graveled drive which ran beyond the window brought her up on her knees to look out. Hardly anyone now used the front entrance drive. This was the trap from the inn, with Jeb. Beside him sat a stranger, a small man with a bushy brown beard.

The trap came to a halt and the small man climbed down from the seat. Jeb handed down a big basket to the man who gave him a short nod before disappearing under the overhang of the doorway. Emmy dropped her sewing on the window seat to run across the room as the knocker sounded. She was cautious about edging open the door of the sitting room to give herself just a crack to see through.

The knocker sounded three times before Jennie the housemaid hurried by, patting down her cap ribbons and looking all a-twitter. It had been so long since anyone had been so bold as to use the knocker. Nobody but Dr. Riggs ever came that way any more, and he only in the morning.

Emmy heard a deep voice, but she could not quite make out the words. Then, as quick as if it were meant as an answer, there sounded a strange cry. Emmy jumped, the door opened a good bit wider than was wise.

At least she could see Jennie show the visitor to the library where Dr. Riggs was always escorted by Miss Wyker to have a ceremonial glass of claret when his visit to his patient was over. The stranger had taken the covered basket with him.

Jennie went hurrying up the stairs to get Miss Wyker. To speed her along sounded another of those wailing cries.

Emmy pulled the door nearer shut, but her curiosity was fully aroused. Who had come visiting and why? And whatever could be in that basket?

She heard the determined tread of Miss Wyker and saw a stiff back covered with the ugliest of gray dresses also disappear into the parlor. Should she try to cross the hall in hope of seeing more of the visitor? She was so tired of one day being like another—all as gray as Miss Wyker's dress—that this was all very exciting. Before she had quite made up her mind, Jennie came in a hurry, probably called by the bell. She stood just within the library door, then backed out to head for the morning room where Emmy had been isolated for numberless dull hours of the day since Great-Aunt had taken ill.

"You—Miss Emmy," Jennie was breathless as she usually was when Miss Wyker gave orders. "They want to see you—right now— over there—" she jerked a thumb toward the library.

Emmy was across the hall and into the room before Jennie had disappeared back down the hall. As she came in, there sounded once more that startling cry. It had come from the big covered basket which was rocking a little back and forth where it stood on the floor.

"This is the child—" Miss Wyker's sharp voice was plainly disapproving.

The brown-bearded man looked down at Emmy. A big grin split that beard in the middle.

"So—you be th' Cap'n's little maid, be you? Must have grown a sight since he was last a-seein' you. Tol' it as how you was a mite younger."

The Cap'n—that was father. For a moment, forgetting Miss Wyker, Emmy burst out with a question of her own:

"Where is he? Please, did his ship come in? Truly?" There was so much Emmy wanted to say that the words stuck in her throat unable to push out clearly.

"Emmiline—this is Mr. Salbridge—manners, *IF* you please!"

Emmy swallowed and made a bob of a curtsey, one eye on Miss Wyker, knowing that she would be in for a scold when this visitor left.

"Very pleased to make your acquaintance, sir," she parroted the phrase which had been drilled into her.

Mr. Salbridge bowed in return. "Well, now, Miss Emmy, seems like we should be no strangers. Ain't I heard th' Cap'n talk of you by th' hour? Your servant, Miss Emmy. It does a man good to see as how you is doin' well, all shipshape an' tight along the portholes as it were. You probably ain't heard o' me—but I has been a-sailin' with th' Cap'n for a right many years now—would be there on board th' *Majestic* yet, only I had me a bit o' real luck, which gave me a snug purse, an' was minded to come home along of that there windfall. They's none o' us as young as we once was an' me, I got someone as has been a-waiting for me to come home a longish time.

"Th' Cap'n, he gave me a right hearty good-bye but not afore he asked somethin' o' me an' I'm right proud that he did that. I was to see his little maid an' bring 'er somethin' as was give to him by a princess as heard he had a little daughter to home. He was mighty helpful to her paw an' she was grateful to him in return, give him somethin' th' which nobody here at home has seen—somethin' as has lived in a palace right a'long of her. Look you here, Miss Emmy, what do you think o' this?"

He knelt awkwardly on one knee to open the basket. For a minute nothing happened. Then there jumped out of that carrier the oddest animal Emmy had ever seen. It looked like a cat, only it was not gray striped. Rather its face, legs, and the lower part of its slender back were of a brown as dark as Mr. Salbridge's beard, while the rest of it was near the color of the thick cream Mrs. Goode skimmed off the milk. And its eyes—its eyes were a bright blue!

It stood by the side of the basket, its head slowly moving as it stared at each of them in turn, Mr. Salbridge, Miss Wyker, who had drawn back a pace or two and was frowning darkly, and the longest at Emmy.

"Miss Emmy, this here's Thragun Neklop, that there means Noble Warrior. He's straight out o' th' king's own palace. They thinks a mighty lot o' those like him thereabouts. No one as is common gets to have these here cats a-livin' in their houses. The Cap'n now, he was favored when they said this one might go to be with his little missy back in his own country. Yes, this here is a very special cat—"

The cat opened its mouth and gave a short, sharp cry which was certainly not like the meow which Emmy expected. Then its head turned so that it looked directly and unblinkingly at Miss Wyker and it hissed, its ears flattening a little. Miss Wyker's frown now knotted all her long face together.

Emmy squatted down so that she was nearly face to face with the furred newcomer.

"Thragun Neklop." She tried to say the strange words carefully. The cat turned its head again, to stare boldly at her. There was no hissing this time.

"That there is a power name, Miss Emmy. His paw was guard o' th' king. Them as lives there, they do not take kindly to dogs—that's their religion like. But cats, them they train to be their guards. An' mighty good they be at that, too, if all th' stories they tell is true."

The cat arose and came to Emmy. She put out her hand, not quite daring to lay a finger on that sleek brown head. The cat sniffed her fingers and then bumped his head against her hand.

"Well, now, that do beat all. Never saw him do that 'ceptin' to the princess when she said good-bye," commented Mr. Salbridge. "Maybe he thinks as how you're the princess now. Good that'll be. Now—servant, Mistress, servant, Miss Emmy." He made a short bow. "I needs must be gitting along. Have to catch th' York stage."

"Oh," Emmy was on her feet, "please—thank you! And father—is he coming home, too?"

Mr. Salbridge shook his head. "He's got the voyage to make and the *Majestic* warn't due to raise anchor for maybe two months when I left him. He'll be coming through, jus' as soon as he can—"

"It's such a long time to wait—" Emmy said. "But, oh, please, Mr. Salbridge, I do thank you for bringing Thragun Neklop."

"My pleasure, Miss—" The rest of what he might have said was drowned out by another of those strange wails.

Emmy hurried behind Mr. Salbridge who strode for the door. Miss Wyker made no attempt to see him away, as she did the doctor when he came calling. Emmy followed with more eager questions which he answered cheerfully. Yes, the Cap'n was feeling well and doin' well for hisself, too. An' he would be home again before long. He was jus' glad to be of service.

While he climbed back into the rig and drove off down the driveway, Emmy waved vigorously. She was startled by a very harsh piercing cry and she ran back to the library.

Miss Wyker, poker in hand, that deep scowl still on her face, was advancing on Thragun. The cat stood his ground; now that scream dropped to a warning growl. His long slender tail was puffed out to twice its usual size and his ears were flattened to his skull.

"Dirty animal!" Miss Wyker's voice was as angry as Thragun's war cry. "Get in there, you filthy beast!" She poked with the iron and Thragun went into a crouch.

"Thragun!" Emmy ran forward, standing between the war ready cat and Miss Wyker.

"Get that foul thing into the basket—at once, do you hear me?"

Emmy had witnessed Miss Wyker's anger a good many times, but never had she made such a scene as this before.

"Don't hit him!" Emmy caught at the cat. A paw flashed out and drew a red stripe across her hand. But in spite of that the little girl grabbed him up and put him into the basket. "He wasn't doing any harm!" she cried out, braver as she spoke up for Thragun than she had ever been for herself.

In answer Miss Wyker used the poker to flip the lid down on the basket.

"Fasten it!" she ordered, already heading toward the bell pull on the wall.

Emmy's hands shook. She had always been afraid of loud angry voices, and lately she jumped at every sound, especially when she was never sure when Miss Wyker was going to come up behind her with some punishment already in mind. She had done so many things wrong ever since Great-Aunt Amelie had taken ill. Emmy never even saw her any more. Nobody seemed to see much of Lady Ashely now. Miss Wyker was always there at the bedroom door, to take the trays cook sent up with the special beef jelly or a new egg done to the way Great-Aunt Amelie always liked them.

Even at night Jennie was not called to sit with her. Miss Wyker had a trundle bed moved into the room and spent her own night hours there. When Jennie or Meggy came to clean, she was always standing there watching them. Meggy said, " 'as 'ow they was goin' to 'urt th' old lady—as iffen anybody ever would!"

"Yes, m'm?" Jennie now stood in the half open door.

"Take this beast out to the stable at once! I do not want to see it about again!"

"No!" Courage which she not been able to summon for herself brought words to Emmy. "Father sent him—to me. He's Thragun Neklop an' a prince! The man said so!" She caught the handle of the big basket in both hands and held it as tightly as she could.

Miss Wyker, her long face very red, laid the poker across the seat of the nearest chair before taking long strides to stand directly over Emmy. Her hand swept up, to come down across Emmy's cheek, the blow so sudden and stinging that the child staggered backward, involuntarily losing her hold on the basket. Miss Wyker had scolded her many times since the first hour when she had arrived and doffed her helmet of a bonnet to take over rulership of Hob's Green. But until this moment she had never touched Emmy.

"Take that beast out to the stable," Miss Wyker repeated, "and be quick about it. Animals are filthy, they have no place in a well-run household. And you," she rounded on Emmy who was standing staring at her, one hand pressed to her cheek where those long fingers had left visible marking, "go to your room instantly, you impudent girl! You are wholly selfish, unbiddable, lazy and a handful! Poor Lady Ashely may have been hastened to her bed of illness by your thoughtless impudence! Poor lady, she has had a great deal to burden her these past years but there will be a good many changes made shortly—and your conduct, Miss, will not be the least of those! Go!"

So sharp and loud was that command that it seemed to sweep Emmy out of the room. She hesitated for one moment on the foot of the stairs to watch Jennie's apron strings and the tail of her skirt vanish toward the end of the hall. The maid had taken the basket. What was going to happen to Thragun Neklop? Emmy's tears spilled over the fingers which still nursed the cheek which was beginning to ache as she went up the stairs slowly, one reluctant foot at a time.

There was a strong smell of horses, but there were other scents which were new. Thragun stretched himself belly down in the basket to look through a spread in the wicker weave which had served him for some time now as a window on a very strange and ever-changing world. He saw an expanse of stone paved yard and there was a flutter of pigeons about a trough out of which water was being slopped by a young man whose shirt sleeves were rolled clear to the shoulder. Thragun sniffed—water—never before had he been kept shut up to receive food and water only at the pleasure of another. However, if this must be so for some reason he had not yet discovered, then let those who were to minister to him, as was correct, be brought to attention of their duty.

He voiced a call-cry which in his proper home would have brought at least two maids and perhaps a serving slave of the first rank to answer and make proper apologetic submission, letting him out of this strange litter and treating him as Thragun Neklop should be. Was he not second senior of the Princess Suphorn's own household?

The young man turned his head toward the basket. However, he made no attempt to come and act in the proper fashion. This time Thragun gave a truly angry cry to inform this odd looking servant that his superior wanted full attention to his desires. The young man had filled two buckets with water which sloshed back and forth, wetting the yard stones, as he came. Thragun waited, but the slave made no attempt to approach. Instead, inside this place smelling of horses, he was starting to pass Thragun's cage when there was a voice from the general gloom behind.

"Asa, you lunkhead, you messin' with th' Knight agin?" The voice was drowned out then by the shrill squeal of an aroused stallion. Then there were whinneys and the sound of horses moving restlessly.

Asa moved out of the cat's sight even though Thragun

turned in the basket and tried to see through another small opening in the wicker. That was too narrow, even though he had been working on it with explorative claws for several days.

He heard two voices making odd noises, some of which he recognized. So did the grooms soothe and tend their charges in the royal stable. Apparently even in this strange land horses were properly cared for. If that much was known, why were cats not properly attended?

Heavy footsteps came toward the basket. Thragun waited. There was more than just hunger and thirst to mark the change in his life now—there was a strange unpleasant feeling. The hair along his spine and his tail lifted a little, his ears flattened.

He was Thragun Neklop—Noble Warrior, acknowledged guardian of a princess. It had been his duty and his pleasure to patrol palace gardens at night's coming, to make sure that nothing dark or threatening dared venture there. Had he not in his first year killed one of the serpent ones who had been about to set fang in the princess' hand when she had reached around the rocks to recover her bracelet? Perhaps he had not sprung on a thief to rip open his throat as had Thai Shan, the mightiest of them all, trusted warrior for the king. But he knew what must be—

"So this 'ere's th' beastie? That there Wyker's got a wicked tongue an' a worse eye, that one! Jennie says that this was brot 'ere special—for Miss Emmy—present from 'er paw. So do we do what that long-nosed witch wants, then what do we say when th' Cap'n comes home an' says where is what 'e sent? An' who, I'm askin', made 'er th' Lady 'ere? M' wage is paid by th' Lady Ashely as 'as been since I was six an' came a-helpin' for m' paw. I takes 'er Ladyship's orders, an' that's th' tight an' right o' it!"

"She's got 'er a thing 'bout cats. Th' moggy to th' kitchen disappeared. It showed claw to that one first time it saw 'er when she came down givin' orders right an' left to Cook 'erself. Then come two days past and moggy was gone. Saw 'er a-talkin' to Rog out in th' garden—'im 'as no feeling for beasties. But he 'ad 'im a sixpence down to the Arms that week. An' sixpences don't just grow in that there garden 'e's supposed to be a-planting of.''

"So—''

There was a moment of quiet. Thragun's eyes were hardly more than slits, and with his ears so flat he looked almost like one of the big carved stone garden snakes on which he used to sun himself in the old days when all was well with his world.

Something deep in him stirred. Once before he had felt its like and that was when he was shedding the last of his kitten fur to take on the browning of his mask, tail, and four feet. His mother had gathered up her family just at twilight one night—there were the three of them, Rannar, his brother, and Su Li, his sister. They had followed their mother into a far part of the largest garden. There, trees and vines and full formed shrubs had grown so closely together there they had formed a wall and such a one as only the most supple of cats could get through. There was something in the heart of that miniature jungle—a gray stone place fashioned as if two of the Naga Serpents had faced one another before a wall, with another piece of wall above which they supported on their heads. They were very old; there was the green of small growth on their weathered scales.

Mother had seated herself before them, her kittens a little behind her. Then she had called. The sound she made was the sort to stiffen one's back fur, made claws ache to be unsheathed. Something appeared between the serpents, under the roof they supported. Mother had sat in silence. Only they were not alone, cat and kittens. Something had surveyed them with cold eyes, and colder thoughts—yet they remained very still and did not run even though they all smelled the fear which was a part of this meeting.

That which had come, and which they had never seen clearly, went. With mother, the kittens scrambled into the freedom of the real garden again. However, from that moment Thragun knew the stench of fear, and that wrongness which is a part of evil to be ever after sensed by those who had met it. Also, he had learned the warning which came before battle to those born to be fighters and protectors.

These two who stood over his basket now did not radiate that smell. But that female in the house did. Thragun knew that it was of her that they spoke now. He had come to this place because his princess had asked him to do so. She had explained to him that there was a great debt lying on her because the man from the far country had saved her father. She had learned that this man had a daughter, and now she wished Thragun to be to that daughter even as he was to her, a noble warrior to be ever her shield and her defense. Knowing that all debts must be paid, Thragun had come, though there were times when he wished only to sit and wail his loneliness to the world.

The man who had taken him by the princess' orders had always sought him out, if he was near, when those times came upon Thragun. He had talked to him, stroked him, spoken of his daughter and the old house where she lived with a kinswoman, waiting for the day when the man's duty would be fully done and he might return himself to be with them. And Thragun understood—to the man, his daughter was a treasure precious above anything in the king's palace.

Now what he felt was that need to be alert before danger, and behind it there was the faint, bitter smell of evil, sly and cunning evil, which could and did slip through the world like one of the serpents-which-were-not-Nagas. He was a warrior and this was the enemy's country through which he must go as silently as wind, as aware as that which hungers greatly. Now he must seem to be as one who had no daggers on the feet, teeth waiting in his jaws. With his mouth he shaped a cry such as a lost kitten might give.

"Like as th' beastie's hungry, Ralf—"

"No one's tellin' me wot is an' 'tisn't right!"

There was a sudden movement and the basket lid swung up. Thragun sat up, his tail top curled properly over his front toes, his unblinking blue eyes regarding the two of them.

The man beside Asa was short and thin and smelled strongly of horse sweat. With his black hair and dark skin he looked almost like one of the stable slaves back in the land where things were done properly. There was none of the evil odor clinging to him, nor to the boy either.

There was a long drawn noise from the man which was not a word, but plainly an exclamation of surprises. He squatted down on his heels, his face not far above Thragun's own.

"Blue eyes," that was the boy. " 'E don't look like any moggy as I ever saw—"

"Sssssisss—" The man held out his hand and slowly, as if he were dealing with one of his horse charges. "You sure be a different one."

Thragun sniffed at the knuckles of the hand offered him. There were smells in plenty, but none were cold or threatening. He ventured a small sound deep in his throat.

"You be a grand one, ben't you! Asa, get yourself over an' speak up to Missus Cobb. She's already got a hankerin' for moggys an' she'll give you somethin' for this fine fellow."

The boy disappeared. Thragun decided to take a chance. Moving warily, with an eye continually on the man, he jumped out of the basket, still facing the small man.

"Yis—" that almost was a hiss again. "You ain't no common moggy." His eyebrows drew together in a frown. "I thinks as 'ow th' Cap'n, he mustta thought as 'ow you was right for Miss Emmy—she likin' beasties so well. An' th' Cap'n sure ain't goin' to take it calm if you go a-missin'—

Standing up, the man rubbed his bristly chin.

"Trouble is, that ole she-devil up to th' house, she's doin' all th' talkin' these days. We don't git to see our Lady a-tall—jus' tell us, they do—that fine gentlemun o' a doctor, an' Mr. Crisp, th' agent—that our lady can't be bothered by anythin' now she is so bad took.

An' Miss Emmy; she ain't got no chance t' say nothin'. Th' Cap'n so far away an' nobody knows when he's coming back agin. It ain't got a good smell 'bout all this, that it ain't. So," he leaned back against the wall of a stall, a proud horse head raised over his shoulder to regard Thragun also.

"Soo—" the man repeated, one hand raised to scratch between the large bright eyes of the horse, "we 'as us a thin' as needs thinkin' on. Now was you," Thragun congratulated himself that he had indeed found a very sensible man here, "to git otta that there basket an' disappear—'ow are you goin' to be found—with these 'ere stables as full of holes and 'idey places as a bit o' cheese. An' out there—" he waved one hand toward the open door, "there's a garden an' beyond that, woods—Our lady, she don't allow no huntin' an' them two what wants to answer fur her—they ain't changed that—yet. So supposin', Rog, 'e comes 'long for t' see t' you an' he finds that there basket busted open an' you gone—might be 'e'd jus' put somethin' in his pocket and say as 'ow 'e did as 'e was told—"

"Now," the man raised his voice and caught up a broom. He aimed a blow at Thragun—well off target and yelled, "Git you out, you many critter, we don't want th' likes of you a hangin' 'round, no ways we don't."

Thragun leaped effortlessly to the top of a stall partition, but he made no effort to go farther for a moment. Then he walked leisurely along that narrow path to a place from which he could jump again, this time to a cross bean. At the same moment Asa returned, a small bundle in his hand.

"Ralf, what you be about—"

The man rounded on him. "Me? I 'as been a-chasin' a beast what 'as no place 'ere. An' don't you forget that, lad."

Asa laughed, then darted into the stall where Thragun had made himself comfortable. Flipping open the hand-kerchief, Asa turned out a chunk of grayish meat, still dripping from the boiling pan, and a wedge of cheese. He hacked the meat into several large chunks with a knife he took from his pocket and crumbled the cheese, leaving the bounty spread out on the napkin well within reach of Thragun. The cat was already licking the meat inquiringly when Asa returned with a cracked cup in which there was water.

"Couldn' get milk," he said as he set the cup down. "Missus Cobb, she's mad as a cow wot's lost 'er calf. Old Pickle-Face is a-giving' orders agin. No tea for Miss Emmy 'cause she's been a-askin' for th' cat. When Pickle-Face tol' her that 'e was gone for good, she stiffed up an' hit the old besom, then said as 'ow her paw would 'ave th' law on Pickle-Face for gettin' rid o' th' cat. She would not ask pardon, so she's not to 'ave no vittles 'cept dry bread and water 'til she gits down on her two knees an' asks for it."

"I'll be a-thinkin' that little Miss is na goin' to 'ave so 'ard of it," Ralf said. Thragun snarled. He had somehow got another whiff of that evil smell. Though the words these two stable slaves used to each other were totally foreign, he could pick out thoughts like little flashes of pictures. Not all the temple and palace four-footed guards could do that. But to Thragun it had become increasingly easy over the years.

Asa kicked at a handful of bedding straw and reached for the broom.

"Meggy, she says as 'ow she 'as heard *'im* two nights now—"

Ralf stopped, his hand on the latch of the stall, but not yet opening it. His face was suddenly blank. There was a long moment of silence before he spoke. Thragun raised his head from tearing at a lump of meat. Back in the dusky stall his eyes shone, not blue, but faintly reddish.

"Missus Cobb, she put out a milk bowl last night," Asa continued, his eyes on the floor he was mechanically sweeping.

"Sooo—" Ralf swung the latch of the stall up. "She's one as can sometimes see moren' most. M' granny was like that."

"There's them what says as *'E* ain't 'ere nor never was."

"Look to th' name o' this place, boy. 'Twas *'issen*

they say a-fore any folks came 'ere. They also say as 'ow *'E* brings luck or fetches it away. Lord Jeffery, 'im as wos master 'ere in m' granny's time, 'e got on th' wrong side o' *'im* an' never took no good of life after that. Died young o' a broken neck when 'is mare stepped in a rabbit 'ole. But 'is lady, she was from right believin' folks an' they say as how she came down by candlelight an' went to *'is* own stone wi' a plate of sugar cakes an' a cup o' true cream. Begged pardon, she did. After that, all wot 'ad been goin' wrong became right agin."

"That were a long time ago—" said Asa.

"Some things there is, boy, wot'll never change. You get a rightful part o' th' land an' do your duty to it an' them wot knew it afor you, will do right by you. But iffen *'E* was to come, aye, it would be o' a time like'n this."

He led the horse into the stable yard and Asa fell to cleaning out the stall. Thragun swallowed the last of the food. Not that it was what should be served to Thragun Neklop, but these two had done their best. He washed his whiskers and prepared to explore the stable.

There was a good deal to be examined, sniffed, and stored in memory. Asa and Ralf were in and out on various tasks for the comfort of three horses.

It was very late afternoon before a man came in, Asa with him. He was grinning, wiping his hands on his stained and patched breeches. Thragun's lip curled, but he made no noise. This was evil again—though not as cold and deadly as that he had met when he had confronted that black Khon in the house.

The basket in which he had arrived still sat there, but Asa had dealt with it earlier. There was a break in the bamboo frame door leaving jagged ends pointing outward. Thragun was critical of the work. If he *had* done that, he would have made a neater job of it.

"Us came back," Asa was saying, "an' thar' it was. Th' beast—'e made his own way out."

The other young man spat. "Think you'd better 'ave a better story when th' Missus asks."

Asa shrugged. "We ain't been 'ired, me an' Ralf, to

take care o' anythin' 'cept th' 'osses. An' Ralf, 'e ain't really got anythin' to watch 'cept Black Knight. She can't come a-botherin' at us nohow. Why tell 'er? Th' beast's gone, ain't it?"

"An' wot iffen 'e comes back?" demanded the other.

"Then you gits 'im, don't you. Ain't I seen you throw that there sticker o' yourn quicker than Ned Parzon can shoot—take th' 'ead offen a 'en that way?"

"Maybe so." The other kicked the basket, sending it against the wall. "You keep your own mouth shut, do you 'ear?"

"I 'ear, Rog, you a-makin' noise enough to fright m' 'osses." Ralf strode in. "You ain't got no right in 'ere an' you knows it. Now git!"

The younger man scowled and tramped out of the stable. Asa and Ralf stood looking after him.

"That's another who don't 'ave no place 'ere. Were th' Lady 'erself, she'd see that in a flick o' a 'osses tail an' 'ave 'im out on th' road with a flea in 'is ear, she would. Asa," he looked straight at the boy, "I ain't a-likin' wot's goin' on over there—" he nodded toward the house. "*She* an' that lardy doctor 'ave been puttin' 'eads together again. Jennie says as 'ow she was tellin' the doctor something about Miss Emmy being 'ard to manage 'cause she ain't thinkin' straight. They don't know as Jennie was in the little room offen th' hall when they was talkin' together. Little Miss—that ain't no one as would take her part was they tryin' to get 'er shut up or somethin'. The old crow she's always smarmy and soft tongued when any of the Lady's friends come askin'. Oh," he raised his voice into high squeaking note, "Lady Ashely, she's no better, poor dear. I fear we 'ont see her long. Miss Emmy, oh, th' little dear is so sad feelin'. She is too sad for a child. We cannot get her comforted— Now that there I 'eard when Mrs. Bateman came a-calling. Told Mrs. Bateman as how Miss Emmy couldn't go to no picnic 'cause she was so worrit about her aunt. Miss Emmy was up in 'er room were Pickle-Face 'ad sent her to be ashamed of herself because she tried to slip in an' see her aunt that very morning."

"Seems as iffen someone should know—" Asa said.

"Who? Supposin' even Missus Cobb were to get herself over to th' Bateman place an' try to tell them— what 'as she really got to tell? An' Pickle-Face would say as 'ow she is a-lyin'—make it stick, too. There ain't any way as I can see that we can help."

"Tain't right!" exploded Asa.

"Boy, there's a good lot what ain't right in this 'ere world an' not much as can be done to clean it up neither. Come on, we've got to see to that tack."

Thragun's well cultivated guard sense might have been confused by the strange language that these slaves used, but he thought he could fit part of it all together. The little princess to whom *HIS* princess had sent him on his honorable task of protection was under threat from that Khon of full evil. She was now a prisoner somewhere in the house. With a knowledgeable eye he measured the shadows in the stable yard. There was a time of dark fast on its way and dark aided both the evildoer and the guard. His kind, for many lives, had patroled palaces, searched gardens, and knew their own ways of taking care. This was a new place and he knew very little about it. The time was ready not only for him to learn but to be about what was perhaps more important, defending his princess. Thragun's jaws opened upon a soundless snarl and his curved and very sharp claws came momentarily out of the fur screening on his toes.

Emmy huddled behind the curtain, both hands pressed against the small panes of the window as she looked down to the terrace. Rog went clumping by, and she scrunched herself into as small a space as possible. Of course, he was not looking in this direction, and, anyway, he was well below her, but she always felt afraid of Rog. Twice he had come out suddenly from dark places in the garden and stood grinning and laughing at her. Also Miss Wyker liked him. He did errands for her. Emmy had seen him take notes and go out the other way—not passing where anyone could see him unless that one was specially watching. He padded heavy-footed along now and it

was near dark. Maybe he was just going back to the
hut where he lived—a nasty, evil-smelling place. But
the worst of it was those nails hammered into the wall
on which hung little bodies, some furred and some
feathered—birds and a weasel, and—Emmy rubbed
both her wet eyes with her hands.

Her eyes hurt because she had been crying. She
tried to see even the edge of the drive to the stable.
What had happened out there to Thragun Neklop?
Somehow now she thought all a lie, he must be somewhere. She had her own plan, but it might be hours
and hours yet before it would be dark enough for her
to put it to the test. With her tear-sticky hands she
tried again with all her strength to push out one side of
the divided panes of the window. Tendrils of ivy waved
in the breeze back and forth, but there was no wind
enough to make a difference, Emmy thought. This
was an idea she had had for some time and she now
had a very good reason to try it.

A door away down the hall Jennie tapped, her other
hand supporting a tray with a porringer on it. The nutmeg
smell was faint, but she could smell it even though the
lid was on the small silver bowl to keep its contents warm.
Cook had made this special—a smooth, light custard
that she said even a newborn babe could take without
any hurt. Jennie gave a slight start and looked back over
her shoulder. Old houses had many strange noises in
the night time. But this evening—She drew a deep breath.
HIM— That patter sound all the way up the stairs behind her—like to scare her into falling or take her death
from it. She knocked again and with more force.

The door opened so suddenly that she might have
skidded right in had she not caught herself.

"What do you mean? All this clamor when she is
asleep! You stupid, clumsy girl!" Miss Wyker's voice
was like the hiss of a snake and Jennie cringed. Somehow she got the tray and the porringer between them.

"Please, Cook did think as 'ow the poor lady might
find this tasty. She used to be quite fond of it—jus'
good milk, and eggs from the brown 'en as 'as the best
and biggest ever—"

With a snap Miss Wyker had the tray out of her hands and was thrusting before her as if to push Jennie out of the room.

"Cook is impertinent," Miss Wyker scowled, enough, as Jennie said later, to make the flesh fair creep on your bones like. "Lady Ashely's food must be carefully selected to match the diet Dr. Riggs has planned. Get back to the kitchen and don't let me see you above the backstairs again or it will be the worse for you." Jennie had backed well into the hall. Now the door was slammed and she quite clearly heard the sound of a key turning in the lock.

For a moment she just stood there and then she gave a quick turn of the head—facing down the hall. Her own face puckered and she put the knuckles of one hand up to cover her mouth as she turned and ran—ran as far and as fast as she could, to get away from that thin high shriek which seemed somehow to echo in her head more than in her ears.

Him! With *him* loose what could a body expect but trouble? Bad trouble. She'd give notice, that she would! There was no one who was going to make her stay here. Her heavy shoes clattered on the uncarpeted backstairs as she sought the kitchen three stories below.

Emmy got to her feet. She had been down on her knees trying to see through the keyhole. These past weeks she had used every method she could to learn things. How long had it been since she had actually seen Great-Aunt Amelie? Three—maybe four weeks, and then she had only gotten a short peek at her through the door before Miss Wyker had come up and pulled her away, her fingers pinching Emmy sharply to propel the girl toward her bedroom where she had also been locked in. That was another night Emmy might not have had any supper, but Jennie had crept up after dark to bring her some of Cook's sugary rolls and a small plum tart. Emmy had discovered some nights ago that, whether she was being openly punished or not, she was always locked in at night. That was when she first began to explore outside the window. She had awakened from a very queer dream.

Emmy had never remembered any other dream so well. This one was different. It made her go all shivery, and yet not so fearful that she was afraid to try what she had done in her dream. Of course, then there had been someone with her—though she never really saw who it was—just knew that the unseen had watched her with approval and that had made her feel better.

Now she stood in the middle of the room and unfastened the buttons of her dress, shrugging it off, so that its full skirt lay in a circle around her. Next came her two petticoats. Gathering up all these, she threw them in an untidy bundle on the bed. Then, stopping to think, she gathered them up to roll into a thick armload which she shoved under the covers, pulling the pillow around so it just might look like a sleeper spent from crying.

Emmy herself was through crying. She went to the bottom drawer of the bureau and opened it. There was her mother's beautiful shawl which she brought home from India when she had come with Emmy to Great-Aunt Amelie's. There were other things mother brought, too, and Emmy jerked out a package from the very bottom, struggling to pull it open. Then she was looking at what had belonged to her brother she had never seen—to remember. He had died in India, that was why mother brought her here as the bad seasons did make so many die.

For only a moment she hesitated. Mother had kept this suit as one of her treasures. What would she think of Emmy wearing it? No, she would understand! It was important, Emmy did not know how she was sure of that, no one had told her—unless it was the person in her dream whom she had never seen.

She pulled on the trousers, and pushed her chemise into the top of them. They were a little too big and she had to tie them on with a hair ribbon.

So readied, she returned to the window. It was dark enough now, of that she was sure. She climbed on the sill and slipped through, her feet finding the ledge which ran along the wall just below the windows.

Taking the best grip she could on the ivy, Emmy began to edge along that narrow footway.

Thragun slipped like a shadow from one bit of cover to the next. There were lights in some windows and now and then he heard voices. The slaves were gathered in the largest room along the wall. He heard their coarse, rough voices. But he was more intent upon the fact that the walls before him appeared to be covered with a growth of vines. Of course, they were not the thick, properly stemmed ones which provided such excellent highways in the palace and temple gardens. However, he would test just what good footholds they had to offer. There were strange smells in plenty, but he was not to be turned away from his firm purpose now.

Cook stood with both red hands planted firm upon the much scrubbed table, looking across the board at Jennie. Her face was as red as her hands and she made it quite plain just what she was thinking.

"M' lady eatin' only what that puffed pigeon of a doctor tells 'er, is that it? I say it loud and clear, that wry-faced Madam who thinks to cut 'erself a snug place 'ere is goin' to find out that she ain't the mistress. No she ain't!"

"An' just 'ow, Missus, is you goin' to git 'er to listen to you?" Ralf emptied his beer mug and thudded it down on the table.

For a long moment there was no answer. Suddenly Mrs. Cobb straightened up, her weight making her look someone to be taken seriously. She reached out her hand and drew closer a basin of thick brown crockery. Then she turned, without answering the question, and hefted a jug of the same heavy earthenware. From that she poured a stream of milk into the bowl. The milk was so rich and thick one could almost see flakes of butter swimming in it, striving to be free.

The bowl she filled carefully within an inch of the top, then she put down the jug, and, from under the vast sweep of her apron, she brought out a bunch of jingling keys.

Ralf's eyebrows slid up. "Th' keys? 'Ow ever did that Madam let 'em git outta 'er 'ands, now?"

Cook's lips curled but in a sneer not a smile. "Oh, she got our lady's bunch to rattle a little song with, may that which waits at water medder git 'er for that! But m'lady, she saw long ago as 'ow it was not 'andy for me to go runnin' to ask for this store and that when I was a-cookin'. Nor was she ever one as begrudged me what I 'ad to 'ave. So I've had m' own keys these five years now."

"An' what are you goin' to do wi' that?" Ralf pointed to the bowl.

"Ralf Sommers, you ain't as big of a ninny that you 'as to ask that now, are you? This 'ere," she looked around her, "be Hob's Green. An' it didn't get that name for nothin'."

Ralf frowned. "'*IM*? You is goin' to deal with '*im*?"

Mrs. Cobb looked down at the bowl as if for a moment uncertain, and then, her mouth firmed, her chin squared. "I be a-doin' nothin' that ain't been done before under this 'ere roof and on this land!"

She walked past Ralf out of the kitchen and down the passage which led to those very dark descending stairs to the vast network of cellars which no one, even in the daytime, willingly visited or if one must go, it would be hurried, lantern in hand and looking all whichways as one did it.

At the top of the stairs there was another door in the wall, opening into the kitchen garden though no one now used that. Mrs. Cobb placed the bowl carefully on the floor. Selecting a key, she forced it into the doorlock and shoved it open a hand's breadth.

She drew back. The way was dark, so much so that she could hardly see the bowl. She cleared her throat and then she recited, as one who draws every word out of some deep closet of memory:

> "Hob's Hole—Hob's own.
> From th' roasting to th' bone.
> Them as sees, shall not look.
> Them's is blind, they'll be shook.

Sweep it up an' sweep it down—
Hob shall clear it all around.
So mote this be."

Mrs. Cobb turned with surprising speed for such a heavy woman and swept with a whirl of her wide skirts down the passage until she could bang the kitchen door behind her.

Thragun stayed where he was crouched, watching through the slit of the door she had opened. He sniffed delicately. That which was in the bowl attracted him. Squeezing through the narrow door opening, the cat looked up and down the narrow stone paved way. He sniffed in each direction and listened. Now he was inside the house again and no one had seen him. He smelled the contents of the bowl, ventured a lap or two, and then settled down to drink his fill.

He jumped, squalled, and turned all in almost one movement. The painful thud on his haunch was not to be forgiven. Thragun crouched, reading himself for a spring.

Crouching almost as low, and certainly as angrily as he himself was, a gray-brown creature humped right inside the door. Thragun snarled, and then growled. In spite of the heavy gloom of the passage his night sight was clear enough to show him exactly what had so impudently attacked him by driving a pointed foot into his back.

Thragun growled again. His right front paw moved lightning quick to pay for that blow with rakeing claws. But the paw passed through the creature's arm and shoulder. Its body certainly looked thick and real enough but what he struck at might only be a shadow.

He straightening up. Thewada! So this new place had such shadow walkers and mischief makers as he had been warned about since kittenhood—though he had certainly never seen one himself before.

"A-stealin' o' Hob's own bowl, be ye?" The creature straightened up also. It looked like a man but it was very small, hardly taller than Thragun. Its body was fat and round, but the legs and arms were nearly stick thin, and it was covered completely with gray-brown wrappings. Only a wizened face, with ugly squar-ish mouth and small green eyes like pinheads on either side of a long sharp pointed nose (like the beak of some rapacious bird) were uncovered. However, the skin was so dark it might have been part of that tight clothing.

"This be Hob's place!" The words bit at Thragun. "Fergit that, you night walker, and Hob'll see you into a toad, so he will!" He stamped one long thin foot on the floor, followed by the other in an angry dance. Now he pointed his two forefingers at the cat and began to mouth strange words which Thragun could not understand.

Thewada could be mischievous and irritating, Thragun had heard, but for the most part they were lacking in power to do any serious harm. He yawned to show that he was not in the least impressed by the other's show of temper.

"I be Hob!" the dancer screeched. "This be my place, this!" Once more he was stamping hard enough to set his ball body bouncing.

"I am Thragun Neklop—guard of the princess," returned Thragun with quiet dignity. "You are a thewada and you have no place near the princess—"

Hob's face was no longer brown-gray like his clothes, rather it had turned a dusky color, and if he tried to mouth words they were swallowed up by a voice which wanted more to screech.

"The bowl is yours," Thragun continued. "I ask pardon for sampling it. It is a good drink," he contin-ued as if they were on the best of polite terms. "What is it called?"

His attitude seemed to bewilder Hob. The creature halted his jumping dance and thrust his head forward as if to aid his small eyes in examining this furred one who was not afraid of him as all proper inhabitants of this house should be.

"It be cream—cream for Hob!" He shuffled a little to one side so he was now between Thragun and the bowl. "Cream they gives when they calls. An' truly it is time for Hob to come—there be black evil in this house!"

Thragun stood up, his lash of a tail moved from side to side and his ears flattened a little.

"Thewada, you are speaking true. Evil have I smelled, ever since I have come into this place. And I—I am the guard for the princess—What do you know of this evil and where does it lie?"

Hob had grabbed up the bowl in his two hands and thrown back his head so far on his shoulders that it seemed to be like to roll off. He opened a mouth which seemed as wide as half his face and was pouring the cream steadily into that opening.

"Where," asked the cat again, impatient, "is that evil? I must see it does not come near to the little one I have been sent to guard."

Hob swallowed for the last time, smeared the back of his hand across his mouth and smacked his thin lips. Then he pointed to the ceiling over their heads.

"Aloft now, so it be. She has a black heart, she has, and a heavy hand, that one. What she wants," his scowl began growing heavier as he spoke, "is Hob's house. An' sore will that one be iffen she gets it! I say that, and I be Hob, Hob!" Once more he stamped on the stone.

"If this place is yours, why do you let that one take it?" Thragun asked. He was staring up at the ceiling, busy thinking how he might get out of here and up aloft as the thewada said it.

"She works black evil," Hob said slowly. "But the law is with her—"

"What is Law?" asked Thragun in return. "It is the will of the king. Is he one to share this evil?"

Hob shook his head. "Mighty queer have you got it in your head. The Law is of us who have the old magic. Only it will do no harm to that one because she does not believe. There are them who lived here long ago and now walk the halls and strive to set fear in her. But until she believes we can no' drive her out. 'Tis the law—"

"It is not my Law—I have only one duty and that is

to guard. And guard I will!" Without another look at Hob, Thragun went into action, flashing away down the hall.

Emmy's fingers were pinched and scraped from the holds she kept on the ivy and she dared not look down, nor back, only to the wall before her as she crept foot width by foot width along the ledge.

She shrank against the wall and hardly dared draw a breath. There was a sound from the next window. The casements banged back against the wall. Then she heard Miss Wyker's voice:

"Miss Emmy, my lady? Alas, I fear that you must be sadly disappointed in her. She is impudent and unfeeling. Why, she has never asked to see you nor how you did."

Emmy began to feel hot in spite of the very cool breeze which rustled the vines around her. Miss Wyker was telling lies about her to Great-Aunt!

"Now, my lady, do you rest a bit and I shall be back presently with the night draught Dr. Riggs has prescribed."

There came an answer, so weak and thin, Emmy could hardly hear it.

"Not tonight, Miss Wyker. I always wake so weak and with an aching head. I felt much better before I began to take that—"

"Now, now, m'lady. The doctor knows best what to give you. You'll be yourself again shortly. I shall be back as soon as I can."

There came the sound of a door closing and Emmy moved, daring to edge faster. Then she was at the open casement to claw and pull her way into the room. There were two candles burning in a small table near the door, but the rest of the room was very gloomy.

"Who—who is there?" Great-Aunt's voice, sounding thin and shivery, came out of all the shadows around the big curtained bed.

"Please," Emmy crossed the end of the room to pick up one of the candles. Going closer to the bed she held it out so she could see Great-Aunt resting back on some pillows, all her pretty white hair hidden away under a night cap, so just thin white face was showing.

The anger which had brought Emmy so swiftly into the room broke free now. "Please, Miss Wyker told you a lie. I did want to see you and I asked and asked, but she said you did not want to be disturbed—that I was too noisy and careless— But it was a lie!"

"Emmy, child, I have wanted to see you, too. Very much— But how did you get here? Surely you did not come through the window."

"I had to," Emmy confessed. "She locked me in my room. And she locks your door, too. See," she crossed the room and tried to open the hall door, but, as she expected, she could not. Turning back to the bed, her eyes caught sight of the tray Jennie had brought with Cook's custard on it.

"Didn't you want this?" She took the tray in one hand and the candle in the other. "Cook make it special—out of the best cream and eggs. She said you always liked it when you were not feeling well before."

"Custard? But, of course, I like Cook's custard. Let me have it, Emmy. Then you sit down and tell me about all this locking of doors and my not wanting to see you."

Lady Ashely ate the custard hungrily, while Emmy's words came pouring out about all the things that had been happening in Hob's Green which she could not understand, ending with the story of how Thragun Neklop had come that very day and how Miss Wyker had acted.

"And father sent him to me—he is a gift from a princess, a real princess. Jennie took him away and I don't know what has happened to him!!" One tear and then another cut into the dust of the vines which had settled on Emmy's round face.

"Emmy, child, can you help me with these pillows, I want to sit up—"

Emmy hurried to pull the pillows together and make a back rest for Great-Aunt.

"Emmy, has Mr. Adkins been here lately?" Emmy was disappointed that Lady Ashely had not mentioned Thragun, but she answered quickly:

"He has come three times. But always Miss Wyker said you were asleep, or it was a day you were feeling poorly, and he went away again." Mr. Adkins was the vicar and Emmy was somewhat shy of him, he was so tall, and he did not smile very much.

"So." Great-Aunt's voice sounded a lot stronger. Emmy, without being told, took the empty bowl on its tray and set it on the chest under the window. "I do not understand, but we must begin to learn—"

"But," Emmy dared to interrupt, "what about Thragun? Jennie said Rog took Cook's kitty away and it never came back."

"Yes, we shall most certainly find out about Thragun and a great many other things, Emmy. Go to my desk over there and find my letter case and pen and ink—bring them here."

However, when Lady Ashely tried to write, her hand trembled and shook and she had to go very slowly. Once she looked up at Emmy and said:

"Child, see that brown bottle over on the mantelpiece? I want you to take that and hide it—perhaps in the big bandbox in the cupboard at the back."

It was when Emmy was returning from that errand that they heard the key turn in the lock. Lady Ashely forced her hand to hold steady for two more words. Then she folded it and wrote Mr. Adkins' name on the fold. Without being told, Emmy seized the letter case with its paper and two pens, one now dribbling ink across the edge of a pillow, and thrust it under the bed, stoppering the small inkwell and sending it after it. Lady Ashely pushed the note toward Emmy and the girl snatched it to tuck into the front of the dusty and torn breeches.

The door opened and Miss Wyker stood there, a lighted candle in her hand. She held that high so that the light reached the bed.

"M'lady," she hissed, "what have you been about? What—"

The light now caught Emmy, and Miss Wyker stopped short. Her face was very white and her eyes were hard and glittered.

"You cruel child! What are you doing here! Shameful, shameful!" Her voice rasped as she put down the candle to bear down on Emmy. She caught one straggling lock of the child's hair and jerked her toward the door. "Be sure you will suffer for this!"

"I think not, Miss Wyker." Lady Ashely did not speak very loudly, but somehow the words cut through. Miss Wyker, in the process of dragging Emmy to the door, looked around, but her expression did not change.

"M'lady, you are taken ill again. This cruel child has upset you. Be sure she will be punished for it—"

"And if I say no?"

"But, m'lady, all know that you are very ill and that you sometimes wander in your wits. Dr. Riggs himself has commented upon how mazed you are at times. You will take his medicine and go peacefully to sleep, and when you wake this will all be a dream. Yes, m'lady, you will be very well looked after, I assure you."

Emmy tried to hold onto a bedpost and then to the back of a chair, but pain from the tugging at her hair made her let go. Great-Aunt was looking at Miss Wyker as if some horrid monster were there. She pressed her fingers to her mouth and Emmy could see that she was frightened, really frightened.

The door to the bedroom was thrown open with a crash and Emmy jerked out into the hall.

"You," Miss Wyker shook her, transferring her hold on Emmy's hair, to bury her fingers in the flesh on the child's shoulders, shaking her back and forth, until Emmy went limp and helpless in her hands. "Down in the cellar for you, my girl. The beetles and rats will give you something else to think about! Come!" Now her fingers sank into the nape of Emmy's neck and she was urged forward at a running pace.

They reached the top of the narrow back staircase the servants used. Up that shot a streak of dark and light fur. It flashed past Emmy. Miss Wyker let go of the child and tried vainly to pull loose from what seemed to be a clutch on her back skirts. Unable to free herself, she tried to turn farther about to see what held her so. Something small and dark crouched there.

Then came a battle scream, answered by a cry of fear from Miss Wyker. Now her hands beat the air, trying to reach the demon who clung with punishing claws to her back. She screamed in terror and torment as a paw reached around from behind her head and used claws on a white face which speedily spouted red. Miss Wyker wheeled about again, fighting to get her hands on the cat. Then she tottered as that shadow hunched before her now at her feet struck out in turn. The woman plunged sidewise with a last cry. Thragun flew through the air in the opposite direction, landing on the hall floor not far from Emmy who had crowded back against the wall, unable even to make the smallest sound.

The cat padded toward her, uttering small cries as if he were talking. That candle which had fallen from Miss Wyker's hand rolled, still alight, down to the stair landing below. Miss Wyker lay there very still. But there was something else, too, something dancing by the side of her body and uttering a high thin whistling sound. Only for a minute had Emmy seen that and then it was gone. Thragun was rubbing back and forth against her legs, purring loudly. Emmy stooped and caught him tight. Though this was hardly a dignified thank you, Noble Warrior allowed it. After all, was he not a guard and one who had done his duty nobly and well, even if a skirt-jerking thewada had had something to do with it? *HIS* princess was safe and that was what counted.

BASTET'S BLESSING

by Elizabeth Ann Scarborough

In memory of Shuttle, trusty companion,
professional hunter, dedicated sunbather
and excavator of cat boxes.

His coat was the tan of desert dunes, ornamented with
bands shaded from pale amber to gold around his legs
and tail and outlining his great peridot eyes with a
tiger's mask. When he moved, it was as if the sphinx
had risen to its massive paws to stalk the paths of men.
The length of his tail and the height of his ears bespoke more than common lineage. When he roared,
unfortunately, it tended to come out as a rasping maoao
noise, in keeping with his size, but one had to be
pragmatic. Probably he would never have been able
to find good help if he roared when he wanted in,
roared when he wanted out, roared when he wished a
change in his menu or wanted his box changed.

And truthfully, roaring would have misrepresented
him, for he was a gentle, scholarly creature, of quiet
dignity and poise. Or so he believed, and so he told
Dr. Mercer the morning he made her acquaintance.
She found him in reduced circumstances, incarcerated
in a wire pen.

"Poor cat," she said, kneeling so that her eyes were
on a level with his. Whether it was because her eyes
were intelligent and kindly that he decided she would
be suitable, or because she had the good sense to
kneel in his presence, he was unsure. But he rose to a
seated position, his front half erect while his back half

supported it. His unusually long tail flicked up and down slightly to indicate that he required her attention.

"Madam, please disregard my present habitation. I was evicted from my former lodgings because of xenophobic tendencies toward my species on the part of Miss Rosamund's new patron. Do not distress yourself on my behalf, however. The arrangement was never truly to my liking. Miss Rosamund, in addition to housing my mother and siblings, kept five others of my species and I am a creature who prefers a degree of privacy and solitude."

He forbore to mention that he also liked digging, which was why he alone of all of Miss Rosamund's boarders had been ignominiously evicted on the patent leather toe of the patron's shoe.

Dr. Mercer did not pry. She jingled a few coins in a small purse and selected one for the jailer. "I'm taking this cat."

The jailer did not argue. The vivisectionists did not pay as well. And Dr. Mercer carried herself with authority.

Her confidence did not come from being an immaculate housekeeper. She was the despair of her twice-weekly cleaning woman. The appointments were nice enough. The rugs were old, rich with exotic patterning and ruddy color. Deep leather-upholstered chairs squatted around the flat in sufficient profusion that they should have provided adequate seating for a Sunday tea. A carved cherry desk with clawed feet took up half the parlor. The bedroom was dominated by the velvet canopied bed but also held a fainting couch, dressing table, and wardrobe. The dining table was a fine old piece, too, inherited, like the rest, from Dr. Mercer's father's estate. The vast walnut bookshelves that lined the walls with heavy old volumes in cloth and leather covers had belonged to the estate, too. If the books had stayed on those shelves, the cleaning woman would have been happy. But they dripped across the dressing table, spilled onto the sofa, flowed onto the fainting couch, cascaded onto the chairs, burdened the bed, and all but drowned the dining table. Piled among the pillars of books were reams of papers, dissertations, notes, graphs, illustrations, and bits of other detritus, pieces of pots and scraps of ancient cloth. The decor, the cat decided upon inspection, suited him nicely.

When Dr. Mercer brought him home, she first filled an old clay dish with water and another with canned fish and placed it on the floor for his approval. For some reason, she put an old pillow near the dishes, beside the coal cookstove. Then she scooted a year's worth of research literature to one side and sat on the couch, watching and waiting for the cat's verdict. He sniffed the fish, sniffed the water, sniffed the pillow, then paced the perimeters of his new domain.

Papers slid under his paws, the musty smell of old ink and a tinge of green mold filled his nostrils, and his claws flicked across the linoleum and across the hardwood, until he padded onto carpet and clicked back again, back and forth from the parlor to the bedroom to the kitchen. Then he leaped lightly onto the desk, the bed, the sofa, and the chairs, feeling knowledge, wisdom, information, and also vast amounts of ignorance and misunderstanding push against his pads.

Dr. Mercer observed his survey with amused tolerance, the same feeling her flat aroused in him. "You're quite the pacer, aren't you? To and fro, to and fro, like a weaver's shuttlecock. Very well, then, Shuttle it is." Perched high atop a trembling tower of tomes on ancient Egyptian archaeology, the cat regarded her thoughtfully for a moment, then blinked his approval.

Miss Rosamund had never called him anything except "cat." His other name had been long forgotten, even by him. "Shuttle" would do.

In a short time Shuttle and Dr. Mercer developed a congenial relationship, based on mutual respect and interests.

During the wet, windy days when Dr. Mercer ventured into the gray world beyond their snug flat to reach her classes and practice her profession, Shuttle drowsed on the books, soaking up images of sun-

warmed sand, tall fronded trees, and the heavy green
Nile snaking through the dusty tombs of kings and
queens, the ancient burial grounds where mummies
lay dry as autumn leaves, withered in their wrappings
and desiccated until their own cats would not have
known their smell.

He learned of the classification of pottery shards by
period and design, the intricacies of hieroglyphics, the
blueprints of tombs, the interesting things canopic jars
held, and about the ka or soul.

Dr. Mercer was cooperative in broadening his education. About the time he had napped on the top book
of every pile in the house, she would come home with
some new problem and a whole new layer of knowledge would be shuffled to the top.

Thus Shuttle's education as an Egyptologist, ranging
over a period of months, was thorough and compre-
hensive if not especially chronological.

Not all their time was spent in study. On occasion,
colleagues or students would stop by, and long discus-
sions and arguments would ensue while they drank
sherry and catnip tea. Shuttle liked to lie along the top
of the couch, basking under the reading light, pretending it was the hot sun of Thebes. He stretched so the
warmth could penetrate his fur, until his body extended the length of the cushion, his tail tickling Dr.
Mercer's neck. He added occasional comments, but
even human beings intelligent enough to read heirog-
lyphics were ignorant of his language, though Dr. Mercer, being his personal protégée, understood more
than most.

He felt as if he had known her since he was a kitten,
and longer, so well suited were they and so comfortable together.

At any rate, he grew very attached to her, and when
she first came home, he would seat himself on her lap
and allow her to warm her hands in his fur and at
night he would first curl next to her head to lull her to
sleep with his purr, then lie for mutual warmth near
her feet. She was very considerate and moved carefully, even in her sleep, never thrashing about as Miss

Rosamund had done. Once she was quite asleep, he would often proceed with his own research, mapping out excavations in the sand in his commode, or lying on the books in the windowsill, to gaze across the rooftops at the thrashing sea and watch the wind scatter clouds across the moon's wan eye.

Dr. Mercer, even while deep in her studies, would rub his ears or tweak his tail affectionately as he passed her chair. Sometimes when he lay near her book, she would seek out his fur with her fingers or read him passages and then argue with him as if she expected him to concur with her opinion. He usually did. She was unusually bright.

And then spring, a season he always anticipated with relish, betrayed him. Dr. Mercer pulled odd smelling receptacles from the closet and began packing heavy, functional clothing he had never seen before, things in desert colors, and a hat. She never wore hats. He sat on the cases and watched with avid interest for a while. He thought the cases smelled something like the books. Like Egypt. The dust was old dust, sand and mummies, he imagined.

One day she snapped the clasps shut and bent down and picked him up, so that his face was so close to hers his breath clouded her spectacles. "Sorry, old dear, but duty calls. Monica Thomas will be here to see to you. You'll remember Monica. I believe you liked her." Nonsense. He barely knew the girl although he was, of course, polite to all of their guests. "I'll miss you, but if I took you along you'd have to undergo quarantine back here, all that sort of thing, and you'd hate that. I will think of you often. I'll be digging outside Bubastis. You'd approve of Bubastis. Sensible people. Thought cats were divine."

And then she was gone and Monica Thomas came. Monica Thomas did not really care for cats as much as she cared for the professor's lovely flat far from the dormitory, where she could study Shuttle's and Dr. Mercer's books at her leisure and, more often, entertain in private. She put all the books back on the shelves and screeched at Shuttle when he sat on the tables or touched his claws, even in thoughtful kneading, to the upholstery. She shut him out of the bedroom many nights, away from the window. Sometimes she would condescend to pat him, but she disliked getting his hairs on her clothing. She let his food get stale or, worse, sometimes forgot to set it out.

At first he was patient, for what is time to a being with nine lives? But by the second round of the moon, he felt Egypt through the pattern in the rug, through the polished hardwood; he felt it through his claws and bones and in the fighting hairs of his back and tail and in the sensitive places where his whiskers touched the world around him. And he knew. All was not well in Egypt.

Monica did not agree. She came in brandishing a letter from Dr. Mercer, chirping to Shuttle that his mommy had said hi. When she went to bed that night, Shuttle hopped upon the desk and sniffed the letter. Her scent was on the paper, salty and faint but distinctive. Hue lay upon it, warming his stomach with it and absorbing the message. If he were human, he would have been reassured. "We have made a find. Of course, it's too early to know quite how important it will be, but already we have located the entrance to the tomb and the shrine. Unfortunately, work has slowed down as our fellahin have deserted us. Some complaints about odd noises at night. Negotiations are in progress, however."

What she said was not as significant as her scent and that of the paper. It carried danger, *wrongness*. Shuttle scratched at the bedroom door and tried to explain to Monica that he needed to look out the window, to see if he could see Egypt, to divine the nature of the problem. She threw a house slipper against the door, but in the morning fed him fresh food and chucked him under the chin as if he were a mewling kitten. "Don't cry, chum. She'll be back in a few months."

Months! He should have insisted on accompanying her.

He spent the day staring at the sea, leaving it only to return, his claws clicking back and forth on the

floor. He scratched at the sill and at the door. He had
to get to Egypt. But it was no use. He was locked in.
At last, exhausted, he fell asleep on the desk, on the
letter and the book whose place Monica had marked
with it.

And at noon he rose and walked through the window, across the housetops, and with a mighty leap
crossed the sea and all the countries between to Dr.
Mercer's tent. She was sleeping, mosquito netting
draped over her, her hair matted with sweat. She
smelled wonderfully like herself, only more so, but she
twitched and moaned in her sleep. Shuttle purred and
she quieted, and he padded out into the night.

The tents would have been easy for him to penetrate as a flesh-and-blood cat. For his ka-form, they
were less substantial than the heat waves that rose
from the sand. Most of the tents held sleeping scientists, sleeping students. The native workers, he knew
from conversations, would be at their villages. He
kept poking, barely interspersing himself with the fabric of a tent before pulling out again, until he found
the ones he sought.

Naturally, in his higher form, the cook tent did not
tempt him, especially since the odors were old and
complicated by disinfectant some conscientious scientist no doubt forced on the native cook.

No, the tents that interested him were those where
finds were already being cataloged and recorded. He
knew that the answer to the wrongness must lie there,
or part of it.

It came to him through the canvas, so that he hesitated before entering. He hissed and all his soft fur
spiked into quills. The pottery shards were there, neglected, on a side table, along with a typewriting machine that bowed the rickety table in the middle with
its weight. On the center table were jars and transcrip-
tions, bits of jewelry, and whole pots. He barely noticed them. It was the stack of cylinders, piled like
firewood on top of and underneath the third table that
sent twitches from whisker to tail tip.

He stalked toward the table, sniffing, but he knew

from the outline of the ears, from the shapes of the snouts pushing their silhouettes against the shadowed canvas, that these were cats. Dead cats. Very old dead cats. Desecrated, deformed, bereft of beauty. He growled uncertainly, his tail jerking. Suddenly, something stirred in the far corner, rustling like a mouse then trumpeting like an elephant, and he shot straight into the air and dashed through the tent wall. When he was safely on the outside, he heard the snoring resume, and realized the mouse and elephant had both been no more than another sleeping scientist. Cautiously, he slipped paw by paw back into the tent and stole past the scientist. He recognized the fellow, of course. Dr. William Parsons. Good pottery man, Dr. Mercer said. Apparently not much for cat mummies, from the casual way they were left lying on top of each other. Much as the mummies repelled him, Shuttle was fascinated by the wrappings, cloth wrapped in intricate patterns around the bodies, paws, and tails. A gummy black substance such as that used on human mummies covered the cats. One stiff was all he needed. What had become of these creatures, he wondered? And what was it about them that felt so wrong? He stopped wondering, stopped sniffing, and stared for a long moment. In his head a chorus of plaintive mews rasped across the ages and he opened his mouth and caterwauled, spooking himself all over again.

He leaped from the tent, leaving Bill Parsons, oblivious to ka-ish caterwauls, still sleeping soundly, if noisily.

The expedition had had unusual luck, locating its first finds shortly after commencing the dig. Dr. Mercer's letter had taken almost a month to reach Monica. The tomb now stood open, with a guard sleeping by the door. A series of ditches and stakes marked the site of the temple and the shrine. The tent town of scientists and their assistants ranged in a crescent surrounding the site.

The shrine was little more than a small stone mound at one end of the crescent. The mound was hollow as an oven and the door was ajar. Shuttle could not bring himself to enter that place. The smell of mummies and misery hung heavily within, and the mews such as he had heard within his head echoed and reechoed through the shrine. This, then, had been the sepulcher of those unfortunate members of his race now lying like so many mackerel wrapped by the fishmonger within Parsons' tent.

The tomb gaped at the other horn of the crescent. A less grisly object of study, more worthy of his scientific attention, he decided. He could hardly be expected to assist Dr. Mercer with her problem, whatever it was, before he had made a survey of the site.

He wafted inside, past the guard, whose head lolled at an angle that looked most uncomfortable to Shuttle, who was himself an expert on comfort.

The tomb was set in the side of a hill. Inside was a downward sloping path. The interior was not as elaborate as the tombs of pharoahs, but quite commodious enough for the dead. Shuttle tried to bump the tops off the decorated chests with his head but found his hardest butts made no impact. He stood on his hind paws and put his front ones on the lips of urns, sniffing the lids for oils, perfumes, or entrails. The odors were strong enough even after so many decades to cause him to curl his lips back over the scent glands at the side of his mouth, as a highborn person might curl theirs in distaste.

His paws made no sound on the tiles beneath them, across which grains of sand bounced and skittered like frightened insects, of which there were also a few. He disdainfully ignored them in the interests of science.

The top of one of the jars had been removed and Shuttle was thrusting his head into its mouth when he heard the scrape, the slither, and the shuffling noise. He froze, suspended by his chin and front paws, as a whisper of chill seeped through the desert warmth that had formerly permeated the open tomb.

And over the scrape, slither, shuffle, the sad mewling cried out within him once more. He shot out of the tomb so quickly that he almost tangled in the bandages of the figure limping relentlessly toward Bill Parsons' tent. This further alarmed him so that he thrust himself across the remaining distance, through tent and mosquito net, to land on top of Dr. Mercer's waist, between her rib cage and her hip, where he dug in so hard that had he had the foresight to bring his body with him she would have borne his mark for weeks.

It would serve her right, too. What was wrong with their nice flat and her teaching position that she had to leave him in the care of Monica Thomas to come to this horrid place? He trembled like a brown leaf in a high wind, huddling next to Dr. Mercer. That awful mewling! How could she be deaf to it?

But suddenly another sound touched his flattened ears. Low and strangled, gargling and full of loathing fear, and then, cut to dead silence. The silence lasted only a moment before Shuttle's sensitive ears detected the slow scraape, slither, shuffle, scrape, slither, shuffle, scrape, slitherr, shufffle, *scraaape, slitherr! shuffle—* SLUMP, SCRAPE, SLITHER, SHUFFLE, DRAG! and the dusty stench of the collection of moldering bandages was within the tent, its hands clawed toward the mosquito netting, ready to dispatch Dr. Mercer as it had no doubt already dispatched Bill Parsons and who knew how many others? Dr. Mercer stirred and mumbled in her sleep, and half wakened to the mummy's presence as she had not to Shuttle's. She began to leak that strangled cry.

That was too much for Shuttle. Mummy's curse, for it was obviously the manifestation of that phenomenon that had haunted at least two other excavations that was now attempting to claim his own colleagues, was all very well. He himself was sometimes cranky when awakened from a long nap. But this tent was Shuttle's territory and Dr. Mercer was *his* companion. Ears flat, fur bristling, fangs bared, claws unsheathed and body four times its normal size, Shuttle launched himself through the mosquito netting at the bandaged apparition, ready to rend it bandage from bandage.

The necessity did not arise. Murderous the mummy might be, but it was an exceptionally well-brought-up spook, nevertheless. Being a supernatural sort, it at once perceived Shuttle and his displeasure, and fell to the ground in a gesture of submission and humility Shuttle recognized from the reproductions of scrolls and paintings in Dr. Mercer's books. This gruesome thing had probably murdered Bill Parsons, but Shuttle, licking himself thoughtfully while watching the mummy grovel, could not bring himself to attack this unusually sensitive and courteous example of Egyptian eternity.

He did spring at it a little, to shoo it off, then followed it from Dr. Mercer's tent, battling at the bandages it dragged to let it know that he meant business. It returned to the tomb, past the body of the guard, now an empty husk whose ka had apparently had more pressing matters to attend to than guarding the tomb.

The mummy returned to its coffin and case, settling itself in with a sigh of dust. It did not replace the lid. That did not reassure Shuttle. Certainly the mummy was obedient now, with a cat-ka to show it its place, but Shuttle had no idea how long he could maintain his present state. Surely, his ka must return to his body again soon and then Dr. Mercer would be once more at the mummy's mercy. And, of course, the rest of the expedition also would be in danger, but he concerned himself with only one aspect of the situation at a time.

The piteous mewling was louder now, closer, but it seemed to Shuttle that it was less a complaint and more a summons. He leaped onto the rim of the mummy case and followed his nose, until he peered over the head-end of the mummy case, where he observed a small mound, little more than earth and sand from the look of it. To this mound he was drawn and he began scratching, scratching, his incorporeal claws flinging ancient ghost-dirt and ghost-sand to either side of him until the real dirt and sand collapsed over a small casket. He took two paces backward as the lid of this casket began to wiggle. The mewling increased in intensity. He extended a delicate paw and slapped the damned thing away, startling himself that he was able to do so, since he had grown used to having no substance. Within the casket lay another cat mummy, golden rings in the ears, bound with basketlike strips confining body, paws and tail. Lovely latticework. Probably indicated a lot about period, craftsmanship, the people who made it. But from within, now, came the compelling cry, "Release us."

Shuttle set a tentative paw on the bandage.

"Release us," the cry rasped again. He pawed loose an end and took it in his teeth. It felt gummy, tasted of dust and ancient herbs. To his surprise, his tugging had some effect. At first the bandages crumpled beneath his teeth and paws, but as he came to the deeper layers, they simply unwound. The sticky substance dissolved as he burrowed deeper into the mummy, so intent upon his labors, upon stilling the cry, that he did not notice at once when the dust rising from the corpse turned to vapor and the vapor formed into a cat-ka.

He was ravaging the last of the bandages when the voice, purring now, not mewling, bespoke him. "You have done well, descendant and disciple. Rest now, and bathe." He looked up and was startled to see another cat, not a sleek ebony figure sitting majestically erect like the statues, but a beautiful four-colored tortoiseshell curled in midair, her tail wrapped comfortably about her feet, her sapphire blue right eye and her emerald green left eye regarding him with beneficence.

Still, it was her territory. "I beg your pardon," he said. Something about her made him roll submissively onto his back. Her spectral tongue licked his spectral fur until he understood that he was not required to submit, and pretended instead to be bathing his left hind leg. "Didn't know there was anyone else about in these parts—"

"Did you not?" she asked. "Then why have you come, if not to release us? You may speak freely."

"It's my job, you see," he said, cleaning between his front toes. "I am an Egyptologist. My people have been digging up your people for many years now. And please excuse my ignorance, but who might you be?"

"We are an incarnation of the goddess Bastet, of course. You weren't expecting Anubis we trust? Good. As for begging our pardon, there is no need, for you have freed us."

"Yes," he said. "Yes, I have. And very good of me it was to do so, too, when your minion here—this is your minion?" he flicked his tail at the larger mummy.

"In her last incarnation, she was our priestess."

"Your mummy killed one of my colleagues and attempted to kill my fr—er—*my* priestess. I thought it was because we had desecrated your tomb."

The jeweled eyes closed for a moment, then opened, the purring growing louder. "She is very diligent, our priestess, but unfortunately a product of the delusions of our civilization. She knows our spirit has been restless and according to her belief, the only way to appease us is sacrifice. That was all well and good while one was embodied, you see, and hungered for offerings of fish and cream, but when one is bound paw and tail, such measures serve only to drive your people away, taking with them my unfortunate children."

"Your children?"

"The litters of my loins from this incarnation, when humans sought to honor us by enslaving our kas within these worldly rags." She flicked her tail derisively at the disintegrating bandages. "Our kind were much honored in our lifetime. Not just the fish and cream, but safely and protection for all in our name. Laying so much as a sandal on one of us was punishable by death, and people made statues of us and mourned us when we died. But then they conceived the notion that since they were attached to their present incarnation, we must be likewise, and they began to enshroud and entomb us as you see here. It was a terrible turn and as they were too primitive to learn our tongue, however devoted they were otherwise, there was simply no way to tell them that what was thought good and desirable for such stylized creatures as themselves was living death to our kind. Many of us sought to escape by leaping into fires when the occasion rose and speeding to the next incarnation, so terrified were we of being body-bound for all eternity. But we who were worshiped directly were far too protected to escape the fate to which our worshipers unwittingly condemned us. Though we would have hidden ourselves from them, still; they found us and left us even as you find us now."

"Appalling," Shuttle agreed. "But my people are not responsible."

"Your people would take us from our native soil," Bastet said. "Lacking the respect of our servants, they would disregard our imprisoned souls and we would never be free to walk the earth on four paws again."

"But I released you. You are free."

"I am a goddess. I have my responsibilities. My kittens remain bound."

Shuttle stared back into the sea-deep eyes, raised his tail twice and flopped it down, "I'd free them for you in an instant, just out of professional courtesy, but this is not the real me, you understand, but my ka."

"Your ka, O deliverer of our spirit, is the real you. But we are curious as to the whereabouts of your physical incarnation and how your ka came to separate from it."

"My—mrrr—physical incarnation lies sleeping across the sea. I dreamed of the danger to Dr. Mercer and our colleagues and since my body could not come, I came without it. Fortunate thing that I did, too. I fear that priestess of yours has already killed two of our party and would have killed Dr. Mercer except that I was there to put a stop to it." He growled a little at the last.

"Our servant is impetuous. But no matter. You will serve us, if we enable it?"

Shuttle blinked slowly. "So I have said."

"You may leave us. Even as your spirit and mine cooperated to free us, so shall we lend weight to your ka-self, sharpness to your ka-claws and strength to your ka-jaws that you may release our imprisoned ones. Go now."

He went, casually, as if it were his own idea. He tried to pass through the walls of the tent where the cat mummies lay, but bumped his nose, and had to enter through the flap instead. Bill Parsons was gone. Shuttle supposed he had gone wherever they took dead humans. Just as well. After all the studying Shuttle had done to learn about the preservation, restoration and storage of artifacts, he did not want even the corpse of a colleague observing him in such unprofessional conduct. There was no way to tell his fellow scientists that these mummies were not mere artifacts, but contained the living kas of cats long overdue for reincarnation. He rather suspected that even if humans could understand the words, they would be unable to grasp the concept. Even Bastet's pet priestess was no brighter.

Something screamed and laughed maniacally nearby and Shuttle froze, his trail bristling. When the noise continued, he realized he must be hearing the cry of a jackal. Dratted dog, he thought with disgust, and went to work.

Life on the street between Miss Rosamund's and Dr. Mercer's homes was excellent preparation for freeing mummified cats. First he gave each shroud a series of good long rakes with his claws, to open the bandages, then he seized the ends in his teeth and pulled, as he had once pulled the ends of the scarlet yarn in Miss Rosamund's knitting basket. The bandages tasted dreadful and the gum on them stuck to his fur, but once he got the unwinding started the contents dissolved to dust. The dust rose and the vaporous ka emerged in shimmering cat form, stretched, gave itself a lick or two, and vanished. Many times he did this, until his whole body ached and his teeth tingled. But finally the last of Bastet's kittens dissolved into nothingness and he sank to his belly among the ruined bandages.

Just in time to hear the slump, slither, shuffle, drag pass beside the tent wall.

Weariness forgotten, Shuttle jumped to his feet and dashed from the tent into the smoky gray dawn. He leaped in front of the mummy just as it reached Dr. Mercer's tent. He did not give the mummy time to genuflect this time but pounced at it so that it stumbled backward. He pounced it all the way back to the tomb and stood growling while it shrank into its coffin. No sooner was it supine than he intended to spring upon it and shred it as he had the shrouds of the kittens.

But suddenly Bastet stood before him, her back raised in fighting position, her mottled fur erect, jeweled eyes glowing.

"So that's how you reward your servants, is it?" he hissed. "That thing tried to kill Dr. Mercer again. Let me rip—let me free it, as I did you and the others."

"Our priestess is human. This is her immortality and her mission. This is her presence. Unruly though she is, we cannot reward her by allowing her to be sundered from her destiny."

"Well, fine," Shuttle spat. "Then tell her to keep away from my people."

"She obeys her destiny even as you have obeyed yours," Bastet said, settling down into her mummy's chest. Shuttle thought he saw the bandages over the skeletal face lift in a smirk through the velvet fur of the goddess. "Even now the strength we lent you is gone. Return to your body, deliverer, and take your servant with you."

Shuttle felt the remaining strength fade from his paws and claws and jaws, and his whiskers and tail drooped and he saw that he could once more see the tiled floor through his own feet. He meowed. "If only I could! But she will not leave."

"Then she should be punished for her faithlessness," Bastet said.

"You simply don't understand the way scientists think, goddess," Shuttle told her. "Dr. Mercer and I are of one mind on this. It is necessary to dig in this land to do one's work—she must dig as you and I must dig and hunt and—er—goddess, for that matter, please do not make me vanish and leave her to that mummy. She is more than a servant to me. She is my comrade, my colleague, my companion, and my comfort. How can you beg me to go against all I have learned to do as you asked and then deprive me of her?"

"Oh, well, if you're going to get maudlin about it," the goddess said huffily. "We *do* reward service."

"Then you'll call off the mummy?"

"We cannot. But we have another idea. You may find it a bit hectic, but if you insist on forming unsuitable attachments you have to be prepared to put up with some inconvenience. You have freed—let us see, seventeen, not counting our divine self, times nine is—153 lives. We suppose one extra for you should not be too much to grant. So be it. You have our blessing."

The soft pressure of a hand across his sun-warmed fur awakened Shuttle. Lazily, he gazed up into Dr. Mercer's sweating face.

"And where did you come from, my friend?" she asked.

"He's colored just like your cat at home, Jane," Bill Parsons said. "Wonder how he got in the tomb."

"Probably the same way that jackal got into the tent and destroyed the cat mummies."

"Now, Jane, I'm sorry. But that nightmare I had was far too vivid for me to remain in that tent the rest of the night. You know very well I have a weak heart."

"I know very well you have a weakness for sherry. As does Achmed, which is no doubt how cat here got around him."

"Watch that beast. He'll bite you."

"Nonsense. He's quite friendly, aren't you, fellow?" Shuttle purred and bumped her hand. "If I didn't know it was impossible, I'd swear this is Shuttle. I shall name him that anyway and adopt him. Surely Shuttle won't mind having a namesake."

And so the cat joined them. He, too, dug, investigated, and studied, and in the evenings slept on Dr.

Mercer's knees and at night patrolled the camp to keep his associates from harm.

When the scientists packed up to return, Dr. Mercer paid a local family well to care for him until her return, but as soon as she left, he crept away into a secret cave and slept a long sleep.

Shuttle raced to the door to meet Dr. Mercer when she returned to their flat. Monica Thomas watched in amazement as the professor set down her bags, held out her fingers to her cat, who bumped against them, and then gathered him in her arms and stroked him while he purred.

"Well," Monica Thomas said, "I'm glad to see the old thing can move. He's always asleep when I'm home and he hasn't been eating well. I think he missed you."

But Monica Thomas, as usual, was wrong. From the moment of Bastet's blessing, Shuttle's ka traveled from his Egyptian body to the one in America and back again, depending on the season. And while in Egypt he might miss his bed and his books as he might, in America, miss digging in the sand and the freedom of chasing lizards through the camp, he never again had to miss Dr. Mercer.